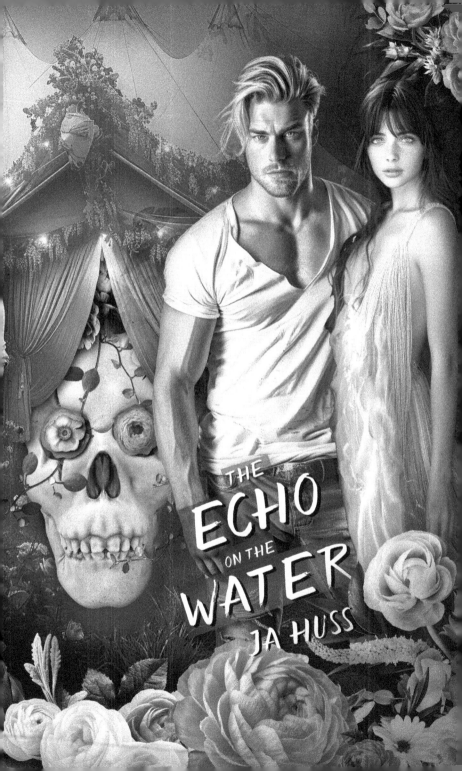

THE
ECHO
ON THE
WATER
JA HUSS

Edited by RJ Locksley
Cover Design by JA Huss
No AI was used in the making of this cover

ABOUT THE BOOK

Rosie Harlow is desperately seeking… well, she's not sure. A romance would be nice but so would a dinner conversation with her pre-teen son. Too bad her boy is way too busy growing up to pay his mama any attention. Rosie never meant to swear off men and she's not frigid—you don't become a single mom at fifteen by being frigid—but this dry spell of hers had gotten out of hand and something must be done.

ENTER AMON PARRISH. Back in high school Amon was voted most likely to get caught with his pants down. He was a trouble maker. The quintessential bad boy. But twelve years away from home, traveling the world and working with Collin Creed doing super-secret (and somewhat illegal) things, changed all that and these days Amon Parrish is a brand-new, stand-up man.

AND, to Rosie's surprise, a romantic man as well. Because he has decided to *court her*. And this is not just any ordinary courting, either. It's… well, a page ripped right out of a bodice ripper.

BUT EVERYONE IN DISCIPLE, West Virginia has a secret in their past.

Even the cheerful, perpetually optimistic, and seemingly innocent, Rosie Harlow.

THE ECHO on the Water is a swooning plate of small-town fiction served up with a side of spice. It honors the themes of friends to lovers, found family, and is filled with bigger-than-life, morally-grey characters against a backdrop of the weird and wonderful.

AMON

Every now and then, ever since Collin and I came home to West Virginia, out of the damn blue, I'll get a weird sense of longin' in my chest. Like an ache, but not a sad one. Like an emptiness, but not a black one. It's more like an itch ya can't scratch or a craving ya can't satisfy.

Standing here in the Bishop butcher shop as I wait on my soup bones, I get that feeling.

Which is weird because I'm really fuckin' satisfied. Like completely fuckin' satisfied. I love being home. And every day, as I drive through Trinity County doin' my business, there is this feeling of belonging. An arrival, of sorts.

Even countin' the little scuffle up on the mountain at Blackberry Hill, this return trip home has been easy and sweet.

Haven't gotten laid yet, which, not gonna lie, kinda sucks. But I've gotten more than my share of women all over the world for the past twelve years. I'm playin' it careful now. Taking my time. Choosing wisely, as they say. Because when one enters Trinity County, West Virginia, one does not just start humping girls left and right like they're water and you just arrived at an oasis after a hundred-mile trek through the fuckin' Sahara desert, dying of thirst.

Especially if one wants a Disciple girl. And I kinda do.

Don't get me wrong. I have pictured myself up in a hayloft dressed in traditional, handmade farmboy attire taking a frilly-dressed girl from behind plenty of times. That was definitely my go-to dream scenario when I was fifteen. And there ain't nothin' wrong with a stripper from Revenant in my book.

But a Disciple girl? Yeah. They're different. They're kinda like a combination of Bishop and Revenant. Playing all traditional on the weekends for the Revival shows, but then bein' all rough-edgy during the week as they just go about their lives.

I like it.

"All right, Amon. Here ya go. Two hundred pounds of soup bones." Johnny Boy Butcher, who is the literal butcher of Bishop, West Virginia, and hasn't been a boy for about fifty years now, pulls my cart piled high with wooden crates out from behind his butcher-shop countertop and lets it come to rest at my feet.

This makes me smile. Not just because Johnny Boy is keeping my entire kennel of super-smart, military-style protection dogs in soup bones, but because the wooden crates are just *such* a nice touch. It's so fuckin' old-timey, I can't stand it.

I could leave Trinity County and find myself a butcher who would wrap my soup bones in plastic instead of white paper and I'd probably pay a whole lot less for the exact same amount of chewing time, but it just wouldn't be the same.

"Thanks, Johnny Boy. I'll see ya next week."

He tips an imaginary hat at me and turns his attention to

the next customer in line. I pull my cart over to the door, where a man wearing vintage-looking overalls is already holding it open to make my life easier, and then I leave the butcher shop with a nod and a 'thank you' for the kindness.

I love that about Bishop. How nice and friendly the people are. I mean, this is the downtown historical district and it's literally the townspeople's job to be pleasant and accommodating. But acting aside, it still works. It still makes me feel appreciated. Like I matter, even to strangers.

Trust me when I say this, it's a rare thing to be welcomed by strangers when you're the actual stranger. Especially when you're traveling the world as black ops military, as I was. I grew used to the indifference, as well as the hostility. Almost forgot what it was like to be somewhere I belonged. But it hit me quick when we came home to West Virginia. And now, knowing what I do of the wider world, I would never leave this place again, not even if someone offered me millions of dollars.

I start pulling my cart down the brick sidewalk, enjoying the clip-clopping sound of the horses as they pull their carts down the brick-paved street, and then stop short when I spy Rosie Harlow leaving a small shop across the road. It's kinda set back, this building, and it's real small. Maybe fifteen feet wide at the most. Like the space it takes up was an empty alley before it was a shop front.

There's a tiny courtyard in front surrounded by a white picket fence, and Rosie is just opening the gate to exit when she catches my eye, waves, and calls my name. "Amon!"

I'm about to cross and go over to say a proper hello, but I've got this heavy cart and Rosie is light on her feet, so before I know it, she's scooted her way through the horses and buggies and is standing right in front of me. "What are you up to today?"

"I was gonna ask you the same thing."

"What's all this?" She makes a circle with her finger, gesturing to my cart.

"Bones for my dogs." I make a circle in the air, gesturing to her clothes. "What's all *this*?" Because she is in a full-on Bishop costume. I'm talking petticoat, gown, apron—the works.

Which is a very nice look on her.

Rosie Harlow is petite and fresh-faced, but she never looks the same from day to day. Oh, her long hair is always brown and yes, she's always lookin' cute as fuck. But since I've been back, I've seen her dressed up in go-go boots, leather fringe, bell bottoms, and gold lamé. She's not afraid of fashion and if she were an actual woman of the vintage sort, she'd be a doe-eyed sex symbol and all the teenage boys would have her poster on their bedroom walls.

But today Rosie Harlow is something all-together different. She's vintage, but not in a Valerie Bertinelli rock-star girlfriend way. Today, she looks very... trad wife. But she's not puttin' off a milkin' cows and makin' sourdough bread kind of farm-y trad wife vibe. More of a powerful high society, wind-beneath-the-wings kinda trad wife, à la Bishop style.

And it's kinda hot.

Rosie raises up both shoulders, shootin' me a smile. "My new dress." Then she twirls for me.

Which again, is kinda hot. "Well, I like it, Rosie. A lot. But... why are you here, in Bishop, wearing a costume?"

"Oh!" Her smile drops into a more serious face as she

leans forward a little. "I work here. Two days a week." Then she turns and points to the sign above the little shop she came out of. "The *Bishop Busybody*. I've been writing this rag for about four years now. Doesn't really make a profit—yet. Start-up costs and everything. But it's finding its audience. It's fun. And it makes me happy, which is the most important thing."

I study the sign, then look her in the eyes, noticing that they're bright gray for the first time ever. "You write for a newspaper?"

"Well, 'newspaper' might be a bit ambitious a word for the *Bishop Busybody*. It's more of a... fictional thing. Which, of course, the *Bishop News* is as well. But it's not really news at all. It's... lonely hearts."

My eyes squint down in confusion. "It's what?"

"Lonely hearts. You know, like... personals."

"Personal ads?"

"Yeah. 'Desperately seeking somebodies.' Mail-order brides and that sort of thing. But it's fake. I just make all the ads up and every edition comes with a little announcement. Like a wedding or a baby. Just enough so readers can keep up with their favorite fictional desperately-seeking-somebodies over time." She pauses to think here, making a very cute face while she does it. "It's like an early version of a soap opera. A very slow-moving one. But aren't they all?"

It takes me a few seconds to catch up with her question mark because I'm still envisioning the soap-opera image she just put in my head. I blink. "I guess. But... people actually read that kind of thing?"

"Well, not many people. Which is why it doesn't make a profit. But I've clawed my way up to seventy-three regular subscribers and sell about two hundred more on a good week."

"Rosie Harlow. When the hell do you have time to run and write a frickin' newspaper?"

Rosie laughs. It's a nice laugh that makes her face look even friendlier than it already does. "Amon, no one ever has time for anything. Time is something you make for things you like doing. And I like doing this on Tuesday and Wednesday mornings." Then she gives me a little curtsey and turns away, walking off in the opposite direction to where I'm heading.

"Bye, Rosie," I call.

"See ya around, Amon," she calls back.

I start walking again, pulling my bones behind me and heading for my truck, which is parked outside the Bishop historical district, since this part of town is horse and buggy only. But she's right, I realize. Time *is* something you make for things you like doing.

THE RIDE **back** to the Edge Security compound is only about twenty minutes. In the crude triangle that makes up the cities of Bishop, Disciple, and Revenant, our place is right off the highway just about halfway between Bishop and Disciple. Which is kinda convenient when it comes to running errands and shopping.

Edge is busy, as usual, when I pull into the long gravel

driveway. There are sixty ex-soldiers living here with us and they are going about their day, training. Getting ready for the big August first deadline Collin has set up with Charlie Beaufort, our DC contact. I'm not sure what the first job is just yet—everything with Charlie is on a need-to-know basis and no one needs to know that but Collin at the moment. But we're on track, so I'm not worried about it.

I drive my truck all the way to the back where my house is, then pass it by and pull right up to the kennel. It's a long brown building that can hold up to sixty dogs. We've only got thirty-six at the moment, but more puppies are on the way.

The dogs are therapy for the men, but we train them up to military specifications and will sell them—eventually. But we haven't sold any yet.

When I enter the kennel, it's empty of dogs because they're all outside with their partners. But I say hi to the men in here who have clean-up duty as I make my way into the walk-in freezer with my cart of bones and unload.

When I'm done, I take the cart out, close the door, and just pause to have a look around. Sometimes it feels like I've died and gone to heaven. Like I need to pinch myself because this life we've created feels more like a dream than anything resembling reality.

I train dogs for a living. Not just any dogs, either. The world's smartest dogs. If you'd have asked me two years ago if this would be my life, I would've laughed. The bad press from all those congressional hearings hadn't faded yet, it was all very fresh. And there was a time when I thought Collin, Ryan, Nash, and I would be spending a few years in prison over our part in the scandal.

But Charlie Beaufort worked it out. As Charlie Beaufort usually does. And, well… here we are. Free, and happy, and well on our way back to successful.

So maybe for the first time since Collin and I were pulled aside by those MP's when we got off the bus for basic training, I let out a sigh.

We made it.

It was rough, and we lost a lot of men, but four of us pulled through.

And now we're here, back in West Virginia, and it's all gonna work out.

I really do believe it.

Just as I'm thinking this a high-pitched whistle to the tune of 'Yankee Doodle' cuts through the silence and a tall man about my age comes around the corner holding a clipboard. He's looking down at this clipboard, not paying attention, and we nearly collide.

"Whoa, there," I say, putting up both of my hands, pushing him back. "Watch where you're going."

The man stops and his eyes lift up slowly, revealing a strange expression on his face that I can't quite place, but comes off a little bit challenging. But just as quick as I catch it, the look disappears and then his blue eyes are smiling as the corners of his lips turn up. "Oh, sorry." He clicks his pen and points it at me. "You're Amon Parrish, right?"

"I am. And who the hell are you?"

"I'm Sawyer." He thrusts a hand at me. "The inspector."

My eyebrow shoots up. "Inspector?"

But just as I say that, Collin comes around the corner. "Oh, there you are, Amon. We were just lookin' for you."

My one eyebrow is still cocked because I'm confused. "*We?*"

Collin nods his head to Mr. Clipboard. "This here is Sawyer Martin. He's here to inspect everything for Charlie."

"Inspect it for *what?*" For some reason I find myself annoyed at this revelation. Mostly because of the near-collision that came with a side of confusion. But also because this is the first I'm hearing about some fuckin' inspection, and since Ryan, Nash, Collin, and I are all equal partners, the idea that some stranger would be passing judgment on my kennel makes me feel put out.

It's not even Collin who answers me, which just escalates my vexation. Mr. Clipboard once again thrusts his hand at me. "Nice to finally meet you, Amon. I've been looking forward to it."

I actually growl. It comes out past an upturned lip and everything. Because there's just something about this guy I don't like. "Why is this the first time I'm hearing about this?" I'm looking at Clipboard, but I'm really talking to Collin.

"Oh, come on, Amon." Collin slaps me on the back. "Sorry I didn't tell ya, but I just found out myself."

"Well, what are you looking at in my kennel?" I jut my chin at Clipboard's little checklist. "What's that?"

"Just basic stuff. Mostly about safety and—"

I'm just about to lose my shit when Collin grabs my arm, turning me. He calls over his shoulder. "You look at whatever you want, Sawyer. We've got nothing to hide here. If you need us, we'll be up at the office." Then Collin gives me a little push towards the back door and we leave.

Once outside, I turn to him. "What the hell is going on? Why is that man here passing judgment on us?"

13

"Forget him. It's just... Charlie. He's..." Collin sighs. "Well, you were there when we rescued Lowyn. You know I had to promise Charlie I'd work for him, right?"

I shrug. But I do.

"Well." Collin shoves his hands in his pockets. "This is part of that. There's no point in arguing. If Charlie wants to inspect the place, then he gets to send a man to inspect the place. It's no big deal, anyway. We've got nothing going on here but what's on the paperwork."

I side-eye the door we just came out of, then meet Collin's gaze. "Yeah. For *now*. But it could take a turn at any time."

"This Sawyer character, he's only gonna be here two weeks, so he'll be long gone before any turning starts happening."

I blink. "Two. Weeks? Who the hell needs two weeks to do an inspection!"

Collin grabs my arm again and starts walking up the driveway towards Nash's house, which is also where the Edge office resides. "Keep your voice down. And forget that guy. Charlie's just nervous about the contract. He wants to see how the men are getting on. And they're gettin' on good, so let's show them off, ya know?"

I huff.

"Anyway, we've got bigger problems, Amon. Because Mr. Martin back there showed up with a delivery for us. And I was just coming to get you so we can have a discussion about it."

"What kind of delivery?"

Collin stops walking to look me in the eyes. "The kind

that brings four stainless-steel canisters inside a cooler of dry ice, that's what kind."

"But…" Once again, I am confused. "We already got our delivery for this week."

"Exactly." Collin starts walking again. "Like I said, we've got bigger problems than an impromptu inspection."

INSIDE THE EDGE SECURITY OFFICE, Ryan, Nash, Collin, and I all stand round a small table looking at the cooler with trepidation. The four of us are the same in some ways, but different in many others. Obviously, Collin and I come from Disciple, West Virginia and grew up together, so we're more the same than different. But Nash is a West Coast guy who came up in big money and Ryan is an East Coast guy who came up in… well, the mob, actually.

But for some reason, it works. At least when it comes to 'security'.

Nash walks over to his desk and picks up a large white envelope, then hands it to Collin. "It came with a package. I opened it because it was addressed to Edge. But it's for you, Collin."

Collin takes the envelope when Nash offers it, then peeks inside. A moment later, he's pulling out another envelope, this time red.

Red is never a good sign.

"Ah, fuck," Ryan says, flopping down into a chair. "Ah,

fuck! What the hell is this shit?" His eyes are a little bit wild as he looks up at Collin. "They said we were good, Col. They said we were *fine*. A cooler showing up with a red envelope doesn't sound fine to me."

Collin puts up a hand. "Just... relax. Don't jump to conclusions."

"Well"—Nash laughs, then takes a seat at the table as well —"he's not wrong, Col. This does not look promising."

I pull out a chair and sit as well. In my experience, red envelopes that come with coolers are never a good thing.

Collin stays standin'. He unseals the red envelope, pulls out a thick stack of papers, and scans the cover letter. Then he sighs and drops the whole stack onto the table. "They've got a new protocol for us."

"No!" Ryan stands up. "No fucking way. I'm not drinking that shit! I'm not doing it!"

Collin rubs a fingertip against his temple like he's got a headache. "It says there's been some complications with other teams, Ryan. And this protocol is just precautionary."

"We haven't experienced any complications," Nash points out. "So why do *we* have to drink it?"

Collin looks at me and I shrug with my hands. "If it ain't broke, ya know?"

"I know. But..." Collin stares at the cooler for a few seconds. "But we don't have much choice, guys."

Ryan is pacing the room now. "We absolutely do, Collin! We absolutely do." He looks at me. "We're just gonna pretend we're drinking them and not do it, right, Amon?"

I don't know what to say. This really isn't my department. I don't even understand why we're drinking the first batch, to be honest. I mean, I know they tell us it's for health reasons. That some of the treatments we were ordered to take while we were under contract with the military had some bad side effects and one of our men even died from them several years back. But other than that, I have no idea what they did to us or why it warrants a weekly delivery of a mandatory frozen fruit drink. I've never gotten sick from anything they did to me in the military. Just that one guy who worked on the team for about a year.

Nash stands up and starts opening the cooler. We all lean in as he presses in his security code to pop the lock and then opens the lid. A mist of dry ice vapor floats up and he waves it off, then grabs a set of tongs from his desk and reaches in, pulling out one of the canisters.

The stainless-steel canisters that get delivered every Monday come with a green ring around the top, but this ring here is orange.

We all look at each other.

Ryan is the first to speak. "Nope. You guys do what you want, but I'm not drinking that shit. I am *not* drinking that shit." He huffs, looking at me. "We've had enough. Right, Amon?"

Raleigh, his name was. The one that died. Nice guy. Kinda quiet, but in a dangerous kind of way. Which is how most men here at Edge present, so it was all fine.

Collin and I were discharged from the marines after two years of training. I spent that first two years learning how to produce military-grade K-9's and Collin spent it perfecting the finer points of counterintelligence. In other words, he did spy shit.

So, after the discharge he and I weren't required to take

any more government mandated 'treatments' and we opted out.

Nash and Ryan didn't join up with us for another year or so. Which means they took a few more of these injections than we did. Raleigh came along five years into this whole thing. He and I were never really friends, so how many injections he took, I've got no idea. Doesn't matter at this point because he's dead now and, according to Charlie, it was an injection that did this. That's when Charlie told us that we needed the fruit drinks to counteract any deleterious side effects from previous treatments.

It felt like a reasonable ask at the time. I mean, Raleigh *did* just die. But that was... hell, six years ago now. And none of us have ever gotten sick. So I'm kinda with Ryan on this one.

This whole time I've been thinking back, Collin has been silent. But he lets out a long breath now. "All right. We won't drink them and I'll try and get more information. But you all know how this works. They're not gonna tell me."

"They're lying." Nash walks around to the other side of his desk and takes a seat, then looks Collin dead in the eyes. "Maybe the one we've been drinking is a treatment to prevent something worse. But then again, maybe it isn't. I say we stop them all. Because they lied to us back then, Col. And once a liar, always a liar."

"None of us have gotten sick though," I say. "I mean, we've been drinking these for years now."

"We don't even know if they're the same protocol, Amon." Ryan's still pissed. He's always been a bit of a conspiracy theorist and we all kinda taunt him about it on occasion. But he's been right about a lot of shit when you look back. "They could've been changing the formula every week and we'd never know the difference."

Collin puts up his hands. "Fine. Let's stop."

I raise an eyebrow, surprised. "Really?" Because Collin likes to follow rules. It's a weird trait considering who he is and what he's done. But he likes certainty, and rules and regulations bring that. That don't mean he's a blind follower —he's bucked his share of the system over the last decade— it's just the drink protocol hasn't ever been part of that.

He really believes that there's something wrong with us and these drinks fix it.

Or, at the very least, he's never been willing to find out if he was wrong.

Until now, I guess.

"All right," Ryan agrees, obviously feeling better about things because he lets out a long breath. "Good. I'm glad. I've been ready to ditch those drinks for years."

Ryan is about to leave, convinced the matter has been settled, but Collin puts up a hand. "On one condition, Ryan."

Ryan turns. "What's that?"

"That we report in every night with how we're feeling. Starting Monday, of course. Since we already took this week's dose."

We all agree, then give each other one final look before going back to work.

ROSIE

I have a small cottage just off Goosebeak Alley and right behind the blacksmith that I use to keep my Bishop life separate from my Disciple one. It was a necessity at first because if you wanna work in the Bishop downtown historical district, you gotta look the part. Which means I have myself a nice little collection of eighteenth-century dresses that need to be kept in a certain condition.

When my son, Cross, and I were still living in our Disciple trailer, there wasn't any room to store these dresses properly. Of course, there's plenty of room now because we're living in Lowyn's house. But driving home in a traditional gown without ruining it is a chore so I decided to keep the little cottage behind the blacksmith instead of giving it up.

This cottage is basically just a ten-by-ten square and doesn't even have a proper kitchen, just a countertop to plug in small appliances, a tiny sink, and a little bar fridge to keep a few snacks. There is a bathroom, but it's just a tall rectangle that hangs off the cottage like maybe it was an outhouse before modern plumbing renovations.

I only use the cottage as a dressing room but it's the most perfect space a girl could ever wish for. The floors are gorgeous wide-plank dark wood, the walls are a cream-colored plaster that looks so soft, ya just wanna pet it, and there's a French chandelier hanging down from the center of the ceiling that originally used wax candles but now has electric ones.

Bishop is a stickler for everything eighteenth-century authentic, but the town makes exceptions for electricity. Fire, it turns out, is a fire hazard. And insurance premiums in the twenty-first century will break the bank even if you're not lighting hundreds of candles every night, let alone when ya are.

I have three vintage armoires that I scored from McBooms because Lowyn didn't think they'd be worth restoring after she got them home from her picking trip. They line the walls of the small space and together they are big enough to store my seven dresses and collection of aprons, stays, and petticoats.

In between two of the armoires I have a vanity, which is new, but it's custom and Amish-made, so it still has the whole Bishop vibe. The last thing along the walls is the dresser that stores my various undergarments.

Right underneath the chandelier in the center of the room is my most favorite piece of furniture ever. A chaise longue covered in light blue silk velvet, authentically restored by Lowyn McBride herself, and gifted to me several Christmases ago after it had sat in the McBooms showroom for over a year and she saw how I longed for it. It's got to be worth ten thousand dollars, at least, but I would never sell it. Aside from my child—who doesn't count because he's not an asset, he's a human being—this chaise is my most prized possession, the best gift I've ever received. Again, aside from my child, who, in retrospect, was definitely a gift, but also wasn't, since I was fifteen at the time when I had him.

My little cottage is full up with gorgeous, frilly, feminine things and every time I walk through the door, I sigh, it's that cozy and comfortable.

A second home for me, actually. I only use it on Tuesdays and Wednesday when I'm in Bishop takin' care of my *Busybody* duties. It's kinda wasteful to spend so much money on such a small part of my life, but it makes me happy. And I think I deserve this happiness.

Besides, Cross has not gone without anything due to the expense of my life here in Bishop. Aside from a father, of course, but that's got nothing to do with Bishop. In fact, I would say Cross benefited from my second life because you really can't buy happiness. Sure, it's fun to try. But after the spending spree is over there's nothing left but the truth. Happiness is a precious thing—it's not for sale nowhere.

Of course, I don't even pay rent in Disciple these days. I'm living at Lowyn's house and she refuses to take money from me. She considers her contribution to my easier, less-stressful life a pay-it-forward gift. And the job of a recipient of such a gift is to appreciate it, which I do. And take advantage of it, which I'm trying to do. I'm just not sure how, aside from saving money, living at Lowyn's helps me get to the next step in my journey.

Philosophical musings aside, I am a very lucky woman and even though the Revival is nothing more than a carnival sideshow when you look too close at it, I sit in that tent every single weekend and count my blessings. Every single 'amen' I shout is honest. I mean it with my whole heart.

It was a rough ride. Felt like a nightmare rollercoaster I couldn't get off for a few years there in the beginning, but it's all worked out for Cross and me.

It truly has.

AFTER CHANGING *into* my McBooms clothes—vintage bell bottoms, halter top, and clogs, which is my most favorite shoe ever—I walk a few blocks over to the printers just outside the historical district and get my copies of the *Busybody* all printed on pretty vintage-like paper. Then I come back to my cottage and sit at the vanity so I can fold and stuff this week's edition of the *Busybody* into vintage-looking envelopes.

After that, I affix the meticulously designed address labels and stack them up all neat so I can get a good look at them. Seventy-three subscribers. It doesn't sound like much, but I'm proud of that number. It averages out to a little bit less than twenty new ones per year, but still—it feels like a win.

I gather them up in my giant purse and head on out the door.

Outside it's hot and sticky, though that is just getting started because it's only June. By July we'll all be melting. But I love summers in Bishop. Everyone's outside working on something. All the downtown ladies are in their backyards gardening, or feeding chickens, or chasing baby pigs. And all the men are doing manly things like making horseshoes and milling grain, or whatever it is these Bishop men do.

There's a lot of activity, but it's not chaos like a big city might be. It's easy, and relaxed, and comfortable.

I love being in Bishop, though I don't mind leaving, to be honest. Disciple is the same way, but on a less rustic spectrum. But before I return, I have two more things to attend to. First, I stop at the post office and hand my envelopes over to Betty Watson so she can run them through the postage machine that will stamp each one with the Bishop postmark. Details matter, after all.

When that's done, I head on over to the Bishop Inn to help out for the lunch rush. I don't have a regular job there, I just fill in on the days I'm in town. And they might have me washing dishes, or bussing tables, or serving. It all depends. But I don't mind it. You don't have to dress traditional at the Bishop Inn because it's right on the edge of downtown and not technically part of the historical district.

When I walk in, Jessica, part-owner and front-desk manager, greets me with a smile. "It's the kitchen today, Rosie. Bryn will fill you in."

I smile and wave as I make my way through the crowd of people waiting for a table or to check in. Bryn McBride is her usual self, mumbling under her breath as she works the grill and the stove at the same time. Mostly she's cursing. But this is what I like about Bryn. She is all drama all the time. When we're together there isn't a moment when she's not complaining, or gossiping, or telling some kind of puffed-up story.

It's off-putting to some people, but not to me. I like it because Bryn is the kind of person who fills in empty spaces. When she's nearby there is no room for loneliness, or silence, or regrets because she is bigger than all of that. She's loud, and aggressive, and I just laugh when she complains about not being able to find a decent man because it's got nothing to do with her looks—she's beautiful, just like her big sister Lowyn. And it's got nothing to do with her ambition—she's successful too. On a smaller scale than Lowyn, but flourishing, nonetheless.

The reason she can't find a man is because she's so damn disagreeable, most people just get tired of it. But I can't tell her this because her confrontational personality is my most favorite thing about Bryn McBride and I never want her to change.

"Oh, good! You're here!" Bryn exclaims this when she finally breaks off from her rant and notices me putting on a plastic apron. "I've got dishes piling up and I need those pots and pans, Rosie!"

"I'm on it," I tell her. I start doing dishes, every once in a while looking over my shoulder as Bryn makes room for me in her private tirade—which is only private in the Bryn sense of the word, in that she's mostly talking to herself, but these external monologues just happen to occur out loud.

But Bryn fills up the space. The emptiness recedes. Silence hasn't got a prayer.

And I like it this way.

AFTER MY LITTLE **shift** at the Bishop Inn is over, I head back to Disciple. But it's only two o'clock, so I don't go home. Instead, I stop off at McBooms to check in and see how things are going. Lowyn made me the manager so she wouldn't have to come into Disciple every day. She's keeping her distance from the town right now on account of all that mess up in Blackberry Hill and Jim Bob Baptist's part in it. Which was tangential, at best, but I can see her point.

Anyway, she left town, renouncing any Revival profit share for good, and moved in with Collin and his gang over at the Edge compound. But she couldn't just pick up McBooms and move it as well.

So. I am the manager. The problem is, I'm not in town every day. I only worked at McBooms part-time. I only work anywhere part-time. So she ended up hiring a gang of teenagers for the summer and I'm loosely in charge of them.

When I walk in the door the music is blaring, two teenage girls are dancing in the middle of the showroom, and two teenage boys are sitting in a nearby 'living room' watching them. When they see me, the music and dancing comes to a screeching halt and the boys all stand up, smoothing their hair and trying to look presentable.

They always treat me like I'm an adult and get all respectful and shit. It's kinda cute.

I act accordingly as well, planting my hands on my hips

and making my eyes wide. "What the hell is goin' on in here!"

They get all scared and fidgety, apologizing profusely. I glare at them a little, then tell the boys to leave and prod the girls back to work.

The problem is, there's really nothing to do here during the week. I mean, *I* have things to do—I'm in charge of cataloguing everything Lowyn brings home from her pickin' trips and coordinating with the warehouse and shipping people—but the teenagers are only here to mind the place. And maybe, if a customer walks in, ring them up. But most of Lowyn's foot traffic happens on the weekends after the Revival show, so it's always dead.

Still, there's not a wooden floor in existence that can't use a good sweepin'. So that's what I have the girls do. But I let them put the music back on. I always play music when I'm here too.

Then I gather up the pile of mail Lowyn never pays any attention to, take it over to my favorite Fifties dinette set in the middle of the showroom, and sit down to sort.

It's a big pile, but junk is easy to filter out and since this is my regular spot, there's a trash can at the ready near my feet.

Almost all of it is junk, so I'm toss-toss-tossin' away when I just so happen to look down and spy an envelope sticking out of a catalogue.

"Oops!" Guess I got a little over-enthusiastic. I pick the envelope up out of the can and turn it over. "Well, that's weird." I say this right out loud because the envelope is addressed to *me*.

It's handwritten too, my full name sittin' right on top of

the McBooms street address in a well-practiced all-caps style. No return address, not even on the back. But the weirdest thing is that the postmark says Disciple.

I release the seal on the envelope and pull out a piece of paper that turns out to be something of a worksheet. A dot-to-dot worksheet, actually. But not in the traditional 1-2-3 dot-to-dot pattern, but letters. And not just in the one alphabet I recognize, but something that looks like Greek and another that looks Chinese.

I flip it over and look at the back, but it's blank. Weird. Why would someone be sending me this?

Maybe it's some kind of promotional thing? I dunno. I'm just about to toss it in the trash when I pause.

Maybe Cross would like to solve it? He's a smart kid. And he used to love puzzles when he was younger. Of course, he's on the verge of being a teenager now so all the things he thought were cool two years ago are now for kids, because obviously, when a boy hits twelve, it's time to grow up.

Those are his thoughts on the matter, at least. Still, this worksheet doesn't look anything like the ones he used to do when he was smaller. It looks... complicated. In fact, it looks a little bit like code. And codes are something totally different than puzzles because codes are things grownups solve for serious reasons, of course.

So I shove the paper back into the envelope and stick it in my purse to take it home.

Even though I still feel a thrill when I park my car in the driveway and walk up to the gorgeous front porch of Lowyn McBride's meticulously restored house, I hate getting home before Cross. During the school year it almost never happens. But summer is all about unexpected plans and spur-of-the-moment adventures, so it's a nightly thing these days.

I do expect him for supper, but the average suppertime in the summer for the people of Disciple is seven-thirty. Parents coordinate this so we can be sure that our children will appear at the dinner table on a nightly basis.

But McBooms only stays open 'till six, and it's my duty as manager to shut it all down when closing time comes around.

So here I am. At home alone.

There is not a damn thing about Lowyn's home that's cold or uninviting. And that helps. A lot, actually. But even though I love this house, it's not my house. Even if I bought this house from Lowyn, it would always be her house. So all the warm and welcoming things she's collected and displayed to maximize a sense of comfortable coziness when I walk through the door only helps so much.

Glancing up at the clock, I set my big purse down on the countertop, put on an apron, and immediately start making dinner.

At seven-thirty on the dot, my son shows up all bright-eyed and bursting with stories of what he and his friends did all day. He's a handsome boy, just like his father was. In fact, he looks a lot like his father. He was always lanky as a child, but his shoulders are gettin' broader and his arms are getting wider now. He's got my eyes and my smile, which looks good on him and makes him appear friendly—most of the time.

We sit across from each other at the table and I genuinely pay attention as he tells me about the woods, and the waterfall, and the girls—he is not into girls yet, but he's going to the junior high next year and so that's all part of it.

I eat it up. I can't get enough of my son.

But this dinnertime conversation is pretty much all we have these days. All he wants to do is be with his friends and think about growing up. And as soon as he's done eating, he puts his plate in the sink and then goes into the living room to play video games.

He's my life. He is my whole purpose. And I don't want to belittle the life I've built after getting pregnant at fifteen and fighting my way through everything that came with it. It's a good life for a woman of twenty-eight.

But children grow up. He's growin' up.

And I'm just not ready for it.

I want to hold on to him for as long as I can.

Still, there's just not much left of those days to cling to and I'm struggling to get a grip on my changing role as a mother of a soon-to-be teenager. I can't seem to hold his attention anymore. I'm just... Mom. And we don't have much in common. I don't play video games and he doesn't collect eighteenth-century dresses. Hell, I'm not even sure he knows I own those dresses. We've definitely never talked about them at dinner, so he might not.

So how do I keep this conversation going? How do I get his attention?

Then I remember the dot-to-dot that came in the mail. While it's really not that exciting, at least it's *something* for us

31

to talk about. So I take it out of my purse and flop down on the couch where Cross is playing his video game.

He grunts at me, probably because I messed up his move. But then he pauses his game and side-eyes me, whining his words out. "What do you want?"

"Look." I thrust the envelope at him.

"What is it?"

"Open it and look."

So he does, but he's not impressed. "A dot-to-dot worksheet? What am I, four?"

"Did you even look at it? It's not a simple dot-to-dot. It's a code."

His face twists a little. "What do you mean?"

"Well, it's not numbers, it's letters. And it's in different languages."

Apparently, this is just enough information to be intriguing because Cross takes a second look at the worksheet. But it's truly just a cursory glance because he puts it down and starts playing his game again. "Cool. Maybe I'll look at it later."

I sigh. Then get up and start cleaning up the kitchen.

A couple hours later after dinner is over, the dishes have been done, and Cross has gone to bed in the very bedroom that Collin Creed spent his entire childhood in, I go upstairs to my bedroom too.

I'm not much of a sleeper. It's a rare thing if my lights are out before midnight. So while I do get in bed, I don't wind down. I pull my Lonely Hearts notebook out of the nightstand drawer and start thinking up new personal ads for next week's issue.

My pen knows just what to write because I do this every night.

Desperately seeking... *somebody*.

AMON

I'm driving the highway loop en route to meet up with my sisters and there's a little bit of traffic when I hit Disciple because tourists always show up on Friday nights, even though there's no Revival until tomorrow.

Everything comes to a stop and I find myself sitting still in my truck right down the hill from Collin's house. Which is Lowyn's house. Which is actually Rosie's house now, and when I glance up, there she is. Coming down her walkway all dressed up in a Revival costume. Which, in this case, is a 1920's era flapper dress. Her long brown hair—which she likes to wear straight most of the time—is piled up on top of her head in one of those messy, sexy updos.

She looks hot as hell.

Rosie Harlow has always been cute, even pregnant. And for some reason, that's my image of her when she pops up in my memories. Probably because she went into labor at school—at lunchtime, in the cafeteria—and I was standing like ten feet away when her water broke. I will never forget that look on her face. It was… terror.

Normally I'm a jump-into-action kind of guy. And I was about to do that—not sure what exactly I had planned, but I was gonna at least go over to her and see if she was OK—

but that look on her face stopped me in my tracks. I couldn't move. And by the time I snapped out of it, other people had rushed in—all the girls, actually. And I wasn't needed or necessary.

Then there was a crowd, and a commotion, and that was the last time I saw Rosie Harlow until the morning I bumped into her at the Rise and Shine coffee shop the day Collin bought the Edge compound.

I buzz my window down and call out, "Hey, Rosie!"

Collin's street isn't directly on the highway. It's one street up. But there are no houses here to block the view and when she looks down, she smiles and waves. "Hey, Amon. What's up?"

"Oh, I just wanted to tell ya that you look real nice in that dress."

She blushes. Actually fuckin' blushes. Which I really like and ups her hotness by a factor of eleven. "Well, thank you. You look pretty nice in that truck yourself."

The traffic starts moving a little, so I'm easing forward, but she skips down the gently sloping grass, passes right by the sidewalk, and comes out into the street holding out a newspaper. When she gets to my truck, she pushes it towards me and I take it.

"What's this?" I ask.

"Tomorrow's Revival paper, of course."

"I can see that, Rosie. But why are you giving it to me?"

"Because Jim Bob said I could put the *Bishop Busybody* inside as an insert. And since you took an interest in it, I thought you might like a copy."

I place the newspaper on the passenger seat and Rosie

walks forward with me as we inch along the highway, waiting for people to turn into the Revival parking lot just up ahead. "Do you wanna go bowling with me tonight?"

Rosie smiles at me. And I've been turned down enough to recognize the smile. It's a no. "Well, I'm real busy right now, so I can't. But maybe some other time." She makes her smile bigger. "You have a nice night now, Amon. I've got to go. I'll see you around."

Then she leaves the highway and gets herself back on the sidewalk, heading towards the Revival grounds.

Of course she's busy. She's in costume. So this asking out thing I just did was a waste and I suddenly feel stupid. But also disappointed.

I like my sisters. I like bowling with the family—who doesn't? But Rosie Harlow has got my interest up and I think I would like to have a date with her.

I've got one strike now, though. So next time, I will plan it better.

The traffic clears and suddenly time speeds up again, the lag gone now. And a couple minutes later I'm pulling into the driveway where three of my sisters live.

I'm the oldest of five and all four of my siblings are girls. My mother was very young when she had me so there's an age gap between Eden and I. She was only twelve when I left for the marines. Angel was ten, Vangie was seven, and little Halo was only four. So when I first got back, I was expecting a sort of adjustment time.

And it was kind of a rude awakening. For me at least, not for them. Because in my head they were all still small and when I walked into my parents' house what I found was a bunch of grown women. Or nearly, in the case of Halo, since she's only sixteen.

It hit me then just how much I had missed. And there's a part of me that kinda wants to take all that time back.

I mean, not really. If I had stayed in West Virginia after high school I'd have ended up in Revenant. And I know we say it's all fake, but it's not. Not really. Just like the Revival is fake, but not. And Bishop is fake, but not.

How could anyone grow up in these places—these towns with such... personality and identity—and not be influenced by them?

So I would've ended up a biker. I would've ended up spending my days sleeping and my nights partying. I'd be playing a role in the Revival, but it wouldn't have been security. I'd have been in that gang that Lucas is running. Hell, if I was in Revenant all those years, maybe I would've been running that gang. Lucas is kinda young, after all.

So I know that leaving was the right decision for me. Collin and I would never have been friends if we weren't both in the same recruiting office that day back in senior year.

Anyway. Eden, Angel, and Vangie share a house across the street from the parents now. Halo still technically lives at home, but that's really only technically.

I don't bother knocking when I get to the door, just try the doorknob, find it unlocked, and walk in on an in-progress conversation about their business. They run all the social media marketing for the Revival. But they do more than that, too. They run marketing for all kinds of companies now.

The front living space has a corporate break room look about it, since the house doesn't have an extra room for an office. Desks everywhere, stacks of paper, whiteboards, and all kinds of other shit that lets people know that this side hustle of theirs has gone serious.

As soon as they notice I'm here, they all get up from their desks and come running at me like a gang of girl-bosses, which is only slightly terrifying, since they are my relations and all. But had I been a stranger, I'd be considering a duck-and-cover move right about now.

"Amon!" Halo exclaims, practically jumping into my arms. "You're back!"

I don't pick her up—though I do allow myself a moment of sadness here that I was gone all those years that I *could've* picked her up—and just hug her back.

Vangie and Eden join in, making it a group hug.

"You guys do realize I've been back for months now, right?" Angel's the one I'm looking at when I say this because she's not a hugger.

She's got her arms crossed and she's scowling at me as she answers back. "They think it's the last time they'll ever see you, Amon. That's why they're hugging you like that."

I walk forward towards her, little sisters hanging off me like fruit, and Angel backs up.

39

"Don't, Amon. I'm serious."

"Don't what? Don't hug you, Angel?"

We lock eyes for a moment, that spaghetti western showdown music playing in both our heads. She breaks first, trying to run. But I tackle her, making her squeal and sending her flyin' sideways onto the couch like we're little kids again.

She fights back as I use my considerable weight advantage to keep her down, and then all the girls join in—taking her side, of course—and pull me off.

Angel's got every right to be mad at me for leaving so long. Because I missed it. I missed all those years of them growing up. And I'm sorry about that, but it's done now and there's no way to change it. Still, my tactical move worked because while Angel hasn't given up cursing me, she's doing it with a smile now.

I flop down in a chair and sigh, looking around their house, wondering how so much could've changed in just twelve years. "We goin' bowlin' or what?"

There's a chorus of yeses, then a bunch of talk about work and whatever. Halo disappears, goin' across the street to the parents' house to grab whatever she needs, and the rest of them migrate upstairs to get ready.

Which leaves me time to spy something interesting. I lean over and grab a piece of paper off a side table. Well, look at that. The *Bishop Busybody*.

It's just copy paper, of course. But it's yellowed, like it's old. And it's nicely designed, like it's vintage. The publication title, as well as the contributors, is all printed in an old-timey font reminiscent of Colonial times, but with better readability.

I stare at Rosie Harlow's name for a moment, thinking about her all dressed up in Bishop yesterday. She looked… pretty. Frilly and feminine, for sure. Which I am not used to because since I've been back, I've mostly seen her in those bell bottoms and halter tops, looking all retro sexy. Which is a weird thing to be thinking about the mother of a twelve-year-old boy, but there is it.

But I like the dress and it looks natural on her. Like she fits in down there in Bishop.

My eyes scan down to the first article—which, of course, isn't an article, it's a personal ad—and I start to read it.

To THE ESTEEMED *ladies of refinement and courage, I am a robust and hearty young man of twenty-four, carving out a life in the untamed wilderness of West Virginia. My days are filled with the pioneering tasks of building, hunting, and tending to the land I am striving to tame.*

I seek a courageous and resilient woman, one who finds excitement in the prospect of a life amidst the wild beauty of West Virginia. A partner who is undaunted by the challenges of pioneer life and who can stand beside me as we forge a future in these uncharted lands. She should be spirited, resourceful, and ready to embrace the thrills and trials of a life less ordinary.

I'M STILL READING, smiling big, when Halo comes back, interrupting my happy vibes.

Rosie Harlow can write. Because I'm kinda jealous of this robust, hearty young man of twenty-four. And also, I like his taste in women.

"What are you doin'?"

I look up at Halo and hold up the paper. "Rosie Harlow writes this."

"Yeah, so?"

"It's... fun."

Halo smiles. "Yeah, it is. I always read them. Every single week." She sighs. "When the grumpy Mr. Stanton finally proposed to the widow Smith, I about fainted to the floor. His letter was so beautiful. They're expecting this October, ya know. Twins!" Her eyes are bright with excitement.

I just shake my head and stand up, reaching out to mess up Halo's hair while she backs off, squealing. A moment later all the sisters are there, ready for a night of bowling. So we leave and walk down the road together, ready for a night of sibling fun.

I love it here.

I'm so glad I'm back.

But as I walk, I can't help writing my own 'desperately seeking somebody' ad in my head.

AFTER BOWLING IS **over** and it's well past midnight, I find myself thinking about Rosie Harlow again as I pull my truck out onto the highway that runs through town.

And then her house is right there. Most of it is dark, but there is a light on upstairs.

She's awake.

I slow the truck, wondering maybe if I should stop by, but then speed up again, because knocking on a single woman's door in the middle of the night isn't something one does.

And then I'm thinking about what Rosie said to me yesterday. *Time is something you make for things you like doing.*

And I promise myself that tomorrow, I will make time for Rosie Harlow.

*E*veryone in Disciple complains about the weekends because we have to work. And not only that, we have to work hard. But it's the kind of complaining one does when they feel tired and wish for some spare time, but aren't unhappy.

Even though I don't really play a regular part most years, I am not unsatisfied with my role in the Revival. I like being shuffled around in the casting of the show because I get different costumes, and new motivations, and most of the time I'm a plot booster. I'm the woman who points to Collin Creed and says, "There he is! That's him! The murderer, Collin Creed!"

And it's always a surprise because script changes are only doled out on a need-to-know basis. So there's lots of gasping, and amazed looks, and smiling, too. Because everyone knows it's fake, so they don't much care when I'm throwing a fit, making them the center of attention.

It's just a bit of fun. And there's nothing wrong with a bit of fun when you're workin' so hard.

As usual, Cross went in early for choir practice, so I leave the house by myself and head on up the hill. When I get to the Revival tent, I immediately go find my daddy and brothers to see if they need any help. My family is in charge of the entire frickin' tent, including the scaffolding and over-tent that pops out in inclement weather.

I find them all hanging out near the maintenance shed, which is near the river. I am the youngest of five, the only girl, and they baby me the way one might expect if one has four big brothers.

But they don't need any help and I am shooed out of the way and told to go on down to the tent.

Even after I got pregnant at fifteen, my family stood by me. My daddy was mad, my mama cried, and my brothers all wanted the name of the boy who did this to me. But they settled down once Cross appeared.

I never did give up that name, but not because I didn't have it. I knew exactly who that boy was and I was a very willing participant. I was a bit of a free spirit in my teenage years—which is a nice way to say 'slut.' But whatever, it is what it is.

I liked him though, and had I given up his name, he would've been dead for certain instead of just presumed. His name was Erol Cross and he was two years older than me and wasn't even from the Trinity area, but lived in a little town about thirty miles down the river. He and his crew used to come into Revenant to party on the weekends in his senior year of high school. And that's where I met him. In the Bong Balls pool hall right there on D Street, across from McGills Tavern.

Erol and I were more than casual, we were planning a future together. I wasn't gonna keep him secret forever. That was not the plan. The plan was for me to have the baby and him to graduate high school and get a job to make him look serious and dedicated. Then we would both go to my parents and tell them we were getting married.

After that, he would move to Disciple, work his job during the week, and take part in the Revival on the weekends, just like most everyone else. He would've ended up working the tent with my brothers. Their hatred of him would've faded over time and by now, twelve years later, we would've forgotten all about how it started.

But that's not how it happened, obviously. Instead, Erol woke up early on his eighteenth birthday and went into the woods. He had a little side hustle trappin' beaver and it was the last day of the season, so he told me the night before that he was gonna go pick up his traps before the partying started.

He never came home.

They never found a body or anything.

Just… gone.

To say that I was devastated would be an understatement. I was eight and a half months pregnant and I went into labor in school the next week. My water broke in the cafeteria at lunchtime. In front of everyone.

But there wasn't much time to feel humiliated. There wasn't much time to feel anything but sad and terrified, really.

And then Cross was there—named after his daddy.

And from that day on, he was my life.

TODAY, *as I sit in the tent* waving my fan to stave off the heat, is another sad day for me. And I am feeling it quite sharply at the moment because the children's choir is singing and for the first time since he was three, Cross is not up there on the stage.

His voice started breaking a few weeks back and this morning the choir director, Mr. Bateman, decided that it was time for Cross to move on to something else. Since this departure was sudden, no one quite knew what to do with Cross this weekend, so he's working the tent with my daddy and brothers, wearing a last-minute hand-me-down costume, and I don't even know where he is right now.

The only thing I do know is that he's not on that stage so I have no one to look at.

But just as I'm thinking that I notice a movement stage left. The tent flap opens and there, of all people, is Amon Parrish. He scans the crowd like he's looking for someone. And then, unexpectedly, his eyes find mine and he smiles.

Now Amon Parrish was *the* boy everyone wanted to date in high school. Collin was too, but Collin was taken. Even before he hooked up with Lowyn, everyone knew he was in love with her, so no one was wastin' any time fantasizing about Collin Creed.

Amon was the biker-jacket-wearing-bad-boy to Collin's golden-boy-jock image. He looked like the lead singer of a rock band with that blond hair and blue eyes of his. Only he was always fit and muscular and didn't look like a drug addict. Every girl in high school had a fantasy starring Amon Parrish and since Amon wasn't a 'goin' steady' kinda guy, most of them got to live it out. He's only gotten better with age, so I imagine he's had all kinds of exotic women over the last decade.

I, of course, never fantasized about Amon because I was younger and busy with my own real-life boy. But he's still smiling so... I smile back.

And there it is—an Amon Parrish fantasy flits through my mind. I see us kissing, and his hands going wild all over my body, and some wall sex suddenly appears. Which makes me blush, so I forcibly push the fantasy aside and come back to reality.

Why is he here? Did he come here for me?

Oh, it can't be. Amon Parrish has no business with me. We bump into each other around town and we chat every now and then, but nothing more.

Except he did invite me to go bowling with him last night, didn't he?

Just as I'm thinking this, he starts walking this direction. It's an unusual thing to do because we're in the middle of a sermon. So there is a rustle of clothing as everyone's head turns in unison to watch him do this, which causes Simon, our pastor, to stutter at the lectern.

Even if Amon is heading my way for a purpose, he's got no endgame because there are no empty chairs in my row. There are no empty chairs at all in the tent—it's a rule. If we're not sold out—and that's a rare occasion indeed—we fill those chairs up with townspeople.

He stops at the end of my row and sighs, knowing he's got no endgame, but willing to stick it out until the show is over, I guess. Because he settles against a post and starts paying attention to the words still spilling out of Simon's mouth.

There's a hushed murmur from the townspeople, all wondering what he is up to. But it calms down quickly because... well, it's Amon. Everyone knows he's a wild card, even if they did kinda forget over the years since he left.

And anyway, he doesn't make any more moves. Just appears to be enjoying the sermon.

I, on the other hand, am so distracted by his sudden appearance that I miss my next 'amen.' And then I spend the next ten minutes running scenarios through my head about why he's here. Most of them comin' out on the sexy side of things.

Which is a fantasy for sure, because I'm not his type. At least I don't think I am.

When the show is over everyone gets up to leave, as do I, but Amon stays right where he is. Obviously waiting for me.

I make my way to the end of the row and stand before him, his eyes dancin' a little. "Amon."

"Rosie."

"Are you here for me?"

"I am."

"Oh. I see. Well. What can I do for you?"

"I asked you to go bowling last night."

"You did."

"You turned me down."

"That's right."

"Well, I was wondering if it was just bad timing or if it was me."

I let out a breath. "Why are you wondering that?"

"Why?" His eyebrows shoot up. "Because if it was bad

timing, I'm gonna ask you again. But if you don't like me, I'll move on."

"That's very forthcoming of you."

"Thanks. I like to be forthcoming."

He's talking with a straight face, but I'm smiling pretty big right now. "Well, can I think about this a little bit?"

"Can you define 'little bit?'"

I smile bigger. "You're flirtin' with me."

"Why does that surprise you? You flirt with everyone."

"Well, yeah. But that's me. You're… you."

"What are you saying? I'm not flirty?"

"Are you flirty?"

He smiles now. But he narrows his eyes too. "Should I ask again? Or should I move on?"

"If I say move on, will you truly move on? Or will you try again?"

His smile grows. "Try again."

"Then I'm gonna tell you to move on."

He nods, still smiling, then leans forward. "By the way, I read your little paper. Not the one you gave me, but the one from last week. My sisters had a copy."

"Oh, right. They do the Revival marketing and I'm part of the marketing now."

"I like it."

"Which part? The whole idea of it? Or just the vibe?"

"The writing."

I nearly giggle. "You like the *ads*?"

"Yeah. I'm kinda jealous of Robust and Hearty because I like his taste in women. And I was thinking that the woman he described sounded a little bit like you."

I nearly guffaw. I manage to hold it in, but my cheeks get

hot and I know I'm probably turning bright red. "You fancy a..." I pause to think back on what kind of partner Robust and Hearty was looking for. "A courageous and resilient woman who is ready to embrace the thrills and trials of a life less ordinary?"

Amon nods. "I do."

"Well." I pull myself together. "I'm sorry to disappoint you, Amon Parrish. But I am not looking for a man at the moment. I am quite happy with my life as it is."

He nods at me. Pretends to take off an imaginary hat and bows a little. And even though he's not in costume—he's wearing his usual outfit of black tactical pants and black t-shirt—I picture him in one. "Well, then," he says. "I will leave you to your day. But I'll see ya around, Rosie Harlow."

I nod back. "See ya around, Amon Parrish."

He turns and walks out, not even looking back. But I'm not unhappy about that because he already told me that he's gonna try again.

I am being *courted*.

By Amon Parrish, of all people.

MY ROLE **in today's Revival** is tea-party participant in the garden party tent. Visitors can buy special tickets for a seat at the garden party tables. Four people to a table. Two are Disciple women and two are ticket-holding guests. That way we can all have a nice chat and get to know one another.

It's not required that the out-of-towners dress up in

costume—not everybody can afford that. But it's pretty common that they do. On this afternoon our two guests are very period-appropriate and my assigned garden party tea partner is MaisieLee Roberts herself, the dressmaker of the aforementioned period-appropriate dresses.

MaisieLee rests both her elbows on the table, propping two fists under her chin as she leans forward in my direction. "So." She cocks her head at me. "What did Amon want?"

"Which one is Amon?" tea-party-participant number one asks.

"He's the handsome fella who interrupted church," tea-party-participant number two replies.

"Oh," the first one says. Then she nods, smiling. "I like him. He's cute."

MaisieLee butts in here. "Isn't he just. Are you datin' him, Rosie? Because last I heard you were datin' a Fayetteville man called Scar."

"Which one is Scar?" Number One asks her partner.

"I'm not sure," Number Two replies.

I wave a hand at the visitors. "He's no one." Then I look MaisieLee in the eyes. "We'll talk about this later."

But MaisieLee is ready for my dismissal and she's got a comeback. "Oh, I think we should talk about this now. Don't you ladies agree?"

The two guests nod enthusiastically. "We do. Oh, we do."

I could put up a little fight, but why bother when I can just lie? And anyway, it's not even lying when you're acting. And I *am* acting. Everything inside the tent grounds is fair game for acting. So I lean in towards our guests, which makes them lean in towards me in turn. "Amon and I were a thing, you see."

"Oh, really?" One says.

"Yes. For a long time. He's my true love, ya know? But he cheated on me." The guests gasp and MaisieLee snorts. "When I was pregnant, of all times."

"Oh, no!" Number Two says. "That's terrible!"

"Isn't it just?" I agree, giving MaisieLee a side-eye. "And that was twelve years ago. He left town for all that time, but now he's back trying to make amends. So I'm not sure, ladies. I gave him my heart once and he stepped all over it. Why should I trust him with it again?"

Two says, "Once a cheater, always a cheater."

And One says, "Never trust a man who leaves you high and dry." Then she gives me a stern look, kinda shaking her finger at me, and for a moment I think I'm about to get scolded. But she says, "A man who can't stand up is not a stand-up man."

Which confuses me, but comes off with too much confidence and a little bit too poetic for me to ask questions about interpretation. And anyway, MaisieLee is sighing and rolling her eyes, because the guests are firmly on my side now and she's not gonna get anything truthful out of me today about Amon. So I guess it doesn't matter that the little quote didn't make sense.

After that we chat about Revival things and an hour later, I'm done for the day. I go looking for Cross and find him with my brother, Pate, who is nearly ten years older than me and the oldest of all us Harlow kids. Cross is up on a scaffold holding a hammer and pounding away on something or another.

"Hey, kid!" I yell up to him. "You about ready to go home and change? My day's over."

"Oh, not yet, Ma," Cross calls back. "Uncle Pate just finally trusted me to get on up here and fix this all by myself."

I shoot Pate a look. "It's a little bit early to have him climbing all over things doing repairs, don't you think? He just started today."

Pate shoots me a look right back. This one comes with low and lazy eyes that say I'm overreacting. "Rosie, you were five the first time I sent you up a scaffold to pound something." He nods his head towards Cross. "He's practically a grown man, for fuck's sake. Stop babying him."

I scoff. "I'm not babying him. And he's twelve, Pate. That's not grown."

Cross calls down. "Alexander the Great was conquering the whole world at age twelve."

I'm pretty sure this is not true, but I'm also a high-school dropout, so what do I know. I look at Pate, but he just grins. Which means he's probably a hundred percent sure it's not true, but isn't gonna intervene on my behalf because he's got Cross doin' all his fixin' work for him.

So I just sigh. "Whatever. Be home for dinner."

"I will, Ma." And then Cross goes back to his pounding.

BUT CROSS DOESN'T COME HOME for dinner. At six-fifteen, he calls asking if he can have dinner at his friend's house and then stay the night. They're working on a car or something.

I want to say no. But I don't. I force myself to smile, even though it's just a phone call, and tell him yes and to call me in the morning.

Then I sit at the table and stare at the spaghetti and meatballs I made.

It's probably gonna be a thing, this going out on Saturday nights. My boy is growing up whether I want him to or not.

I might need to get myself another part-time job.

LATER THAT NIGHT, after I've cleaned up the kitchen, folded laundry, and mopped the floors, I change into my nightgown, get in bed, and grab my Lonely Hearts notebook out of the drawer. I'm just about to open it up and start writing when I remember Amon this morning during Revival. My heart is sad about Cross and how the fast-forward button seems to have been pushed on his growing up, but Amon's little gesture this morning makes me smile.

Amon is nice-looking. He's got that whole 'blond hair, blue eyes' thing goin' for him. It made him more charming than he actually was as a troublemaking kid and definitely got him out of a detention or two if the adult authority was of the female persuasion.

I like Amon. I've always liked him. And we easily slip into a natural sort of banter when we bump into each other. And I like the idea of being courted, but is there room for a man in my life? All my recent boyfriends have been fictional. Like that Scar man MaisieLee mentioned. Fake. I make them up so people don't pity me. These men always live out of town and come with names like Scar, which implies a certain thing about a man. Which implies a certain thing about me, to be honest. But I'd rather be known as the woman with poor taste in men than a spinster-in waiting.

Because the truth is, I just don't date.

It's not that I haven't dated anyone since Cross was born. That's not true at all. There was a time there, right after Cross started kindergarten and my single-mommy routine took a turn, when I dated all kinds of men outside of the Trinity area.

But I compared each one of them with Erol. I was still stuck on the idea that he might come back. I mean, they didn't find a body. There was no death certificate. Even now, there is no death certificate. He could still be out there. Maybe the idea of a wife and a baby when he was eighteen was just too much? Maybe he just needed some space? Some time to think?

That was my daydream back then. That Erol would come back riding a motorcycle or something, with a black leather jacket to match, and he'd take one look at me and little Cross and just fall back in love with us.

But I gave up on that fantasy years back now. And I stopped dating too.

However. Amon Parrish, age thirty, might be worth taking a chance on.

It's just... it comes at an inopportune time. Because I'm feeling this emptiness of losing Cross. This is another transition period in the motherhood experience and my first inclination when these transitions occur is to go hook up with a Scar.

The name Scar is just a euphemism for any man, really. But particularly one of questionable morals and decision-making skills.

And Amon Parrish is a Scar if ever there was one. I don't know the whole story of what he and Collin and the rest of their crew have been up to all these missing years, but I know enough. He might be flirty and fun, but he's also a big red flag. A mistake waiting to happen.

And my lonely heart just can't handle the fallout of such mistakes.

So I open up my notebook, click my pen, and start writing a new ad.

Desperately seeking... somebody who is not Amon Parrish.

AMON

On **Monday morning** I'm glaring at inspector Sawyer Martin from my porch as he pokes around my kennel.

"If looks could kill…" Collin sips a cup of coffee as he approaches my porch steps. "Why are you so bothered about that guy, Amon? He's no one. He'll be gone soon enough and you'll never have to think about him again."

I shrug. "I just don't think my kennel is any of his business, that's all."

"It might not be, but if Charlie told him to inspect things, then the man needs to inspect things. He seems competent, so don't let it bother you."

My gaze slides away from Collin and lands back on the kennel, but this Sawyer guy has disappeared. "Charlie has no say in my kennel. I paid for it all by myself. He didn't give a dime for it. So even if he's got some kind of problem with what I'm doing and how I'm doin' it, it's none of his damn business. Which means this guy's poking is getting' on my last nerve."

"Just ignore him." Then Collin turns his back to me and starts walking up the driveway towards Nash's house. "See ya around, Amon."

"Yep," I call back. "See ya around."

I wait until Collin is out of sight, then I hop down my

porch stairs and head around the side of the kennel where I find this Sawyer character peeking into kennel windows.

"Can I help you with something?"

He turns, startled, then smiles. "Why, yes—yes, you can. This building here seems to be locked. If you could let me in, I'd sure appreciate it."

Though I didn't notice it before, his accent comes off as local. "It's locked because ain't no one got any business in there right now. All the dogs are either training with their partners or resting comfortably because they're about to give birth to puppies."

His smile never wavers. "OK. But you didn't say if you'd let me in or not."

My immediate instinct is to fight with this guy and deny his request for access. But Collin is probably right. The sooner he does his job, the sooner he leaves.

"I'll let ya in," I tell him, "if you tell me what you're looking for."

He's still smiling. Like this is his default expression. "I'm not really looking for anything in this kennel. I was just told to take a look at everything, so that's what I'm gonna do."

"You already saw this kennel. So why the second look?"

"I'm here to take lots of looks, Mr. Parrish. It's not a one-and-done kind of thing. It's a thorough inspection for Charlie Beaufort because, possibly, he's got some concerns about you boys."

Something happens here with this guy. I don't know if it's his tone, or the way his eyes narrow down in the slightest of ways, or the fact that he's way more confident in his interaction with me than most men are. It's possibly all three. Because I take a second look at Sawyer Martin and decide he's not a paper-pusher and I should've seen it immediately.

He's also lyin'. That's something I can see even in the dark. "Charlie doesn't have any concerns, not with Collin in charge. So your script needs work."

Still, his smile does not crack. "Can I see inside, Amon? Or should I just check off the box here that says 'refused access?'"

He holds up his clipboard and sure enough, there is a damn tick-box that says 'refused access.' I wave my hand at the door and bow a little. "It would be my pleasure."

I punch in the code to open the main door of the kennel and the inspector follows me inside. Immediately the mama dogs start whining for attention, but King is in here as well, and he gives me a friendly bark.

"I thought you said there were no workers in here?" When I look at Sawyer Martin, he's got one eyebrow raised.

Which makes me scoff, then nod at King. "This dog's with me today. He and I have an appointment down in Fayetteville."

Sawyer scribbles something on his clipboard. "Is that right?"

"That's right." I punch in the security code to open King's kennel, then point at my left side. The dog trots over and sits at my knee. "He's gettin' fitted for a new vest today."

Sawyer wants to say something here, but he's been schooled in the art of composure, so whatever it was, he holds it back and gives me a fake salute. "Well, you and your dog have a nice day now."

Which is, essentially, a dismissal. And I feel my temper getting ready to rear up. But I too have been schooled in the art of composure and even though my vest-fitting appointment with King isn't for hours, I decide to turn away and leave things here.

Outside I direct King to get in my truck, then I get in as well. But on my way out of the compound I stop at Nash's house, tell King to stay in the truck, and go inside to find Collin. He's sitting in Nash's office going over some paperwork, so I stand in the doorway, waiting until they're finished talking.

Collin turns to look at me. "Why are you loomin' in the fuckin' doorway, Amon?"

"He's up to something. I can tell. It's a mistake letting that man have free rein over our compound."

"Dammit, Amon." Collin is frustrated with me now. "I told you to ignore him. Just let the man do his job. If Charlie wants him to look around, I'm gonna let him look around."

Collin is typically the suspicious one, not me. I'm the easy-going dog trainer. Happy and content is my default setting. So I'm irritated that he's so indifferent about this whole thing. "You're not the least bit bothered that Charlie Beaufort is sending people up here like he's our boss? Because I am."

"Amon, I gave up trying to fight Charlie years back now. He and his government contracts are the only way Edge gets off the ground. We talked about this and we all agreed he is a necessary evil. So even if I am unhappy about this Sawyer guy, it doesn't do any good to complain about it. For all intents and purposes, Charlie *is* our boss. If he wants Sawyer up here looking around, then we should just let the man do his job and hope he really is gone in two weeks."

I want to say a lot of things about this little speech Collin just gave. I want to call him a sell-out. I want to call him beholden. I want to accuse him of things.

But I don't, because he's right. We've hashed this out and we all agreed to work with Charlie for a couple of years until Edge could support itself. We're a brand-new company that just hired sixty employees who aren't actually ready to work yet. Not to mention all the dogs.

We came into this project with millions in the bank, but it literally costs us a hundred thousand dollars a week just to keep up with expenses. Without the government contracts, we can't afford this place. And we've got sixty men and dozens of dogs countin' on us to make it all happen.

So I just sigh.

"I get it, Amon," Collin says. "It sucks. I don't want to be under the thumb of Charlie Beaufort any longer than we have to. But right now, we have to. So whatever's up your ass about this Sawyer guy, just... let it go."

I look at Nash for his opinion on the matter, but he shakes his head. "It's gotta be somebody, Amon. We're not self-sustaining yet. So it's either Charlie or your friend Jim Bob Baptist down there in Disciple. Both are bad, but at least one is necessary. And we already burned a bridge with Jim Bob, so..." Nash shrugs with his hands. "Get over it, dude."

"Fine," I say, giving up. "I'll let it go. But I don't want him fuckin' with my dogs. Whatever he's doing, he can leave them out of it." I look Collin in the eyes. "Fair?"

Collin nods. "Fair. I'll let him know."

"Thanks."

Then I turn and leave, but Collin says, "Hey. Before you go. Got any complaints about how you're feelin'?"

I turn back to him, squinin' my eyes. "What?"

"The drinks," Nash says. "It's Monday. They're coming this afternoon so we gotta decide if we're gonna drink them or not."

"Oh, right." I pause here to think about how I'm feelin'. Then shrug. "I don't feel any different. How about you guys?"

They both shake their heads. "Nope," Collin says. "I feel OK."

"Then it's settled, I guess." I leave the house rollin' my eyes about the drinks and still kinda agitated about the interloper, but once I get in the truck King is there. Sittin' in the passenger seat like he's my best friend and despite a natural urge to remain sour, I smile instead.

Dogs. They are the salve for the wounds of men.

THIRTY MINUTES *later* I'm just entering Revenant when I decide to stop at the diner to kill some time and have some breakfast, since King and I are way early for our vest-fitting appointment. Even if it wasn't Revenant, I could take King inside any establishment I wanted to because he's a service dog. So I snap a lead on him and we go inside for some pancakes. He likes pancakes.

I'm standing at the cash register waiting to be seated

when all of a sudden, I spy Rosie Harlow across the diner. Her long, brown hair is pulled up into some kind of messy beehive thing and she's wearing a pink waitressing outfit reminiscent of the ones they used to wear in the old days. The whole thing really works because she is truly looking very cute.

Rosie's pouring coffee and chitchatting with the customers at her table, so she doesn't see me right away. But once she turns and our eyes lock, her mouth goes up into a grin. And as she walks over to me, it grows wider.

"Rosie Harlow. What the hell are you doing?"

"What do ya mean? I'm working."

"You work here?" I point at the floor.

"Sure do. For the past two years. Only Monday mornings though."

"Monday mornings? That's it? How does that make sense?"

Rosie cocks her hip and her shoulder at the same time. "Well, I didn't have anything else to do on Monday mornings. So why not?"

"Is that what you do then? Fill up every bit of empty space?" It wasn't meant to come out serious, but it kinda does.

Doesn't faze Rosie, though. "Maybe. Table for"—she looks down at King, then back up at me—"two?" We both laugh. "Let me ask you something then, Mr. Nosypants. How come you're bringing a dog to breakfast with you instead of a woman?"

Oh, she walked right into this one. "Because the woman I'm interested in is standing right here in front of me."

Rosie smiles. Maybe even blushes a little as she grabs two menus and turns on her heel. "Follow me."

She seats us at a booth, putting one menu down in front of me and the other across the table, like she knew King was gonna jump into the opposite side of the booth—which he does—and I think it's kinda fun that she gave him a menu even though he doesn't read much.

Rosie stands there for a moment, like she's got something to say, but can't quite find the words. In another moment she's gonna give up and just walk away, so I preempt that with an answer to the question she hasn't yet asked. "Because I like you." Then I hold up a finger so I can tick off a list. "You're fun. You're pretty. You're industrious." This makes her huff, but it's more of an incredulous laugh than some kind of exception to my characterization. "And we're friends, right?"

"I suppose."

"You're not seeing anyone, right?"

"I'm not. That's correct."

"And I'm not seeing anyone. So…"

She's not convinced. "I dunno, Amon. Are you telling me we should date because we're leftovers?"

"No. That's not what I'm saying. I'm saying the timing is right, when maybe in the past, it hasn't been."

"Oh, please. You never took any notice of me at all before you got back."

"That's because I was gone twelve years, Rosie. And you were very fuckin' pregnant, not to mention fifteen years old, the last time I saw you." Again, I have a flash of memory of her standing in the cafeteria when her water broke, that look on her face like her world was ending. "You know what though?" I say, because she and I were looking right at each other that day twelve years ago and I think she's remembering that right now. And I don't want her to think about that day, even if she did get a baby boy out of it. Something bad was happening to her and it had nothing to do with the baby. Something else that I don't know about.

"What?" Rosie says.

"Your boy? He's amazing."

She narrows her eyes a little. "What do you know about my boy?"

"He hung out with me those couple days we were part of the Revival when we first got back. He made sure the dogs always had water in the security tent."

Rosie smiles. Big. "He is a good boy, Amon. I don't know how I got so lucky."

"You didn't get lucky, Rosie. You got exactly what you deserved."

ROSIE

I *get flustered* as all hell when Amon Parrish compliments me this way. My face and chest go all hot, like I'm blushing too.

Amon notices this and chuckles. "Come out with me. Just once. We won't go bowling. We'll do something better."

"Better like what?" I'm still trying to get a hold of myself, so my answer isn't very original, but it's all I've got at the moment.

"Oh, I don't know. I'll figure something out."

"Hmm. Well, I think maybe you should come up with a better plan before you ask a woman out, Mr. Parrish."

Amon laughs too. "All right. That's fair." Then he's about to say something else, but Geraldine Guffie—the head waitress, who's well into her retirement years and has been working here since she was a teenager—calls my name from across the diner.

For a moment I think she's mad that I'm doing too much chatting, but she's holding an envelope up in the air, waving it at me. "You've got a letter here, Rosie."

"What?" I call back. "What kind of letter?"

Geraldine shrugs. "The kind that comes in the mail?"

I huff, then look at Amon. "You two decide what you want and I'll be right back."

Geraldine put the letter on the counter and went back to

71

her business, so I just pick it up and look it over. It's familiar. As it should be, because I got one just like it at McBooms. Sure enough, when I open it up, there's a worksheet inside. This time it's not an extreme dot-to-dot but a maze. A very complicated maze that isn't the kind where you simply find the path to the center, but has little equations to solve along the way. There's a key at the bottom with numbers—presumably the answers to the equations—and a direction to turn. When I look closely at the center, there appear to be six different ways to arrive there. But when I look for the entrance to the maze, I only find one.

"Huh."

"What is it?" Taylor Hill asks. She works here in the Revenant diner weekday mornings when the Bishop Inn is slow.

I fold the paper back up and tuck into the envelope. "Oh, it's just some junk mail."

Taylor throws me a confused look. "Junk mail? Here? That's weird, isn't it?"

"Geez, Taylor. It's not that big of a deal. It's like… a sample, or something. For a kid's workbook. Tryin' to sell me stuff, that's all."

She shrugs, then bounces off to deliver some scrambled eggs and hash browns.

But it *is* kinda weird. What I said makes sense, if there were marketing material inside, but there isn't. But it's really not worth worrying about. I look over at Amon's table and find him smiling at me from across the diner. So I just stuff the envelope into my apron to think about later.

"OK. I've got an idea for a date." Amon says this as I

approach his table, getting my server pad out and clicking my pen.

"I'm all ears, Amon."

"Is that real interest? Or are you just humoring me?"

"Well." I let out a breath. "I guess I'm not sure. Are you truly interested? Or just bored?"

He looks a little sad for a moment, but this look disappears so quickly, I almost think I imagined it. "I'm interested. For real. But how about we leave the date as a surprise?"

He didn't answer my question. "A surprise, huh? Well… how about I check my schedule and get back to you?"

He's about to say something. Probably something about my schedule not being so full that I can't give him an answer. But in that same moment I think he gets it. This schedule-checking thing isn't some kind of lie and he knows this because he's seen me working all over Trinity County in the last week. So he rethinks his objection. "OK. I'm sure we'll bump into each other again soon. So you check your schedule and then I'll plan a date."

I smile. It's a customer smile, not a flirty one. Because I think he *is* bored. I think he's been all over the world, and seen some really cool things, and being back in West Virginia is all kinds of normal. And so are the women here. I'm probably the most eccentric one around, actually, which isn't saying much. "Now, what can I get you two boys for breakfast?"

*I DIDN'T SEE **Amon*** and his dog leave because I was in back mopping up a mess one of the new cooks made with some bad egg-flipping, but he left me a nice tip. Twenty-five dollars. Which I give to the bus boys to split because I don't actually work this job for the money and I like tipping bus boys. He also left a note that said, *I'll be in touch.* And this makes my heart flutter a little bit because it's promising something. That he will get in touch, obviously. But something more than that. It's hinting at… change. And I've got quite a bit of that going on in my life at the moment, so I'm just not sure I need more.

But that's a worry for another day because Amon left and went on with his business and now it's time for me to do the same. I change into my bell bottoms and halter top, leaving the diner just as the lunch rush is getting started because there are plenty of Revenant waitresses who like to work lunch and dinners during the week and I'm just not needed. But that's fine. Because I am needed down at McBooms.

I'm always needed at McBooms because Lowyn is so damn good at buying new pieces of old junk that those catalogues constantly need attention. Plus, I am in charge of the teenagers and there ain't a teenager on the planet who can't use some extra supervision. My past teenage self included.

There is some squealing going on when I enter the store, and the same two boys are hanging about. These boys and girls are Lowyn's helpers in her tent during Revival this season, so naturally they are getting close and even though the boys aren't needed here at the store, it's not surprising that they're showing up. It's summer, after all. Chasing girls is pretty much what all high-school boys do during the summer.

Still, things must be guided or they will go off the rails. Having once been an out-of-control teenager myself, I understand that persons of this age are often unreliable, overly emotional, and impulsive.

The adult in the room can handle it in one of two ways:

One, forbid them from doing things. Like telling the boys they can't hang out. Or telling the girls they can't have music.

Or two, you can give them a project.

I don't actually wish someone had given me a project at fifteen because then I would not have Cross. But I do generally subscribe to option number two.

So let me think… what might be a good way to keep teenage boys busy while showing off for the girls they like? Why, moving heavy objects in the heat of midday, of course.

I call them all into the back storage area where Lowyn keeps the pieces she hasn't had time to stage yet. She's been so busy with her new life with Collin down at the compound that this area is starting to become a bit of a mess. So I tell the teenagers to put all the pieces out on the floor in a place that makes good design sense. Girls decide where and boys do the moving.

The girls are excited. This is fun for them. The boys, not so much. But that's just because they haven't thought things through yet.

You see, it only takes about ten minutes of moving armoires and bookshelves before they need to take their shirts off. Which allows them the opportunity to show off the muscles they've worked so hard to build all year doing sports. Which in turn allows the girls the opportunity to admire them.

Everyone is satisfied and I don't come across as the 'mom' in the room, even though I am. Once they are all settled into their new project, I gather up the stack of mail, take it over to my favorite dinette set, and plop it down so I can go through it.

Now this is when I pause and remember that letter that came to the Revenant diner. It's still tucked in my waitressing uniform, which is in my car, so I go out and get it. Then bring it back inside with me and study the pattern.

Of course, the most obvious thing is that they are both worksheets. The other thing they have in common is that they are not simple worksheets. They are not for small children. They were both made for adults. Or maybe a really smart teenager who enjoys a puzzle challenge.

I don't have the other one, it's at home on the kitchen counter, so I can't try and solve it. And that one seems like a long project, what with all the different languages involved.

But I feel like I could solve this one. The equations are mostly simple. They start out that way, at least. It's not 2+2 or anything that easy, but more like $x + 5 = 21$. Which looks special because of the x, but all it's really asking is what is twenty-one minus five.

"Sixteen," I mutter, my finger tracing down the key at the bottom of the page. And sure enough, there's a number sixteen there and it comes with instructions: *Turn right.*

I turn right in the maze until I bump into another equation. It's much the same, just slightly more difficult.

Still, it's solvable with half a minute of figuring. This time, the answer tells me to continue straight. I keep going, solving the equations and tracing my pencil through the maze, until I realize that the line I'm drawing has nothing to do with getting to the center of the maze, because this little pathway is turning into a picture.

A cross, to be specific.

I stop solving and take a breath, a sinking feeling suddenly flooding through my body.

What is going on here?

Do I have a stalker?

As soon as this idea hits my brain, I know it's true.

I look around. There's no one in here. It's Monday. They're always slow. So there's just the echo of the teenagers in some far corner of the back storeroom to break the silence and nothing else.

Who would be stalking *me* though?

Immediately I rack my brain trying to think if anyone has been paying me more attention than usual. Or if someone new has popped into my life all of a sudden.

My heart actually thumps when Amon Parrish's face pops into my head.

No.

Could it be?

But why?

No.

Except he is the only new person in my life. Period. There is no alternative possibility. And hasn't he kinda been not-so-secretly stalking me? When I came out of the *Busybody* last week, there he was. When I came out of my house on Friday night, there he was. Sure, he was stuck in traffic, but what are the odds of that? He asked me to go bowling with him, and I said no, of course. Then on Saturday he came into the Revival, interrupting everything, and asked me about why I was telling him no. And today he just happened to wander in to the Revenant diner on the one morning a week when I work there?

Suddenly, my cheeks are hot with anger and I go for my phone, ready to press his contact and give him a piece of my mind. If he wants to court me and ask me out, that's fine. But this… this stalking and letter-writing campaign is a tick too much. It's not right. Especially coming from a man like Amon Parrish, who has been all over the world for the past dozen years doing God knows what. Something dangerous, that's for sure. And something illegal, since everyone knows about those congressional hearings.

It's wrong, and it's scary, and I am angry.

But calling him up and yelling at him because I've figured it out might just be playing right into his hands. He's trying to get my attention, obviously. And if I give it to him, then he wins. It doesn't matter if I'm angry, or happy, or scared. The emotion is beside the point.

A man who acts this way just wants to be noticed. He doesn't care how he gets that attention. It's sick. And I'm actually a little bit shocked that Amon Parrish has turned out this way.

I SPEND **the rest** of the afternoon absently shuffling through photographs and making new entries in Lowyn's catalogs, but I'm watching the clock the entire time. And at five-thirty I tell the teenagers to show me what they've done. They've been busy all afternoon, which is a good thing for me because my head is filled with questions and I don't actually have the capacity to function outside my own thoughts.

But the day is over now, the girls did a good job arranging things, the storeroom has been cleared out a bit, and the boys are proud as punch that they scored some points today and all four of them are meeting up at the ice cream shop on the corner of Walnut and Fourth.

Good for them. I smile, wave, and lock up after they've gone.

Then I leave by the back door, lock up, and drive home.

Since I've had several days in a row filled with nothing but disappointing mom moments when it comes to my son, I don't expect him to be there. I expect the house to be empty, and for the phone to ring, and for him to tell me he's got such-and-such plans that do not involve his mother.

But I am very pleasantly surprised to not only find him home, but waiting on me with dinner. It makes me so happy I want to cry. But I don't.

Instead, I beam a smile and say, "What's all this?"

Cross is also smiling. "Well, I've been kind of ignoring you. And I saw the leftover spaghetti when I got home yesterday, so I felt bad for missing dinner."

I touch my hand to his cheek, wondering how he got so big. "Oh, you don't have to feel bad, Cross. Everyone knows that spaghetti is better two days left over than it is served fresh."

"I know. So that's what we're having tonight. You don't have to cook. You don't have to do anything but sit down. I even picked up fresh bread from the bakery."

My son. The angel. The most perfect thing ever to grace this world.

I forget all about Amon Parrish and his stalker business and instead, I count my blessings.

THE NEXT MORNING is a Bishop day. Which always puts me in a good mood because I just love my little pied-à-terre, and choosing a fancy dress to wear on Tuesdays and Wednesdays might not be the highlight of my week, but it runs close.

I choose one with a bright pink and yellow pattern and spend an entire hour getting ready. This whole thing I do here with the *Busybody* is kinda stupid and wasteful because almost no one ever comes into my little shop, so the only people who see my dress are the townsfolk and the odd tour group that prefers Tuesday and Wednesday mornings for their historical learning time.

But people seeing me isn't really the point of what happens in Bishop. It just makes me happy. So that's what I am when I open my store, raise the blinds, and take myself over to my writing desk to think up what I want my little paper to say this week.

Tuesdays are my writing days and Wednesdays are my printing days. I have an old-fashioned press, which is a time-consuming pain in the ass, but my paper is so small, it only takes a couple of hours to set up. I don't print them all that way. Just the original, which I save for myself and put into a book filled with all the other editions inside page protectors. The rest get printed on vintage-looking copy paper at the copy shop just outside the historical district.

But today is a writing day, so I get to sit at my desk and think up stories. To imagine one could make a living doing this. Though I don't actually make a living, I am acutely aware that I am insanely lucky that anyone buys anything I write and I enjoy every bit of this process.

After one last look in the mirror, I leave the cottage and head to the shop. When I get there I open the shutters to let the sunshine in and then scoop up the mail from the little slot attached to the door and take it over to my desk to look through.

Sometimes I get real ads. People send them in to me because I print the address of the paper on every edition of the *Busybody* and I don't charge for them. Today it's mostly junk mail, but as I sort, I see a familiar envelope.

Oh, my God. Another one! He sent one here too!

I rip it open and sure enough, there's another worksheet. This time, it's a word search. But, of course, it's not that simple because it's not for kids. There is no word bank at the bottom of the search, so there's no way to know what words you're looking for.

But just a moment of staring reveals the pattern to me.

Cross.

Cross. Cross. Cross. Cross. Cross.

It's everywhere, all through the puzzle.

I stand up, breathing hard. Why the hell would Amon Parrish do something like this? It's not cute. Not at all.

It's creepy and I want him to stop.

AMON

$\mathcal{I}$ *wake up on Tuesday morning* with an idea. A very good idea. One that involves Rosie Harlow. In fact, this is such a good idea I nearly get up and get on it before I've even had my coffee. But I recognize this behavior—rash decisions typically precede bad outcomes in my experience—so I don't get right on it. I make some coffee and go out and sip it on the porch as I watch the men start bringing their dogs out of the kennel for training

This is my most favorite part of the day because I get to see the progress they're all making. Both with the dogs and themselves. And these men aren't the kind who want, or need, a babysitter. So now that we're several weeks into the program and they know exactly what to do with the dogs, it's just a matter of practice.

Some of the dogs are already very accomplished. But most are juveniles and puppies, and training them takes a lot of time. At first, I was worried because we didn't have enough dogs to go around so some of the men had to double up with a puppy, but it's working out just fine. I actually think they like working in teams. Collin's noticed it too, so this will probably be something we do going forward.

After my coffee I walk down the driveway and check on each dog's progress in person and give feedback. Every two weeks we put the dogs through a test and this is a test week. So everyone's working hard.

It's funny how a dog can make a person gentle. Every single one of these men came from the military. They are all killers. They are all dangerous. Some, before they got here, were drug addicts. Some were in prison. Some were homeless. But none of them are stupid and all of them understand that this is the best and only chance guys like them will ever get.

Maybe they take this opportunity and use it as a stepping stone. Get all the training, make us pay for it, and then take off for a better offer. Collin and I discussed this already, and it could happen. But we don't think it will. We think they'll stay and our investment in them will last years. Maybe even decades.

I watch the guys work the dogs, going to each group and offering tips and praise. And once that's over, I turn and start walking back down the driveway.

I'm just about to head up my porch steps to grab my truck keys when I see that stupid inspector sneaking off into the woods. I pause, wondering if I should follow him. I know Collin said to leave him alone, but Collin wasn't against us figuring out what he was up to. He just didn't want me to make things worse than they need to be.

Of course, we're all thinking that this inspection is just Charlie keeping an eye on us. But if that's really it, then why is he going into the woods?

The only thing out in the woods—aside from trails to run—is the shootin' range. But the inspector isn't heading in the direction of the range, he's actually heading in the direction of the old mine. And now I'm thinking... maybe he isn't here just to check on us? Maybe he's here for something that has nothing to do with us at all.

And maybe that all leads back to Blackberry Hill?

Am I jumping the gun with this conclusion?

Maybe.

But it is sorta weird that there's some kind of secret military base up there in those hills. Collin mentioned that he thought it was an underground base. I didn't get all the specifics about Lowyn's connection to Ike Monroe because that's personal and none of my business. But Collin did tell me that he thought there were tunnels up there and that Lowyn said she saw some kind of basement control room inside Ike Monroe's house.

I should follow that inspector. I should figure out what he's up to.

But as soon as this idea floats around in my head, I hear Collin's voice—*just let the man do his job.*

So fine. That's what I decide to do because I've put Rosie Harlow off for too long this morning already and I know that she's working in that little shop down in Bishop. So I push Sawyer Martin to the back of my mind and bring Rosie to the front.

THIRTY MINUTES **later** I'm walking down the little pathway that leads to the *Bishop Busybody* and then I'm pulling open the door. A little bell jingles above my head and since I wasn't sure what to expect, I'm slightly fascinated about what I find inside.

An ancient printing press—I think. A desk. A counter covered in ancient printing paraphernalia. And, of course, Rosie Harlow.

She does a wild turn that makes her elaborate dress swish, and then gasps with her hands up to her heart. Like I scared her.

"Hey, Rosie."

"Amon! What are you doing here?" This comes out a little bit too loud and kinda frantic.

Which surprises me. I mean, it's not like we haven't been bumping into each other nearly every day for the past week. "I... just... thought I'd stop by."

Rosie takes a step backwards, kinda giving me the side-eye. "Any... particular reason?"

"What's wrong with you, Rosie?"

"Nothing. What's wrong with you?"

I narrow my eyes at her. Because she's acting weird. Like she's in some kind of trouble, but trying to act natural and shit. I shift my gaze from her to the room, looking for anything that might come off as suspicious. Then I reach for my sidearm, but of course, it's not there.

When Collin said he was gonna carry after that whole thing up on Blackberry Hill, I laughed at him. "This is Trinity County, Collin. Of all the places on the earth, this is the last one I'd expect us to be carrying heat."

He didn't care what I thought. He open-carries every fuckin' day. And right now, I wish I was carrying too.

"Did you just reach for a weapon?"

I glance over at Rosie. "Huh?" I'm distracted by my heightened sense of alert and lack of firearm.

"Amon, I would like you to leave."

I look around, nodding. Then I wink at her. "OK. I'm going..." But I'm not going. I'm slowly and silently sidestepping so I can get a peek around the counter.

"Amon!"

"I'm leaving." But I'm not, I'm just saying that so whoever is hiding out in here, trying to make her make me leave, will think that I am.

Rosie makes a sudden movement, which kicks in my extensively honed self-defense skills, and suddenly she's coming at me with a fancy umbrella. I deflect, grab the umbrella, and toss it aside.

Rosie gasps, screams, and then I'm whirling in place— really wishing for that fuckin' sidearm—trying to figure out where the intruder might be hiding in this tiny little space. Rosie makes a dash for the door, swishin' right past me, opening it up, and rushin' through it.

I ignore her and keep looking for the cause of all this drama.

But now that said drama is over, it is very clear that there is no one here but me. I go outside, shaking my head, and find Rosie Harlow rushing through her little gate like a bat out of hell.

"Rosie!" I call. "What is goin' on?"

She turns—well, everybody on the street turns. Even a couple of horses look our way—and points at me. "You're stalking me!"

I point to myself as well. "What?"

"You've been popping up at all my jobs. Which is fine, I

guess. It's a free country. But sending me those letters, Amon? It's creepy."

"What letters? I don't know what you're talking about. And I'm not stalking you! We just seem to frequent the same places."

She plants her hands on her hips. "Oh, so you didn't mean to come into my shop this morning?"

I sigh. "Well, yeah. *Today*. But not all those other times. And I haven't sent you no letters."

Rosie lets out a long breath, then suddenly becomes aware of all the attention we are garnering from the good people of Bishop. They are all open-mouthed staring at us because we have created—in the words of old-timey people everywhere—a spectacle. Which is highly frowned upon when one's downtown is a stage filled with actors just trying to do their jobs.

Even though Rosie is on the other side of the gate, I extend my hand in her direction. "Come back inside, for fuck's sake. Whatever you think is happening, I'm not a part of it."

She eyes me suspiciously one more time, then the people and horses, who are still watching her, and lets out an exasperated breath. "False alarm, people!" She calls this out brightly, letting all the busybodies know that the show is over. Then she gathers up her skirts and swishes her way back through the gate, past me, and back inside.

I tip an imaginary hat in the direction of a group of men, begging their pardon, and follow her back inside. "Should I leave the door open?" I ask, annoyed with her and the scene she just made. "Since you obviously think I'm some kind of pervert."

Rosie walks over to her desk, collapses into the chair, and lets out a dramatic sigh. "I'm sorry. It's just... I've been getting letters and you've been everywhere this past week and... well." She sighs. "I'm rattled, that's all. So I jumped the gun, I guess."

I grab the only other chair in here and drag it over next to her desk. Then I sit down. "Start over, OK? What the hell is going on?"

Rosie starts from the beginning and tells me about the first letter that was sent to McBooms while showing me the one that came here. When she tells me about the other one that came to the Revenant diner, her paranoia is understandable.

"And they're all in code, Amon! Like... military things or... homeschool."

I can't help but crack a smile. "Military or homeschool, huh?"

She lets out an exasperated sigh. "Whatever. Make fun of me, if you want. But it's weird! Someone is stalking me!"

Someone *is* stalking her. And they're doing it in a very strange way. "Can I have the worksheets?"

"What for?"

"To run some forensics. I've still got good DC contacts for that sort of thing. I can send it in and see if they can find anything."

Rosie nods, folding the one she's holding back up and setting it on the desk in front of me. "The second one is in my purse. And the third one is at home. What kind of forensics are you gonna do?"

"Fingerprints, for sure. But we can do DNA, ink, and paper analysis as well as check it for chemicals. Some of that might take a few weeks, but we can get fingerprints in a couple days, I suspect."

"Oh, that sounds complicated, Amon. Maybe I'm just being stupid. Does it really deserve all this attention? Maybe someone is just trying to sell me homeschool curriculum and I'm completely overreacting?"

One of my eyebrows cocks up. "What is going on with this homeschool thing?"

"Well, it's kinda popular these days. There's always a couple articles about it in my mommy magazines. They like weird shit like this."

"OK. Well, I'll take your word on that. And if that's what it is, fine. There's nothing to be worried about. But don't you think that if someone was trying to sell you homeschool books they'd have put the name of the company on the paper? So you could look them up or whatever?"

She chews on her lip a little, then sighs again. "Yes." Her eyes go all serious now, getting wider and worried. "It's not homeschool stuff, Amon. Someone's sending these things to me on purpose."

"Yep," I agree. "And that's dangerous. But don't you worry, I'll take care of it."

She exhales, her shoulders relaxing. "Thank you." Then she smiles at me. "I'm really sorry I overreacted. But I had just started putting it all together a few moments before you walked through my door, so—"

"It's understandable. Do you want me to stay while you work? Because I will."

"No." She says this, but it's not a firm no. "I'll be OK."

"How about I leave, but come back when you're done and walk you to your car?"

Her gray eyes go bright. "You'd do that for me?"

"Sure I would."

"Because you're courtin' me?" She smiles here, so I know we've changed subjects now and we're on to lighter banter.

"I might be."

"Did I just ruin it by throwing a scene?"

I turn my head, laughing a little. "Nah. You're fine. Forget about all that for now. When do you leave work?"

"Oh, I only stay a couple hours. Then I go to McBooms for the afternoon."

"Well, how about I grab some breakfast at the inn, come back here in two hours, and I'll be your chaperone. Sound good?"

Rosie nods. "Thanks, Amon. I'm being a big pain in your ass today and you're handling it quite well."

"I'll take that as a compliment." Then I get up, open the door, give Rosie Harlow one more look over my shoulder, and leave.

THE BISHOP INN is just a couple blocks away and when I get there it's not too busy, so I bother Jessica, part owner and front-desk manager, for a notepad and pen and then take a seat in the dining room near the window where I still have a good view of Rosie's place.

I hadn't planned on spending my whole morning in Bishop, but I'm concerned about these letters she's getting. More concerned than I let on. Stalkers are unstable people. They come in a few types, all of which I'm familiar with since Edge specializes in political clients. People stalk others for three reasons: Rejection, predation, and ideology.

I very much doubt that Rosie is being stalked by some anti-Revival zealot. It's more likely that this is a past boyfriend. If it's not a past boyfriend, then it's a predator. Which is the absolute worst kind because they are not actually interested in Rosie, but how Rosie makes them feel, and that makes them unstable. At least the other two reasons for stalking are understandable.

Predation is... well, a hunt. Which makes the stalked nothing but prey.

At any rate, I'm gonna get to the bottom of it. And while I do that, I'm gonna make her an Edge client.

Now that that's over, I turn my attention back to the original reason I came into Bishop this morning in the first place. Which was to insert myself into Rosie's life by writing up a personal ad.

I look down at the empty pad of paper, trying to get my thoughts together. Robust and Hearty is my baseline, but when a man decides to court a woman, he can't just give his baseline. He needs to amplify that shit.

So I begin, startin' and stoppin' dozens of times over the next hour as I pick at my breakfast. I am not a writer, let alone a poet, but eventually I am content with the words I have managed to string together.

Jessica gives me an envelope with the Bishop Inn logo on it on my way out, and as I walk back over to the *Bishop*

Busybody, I seal it up with my note inside.

Rosie is standing at the printing press wearing an apron when I arrive. Her hair's a little bit disheveled and her brow is glistening from effort, even though all the downtown shops have AC—this one included.

Historical accuracy only matters if people are comfortable. No one likes to be too hot and no one likes to be too cold. That was a lesson this town learned early. So Bishop said yes to the air conditioners the same way Disciple said yes to garden-party fashion.

It's not authentic, but no one cares.

"I'm just about done, Amon. Give me fifteen minutes."

"Take your time." I lean on the counter and place my envelope in front of me.

Rosie glances over, squinting in suspicion. "What's that? You didn't find another letter—"

"No, no." I put a hand up. "This one's from me. I just wrote it while I was having breakfast."

Rosie's furrowed brow straightens right out and she smiles. "You wrote a letter? To me?"

"Well, kinda."

"What's that mean, Amon?"

"It's…" I grin. Because it's clever. Not just a little bit clever, either. But like actually fuckin' clever. "It's an ad. I want to place an ad."

Rosie laughs. I don't even think she means to, it just comes bursting out. "Here?" She points to the ground. "With the *Bishop Busybody*?"

"That's right."

"You do understand we don't do 'help wanted' here?"

"I do."

"We don't do 'for sale' either."

"Rosie, I promise, it's publication appropriate."

She laughs again, then starts wiping her hands on her apron as she makes her way over to the counter. "You want to put in a lonely hearts ad?"

"Yep." I'm trying my best to keep a straight face, but it's not working out for me. I'm grinning pretty big.

She picks up the envelope. "Can I open it?"

"Please do. I hope I have made the deadline because I would like it to be in the next issue."

Rosie unseals the envelope, pulls out the piece of notepaper, and gets a wild smile on her face as she reads.

When she looks back at me, I'm someone else.

ROSIE

I just stand there in my shop looking at Amon Parrish like he is a stranger. Well, that's not actually right. I look at Amon Parrish like I'm seeing him for the very first time because... well... I just never expected him to be so... romantic.

His ad reads: *Rugged and worldly man seeks small-town woman with shining gray eyes and a personality to match. Must love dogs. He is charming, handsome, protective, and part-owner of a suspicious (but entirely legal) elite security service. She is smart, funny, adorable, and a good mother who did not get lucky, but got exactly what she deserved. She can pull off every kind of vintage and if she chooses him, she will never be alone and scared again. If this sounds like you, Gray Eyes, please respond to me, Rugged and Worldly, in the next issue so we can start a public correspondence.*

She giggles at the last part. "Amon Parrish?"

"Rosie Harlow?"

"Did you just ask me out using a lonely hearts ad?"

"I did."

"Is this... some kind of gesture?"

"As opposed to...?"

"You don't really want to print this, do you? I mean, it's just a clever trick, right?"

"Well, of course I want you to print it."

"You want the whole world to know you're asking me out?"

"The whole world?" Amon shrugs. "Well, I don't mind if the whole world knows, but my target area is really just Trinity County."

I let out a long breath and suddenly, the world is much brighter than it was two minutes ago. "Do I say yes right now? Or do I have to respond in kind?"

"Well, I really am looking to start a correspondence, but I'm also aiming for a lunch date tomorrow. So if we could just do both, that would be great."

The laugh that comes out of me is a bit shocking. Not just because it's loud, but because it comes with so much happy, I almost can't categorize it.

"So," Amon says. "What do ya say? Lunch tomorrow and a proper response next week?"

"I work here tomorrow until noon or so."

"Well, that works out perfect since noon is the customary time for lunch."

We stare at each other for a moment. I don't know what he's thinking, but I'm thinking that this is just... good. He's good. Despite the fact that I put him firmly into the 'Scar' category the other day, he's not a Scar. He's not. He's... real. And protective. And while a Scar can be protective, it comes across in all the wrong ways.

Amon Parrish doesn't come across wrong at all. Life is so weird because Amon Parrish was not even on my radar when I woke up this morning and now, he's the only thing on my mind.

I nod. "OK."

He smiles. "OK." Then he looks around. "Take your time finishing up. I'll keep myself entertained."

I let out a breath. "Just let me clean up and we can go."

He knocks his agreement out on the counter with a couple of knuckles and then takes himself over to the wall where I've framed past issues of the *Bishop Busybody* and starts reading them.

I turn my back, trying to get a hold of myself, then walk over to the press and put a few more letters in place to make it look like I'm working.

But actually, all I can think about is his ad.

And what I might write in response.

I'M LOCKING **up the shop** when it occurs to me that I have to change before going home. "I have a place here in town," I tell Amon. "Where I keep my dresses. Is it OK if we stop by there first?"

Amon nods. "Sure."

"It's just right down this way, behind the blacksmith." We walk down Goosebeak Alley together in silence, looking around at all the backyard ladies tending their gardens and small animals. But when I stop at the bottom of the three steps that lead to my cottage, I realize that I've never let a man inside before.

Amon says, "This is your place?" like he's both surprised and delighted.

"Yes. I'll just be right back."

Amon raises an eyebrow. "You don't want to invite me in?"

Oh, I blush. I can feel it. "It's just a really small space. And… nothing but dresses, really."

Amon tries to peek in a window, but I've got curtains, so he can't see much. "It's a mystery, huh?"

"No. Not really. It's just… dresses. That's literally it."

Then he's touching me. Well, not me, but my dress. His fingertips have gotten a hold of a piece of lace on my sleeve. "Dresses like this?" And is that a little bit of desire I hear in his voice?

"Yes." I say this, but it's a bit hesitant. "Like this."

"They're pretty. I always liked coming into Bishop just so I could look at all the costumes."

"Do you… want to see them? My dresses, I mean." I add this quickly because his eyes actually flit down to my chest. I try and recover before they flit back up to me again, but only barely manage. "Because never in a million years would I ever have pictured Amon Parrish interested in my dresses."

"Come on, Rosie. It's not the dresses. It's the woman wearing them. And it's not the cottage, it's the woman who owns it. I'm just interested in you, that's all."

Holy shit, he's coming on to me. He *really* is. I mean, it's not a surprise. I knew this was happening. I just didn't imagine that it would start in my Bishop dressing room. I kinda pictured a drunken night out in Revenant, to be honest.

That is not to say I don't prefer the dressing room to the drunken night out.

"Speechless?" Amon asks. "Really? That was enough to make you speechless?"

"Well..." I huff out a small laugh. "You've taken me by surprise, Amon. I never imagined you as a romantic and those words you just said were truly on the verge."

He grins. "Just the verge, huh? Well, there's room for improvement, I guess."

I... don't even know what to say to that. And because I'm a little bit flustered, I default to manners. "Would you like to come in?"

His grin is wild and his answer is evident.

I quickly turn so he can't watch me get flustered, then go up to the door, unlock it, and open it up. I don't look over my shoulder at him, just walk in and scan the space, trying to see it through his eyes.

"Wow." He comes in behind me, closing the door. "I've never seen anything like this."

I turn and look at him. "Um... thank you. I think that means you like it."

"I do." Amon is still looking around, but now his eyes find mine. "But the thing that's really got my interest up—aside from you, yourself—is that you've got a secret life here, Rosie."

"What? No, I don't. Everyone knows I work in Bishop and wear costumes two days a week."

"I didn't know."

"Yeah, but that's only because you were gone."

"Hmm." He hums this, so it comes out low and growly.

And now what do I do? I can't just... undress. I mean, there's a privacy screen in the one corner, but I've never actually used it for changing because no one has actually ever been in here but me.

But I guess... I *could* use it. I could just act like it's no big deal that he's in here. First, though, it would be proper to invite him to leave. To give him the choice.

"Well, I guess I should get changed. There's a lot more to taking off these dresses than one might imagine, so it could be ten minutes or more."

Amon looks me up and down, grinning like a boy, probably peeling back the many layers of my dress and petticoats with his imagination. When he meets my gaze, his smile is a smirk. "Do you need any help?"

I stepped right into that one, for sure. But honestly, this is going too fast. I mean, it's not that I haven't been having sex, it's just I tend to do it with strangers in towns outside the Trinity and not with men I've known since childhood and who are handsome enough to star in their own action movie.

But. At the same time, it's exciting. Something right out of one of those historical romance novels where the duke, or whoever, has to unhook the new governess's corset because she can't breathe or something.

I fan myself with my hand. A weird gesture outside of the Revival tent, but also a practiced one, so it's happening before I can stop it.

"It's fine," Amon says, chuckling at my reaction. "I'll wait outside." And then, before I can pull myself together and stop him, he's walking through the door, closing it behind him.

I let out a breath. It's a mixture of relief and regret. Letting Amon Parrish see my private dressing room feels a bit scandalous, but it's a sexy kind of scandalous. The kind that comes charged with the potential for out-of-control emotions. And if he ever comes in here again, things will go very differently.

Because Amon Parrish has got me very hot and bothered and all he did was undress me with his eyes. What would happen if I let him undress me for real? I would probably lose all control. I might even faint, the way I pretend to in the Revival.

I laugh, internally chastising myself for thinking like a teenager. Then start taking off the many layers of my dress and replacing all that with my more typical style—bell bottom jeans and halter top.

I hang everything up, making the room all neat and organized, and then pause at the door to take one final look, picturing the room from Amon's point of view. The dresses, the petticoats, the undergarments. Even the shoes and parasols.

And that chaise longue right there in the center of it all.

I imagine what it might be like to lie on that smooth, silk velvet with Amon Parrish on top of me and get lightheaded again.

But I shake it off, go outside, and meet him at the bottom of the porch, my modest Colonial façade tucked away until tomorrow and my McBooms persona taking over.

Amon nods at me as I walk up to him. "I like this version too, ya know. I like all your versions, Rosie."

"Oh, my God, Amon. Calm the fuck down. They're just clothes."

He laughs. Probably at my change in personality. I guess I never thought about how much I transform every time I put on a new costume. "The clothes are all nice. But Rosie, it's just you I like."

I fall in next to him and we start walking down the alley, heading towards the edge of downtown. "OK, I guess it's all out there now. So let's talk about this. You've been back for over a month now and you've never looked at me twice."

"That's not true. I checked you out pretty hard that first week. You were the first person I saw when I got back. Remember? In the Rise and Shine getting coffee?"

"I do. That's right. But you were never interested enough to get all flirty with me until you saw me in my Bishop dress."

He clicks his tongue. "It's a good look on you. I might even go so far to say that life in Bishop suits you better."

"But why do you think that? This is a real question because to me, it's just another role to play."

"Oh, come on, Rosie. You're not playing a role here."

"What do you mean? Of course I am."

"There's no audience. It's just you and that printing press in that little shop. It's just you and those dresses in that little cottage. You're not doing this for anyone but yourself."

"Hm." He's right. And I already knew this because every time I start to feel a little guilty about coming here and spending money on the print shop and the cottage I justify it with happiness. "Is that a bad thing? That I do all this for selfish reasons?"

Amon glances down at me. "Of course not. Why would it be?"

"Well, when you explain it the way you did, it feels like maybe I'm hiding from something."

"That's not how I meant it. I was reacting to how natural

it all was. And how you seem to really like the dresses and the old-fashioned shit they do here."

We've reached my car so I stop and turn, leaning against it. I have no idea where he parked his truck. "I do like the dresses. I like how slow it is. I like how people try hard to be polite and friendly. And it's not that Disciple isn't like this, because it is. It's just… different. I can't really explain it."

Amon agrees. "I know what you mean. Disciple is… entertainment. It's like 'friendly and polite' had a baby with 'fantastic and peculiar.'" This makes me laugh right out loud as he continues. "Revenant is kind of the same way. But Bishop is…"

"The ordinary," I fill in for him. "The usual."

"The mundane, amplified to a level of…"

"*Extra*ordinary."

"Exactly." He points at me. "It's fuckin' weird how things go around in a circle like that. Echoes of each other. One extreme to another, some might say. I mean, people wanting cows in the backyard phased out a hundred years ago with the invention of the milkman because they're too much work, ya know?"

"But the people who come here to visit, they eat it up, don't they?"

"Doesn't everyone want to try their hand at milking a cow if they know they don't have to get up every morning at dawn and do it because it's mandatory?"

I laugh. "I don't mind milking a cow every now and then for fun, but I do not want one in the backyard."

"That's my point."

"So it's all just… romanticized." I sigh. "I like it here because it's fake."

Amon turns to me with a small smile on his face that is mostly filled with sympathy, not happiness. "It's not fake, Rosie. It's... a dream. And doesn't everyone wish they could spend two mornings a week inside their dream?" When I don't say anything, he continues. "Anyway, I'm parked over there. When I come up behind you, pull out and I'll follow you home."

It all suddenly feels a little ridiculous. Him acting like I need a bodyguard or something. "You don't need to, Amon. I'm fine. I drive the highway between here and Disciple by myself all the time."

"I'm not doing it because I need to, Rosie. I'm doing it because I want to." Then he turns, fishing his keys out of his pocket, and heads down the street where his truck is parked.

I watch him for a few moments before getting in my car, stunned and amazed that he and I are here already. Talking about dreams and... other things that just didn't get said.

WHEN HE PULLS UP, I pull out, and he follows me all the way into Disciple. I park in front of McBooms, but Amon doesn't find a spot. Just sits in the middle of the road, idling with his window down like we've got unfinished business.

"The letter?" he says. "The one in your purse?"

"Oh, right." I fish it out and hand it to him. "The other one is at the house. Do you need it right now?"

"I think these two will do. So…"

"Tomorrow?" I ask, hoping he didn't forget.

Amon nods, kinda hypnotizing me with those blue eyes of his. "Noon. I'll pick you up at the print shop."

"But I gotta change before our date. Pick me up at the cottage."

Amon shakes his head. "The print shop. Noon." Then he salutes me, like he might one of his buddies, and takes off down the road, his truck rumbling along like the thunder that comes just before the glory.

THE NEXT DAY at the *Busybody* flies by because it's Wednesday and I've got so much to do in order to get my prints ready and it doesn't help that I'm completely distracted by my date with Amon this afternoon. I must read his ad a million times while I set the type. *She is smart, funny, adorable, and a good mother who did not get lucky, but got exactly what she deserved.* That's my favorite part. And I love that he put it in there because it's a sign that this isn't just some one-night thing. He said those same words to me at the diner the other day. And if he's repeatin' them, then he was sincere.

And this means the world to me.

I want to get everything done before he gets here, including stuffing and mailing envelopes, so I came in two hours early and still the time ticks off so fast, I'm barely back from the post office when the little bell above my door jingles.

I turn to look and have to catch my breath. "Amon? Is that you?" It is, of course, but I have to ask because he's wearing a full Bishop summer costume of breeches, boots, and waistcoat and coat. Which, like Disciple, isn't precisely historically accurate but comes close enough. He's all color-coordinated in varying shades of gray, including bits of smoky blue, which complements my own silver-pink ensemble.

Amon's smile could brighten a pitch-black room, it's that lively. "Surprise?"

Oh, my God. He's... well, I'm not sure there is one word that could accurately describe Amon Parrish all dressed up like a Bishop gentleman because handsome just doesn't cut it. He's... everything. "Did you dress up like this for me?"

He makes a face. "What do you think, Rosie? Why else would I be wearing this outfit?"

I smile, then bring my fingertips up to my lips so I can chuckle.

"Do I look ridiculous?"

"Ridiculous? No, Amon. You look positively... *fetching.*"

He laughs now too. "Fetching?"

"Well, I'm trying to stay in character here. But if you'd like the Revenant version of that word, it would be... fuckable."

He laughs again. "I'll take either." Then his eyes slowly glide down my dress. Like he's studying every bit of my body. "Speaking of..." His eyes find their way back up to meet mine. "I really like you in these dresses, Rosie. Of course, I like you in all the outfits you wear, so maybe it's just you I like."

I sigh, fanning myself like I'm in church. But the fact is, he is kinda making me hot. "You're charming, Amon. I always did know that. But you have definitely been upping your game since high school. How do you not have a wife already?"

"Oh, that's an easy one. I was waiting for you, of course."

Which is a lie, because we never had no interest in each other as kids. I was too young when he left, not to mention pregnant. So I tsk my tongue at him and shake my head.

"Do you need any help with anything, Rosie? Or are you ready to go?"

"We're going out like this?" I pan my hand down my dress. Of course it's kind of a dumb question because he's here, dressed up in costume, which makes it obvious that we are. But I'm just surprised, so it comes out before I can think it through.

"I've got a table reserved at the Ordinary."

"Oh." I smile, pressing my lips together. An 'ordinary' restaurant in Colonial times would be just that. Ordinary. But in Bishop, the Ordinary is a special place that tourists need reservations for well in advance because unlike the Bishop Inn, everyone is in costume, including the guests.

It's a requirement. It doesn't matter if they rent their attire from a shop just outside downtown or have them specially made by one of the seamstresses and tailors in the Trinity County area, but they must show up in period-appropriate attire or they do not get through the door.

I've never actually been inside the Ordinary because...

well... I dunno why. I guess no man ever thought to take me there.

Until now.

"Sound like a good plan?"

I nod my head at Amon, feeling a little bit like a lovestruck teenager. Which is a foreign feeling to me since it's been twelve years since I've felt that way. "Sounds like a perfect plan, Amon."

He holds his arm out for me and I come around the counter and take it. Then he leads me out the door and we walk through downtown Bishop looking like a piece of history.

AMON

I've seen Rosie Harlow dressed up many ways now. Retro flower girl from the Seventies, sassy diner waitress from the Fifties, and, of course, Twenties-era garden-party socialite. But I like how she looks in these Colonial dresses the best. She's… different. More demure. Maybe even a little bit shy.

Not that I don't like her more typical bigger-than-life personality, I do. But it's nice to see her in a different light.

The dress she's wearing today is a combination of silver and pink and obviously made of some kind of luxurious fabric. Probably silk. The bodice is pink and it's got laces holding her breasts in like a corset. But she's wearing a dress underneath this corset as well, and this one is silver. The sleeves stop at her elbows and are trimmed in pink lace, matching the corset. There are at least two skirts, one over, one under, and they are contrasting colors so the whole thing is very… *feminine*.

Which Rosie is. But she doesn't typically show it off this much and I really like it. I think she likes it too. I mean, why else would she spend so much time and money in Bishop if this wasn't her thing? She doesn't have a place in Revenant, as far as I know. It's not like she's got a little flophouse above a pool hall and a closet full of biker jackets down there.

Bishop is romantic. I mean, it's all bullshit, just like Disciple, because I doubt people had much time to think about romance in Colonial times. Life was hard and the work was endless.

But Trinity County is selling a fantasy. That's why people come here.

The reason Rosie Harlow has a place in Bishop filled with period-appropriate dresses that probably cost a small fortune is because time is something you make for things you like doing.

And this is something she likes doing.

At least, that's how I put it all together. And maybe I'm wrong, but the look on her face when I walked through that door and she saw me making a fashion statement—well, it was a combination of amazement and joy. So I think I got it right.

As Rosie and I walk arm in arm down the main street here in the historical district, no one really pays us much attention. If they think it's weird that I'm dressed up in Justin Carter's clothes, they don't much care, I guess. Because no one seems to be staring or chuckling behind my back as we pass.

Something Ryan and Nash would probably do. Though I feel like they have both accepted the weirdness of these towns without much protest. Ryan is even dating a Disciple girl, though it's a relatively new thing and whether it lasts or not remains to be seen.

When we get to the Ordinary there is no wait and we are taken right to our table. It's hot outside, but in here it's on the verge of frigid because they keep the AC cranking. Hot people wearing ten layers of clothing aren't happy customers, after all. And if there's one thing Trinity County understands, it's happy customers.

Rosie and I are seated at an intimate table in front of the window so we can see everybody outside, adding to our experience.

There is no menu, you eat what they cook and today it's turkey, duck, and fixin's. Once our server leaves, Rosie smiles at me. "OK. I give."

"You give what?"

"What is this all about?" She waves her hand in the air, gesturing to me and the restaurant at the same time.

"Why did I choose this place for our first date?"

Rosie nods. "You have to admit, it's a little bit out of character for you."

"But not for you. And the only reason a man has a first date with a woman is to make her happy. I figured this would make you happy. Have you ever been here before?"

Rosie shakes her head. "No. Never."

"Have you wanted to come?"

"Are you serious? Yes. Since I was little girl. But"—she points to herself—"I got four brothers. It was never gonna happen."

Now this makes me laugh. "Well, that's funny, ya know? Because I have four sisters."

"Oh, my God. You've been here before!"

I nod. "I have. We came here as a family once when Vangie turned nine. That's all she wanted for her birthday since she was four years old and finally, she got her wish. So we all put the clothes on and came in for a Colonial dining experience. I was like seventeen, I think. So of course, I was all put out about this. But I still remember Vangie's face. She was in heaven. Hell, even Angel enjoyed herself and she hates everything."

Rosie smiles. "So that's where you get it."

"Get what?"

"That... charm or whatever. That... romantic side, I guess. Four sisters. It's hard not to pick up on the ways of women when you're surrounded on all sides."

I point at her. "And that's why you're so damn easy to be around. It's hard not to learn how to be one of the guys when you've spent your whole life being poked by them."

"Oh, that's true. You learn to let things slide off your back when you grow up packed between brothers like cheese in a boloney sandwich."

I smile and lean back in my chair, fully satisfied with this date even though we just barely got started. "I like you, Rosie."

"I like you too, Amon." Rosie blushes and fans herself with her hand. Which is no doubt a habit she's picked up from being the Revival tent all these years and I find that adorable.

Me. With a Disciple girl. Not sure how I got here, but my arrival feels like fate.

WE TALK EASILY about everything after that. Like we're old friends, which we kinda are, who are picking up where they left off, which we're definitely not. But it's all very familiar and casual. Lunch comes, we eat, and we laugh a little, talking about small things in our lives. She asks 'bout my dogs, which I talk about for far too long. And I ask about Cross. Because Cross is Rosie's everything and once she starts in with him, she just keeps going.

She doesn't mind that all I talk about is dogs, I don't mind that all she talks about is Cross, and I can feel us fitting together like puzzle pieces.

After the meal is over and the easy conversation ends, we both sit back in our chairs, relaxing. Though how she relaxes in that tight dress is something I'll never understand. This thought leads down a trail I didn't expect to be traveling on the first date, but it shows up nonetheless. Because I find myself fantasizing about unlacing that corset and slipping that dress down her shoulders.

"I've had a nice time, Amon."

I snap back from my fantasy and gaze into those gray eyes of hers. "I'm glad. I did too. What are you up to for the rest of the day?"

"Well, it's a McBooms afternoon so I gotta go change and head back to Disciple. What are you doing?"

She's smiling when she asks this. So naturally, I jump to conclusions. "I'm walking you home. Then..." I pause, pretending to think because she's blushing a little. "Then I dunno. Depends, I guess." *Maybe I'll follow you into that cottage of yours and carefully undress you, layer by layer, until you're naked, and then make love to you on that lovely velvet chaise.* But of course, I don't say that last part out loud. "Shall we go?"

Rosie sucks in a deep breath, like maybe she heard my

thoughts, and then I get up and grab her chair so she can stand.

Then I offer her my arm and she takes it. We leave the Ordinary like that. Like we're a thing. Which we're not, officially. Yet. But in Bishop, especially dressed as we are, what we're doing is certainly sending all the signals.

Outside it's hot, but the whole downtown is lined with old sugar maples that tower above us, providing a canopy of shade, so it's a nice walk along the brick-paved sidewalks. Downtown is not too busy with tourists today. There are a few groups of schoolkids, but mostly it's local people just going about their day.

The gravel alley where Rosie has her little cottage is bustling with backyard activity. There are pigs running around, and roosters hollering, and groups of women chatting across clotheslines. Their husbands go to work every day and do things like horseshoeing, and butchering, and woodworking. It's weird to see this as normal in this modern era we all live in, but it's kinda cool too.

We stop at her cottage and I'm just about to offer my services to help her take that dress off when Rosie says, "Thank you for a very nice time today, Amon."

Which is code for, *Sorry, Amon, but I don't put out after just one lunch date. Even if you are dressed up like an eighteenth-century gentleman.*

But that's OK. I don't mind the chase. In fact, the chase is kinda fun. "You're very welcome, Rosie. How about we set up another date so we can continue our courtship?"

She shakes her head, blushing. "You're so funny."

"Why?"

"Courtin'? This costume?"

"You don't like it?"

"Well, of course I like it, Amon. It's…" She looks me up and down. And for a moment I think she might change her mind and allow me to relieve her of that corset. But no luck. "Very romantic. And… well, it suits you."

"It suits me, does it?" And I chuckle. Because Rosie Harlow doesn't know me. She has no idea who I was before I came back to Disciple. Which only makes this whole thing better. Because I don't wanna be that guy anymore. I'd choose this guy over that one any day. "Well, this certainly suits you as well. Maybe we were born in the wrong town, Rosie? Maybe we were meant to grow up here."

"So you could, what, be a blacksmith?"

"And you could be… one of those wives over there. Hanging laundry and feeding chickens."

"Chasing pigs and gossiping all day?" She laughs. "It's not a bad life."

"I never said it was."

"But… nah. We were born where we were meant to. I doubt that even I could've talked my way into sticking around for profit share after getting pregnant in tenth grade if I was part of Bishop instead of Disciple."

"Well, if anyone could pull that off, it would've been you, Rosie. Now let's talk about that next date."

"Well…" She pauses. "How about we don't?"

I point to myself, a little bit stunned. "You don't wanna go out with me again?"

"I never said that. It's just, asking me to make plans with you is… a little forward, don't you think?"

"Oh. Right. Fine. I guess I started it, didn't I? We're playing lady and gentleman of Bishop now, are we?"

Rosie shrugs. "Well, I don't think we have to limit our courtin' to Bishop."

Which makes me picture myself dressed up like James Dean ravishing her in that waitress uniform. "We don't?" And now I'm grinning wildly, my imagination goin' crazy with possibilities. "Well, OK then. Challenge accepted." I bow a little, then straighten up so I can grab her hand, slowly lifting it to my lips, and kiss her knuckles while staring her straight in the eyes. "I'll see you soon, Rosie."

She fans herself with that hand when I let it go. And her cheeks go hot and pink. "See ya around, Amon."

BY THE TIME **I get back** to the compound my face hurts from smiling so much.

When Collin and I started making plans for buying this compound, I did envision myself settling down with a Disciple girl. But Rosie Harlow was never part of that daydream. My last memory of her, before I saw her in the Rise and Shine that first morning I was back, was her pregnant. Her water breaking in the cafeteria. That look of utter fear on her face.

But look at her now. She's beautiful, and smart, and funny, and ambitious, and even though she's the only woman I've dated since I've been back—she's the one.

I'm gonna marry Rosie Harlow and then we're gonna settle down and have ourselves a bunch of asshole kids.

Well, with Rosie as their mother, they won't be assholes like I was. They'll be good, like Cross.

Damn. I've made a good choice here. I need to go all out and make sure that she sees me as her 'one.'

The compound is buzzing with ex-soldiers and dogs as I pull in to the driveway, but I just go right on past, all the way back to my house near the kennels. I park, get out, and I'm just about to head inside to change out of my costume when I see that fucker Sawyer goin' into the woods again.

I want to follow him and see what he's up to, but then I hear Collin's voice in my head. *We should just let the man do his job and hope he really is gone in two weeks.*

But when I look around, and over my shoulder, Collin is nowhere to be found. So I make an executive decision and head in that same direction.

I've been all over these woods since we bought the compound and I know them pretty well. So I know that this trail that Sawyer is taking leads in the direction of the old mine. It's mostly a well-worn deer trail, but at one point there's some actual hill climbing involved. Then it evens out into a little meadow, and on the opposite side of that is the main entrance to the mine.

When I get there, Sawyer is nowhere around and the entrance to the mine is blocked with rocks. Which probably how it's been for ages. Either an accidental cave-in, or, more likely, a deliberate one to seal it off so curious teenagers didn't get themselves killed.

I look for tracks, but it hasn't rained in over a week and I'm out of practice in this skill, so as I turn and go back down the mountain, I find myself wishing I had brought a dog with me.

I almost get one and go back up, but then I see Collin coming down his porch steps. "Hey!" I call to him.

He raises a hand back at me. Then he starts laughing. "What the hell are you wearing?"

I look down at myself, then back up at him. I forgot about my costume. "I took Rosie to the Ordinary for lunch. So..." I shrug. "When in Rome."

Collin chuckles. "You took Rosie... *you* and Rosie?"

"Is that weird?"

"Well." Collin pauses to think. "Not really, actually. It's just surprising. I didn't know you were interested."

"Well, neither did I, but turns out I am. She's a very rare gem. Did you know she's got jobs all over Trinity County and she wears costumes for all of them?"

Collin beams an amused smile at me. "I did not know that."

"Well, she does. She's got a printshop in Bishop, Collin. She writes a lonely-hearts newsletter or some such thing. And it's going big-time now because it's gettin' inserted into the Disciple paper every weekend."

Collin makes a face of confusion. "She writes a what?"

"You know. Those 'desperately seeking' personal ads? Only more old-timey. I wrote one. It's going in the paper this weekend." Collin has now been rendered speechless, but his face says what his mouth doesn't, so I clarify. "I wrote one looking for *Rosie*. And then in the next issue, she'll write me back." He still looks confused. "It's a *romantic* thing. Fuck's sake, Collin. I'm courtin' her."

Now he bursts out laughing. He laughs so hard, he bends over, grabbing his stomach.

"What? Why is that funny?"

Collin straightens up, still laughing. "You're *courtin'* her? Oh, Amon. I need to record this shit. It's gold." Then he points to my outfit. "This is above and beyond, brother. Above and beyond."

"Whatever. Anyway. I just followed Sawyer into the woods and—"

"Dammit, Amon," Collin interrupts, his face all business now. "I fuckin' told you not to bother that man. Just leave him alone."

"You and I both know this is about Blackberry Hill. And he's doin' it right under our noses. We need to figure this out because those men are dangerous, Collin. I know we got the upper hand that last time, and we haven't seen them since you threatened Ike Monroe, but it's not a forever thing. It's a temporary truce as they circle the wagons and call for reinforcements."

Collin sighs, but doesn't disagree. "I know. That's probably all true. But this isn't about us, Amon. It's about Charlie. If Charlie's involved, then he's taking care of things."

"You give him way too much credit. He's a dirty, two-faced politician, only worse. Because he was never elected. He's nothing but a corrupt bureaucrat."

"As I well know, Amon. Trust me. But you know why I put up with it. And I'm tired of saying this—he's paying the bills right now. His contracts keep us afloat."

"I get that. But it doesn't mean we have to let his man use us to rile up Blackberry Hill or whatever the fuck he's doing. I'm not saying we need to interfere with Sawyer, I'm just saying that sticking your head in the sand never made anyone's life better in the end. We need to find out what he's doing, even if we never do anything with that information."

Collin sighs and I know him well enough to interpret this sigh as giving in. "Fine. We'll track him." He shoots a look over his shoulder, then lowers his voice. "But we're not gonna interfere and we're not telling anyone else. It's me and you and that's it."

"Let me change and get the dogs. We'll go now."

"No. I gotta run into Richmond this afternoon for a meeting."

I raise my eyebrows. "With Charlie?"

"Who else." He points a finger at me. "Don't take a dog into those woods without me. We'll do it tomorrow."

I sigh, but give in because I basically got my way, even if it's not on my schedule. "Fine. Tomorrow morning, but we're doing it first thing, so don't make any other plans."

Collin agrees. Then smiles at me. "Who ya gonna be tomorrow? Daniel Boone? Or James Joyce?"

"James who?"

Collin raises his eyebrows. "You skipped school that day, didn't you?"

"What are you talking about?"

"That day in Mr. Coswell's English class when he told us to absolutely never, ever read James Joyce's letters to his wife because they were not for Trinity County eyes."

I laugh. "Let me guess. Everyone left school that day looking for those letters on the internet."

"He nearly got fired for that remark."

"Where the hell was I?"

Collin shrugs. "Probably hungover in Revenant." Then

he winks at me. "But I know what you'll be reading tonight. And you'll be penning smutty letters to Rosie by tomorrow."

"Fuck off." But when I turn away, I'm smiling. Because Rosie Harlow is a dramatic girl if ever there was one and my little plan to court her using costumes and personal ads is absolutely brilliant.

There ain't another man alive who can compete with me now.

I go inside my cottage, close the door, and rest my back against it so I can sigh. Then I fan myself with my hand. A stupid habit that I wish I hadn't picked up, but up until Amon, it's never been a literal gesture.

But boy, does that man ever make me hot.

Courtin'. In costumes! And he put an ad in my little paper—desperately seeking me. Everyone in Disciple is gonna see it this weekend. People in Bishop too. Though most of them don't know Amon, so it's not as big a deal.

The really fun part about all this—aside from the costumes, of course, and the inevitable removing of said costumes, of course, of course—is that I get to write him back in the *Busybody*.

I push off the door, walk over to the chaise, and start unhooking my corset, trying to think about how I would like to handle that. In the olden days, I guess they would've posted a letter and put in an ad. But that's no fun for the paper. Readers want a correspondence. They want to watch the relationship develop. They want a wedding announcement, they want a baby announcement, they want updates. Like the kind some people send at Christmas time to relatives who live far away. I've never sent one of those, but I get one in the mail every year because Clover's family always sends them out. Even back when they still lived in

Disciple and everybody knew their business, they sent out one of those updates.

And people would roll their eyes like the Bradleys thought their family life was so damn fascinating it needed to be spelled out in detail at the end of every year.

But the fact is, the Bradleys *are* fascinating. Back then, they were the richest people in town and they owned that big old mansion. Well, they still do own it, but it's been undergoin' renovations for years now and the Bradleys moved away from Disciple right after Clover left for college.

She was the popular girl in school and she had horses. And all those woods to ride in. Everyone wanted to be Clover's best friend because they wanted an invite to go horseback riding in the woods. Lowyn was Clover's best friend. She got all the horse perks.

But anyway, the point is, her family was interesting so people didn't mind reading that newsletter every year. I still look forward to it.

I take off both of my skirts so I'm just left wearing my drawers and camisole as I think about how I might plot out my literary romance with Amon Parrish, which will run side by side with the literal one, because a girl only gets the full-on swoony courtship treatment once in her life and—

My thoughts are interrupted by a sudden flash of memory.

I pause in the middle of the room, squinting my eyes, trying to bring that memory into focus. The park. The forest. The waterfall. And that tree stump.

It's not true. This isn't the first time I've been properly courted. The first time was—

I gasp right out loud, then turn, my eyes searching for the letters, even though I know they're not here. I gave two of them to Amon so he could have them forensically tested and the third is still at my house.

I sit down on the chaise, suddenly light-headed.

The maze turned out to be a picture of a cross.

A *cross*.

How the hell did I not immediately make this connection? I mean, it was his last name! It's what I named my son! And not only that, he was my first love and the only other time in my life that I was given the full-on swoony courtship treatment.

Erol.

He's... back?

I stand up, whirl around, wishing for those letters so I can look at them. Why did I give them to Amon? Why?

Then I realize that I haven't checked the mailbox here at the cottage. I rush outside, not even caring that I'm only wearing eighteenth-century undergarments, and practically skid to a stop at the mailbox. I close my eyes, take a breath, and then open it.

There is one letter.

I take it out and stare at the front of the envelope. My name is handwritten in a well-practiced all-caps style above my little Goosebeak Alley address.

I look around, realize the backyard ladies—and a few tourists—are all staring at me, then wave and smile and run back inside.

My body is all hot and my face all flushed, so I sit down on the chaise to give myself a moment. Because I am jumping to some pretty big conclusions here. I mean, more than likely it's a stalker. Erol's been gone for twelve years now. Why on earth would he suddenly come back? And if he was intent on coming back, why all these stupid worksheet letters written in code?

No. It's not him. It's a stalker. And I should not even open this letter. I should just hand it over to Amon and...

I let out a breath and with it goes my fortitude. A moment later, I've got a fingertip under the seal and I'm poppin' it open.

I hold my breath as I unfold the paper, then let it out in a rush. "What the fuck is this?" I'm confused as I look at the letters. They don't say anything and it's not a puzzle like the rest. It's just... letters. But they are paired up in a weird way. ZC. RN. ZC. LS. HW. AS. JK. UC. EC.

What does this mean?

I flip the paper over, hoping there's something on the other side, but there's not. It's just blank. Then I just sit and stare at them, trying to figure it out. Do I rearrange all the letters until they spell something? How do I figure it out?

Well, despite where I'm currently sitting, I do live in the modern age. So I pull out my phone and type the letters in just as they appear on the paper.

I get nothing, of course. My fingertip taps out a pattern on my chin as I think. There has to be a way to understand the message, or why send it? Furthermore, I know it is a hidden message because the three prior worksheets made it very clear.

I add the word 'code' to the end of my string of letter pairs, but again, the search pulls up things that don't make any sense to me. It's a lot of computer stuff. I study them for several minutes anyway, thinking maybe I'm just too simple to understand the results.

But no. I decide this search is not helpful.

What other way could I phrase it? Then a lightbulb goes off—they're not *codes*. Not really. Because these things actually have a proper name. They're called *ciphers*.

I type that in with the keywords 'double letters', and bingo! The third result down says, 'Key for the Digraph Cipher.'

When I click the link it's a decoder! I quickly type in my letter pairs and hit the decode button.

Meet me. You know where.

Ho-lee shit. It's real. It's a code and it's from him! Erol! After twelve years, he's finally gotten in touch with me. He sent the worksheets to like... prime me, or something. To make me think about codes and puzzles so that when he sent the message, I wouldn't just dismiss it and toss it in the trash, but try and figure it out.

You know where.

And I do know where.

I quickly strip off the rest of my clothes and start pulling on my jeans. I don't even hang up my dress, I just leave it all on the floor, grab my purse, and leave, my keys already jingling in my hand as I power-walk to my car.

Five minutes later I'm zooming down the loop towards the main highway. Once I get there, I turn left and start heading down into the valley. I pass the turn-off to Revenant and just keep going, all the way down the river to Fayetteville. It's not a big place in the grand scheme of things—less than three thousand people call this area home

—but compared to the Trinity towns, it's downright big city.

Even though I have claimed to have dated many a man from Fayetteville over the years, I actually haven't. It's just a hookup location because it's got a couple of motel choices.

But before it was that, it was something special because it was where Erol and I would go. I would take the bus home from school, but instead of getting off in Disciple, I'd ride it down to Revenant. Erol would be waiting for me at the highway loop intersection and we'd drive down into Fayetteville and hike a trail up to a little waterfall that wasn't on any of the maps. It wasn't a river waterfall, just a creek. But it was pretty and always changing. The water might be a soothing trickle down the rocks one day, then gushing over like a dam broke the next.

There wasn't a picnic table, but there was a collection of stumps that we used to sit on. Of course, we did other things there too. It's entirely possible that Cross was conceived in that very clearing.

When I arrive at the trailhead, I park my car, get out, and start up the main trail, searching for the smaller one that will lead me to our spot. I have to backtrack a few times, it's been so long since I've been up here, but about a half hour later, I find it.

Erol was my first. And if he hadn't gone missing, he might've been my only.

I scan the clearing, taking it all in, memories flooding back like it was yesterday instead of twelve years ago. And that's when I see it. A plastic baggie sticking out from underneath a rock, which is on the very stump I used to sit on when we were up here together.

I approach slowly, looking around. Like maybe he's watching.

How long ago did he place it here?

How long has this message been waiting for me?

I just stare at it for a few moments, unsure if I'm ready. Then I feel a little stupid because it might just be a piece of trash. So I walk over, shove the rock off the stump, and pick up the baggie.

The moment I do this, I ache. Because it's the same kind of envelope that I've been getting all week at my jobs. It's got my name on it—just Rosie, no Harlow—and it's the same stylized, all-caps handwriting.

I want to open this envelope so bad, but I can't bring myself to do it. What if it's not another puzzle but an actual letter? One that comes with an explanation?

I'm not ready for this moment. I'm not ready to hear what he has to say. His... *excuse.* All these years I've pictured him dead. That was the only reason I could imagine that would make him stay away. After all our plans. After all those declarations of love. After him knocking me up at age fifteen.

And he's *not* dead?

He just... walked away?

My legs go soft so I sit down on the stump, just staring off into the clearing. Picturing that last time we were together. Erol already knew I was pregnant. It had been a couple of weeks since the stick turned blue.

The night he found out I was pregnant we didn't come all the way up here. We were eating hamburgers in his car in the Revenant diner parking lot. I ate two, plus a strawberry milkshake. It's really weird how you can remember stupid details like that a dozen years later. After we were done eating, I told Erol my big news and at first, he was stunned. Speechless. But he didn't avoid eye contact and he didn't deny being the father or insinuate that I had been sleeping around. He handled it like a gentleman. Like it was a duty. The way I imagine a teenage boy from Bishop might.

I was relieved. And things were just fine. We kept our regular schedule. Me taking the bus down to Revenant after school, him meeting me there and picking me up.

That last time we came up here, he was excited. He was making plans for our future.

Then his birthday came. We had made plans, but not definitive ones because even though it was his birthday and not mine, he was planning a surprise for me. He was gonna pick up his beaver traps that morning and call me when he got back.

But he never did. He was just... gone. No note, no phone call, nothing.

I had never been to his house, just like he had never been to mine. I didn't know his people, he didn't know my people. So when he disappeared, I didn't have anyone to question. I did look up his family in Fayetteville, but there was no one in the phone book, or 411, or online who had the last name Cross in the entire town.

The next six months were agony for me. Not just the whole 'telling my parents' thing or going to high school with a rapidly growing baby bump. I mean, all that was bad, but it was the emotional turmoil that nearly did me in and make me give up.

Give up. As in give Cross up for adoption.

God, that would've been a mistake. I love my son. He's

my everything. My life would be incomplete without him. Luckily, my family rallied behind me when Jim Bob Baptist came over to 'talk about Rosie's future in Disciple' and my daddy, plus every one of my brothers, stood up and my daddy said, "No. Rosie is staying right here and you best get over it."

I had people. I know I was lucky. Of course, my mama cried and my daddy was mad. But it was a short thing. Didn't even last a month, I'd say.

And after Cross came, they forgot I was a child and just treated me like any other adult family member. Their parenting of me was over. It was too early, but I see why they did it this way. I was in charge of this tiny human's life and they wanted me to know that, while they would be there to help, they were not gonna let me out of that responsibility.

There was no way I could go back to school. Everyone in my family works full-time. Most families in Disciple do their Revival duty part-time because they work other jobs, and everyone in my family has two jobs too, even if the second one is mostly just a hobby. But we're in charge of the tent. And after all the modern-miracle scaffolding went up several years back, it turned into more than a full-time job.

Of course, everyone could've shuffled their days around to watch Cross and create time for me to go to school, but it wasn't their responsibility to do that. So I never asked.

Besides, I liked being home with baby Cross in those early years. It was good. I didn't have to pay rent, or work an outside job, or worry about babysitters. And anyway, I passed the GED test right after I turned seventeen and so I am technically not a high-school dropout.

But once I turned eighteen everything changed. No one warned me, but I saw it coming. Cross was about two and a half at this point and my older brother, Pate, had just married Chalice Guffie, the niece of Geraldine from the Revenant diner, and she was staying at home at the time because she was pregnant. So Cross spent his days with her and I got a job at the Revenant diner.

The other jobs just came gradually as more and more of Cross's time was spent away from home doing things. Lowyn hired me at McBooms and that's been a regular thing for a long time now. But there were others here and there before I started the *Busybody*. Waitressing at the Bishop Inn. I was a parts girl for the Sardis Mechanic Shop on Third and Maple. I washed dishes for April Laver in the bakery for a couple years.

But none of this was about money. I actually have plenty of money. I mean, my childhood profit share added up to about thirty thousand dollars by time I turned eighteen and could cash out. And even though I'm not a business owner or a town partner, so I don't get the big contracts like other members of my family, I have way more money than I need.

I don't work the jobs for money.

I work them so I don't have to think about the man who wrote this letter and how he ruined me. Not by getting me pregnant—I do not regret my son. Not one bit. But his abandonment nearly did me in.

Even if I did mostly think he was dead, I never really believed it. I always held out hope that he'd come back. It was this hope that killed me. Inside. Erol Cross ruined my heart. He tore it out, ripped it to pieces, and then stomped on it for good measure.

All this time I've been holding the baggie with the envelope inside, so now I look down at it. Do I put it back? Or open it?

It would be stupid not to look at it because then it would just be this mystery that would linger in my head like the smell of something rotten in the back of the fridge. Is it a puzzle? Is it a letter? What's inside the fuckin' envelope?

And I don't need that lingering in my heart and head for years to come, so I open the baggie, take out the letter, and slip my fingertip under the seal. I hold my breath until I pull the paper out and see that it's on lined paper and it's not a puzzle, it's words.

Then this breath comes out in a rush and my hand shakes as I tug on the folded edges, open it up, and read...

DEAR ROSIE,

I HOPE YOU ARE WELL. I have seen you from afar and you are as beautiful as ever. I've seen our son, too, and he's better than perfect. I'm sorry for the way I left. It wasn't my fault and if you just give me thirty minutes, I will explain everything that's happened to me since that day I disappeared.

I'll be at the Fayetteville Burger Boy from eight to ten p.m. on June twenty-sixth. Please come. Please give me a chance to explain. I have never stopped loving you or dreaming of the day when I could see you again and meet our boy.

FOREVER YOURS,

Erol

I PAUSE after reading the last few words, stunned. Then I scoff. *Yours forever? Never stopped loving you? Dreaming of the day?*

My hand starts fishing through my huge purse almost of its own accord and then the next thing I know, I've got a pen and a notepad and I'm jotting down a reply.

DEAR EROL,

YOU CAN GO to hell for all I care. I will most certainly not be meeting you anywhere and this boy of mine is not yours, has never been yours, and never will be yours. Stop stalking me, stop sending me creepy letters, and just go on your way and forget you ever met me. There is no room for you in my life.

NEVER YOURS,
   Rosie

I RIP the page out of the little notebook, stick it back inside the baggie, and put the rock back on top.

Then I walk out of the woods and leave my past behind for good.

AMON

Bright and early Thursday morning I go outside and find Collin sitting on my porch messin' with his phone, Mercy at his side. She wags her tail at me, then licks my hand. Collin turns his head up as he stands and pockets his phone. "Ready?"

I nod. "Yep. I'll get King from the kennel. Two dogs are better than one." I do that and a few minutes later I'm back and we head into the woods with the dogs.

King and Mercy could be related, that's how much they look alike. Mercy has a fluffier coat, and King is a good twenty pounds heavier than her, but they are both all-black German shepherds. And even though I was told that Mercy was a cadaver-school dropout, it must've been some kind of mistake because she's a helluva tracker and King has earned the highest certifications for both urban and wilderness search and rescue, so I'm pretty certain that we're gonna get to the bottom of this mystery in quick order.

"Did you bring the scent?" I ask Collin once we get a little further up the trail I saw Sawyer take.

Collin nods and pulls a pen out of a sealed plastic bag. He holds it out for the dogs and lets them get a sniff. Then he says, "Seek."

There is a pause here and I relish it. It's my favorite part of training dogs like this because they actually stop and think once you tell them a job. It's a small pause and if you're not looking for it, it flies by so fast most people miss it.

But I see it. Their brains are working. They're getting ideas. And then they're off.

Neither of them are wearing bells, but Mercy and King work well as a team and one will go up ahead to stay on track, while the other will hang back so we can keep up and follow.

When Collin and I catch up, it's King waiting and Mercy is long gone, on track. Then King takes off again, and we follow.

I already know we're going to that old mine, but that was just a guess on my part. The dogs taking us there is the confirmation we need in order to take the next step.

When we come out of the woods and the mine is directly in front of us, Mercy and King bark, then sit. Their signal that the track has ended.

Collin studies the rocks covering the entrance. There are quite a few big boulders that we'll never be able to move unless we get a front loader out here. He looks at me and shrugs. "It doesn't make much sense, Amon. If the scent ends here, and here is a wall of rocks, then where did Sawyer go?"

It's a good question. "He had to have gone in, obviously."

"When you followed him, did you see any missing rocks to indicate he went inside?"

"No," I admit. "But he probably knew I was following him and doubled back."

"Hmm." Collin considers this.

And while he does that, I grab one of the smaller rocks, about the size of a bowling ball, and pull it out. Behind it is nothing but darkness. But that's just proof that there's a space back there.

Collin bends down, snapping a flashlight off his belt and clicking it on so he can shine it into the hole I made. "There's a door. It's only a few feet in. Steel, definitely locked because I can see a little lit-up security pad. But I don't think Sawyer went in. At least not this way."

I lean in and he moves out of the way so I can see, and sure enough, he's right. "You think there's another door and Sawyer disappeared through there?"

"Maybe." I straighten back up and so does he. "But there's a creek over there. Maybe Sawyer just left this track on purpose? Or suspected he was being followed so he doubled back in the creek?"

I look over at the creek. It's only twenty feet or so. "He suspected I was following him yesterday and took precautions? Wouldn't the dogs go to the creek if this was the case?"

Collin shrugs. "There's probably a million ways to trick a dog, Amon. And I know yours are all extra-special smart, but doubling back is the logical answer. If there was another way in, why would Sawyer bother coming out here at all? Why not just go straight to that door?"

He's right. I think Sawyer's interest, and by extension, Charlie's as well, is due to the fact that they do not have access. "Well, what should we do?"

Collin thinks for a moment, then clips his flashlight back

on his belt. "Let's leave it alone for now. I'm sure we could remove enough rocks to get in there, but then what?" He shrugs. "We can't break that door. We'd need a front loader or some explosives to do that. And we don't have either of those things."

"So we just let it go? We just let him come up here and do secret shit on our fuckin' land and pretend it's not happening?"

"I didn't say that," Collin says. "I'll talk to Ryan and see if we can get some equipment up here. We'll get that door open, but it's not happening today, Amon."

"It goes to Blackberry Hill, doesn't it?"

"Probably."

I let out a breath. "Should we call General Forbe?"

Collin considers this, then shakes his head. "Nah. It's really none of his business what we do up here, is it?"

"It's not," I agree.

"So fuck him. And fuck Charlie. I'm tired of this shit. We bought this land to get away from them and now it's starting to feel like we're just digging ourselves in deeper."

Part of me feels guilty about this because I was the one who showed Collin the compound back when we were looking for real estate—on the suggestion of Charlie Beaufort, I realize. But I was so excited about coming home, I didn't really question Charlie's motives. It was a serious mistake, but it can't be undone now. We're here. And we're staying here.

So I just sigh. "Yeah. It does feel that way."

THE NEXT MORNING it's raining buckets so there is no chance of doing anything out at the mine, and it's Friday, so the guys only have half a day of dog testing before they are released for the weekend. I do my part in the testing—which takes place in the big outbuilding when the weather's bad—and then turn my attention to more intriguing things.

The continuation of my courtship of Rosie Harlow.

This involves a ride down into Disciple and an unscheduled meeting with Jim Bob Baptist. Ester Adkins, Rosie's great-aunt, is typing away on her keyboard when I enter the little stone building that acts as the government office of Disciple.

"You wipe those muddy feet, Amon Parrish." Ester says this without even looking up from her computer tasks. "I am not a maid and I do not do floors."

I chuckle. Some things never change. But I do wipe my feet before I approach her desk.

"Can I help you with something, Amon?" Ester doesn't look at me. Just keeps going about her business.

"Does Jim Bob have a minute? I need a favor."

Ester stops typing and then tilts her head down so she can look up at me from over the top of her glasses. "Is this Revival business? Because it's Friday, Amon. And we only do Revival business on Fridays."

Ester will tell you this no matter what day you walk in, but it's fine. Because it actually is Revival business. "It is, Ester. It is."

"Well, go on in then." And she nods her head towards the thick, maple double doors that lead to Jim Bob's office.

So that's what I do and on the other side of those doors I find a contemplative Jim Bob standing in front of the large window behind his desk with his back to me. Jim Bob is a big man. Big as in muscular and imposingly tall, not heavy with extra weight. I suspect he had his share of traveling when he was my age because there's a picture of him all dressed up in military police uniform sittin' on his desk.

It's not facing out, so I suspect most people don't even know it's there. And hell, maybe it isn't no more. But I was in this office nearly every week when I was a teenager and at least a dozen of those times I was alone because Jim Bob was busy elsewhere. So I would sit in his desk and poke through it like the heathen criminal I was wont to be and I always paused to reconsider our mayor when I looked at that picture of him.

In fact, that picture might actually be where I got the idea to join the marines.

I walk up to the desk and clear my throat. I have not talked to Jim Bob since that whole fiasco up on Blackberry Hill when Collin chewed his ass out on the helicopter ride home. So I'm maybe a little bit nervous. "Jim Bob? Can I have a moment?"

He turns his head, but his massive body stays where it is. "Amon. What can I do for you?"

I look out the window to see what's got him so pensive. It's a nice view of the Revival tent up on the hill. Since it's raining, all the scaffolding is up and there are white lights shining dimly against the contrast of the sky, which makes the whole thing appear very fairy-like since the sky is dark purple and gray, covered in thunderheads. "Well, I was wondering if I could ask you for a favor."

Jim Bob turns, smiling. Which surprises me because I thought he might be a little put out about this favor. He waves a hand at the chair behind me, then takes a seat behind his desk, making the old leather chair creak from his weight. "Have a seat, Amon. Would you like a cigar?"

I sit and decline the offer. "No, thanks."

"Well, what can I help you with?"

He's still smiling, and this kinda worries me. So I ask this question first. "Are you mad at me?"

"Am I mad at you?" He leans forward a little, putting his elbows on the desk. "No. But I'm not gonna lie, I am disappointed that you boys don't want to continue a tradition that is so important to this town."

I nod. Because I can see his point. "Well, the fact is, I'm here to ask you if I can participate in the Revival next weekend."

His eyebrows shoot up. "Fourth of July?"

"Oh, wow. I guess I hadn't realized it was coming up so quick. But... yeah. That's what I'm asking."

"Why?" His brow furrows. "Why now? I mean, you boys did basically tell me to go fuck myself."

"We did." There's no point in denying that. "But you see, Rosie Harlow and I are starting up a thing and I would like to surprise her next weekend by showing up at the Revival in costume. So we can have a date. You know, the way Collin got one with Lowyn."

Jim Bob frowns. "The Revival is not a fantasy dating service, Amon."

"I know that. I'm not trying to be disrespectful or nothing. I just want to make Rosie happy."

Jim Bob leans back again, letting out a long sigh. "Well, I like Rosie. She's Ester's grandniece, after all so I feel like she's family. And I want the best for her, of course, so... I will let you participate. On one condition."

Here it comes. But I was prepared for this, so I'm ready to negotiate. "What is it?"

Jim Bob smiles big. "You stick around for the whole season."

"As security? Because I will, but I'll be alone. Collin won't—"

"No," Jim Bob interrupts. "Not security, son. As a player." He smiles big again. "A major player. How about that, Amon Parrish? I'll rewrite the script for next weekend, putting you in character, giving Rosie a complimentary part, and I'll even throw in a big ol' basket on her front porch bright and early on Sunday morning with a costume change inside."

I picture this. I picture my date with Rosie happening just like it did for Collin and Lowyn. It was a pretty good day. "Can we do the dance?" I ask.

Jim Bob nods, his grin wild now because he knows I'm gonna agree. "Oh, I will make sure there is lots of dancing. I'll go all out, Amon. We'll give Rosie the date of a lifetime— which she deserves—and she'll be smitten with you for the rest of her life."

Again, I'm picturing this. Never in all my years of man-whoring around the world have I had such an elaborate date with a woman. But Jim Bob is right, Rosie does deserve this. "You got a deal, Jim Bob."

His eyebrows go up again. "No limits? No questions? I

mean, what if I cast you as a Depression-era farmer and her as a downtrodden wife?"

I shrug. "It's not about the costumes or the role-playing. It's about Rosie and me. I'm only asking for an opportunity here, Jim Bob. Making it special is up to me."

He stands up and extends his hand across the desk. "You've got yourself a deal."

*O*n *Saturday morning*, I'm having regrets.
You can go to hell for all I care.

My response to Erol's renewed interest in me and my son was maybe a little bit reactionary. But in my defense, this man was the love of my life as a teenager and he left me. Pregnant. And for twelve years, I mostly presumed he was dead. Which is worse than actually presuming he was dead because every now and then I'd get the itch to picture he was not dead and then…

I sigh.

Because then I would get sad all over again.

Now I know how Lowyn felt that first day when she learned Collin was back. She denied her love, but it wasn't the kind of love that allows denial. And it caught back up to them.

But this is different. Oh, I know every woman probably says that. But it is. Because Lowyn and Collin were a thing. Knew each other their whole lives, dated in high school, made plans. In other words, it wasn't a whirlwind like Erol and I had.

And Collin didn't abandon a baby.

It's not gonna end up that way for me. I'm not getting back together with this man because I don't even know him. It would be like being with a total stranger.

Amon, on the other hand, is not only the safer choice, but the obvious one. Despite his reputation in high school and the ensuing dozen years he was gone doing secret military things, he's everything I never knew I wanted in a man. Strong, protective, smart, gentle, romantic, and fun. He was gone the same amount of time as Erol, but when Amon came back it was like he never left. Things were easy. And I know that in books and movies and such, women like to swoon over the broody, enigmatic loner, but in real life, that guy is almost certainly just another Scar.

So why are you even thinking about Erol, Rosie? If Amon is so perfect?

It's a good question. And if I'm the one asking it, it's kinda hard to deflect. But there's an easy answer for my fixation and it's called closure.

I need closure. I haven't seriously thought about Erol Cross in probably six or seven years. I cried over him good when he first disappeared, but I was pregnant and hormonal. He faded over time.

But if he's back... then that bastard owes me a fuckin' explanation.

Yeah. That's how I see it. That asshole owes me an explanation. I don't need it to be in person, a letter will do just fine. But I'm gonna get this answer.

And then... well—I pause here to smile—then I'm gonna enjoy being courted by Amon Parrish.

God, when we were growing up he was the boy every girl wanted. Not the same way they all wanted Collin. All the good girls wanted to be Lowyn so they could date Collin. But the bad girls like me, it was Amon who prowled our dreams at night. He was always a one-night-stand boy. All the girls who got mixed up with him back then knew it was a booty call and nothin' else. And most of them took it well when he moved on to another girl the very next weekend.

But he's different now. And isn't this every rogue-lovin' girl's dream? To tame the bad boy's wild ways? To settle down with him and redirect all that savage masculine sexuality and swagger into tribal devotion and protectiveness? To gentle the angry man and wrangle that leather-jacket-wearing outsider into a husband and a father?

It is. Capturing the feral heart of a man like Amon Parrish and keeping it all for yourself is the plot of a teenage romance novel.

Or—I stop to chuckle here—a really good personals ad.

Which reminds me... I turn over in bed and grab this week's edition of the *Busybody* off my nightstand. There is just enough of the dawn-breaking light leaking through the curtains for me to read it.

Rugged and worldly man seeks small-town woman with shining gray eyes and a personality to match.

I sigh. Rugged and worldly is a good combination. Amon's always been blond. Not the dirty light brown of most boys around here, either, but a true blond. Add that to his blue eyes, squared-off jaw, and easy grin and this man is more than handsome, he's downright sexy.

Must love dogs.

What kind of woman is gonna object to that? I mean, a rugged and worldly man with a dog? It's like winning the jackpot twice.

He is charming, handsome, protective, and part-owner of a suspicious (but entirely legal) elite security service.

Now, some women might balk at this, but me? I just find it fascinating. I want to know all the little details about that Edge Security they've got goin' up there in the hills.

She is smart, funny, adorable, and a good mother who did not get lucky, but got exactly what she deserved.

Honestly, this is what won me over. Because the last part, 'got exactly what she deserved', could be a very negative thing in my case. So it's the context that makes it dreamy. Because my prize in this particular instance is Cross. It's the perfect thing to say to a proud single mother.

And the ending, of course. *She can pull off every kind of vintage and if she chooses him, she will never be alone and scared again.*

Alone and scared. It's an interesting addition to his ad. One I don't quite understand yet. But I can't wait for him to explain.

Even though I would never have labeled Amon Parrish as 'most likely to be a good father' back in high school, I can see it now. Yes, he's still wild. But his worldliness has also made him wise. And not only that, he is kind. All men who love dogs as much as he does have kindness in them. He would be a good role model for Cross. Not that my son doesn't have his share—all my brothers stepped up for Cross. Pate, Rush, Ash, and Lecter are all in their thirties, settled down now and with families of their own.

But it would be nice to have a man in the house again. To sleep next to someone every night. To be there when he got home from work. To talk about my day with a grown-up. Not that I don't have friends, I do. But it's not the same as discussing life with a partner.

I sigh again, closing my eyes to daydream a little before I get up and get ready for Revival. I gotta be there early because it's a dramatic day. The conclusion to all the tension that has been building since Easter Sunday reaches a crescendo next weekend on the Fourth of July and the final act begins.

This is my favorite part of our modern Revival season. The slow and lingering nature of the final weeks of summer when the plot is low-energy and a little bit sad. We're still playing out the Prodigal Son story from the beginning of the season, even though Collin and Lowyn are gone. They were replaced by Jameson Grimm and Taylor Hill—who really kinda hate each other, so everyone is ready for this season to be over.

The guests don't seem to mind, though. The regulars who come are caught up in the costumes, and the parties, and the atmosphere. And the first-timers care not a bit about the continuity of the story. They barely know it's happening. It's just a sideshow for them. A carnival. One of three stops on their tour of Trinity County.

But in my opinion, the weeks after Fourth of July give everyone time to breathe, and appreciate the beauty of Revival, and bask in the late summer sun as the story builds again, coming to a final climax around Thanksgiving and then, of course, the real turn into the next year's story.

It's a weird cycle, but I like it.

If this sounds like you, Gray Eyes, please respond to me, Rugged and Worldly, in the next issue so we can start a public correspondence.

This part says... *I see you, Rosie Harlow. And I like what I see. Not only that, I want everyone in town to know it.*

I throw the covers off, get up, and start getting dressed in my costume for the day. But I'm just going through the motions because in my head I am composing my first correspondence with Rugged and Worldly.

AT THE REVIVAL I fan myself and shout, "Amen!" at just the right time. I faint in the middle aisle of the tent—just once this week—and get covered in sawdust. And then I flit down the aisles of the over-tent—which is in place because it's raining—starting scenes, and finishing scenes, and generally doing what I do every weekend. Just... filling in where they need me.

At four-thirty April Laver pushes aside the tent flap of her bakery and joins me in the back alley where I am sitting on a crate, taking a break. There is a scent of baking bread that lingers on her like perfume. Sometimes she smells like cupcakes.

April waves the *Busybody* at me. "What's this?"

I play dumb. "What do ya mean?" Everyone was murmuring about the ad this morning, but it was too busy for any of my close friends to question me about it. Now that the day is over, it's time. And I'm ready. More than ready. I'm excited about it.

"This ad, Rosie. What is going on with you and Amon?"

"What makes you think it's Amon?"

Her eyes go big. "Rugged and Worldly? Who else would it be? It's not Collin. And I doubt those other boys up there at that compound would even think to place a personal ad in an obscure, and fake, Bishop newspaper. Besides"—she smiles at me—"you've got the eyes of a thunderhead, Rosie. They're a storm."

I roll these gray eyes right to her face. "Like the rumble before the glory?" Which refers to the famous Revival sermon that plays every week on the loudspeakers.

"No. They're the echo on the water."

I scoff. "What the hell does that even mean?"

"You know. When you're out by the river, and the sun is going down, and the loons are calling, and you get those chills up your arms. That's the echo. The chills, Rosie." She laughs now. "'Small-town woman with shining gray eyes and a personality to match.' That's got Rosie Harlow written all over it right there. And anyway, the 'good mother' part gave it away."

I actually go speechless.

"What?" April asks.

"Nothing, it's just…" My eyes squint down a little. "You think I'm a good mother?"

"Oh, hell, Rosie. Everyone thinks you're a good mother. Even if you do cat around with questionable men called Scar from Fayetteville."

April winks at me. Like she knows I don't cat around with anyone. Like she knows I spend every moment of my day being busy so I don't have to remember that I'm alone at night. Like she knows I haven't been on a date in years now.

Then, suddenly, she grabs my hand and looks me right in the eyes. "Don't let him get away, Rosie."

"What?"

"Amon. He's a keeper. And this ad?" She holds up the *Busybody* and shakes it a little. "It's proof. So whatever hesitation you have, get rid of it."

"I'm not hesitating. I like him. Hell, I was daydreaming about him when you came out here. I've been daydreaming about him all day."

"Then why am I hearing rumors that you've got a secret admirer?"

My heart skips a beat. "What?"

"Come on, don't play dumb with me. Everyone in Trinity County knows you're getting letters."

"People are talking about that?" I'm shocked.

"Not only talking about it, they're taking sides."

"What do you mean?"

"Amon or the admirer, of course. A love triangle? We've done enough of them in the Revival stories for you to know better. The woman always loses, Rosie. And after this?" She shakes the *Busybody* again. "They're mostly rootin' for Amon. And if you drag it out too long, they're gonna get mad."

"What the fuck? My life is no one's business."

April scoffs. "This is Disciple. You, of all people, know that your life most certainly *is* our business." She looks down her nose at me, making her lips thin with disapproval. "Put an end to those letters, Rosie. They need to stop."

Then she turns and goes back inside her tent. Leaving the scent of fresh-baked bread behind her.

I sit there on the crate, confused. Because I didn't ask for any of this. People should just butt out.

But I know I need to do something about these letters. And tonight is the night Erol will be waiting for me at Fayetteville Burger Boy.

I wasn't gonna go. I wasn't. I wrote my response and that was it, as far as I was concerned. But everything April just said has me worried. Not about the opinions of the town—obviously, I don't care what people think about me—but I don't want this to get back to Amon. It's gonna ruin everything. There is no love triangle here. I've done nothing but open letters that were addressed to me. Why is this my fault?

Why, Rosie? Come on. Because you're the woman. Clearly, I'm a harlot who wants to have her cake and eat it too.

I roll my eyes. But April isn't wrong. If he keeps sending me letters, people will keep talking. And then Cross is gonna hear about it.

No. Nope. That right there is my hard limit. No, no, no. My son will not be hearing gossip about some fake love triangle. I absolutely need to put an end to this. I had no intention of meeting Erol at the Burger Boy tonight, but I'll be there. And by the time I leave he will know exactly where I stand and can be on his way to wherever it is he's going.

That's one thing I like about Trinity County. There are no apartments for rent to outsiders. Even the trailer I vacated to move into Lowyn's house was snapped up by graduating high schoolers. There are no houses for sale, either. And even if there were, they would not be listed anywhere else but on the bulletin board inside the little stone building where Jim Bob Baptist does his government business.

I guess Erol could come into town—attend a Revival, or something—and make trouble for me. But that would be a mistake. I have four brothers and they would not be swayed by a silly love-triangle story. They would chase him out.

But the letters, they're different. They come from outside and sneak their way in without permission, but there's no way to prevent them from coming.

So after Revival I go home—Cross is out with friends again, of course—and change into regular clothes. Because I'm going down to the Burger Boy to send this man from my past on his way.

*I WAIT THERE **for three hours**.* I sit in my car at the fuckin' Burger Boy for *three hours*.

And he never shows.

My anger builds as I drive home. What a waste of time. This jerk, he hasn't changed. And I don't even want to see him again. I only went so I could tell him to stay away. And now it looks like I was rejected again.

Never. He's dead to me now.

When I park in my driveway it's nearly midnight but I notice that there's a light on inside the house. I grab my purse and go to the door, unlock it and push it open. "Cross?" The light is coming from his bedroom. "Are you home?" He was supposed to stay the night at his friend's house. But when I look in the bedroom, it's empty. He's not here. I flip the light off and go back into the living room, looking around, suspicious now.

It's probably nothing, but... I dunno. I get a weird feeling, like someone was here.

Someone like Erol?

Calmly, I walk into the kitchen, open up the pantry, and grab the shotgun. I check all the bedrooms on the first floor first, then the basement. I do this just in case someone is still here. It gives them a chance to escape. I would much rather an intruder escape than shoot them.

Flashes of memory from when Collin had to do just that, in this very house, start flipping through my brain like someone's shuffling a deck of cards.

I take my time in the basement, listening for creaking floorboards. Then I go back up and check the master bedroom on the second floor.

No one.

I go back down and check the locks on all the doors and windows. Then I take my shotgun back up to my room and lay it down in the bed next to me.

Maybe it's crazy.

But then again, maybe it's not.

AMON

ven though my weekend was very busy with work at the compound, I could've found time to swing by Rosie's place at some point. But I had already planned this day and anyway, absence makes the heart grow fonder.

It's Monday, which means Rosie Harlow is working at the diner in Revenant. She's gonna have her hair pulled back in some messy old-timey updo, she's gonna be wearing a pink waitress uniform, and she might even be clicking some gum.

So I'm gonna pay her a little visit down there and I'm gonna show up in style.

The motorcycle isn't mine—it belongs to Lucas, the leader of a colorful motorcycle club here in Revenant called the Deceivers that riles up the Revival people up in Disciple every now and then as part of the script. He's Collin's cousin. But it's a nice bike with a stars and stripes theme to it.

I'm dressed like Lucas's twin—clothes not borrowed—with a black biker jacket and boots to match, a white t-shirt underneath, and some faded, nearly threadbare, jeans.

I park the bike in front of the diner, revving it up and making noise to announce my arrival. Things are always dead down here in Revenant on Mondays, so there's really no one to see me. Just the woman who matters.

Rosie is peeking out the window as she wipes down a table and when she realizes it's me, her whole face lights up. And that smile makes all the trouble it took to create this moment worth it.

I open the door to the diner and find her waiting for me at the hostess station. Now Rosie Harlow is an actor. She don't live in Hollywood and she's never played a part outside of the Revival, but she knows a scene when she's presented with one. And besides, I already told her we were gonna court in costume.

So she's ready for this and when she says, "Good morning," to me, it comes out like a coo. "Table for one?"

"How about… table for none?"

One eyebrow goes up. But she doesn't break when I turn and start walking over to the jukebox. I brace myself with both hands as I lean down, pretending to study the songs inside. Then I casually look over my shoulder so I can side-eye her.

Rosie Harlow is smiling, wondering just what the hell I am gettin' up to. I glance around the diner, which isn't empty, but nowhere near full, either, and find Jonesy Price, the cook and owner of the Revenant diner, winking at me from behind his kitchen counter. I cleared all this with him first, as one does when they are about to disrupt a working day to charm the skirt off a woman.

I turn, just as the distinctive opening of 'Stand By Me' begins to play. Then I lean against the jukebox, letting her get a good look at me. Her smile grows and when I push off, extending my hand in her direction as the song eases into that first verse, she blushes.

We're only about ten steps apart, so it's just moments

later when she takes my hand and I spin her around in a complete circle, hugging her up close to me when she stops.

She's looking right into my eyes, her face filled with intrigue, fascination, and probably a little bit of embarrassment too, since we're dancing in a diner, she's on the clock, and there are a dozen people watching us.

I hold her close, my arms all the way around her waist, our bodies moving slowly to the beat of the song, and I whisper in her ear, "Let's go for a ride on that bike outside."

She huffs out a little air. "I'm working, Amon."

"Well, if you want to come with me, I've taken care of that little problem ahead of time."

We stop dancing and she looks up at me. "In my waitress uniform?"

"Go check your locker." She huffs again. But I just encourage her. "Go on. Check it. I'll be waiting out front."

Rosie looks around, finds Jonesy's beaming face on the other side of his kitchen counter. He says, "Go on. Get out of here. We got ya covered."

She looks back at me one more time, then lets out a breath and makes her way to the back where the break room is.

I salute Jonesy with two fingers to the side of my head. "I owe you one." And then I go out front and arrange myself on the bike, sitting sideways with legs kicked out in front of me, arms crossed, so when Rosie comes out a few minutes later, she can get a good long look at me.

Her laugh is immediate. It's neither a mocking laugh nor a bemused one. It's good-natured astonishment. "What are you doin?"

Her outfit is a more feminine version of mine and it

came straight out of McBooms because I went over there on Sunday and I took Lowyn McBride with me. So this outfit right here that she's wearing is right up Rosie's alley.

I stand up, unbuckle two helmets from the handlebars, swing my leg over the bike, put my helmet on and offer her the second. Then I nod behind me. "Get on and find out."

She doesn't even hesitate. She comes over, takes the helmet, and a moment later her breasts are pushing up against my back, her sweet, warm breath gliding over my neck as she coos, "You're fun, Amon Parrish."

I smile, kick the bike, and tell her, "Hold on," as I pull away from the curb and point us downhill on the loop highway.

IT's *a beautiful summer* morning and the ride down the highway is picturesque. Every time I drive around, I marvel at how pretty West Virginia is. There are lots of pretty places in this world. It's easy to get lost in the ugly, especially with the job I had. It was a lot of cities—which can be beautiful in their own way if you've got a forty-thousand-foot view and all you see are the tall buildings, or the waterfront, if it has one, or the exotic things to do. But cities are mostly just a collection of chaos when you get up close.

So when I had the chance I would remind myself to appreciate places filled with nothin' but slow livin'. And

West Virginia is like this. We've got our own chaos here, of course. But we've wrapped a little bubble around Trinity County and the surrounding areas.

This is not a bad thing, in my opinion.

I'm taking Rosie to the Canyon Rim Boardwalk just outside Lansing because it's close, it's pretty, and it's got a helluva view of the New River Gorge Bridge. Of course, I've been here many times—as has Rosie, I presume. We came as a class three or four times in school. But I haven't seen it since I've been back and I doubt very much that Rosie has been here recently either.

We arrive at the visitors' center and Rosie hops off, removing her helmet. I kick the stand down on the bike and do the same, then secure both helmets to the rear seat.

When I turn back to Rosie, she's smiling at me. "What?" I ask.

"You. You're so… different."

"Different good or different bad?"

"Neither. I mean, as a boy, and from a distance, you were always nice."

I grin. "Always in trouble too."

"Yeah. You were. But that was the outside you. The inside you has always been considerate. You were just a little bit wild, that's all. Itching to see the world, maybe."

"I guess I was. And I got my wish. But now all I want is to be back." I could say more here. I could make the whole declaration. Move things along, get her to agree to be exclusive. But I don't want to miss out on the stuff that comes before that. I want us to take our time.

"And settled?" Rosie asks. Like she's reading my mind.

"Something like that." I point to the path that leads to the boardwalk. "Ready?"

Rosie takes a breath and chuckles. "Well, the walk down isn't the part you need to be ready for, is it? It's the walk back up."

"Don't worry, I'll piggyback you if ya get tired."

And this makes her blush. While she's doing that, I offer her my hand. She looks at it dubiously. "Seriously, Amon? You wanna hold hands?"

"Why not?"

"It's just... kinda high school, don't you think?"

"You don't like it?"

"It's not that I don't like it. It's not that I don't like any of this. The costumes, the dates, the *effort*." She stresses that last word. "Because you are definitely putting in the effort. But... why me?"

I wiggle my still-open hand at her. "Walk with me and I'll tell ya."

Rosie's eyes roll up a little, but only a little. She likes this courting thing I'm doing, but she's wary. She wants to fall for it, but at the same time the rational part inside her is filled with caution. Telling her to guard her heart.

And once again, in my head, I see her that day in high school. Standing there in the cafeteria with that look of horror on her face as her water broke.

That was the first time I ever saw fear. Like *real* fear. I would witness thousands of ways in which fear could manifest in the years after that, but Rosie Harlow, a teenager on the verge of giving birth, was the very first time and I will never forget it.

She comes towards me and slides her hand in mine.

Instantly, there's a connection. I didn't come back with Rosie in mind, but she was the very first person I saw from Disciple when I got coffee that morning. And ever since then, we just seem to find each other.

We're quiet at first as we make our way down the first part of the boardwalk, which is an easy-sloping ramp, taking our time and just looking at the forest all around us as we descend into the New River Gorge. It's still very early, but getting to the first lookout to see the magnificent single arch bridge is easy, so there's a small crowd of families.

If you keep going to the lower one, the rest is mostly steps.

We keep going and Rosie doesn't complain, even though the way back up is gonna be a hike.

When we get down to the lower platform we lean on the railing and take in the view. It's a sea of green trees with the bridge and river below as the main focus.

Rosie turns a little, looking at me. "It's nice."

"It is," I agree.

"You're a good date planner, Amon."

"You're worth the effort, Rosie."

She laughs. "Oh, my God. You're so…" But she can't find the word, so she just shakes her head.

"So… perfect?" I ask, teasing her a little, but only a little. Because I am making an effort.

To my delight, she agrees with me. "Yes. That. But… seriously, I'm not the only single woman in Disciple, Amon. You could have your pick. You know that, right?"

"Well… I *did* have my pick."

She blushes pink now and I turn away, looking at the bridge again to give her a moment. But I've got things to say to her and right now is a good enough time to do that. And anyway, this is what she's looking for. She wants to know why I'm putting in so much effort and it's a reasonable question that I am more than willing to answer.

So I turn back to her, ready to say all the things and put her heart at ease, but I find that she is frowning. And not some slight frown, either. But a deep one that goes all the way up to her eyes. "What?" I ask. "What did I do?"

"You? Nothing, Amon. You didn't do anything. But before this goes any further, I need to tell you something."

"OK." My heart beats a little faster. Because this was a little speed bump I wasn't expecting. "What is it?"

"Remember those letters?"

"The ones I sent into the lab for testing?"

"Yeah. Those. Well…" She bites her lip and wrings her hands a little.

"What, Rosie? What is it?"

"I know who they're from."

"Who?" This comes out a little bit too loud and a little bit too surprised as well.

"Cross's daddy."

"What?" Now that right there is a little more than a speed bump. "How do you know?"

She begins to tell me the story of her illumination and how she ended up at some waterfall just outside Fayetteville. Not far from here, actually.

"It's where we used to go," Rosie says. "When we were kids, ya know?"

"What's his name?" As soon as it's out I know I shouldn't have asked. Especially since it comes out kinda mean. So I really don't expect an answer, but she surprises me.

"Erol Cross."

"Cross?"

"Yeah. I named our son after him. By the time Cross was born Erol had been missing a few weeks already."

"Missing? What kind of missing? Like people kidnapped him or he fell off a cliff or something? What happened to him?"

Rosie shrugs. "I don't know. I still don't know. But he was gone before I even gave birth."

"So that's why you were so scared that day."

She crinkles her face at me. "What?"

"When your water broke at school. I was looking right at you when it happened and I had never seen somebody look so scared."

Rosie smiles, then laughs. "Oh, wow. I haven't thought about that moment in years." Then she frowns again. "So that's why you said that."

"Said what?"

"Alone and scared. In your ad. That's how you remember me. Pregnant and terrified. On the verge of giving birth. All by myself."

"Was I wrong?"

"No. I was scared. And sad, too. Erol and I had made a lot of plans."

"And that was the moment that you realized they were ruined?"

Rosie nods.

"OK. All right. So..." I look at her in earnest now, staring deep into those gray eyes. Because there is only one reason why she felt so compelled to tell me this story right now, in the middle of our date. And that's because she loved him.

"So…" Rosie picks up the sentence I didn't finish. "So I just figured you should know. He's back. Cross's father is back and wrote me a real letter."

There is a crushing feeling inside my chest. Like I just got the worst news ever. My mind is jumping with scenarios, trying to figure out which way is up, as I come to terms with the idea that this… might not work out.

She might not want me.

Which leaves me with only one more thing to say. "Do you want him, Rosie?"

ROSIE

mon Parrish plays his cards close when he says these words. But I can tell that he's a little bit afraid of my answer. And it wasn't a question I was expecting, so I don't actually have an answer ready.

So Amon asks again. "Do you want to try again and see if all those plans the two of you made can still work out, Rosie?"

"The answer is easy to the first question, Amon. It's no."

His eyes narrow down a little. "Just no?"

"Like I said, that one is easy. So yes, it's just no. I don't want him. I don't even know him. But do I still long for the plans we made? That's another question altogether."

"How so?"

"Well, those were my dreams. So it's just different."

Amon lets out a breath, relaxing a little. "So you want the dream, but not with the man you planned it with?"

"Yeah, I guess. If Erol had done this when Cross was still little, I'd have settled, I think. I'd have given in to the old longing. Because if I could've given Cross a father, I would've. But he's twelve now. Erol missed it, ya know? My daddy and brothers taught him everything a father should teach a son. So that part is over."

Amon nods thoughtfully. "I agree, to a point. He still needs a role model."

I smile at Amon, wondering if he's offering to do the job.

Of course he is. That's why we're having this conversation in the first place. But it's not a decision that can be decided by a mother and her love interest. At this age, a boy's role model is chosen by the boy. Even if he did have a father at home, Cross is just about ready to start questioning authority, blood relations or not.

"I wrote a reply when I went out there to the woods," I tell Amon.

"What did you say?"

"Something along the lines of... 'Not even if hell froze over.'"

Amon smiles and this time, when he breathes out, all the leftover tension goes with it. Then he asks the real question, which has nothing to do with Erol. "Do you want me?"

I don't answer right away. Not because I'm hesitating, I just want to enjoy this moment. I want to memorize it. Because this is it. This is all there is to my dating life.

It's over now.

"Yes, Amon. I want you."

He chuckles, but looks down. Maybe to hide his relief or maybe just to take his own moment to fix this morning in his head. When he looks up, he's still smiling and things are different now. "All right then. Let's go back up." He nods his head to the stairs.

I sigh, but smile too, and look up at all those stairs.

When I look back at Amon he winks at me. "I'll carry you if ya want."

"I think I can manage, but I'm not saying no to that offer just yet."

He takes my hand and we climb back up.

. . .

AMON DIDN'T NEED **to carry me**, I made it up those stairs just fine. Very out of breath and my legs will probably be aching tomorrow, but I made it. We walk back to the motorcycle and he unlocks the helmets, but when I reach for mine, he doesn't let go of it. Which forces me to meet his gaze with a questioning look. "What?"

"I have one more question."

"OK."

"Can we have dinner tonight?"

"Um… Cross is actually gonna be home for dinner tonight, so—"

"Well, I was including him in the 'we.'"

"Oh." I am a little taken aback because number one, I have never dated a man from Disciple and number two, Cross was never involved in my love life—lackluster as it was.

Amon, reading my hesitation, jumps in here. "Never mind. It's a bad idea."

"Well, just hold on now. I'm not convinced it is a bad idea. It's just… I've never introduced Cross to a man before. I mean, you know. One I was datin'."

Amon nods. "Right. But… I already know Cross." Then he smiles. "We've already met, Rosie. That cat is out of the bag."

He's not wrong. I mean, I've never seen Cross and Amon

having a conversation, but I'm sure, at one point during that first week when Collin and Amon were all over town, Cross did bump into Amon and say a few words. And all the older teenage boys have been talking about joining up with Edge Security when they graduate. So I'm sure that Cross, as an up-and-coming older boy himself, has also participated in such conversations.

When I take too long to answer, Amon keeps going. "Your place tonight at seven-thirty. I'll bring food, you make dessert, and the three of us will have a nice time. That's it. That's all it'll be. Just a nice time."

I nod. "OK. Dinner at my place tonight."

The whole ride back up to Trinity County I find myself grinning like a stupid teenager. Amon Parrish and me. Together. As a real couple.

It's not something I had ever considered. I mean, not seriously. Of course, everyone loved Amon in high school, but any thoughts I had of him were tempered by the fact that he was two years older and I was pregnant with another boy's baby.

But I will admit that when I first saw him in the Rise and Shine getting coffee that first morning he was back, and before I recognized him for who he was—which was only a few seconds. He aimed that smile at me and the little recognition centers in my brain went off pronto—but in those few seconds when he was a stranger, a tourist passing through, oh, you bet I was interested.

And now, just a few months later, I'm leaning my face into his leather jacket as we fly up the highway on a motorcycle and not only are we having dinner tonight, but it will be our third date.

Yes, my brain went there. Third date implies something. Something I am more than willing to try out. But Amon and I won't be having sex tonight because I am gonna introduce him to my son.

It's a big step but when I start picturing a life with Amon my heart goes soft, and my head gets light, and if I were standing right now, my legs would be weak.

He's the one. I feel it.

Amon Parrish is my forever man.

AFTER AMON DROPS *me off* at my car and leaves, and I drive back up to Disciple, I walk into McBooms on a high I haven't felt in over a decade.

Lowyn is at the front counter doing something with a serious look on her face. The teenagers are sweeping the floor and goofing off in the back corner of the store, and there's some music on, so it's a nice buffer between them and us when I lean my elbows on the counter and sigh.

Lowyn looks up. "Hi, Rosie. I didn't hear you come in."

"I came in the back." I sigh again, louder this time.

Which makes Lowyn grin and redirect her attention to me instead of the papers in front of her. "Well, did you eat a canary or something? Because you look like you've just been doing something devious." She side-eyes me for a moment. "What? Did you have a quickie with that Scar guy down in Fayetteville?" But she winks when she says this. So I know she's teasin' me.

I giggle. "No." Then I turn my body so I have my back to her and prop my elbows up on the counter while looking over my shoulder. "I was never datin' no guy named Scar, Lowyn. He was just made up so people wouldn't ask me why I wasn't datin'."

Lowyn cocks her head at me. "Really?"

"Truly."

She laughs. "I know all about Amon. I live next door to that man and this here outfit you're wearing? I picked it out yesterday afternoon while you were busy with Revival."

I turn back around and practically explode. "You did!" I smile big.

"I did. Amon wanted me too, of course. Because he had this date all planned for you. So. Was it everything you thought it would be? He was aiming for perfect, and I'm rootin' for him, so I hope he pulled it off."

"He did, Lowyn."

"Really?"

"Truly. It was dreamy. And not only have we dated twice now, but we date in costume! Can you believe that?"

"Dating in costume is adorable, Rosie."

"Isn't it, though? For our first date he dressed up in a proper Bishop gentleman's outfit. And then took me to the Ordinary for lunch!"

"Oh, Collin laughed about that Bishop costume pretty hard the other night. And the Ordinary? For a first date? Now that's what I call an effort."

"It is, isn't it?"

Lowyn leans back in her chair, making it creak a little.

"Well, I guess that settles it then. Date number three is a sure thing."

I slap my hands on the counter and burst. "It does, doesn't it! It's settled all right. We're having dinner tonight. At my place. Well, he's bringing dinner. I just have to make dessert. Date number three, Low." My head is nodding in a furious manner and I'm making one of those all-teeth smiles.

Lowyn's stoic face breaks into a wide grin. Then she leans forward, like she's gonna tell me a secret. "You're gonna live next door to me, Rosie Harlow. We're gonna be neighbors."

"What do ya mean?"

"Well, Amon's house is right next to mine. And Amon, well, he's got 'ready to settle down' written all over him, Rosie. And you're it. He wants *you*."

I turn away again, pressing my back into the counter, and *sighhhhhhhhh*. Because while my life has not been terrible at all, I had given up on finding romantic love. I was satisfied with loving my son. And now, on the turn of a dime, just like that—everything is changing.

And I couldn't be happier with where this might end.

Amon Parrish is... *mine*?

"I gotta go," I say, rushing towards the back of the store. "I gotta figure out what I'm gonna wear and rustle us up some dessert!"

Lowyn calls out a goodbye, but I'm already gone.

PICKING **an outfit** for a date with a man at your house is not an easy thing when your soon-to-be teenage son is gonna be there too. And Cross is the whole point of this date. I had to remind myself of that. Amon wants to formally meet him. And even though Cross and Amon already know each other, this is a big step.

I need to come off as motherly, but still a woman in her prime. Because I am. I only just barely turned twenty-eight last month.

My go-to summer outfit is cut-off denim shorts and a halter top. Which isn't very motherly, but it makes sense in my little world. Which means it makes sense to Cross because this is what he's used to seeing me in when I'm just hanging out at home in the evenings.

So this is what I go with instead of a dress.

Hair, on the other hand, is easy. Because ninety percent of the time I just wear it long with no ponytail or nothing. So that's how it is tonight as well.

I don't wear shoes inside, so I'm barefoot.

I decide to do two things to make this night stand apart from any other night at home. The first is paint my toenails. They are the prettiest shade of light green and they match my halter top—which is a crocheted number with full coverage over the breasts and lace that hangs down my belly. That's the motherly part, I guess. Because while you can still see my sexy little button, it's a peek-a-boo look at best. The shorts are just your regular bleached-out cut-offs with lots of tantalizing white strings flirtin' with my upper thighs.

The other thing I do, which I don't normally do, is put on a little make-up. Just a bit of rouge to brighten up my tanned face, some shimmery eyeshadow that matches my top and toes, and lip gloss. I love me some lip gloss. Shiny lips are still a thing in my world.

I was gonna cheat on dessert and just pick up a cake from April Laver's bakery, but… this is Amon. And I want to impress him. Besides, I'm a damn good baker. I worked for April and her family when Cross was just a baby because it was an early-early morning kind of job. And while I mostly did dishes, I worked there long enough to end up helping with the donuts while Cross snoozed in my baby wrap.

The point is, I can bake. So I decide on strawberry shortcake. An easy dessert that no one hates. Amon's bringing dinner, so—

"*Mooooom!*"

"What?" I turn to my son.

"Stop pacing in front of the window like a crazy person. It's just Amon."

He and I already talked about this dinner and he wasn't impressed. Not wasn't happy about it, but literally wasn't impressed. When I told him to go comb his hair and wash his face he scowled and said, "Why do I have to look nice for Amon?"

"Because I like him," I explained in my soft motherly voice.

"*So?* Everyone likes Amon. What does that have to do with him bringing us dinner?"

I wanted to roll my eyes here, but instead I mentally patted myself on the back for my son's cluelessness on the subtleties of dating.

I'm still pacing—though Cross has decided to ignore me and is playing video games on the couch—when Amon's truck pulls up in front of the house.

I let out a breath, just looking out the window.

And while I'm doing that, Cross gets up and opens the door before I can stop him.

I turn, and there he is. Amon Parrish comes up my walkway holding a brown paper take-out bag from the Revival Café and a bouquet of flowers and I go speechless as I take him in. He's wearing the same thing he was this morning, minus the leather jacket. So it's just jeans and a white t-shirt. And he's got his sunglasses on—mirrors, which I have always been partial to, as they are sexy as hell. Normally that blond hair of Amon's falls all over like an unruly child on a jungle gym, but this evening it's been combed back just enough to make him look presentable.

"You better get in here," Cross says. "She's been looking out the front window waitin' on ya for the past half hour."

My face goes hot, but Amon is smiling when he meets my gaze, walks up the porch steps, and hands me the flowers. "I picked them from the woods behind my house, so they're nothing special. And Lowyn tied them up with the ribbon." When he takes his sunglasses off, a few stray bits of hair fall into his eyes and he rakes his fingers through it, trying to tame it back in place.

Oh, my God, I might faint when I look directly into those blue eyes of his, so instead I concentrate on the flowers, sniffing them. They are wildflowers. Small, but colorful. And they are wrapped in a light green satin ribbon that matches my toe polish.

I look up at Amon once again, blinking a little, flattered

and feeling a little gushy that he actually picked flowers for me. But it's not surprising, really. Because Amon Parrish is a fuckin' romantic and he's not shy about pulling out all the stops.

Cross grabs the bag of food and peeks inside. Then he turns and scoots past me, back into the house, muttering, "Yum. Burgers and chicken. I'm hungry." Like this isn't a big deal. Like Amon Parrish brings us dinner every night of the week.

Amon and I both ignore Cross as we gaze into each other's eyes. He speaks first. "You look real nice tonight, Rosie."

"Thank you. And thanks for the flowers, I love them. Come on in." I slip past the screen door and hold it open for him as he comes up behind me. And just the mere presence of his body so close to mine is enough to make me wish that Cross wasn't here right now. Because I am getting hungry for something all right, but it's not food.

It's this man.

*W*hen *I enter Rosie's house* something inside me flips. It's a flip I felt coming since the very first day I came back to Disciple and saw her in the Rise and Shine coffee shop. It's a sense of being home.

A similar flip was felt when I met up with my parents and my sisters, but there was no accompanying longing.

This time, here with Rosie and her boy, I feel a longing.

"Come on in, Amon," Cross tells me. He's in the kitchen, on the other side of the counter, his plate already full of fried chicken and a burger. I was a growing boy myself at one point and my most prominent memory of being twelve was the hunger. Not like I was starving or anything, but I *felt* like I was fuckin' starving. All I wanted was food.

And Cross is no different than any other boy that age. He's stuffin' his face right there at the counter.

Rosie admonishes him. "My God, Cross. You're sending neglect messages the way you're eating. Sit your butt down at the table!"

Cross shrugs like he can't help himself, then walks over to the far side of the kitchen where a mid-century modern dining table is waiting. This is when I remember that Rosie's house is Lowyn's house, and Rosie moved in after Lowyn moved out to be with Collin at the compound. So this whole place is a like an advertisement for McBooms.

Which fits. Because Rosie Harlow dresses like she was born in the wrong century. Her outfit tonight is retro-reminiscent. Cut-off denim shorts and a light green crocheted halter top that could come off as slutty, but doesn't because Rosie Harlow isn't slutty, she's... cute. And in my opinion, you can be cute *or* slutty, but you actually can't be both.

"Here you go, Amon." Rosie hands me a plate and I take it, nodding at her like a gentleman to help herself to a burger and fried chicken. This makes her blush a little. But she grabs her food and a drink and takes it all over to the table.

I get mine as well, then join them.

It should feel a little bit weird because I've never dated a woman with a child, let alone had dinner with them, but there is nothing weird about this moment when I finally look across the table, right into Rosie's gray eyes. Everything about it feels like... providence. "Like an echo on the water."

"What?" Rosie, who is still looking me in the eyes, is confused.

"The call to Revival."

"What about it?" Cross says, his mouth full of food.

I'm still looking at Rosie. "The echo is the past and the water is the future. That's how I always thought of it. Which means it's not a passing, or a coming, but an arrival. 'Let it be a sign,'" I say, reciting the words from memory. But not in a preacher way, just a matter-of-fact way. "'A sign that the righteous will find comfort in the brave. And the danger will exist only in the damaged. Because when you give yourself to something higher, you will feel the relief that comes with the emptiness of anger and you will know, in your heart, that the blessing of grace is now upon you.'"

"Amen!" Cross bellows, then burps, laughing.

Rosie and I also laugh. And she just shakes her head. "Don't go reciting no holy words to me now, Amon. You might just make me blush."

"Oh, my God, Mom. Don't be gross. Your child is sitting at the table." Cross takes a breath from his eating and looks at me. "Can I come work for you?"

"What?" I laugh, thankful that he has changed the subject because I was about to let my eyes wander down that light green crocheted halter top of Rosie's because she fills it up in the most spectacular of ways.

"At Edge Security," Cross says. "Every boy in town is talking about how they're all gonna join up with you guys and let me tell you, they are jealous as all hell that you're at my house right now."

Rosie tsks her tongue. "Cross. Watch that mouth."

But Cross is still focused on me. "So I wanna know if I can join up." His eyes are intent and filled with a sort of hungry ambition that I've only seen on grown men as he waits for my reply.

Rosie doesn't give me time to answer. "Absolutely not, Cross." She doesn't say it mean and there isn't much reproach in her response, but she is firm. "You won't be joining up with no elite security outfit because you'll be in college."

"College is dumb." Cross is talking to me, not his mother. "Right, Amon? I mean, you didn't go to college. You went into the military. Do I have to spend time in the military in order to join your operation?"

"Military!" Rosie is fully paying attention now. "Why, that's just not in the cards, son. There will be no military."

"But do I?" Cross asks me again.

"No," I say before Rosie can lose her shit. "No, you don't need military experience." Which is a lie. There is no other way to get the knowledge and background necessary for what we do without a little bit of black ops under your belt. But I know better than to say this in front of Rosie. "You just need to train real hard, be real sensible, stay calm in every sort of situation you can think of, and"—I pause to wink at him—"grow up, of course."

Cross is with me for all of that until I get to the growing up part. His face twists a little as the words leave my mouth. "Well, I'm twelve now, you know. I'm not a baby no more."

Rosie sighs, like she's got a motherly sermon coming, but I interrupt because that's not what Cross needs to hear right now. "Nah, you're not a baby, Cross. Of course not. Everyone can see that. But you're gonna grow... hell... six to eight more inches, maybe? And gain another forty or fifty pounds. You gotta be a full-grown man to join our operation because we do serious things."

Cross, who has eaten everything on his plate at this point, leans back in his chair with his arms crossed. "Fair. I guess." But he's not all that satisfied with my answer. "But" —he holds up a finger—"there's nothing wrong with training when you're young. It's like being in martial arts, right? You start early and go up the levels. That's all I want. The chance to go up the levels."

"Can you shoot?" I ask.

"Of course I can shoot. I go huntin' every year with my friends and their daddies. I've gotten loads of turkeys and rabbits and I'm gonna get my first buck this fall, you wait and see."

"Can you... fight?"

"Amon?" Rosie is looking at me like she wants me to shut up now.

But I don't shut up because her boy and I are having a serious conversation. "Can you, Cross?"

"I'm joining the wrestling team next year."

"Good. You should definitely do that. Collin was an athlete when he was your age but I wasn't in any sports, so it's not strictly necessary."

"Yeah, but you were a marine. So you got outside training too, just like Collin."

"Cross." Rosie is done with this conversation. "You're not joining the marines, OK? Just... don't be in such a rush to make life-changing decisions."

We're still ignoring Rosie. "If you want, I'll take you hunting this year. We'll practice first. Do some shootin' out on the Edge range. And we'll tag that deer together. How's that sound?"

Finally, this boy smiles. "That sounds great, Amon. Thanks."

Rosie's still in mother mode, but the moment his attitude changes, she lets her objections go with a breath. The three of us look at each other for a moment, then Cross's chair is scraping across the floor and he's bolting up.

"Where do you think you're going?"

"It's not dark yet, Mom. I'm meeting up with the boys. I'll be back when the streetlights come on." Then he is out the door like a flash.

When Rosie turns back she and I lock eyes. "Thanks, Amon."

"For what?"

"Settling him like you did. You didn't have to. And don't feel obligated to take him hunting."

"Well, of course I'm obligated. I said I would, so I will."

"It's just..." Rosie shrugs up a shoulder. "What if this doesn't work out? Won't it be weird?"

"Why wouldn't it work out?"

"Oh, I dunno. A million things could get in the way. Maybe you don't like the perfume I wear. Or maybe... you don't like the way I chew."

My grin goes lopsided. "The way you chew?"

"You know, little things like that. Things you can't figure out you hate until you're in deep with a person."

"Well, if you're in deep with a person, then little things like that shouldn't make a difference."

This is the right answer because Rosie's grin is wide and real. She gets up from the table and walks across the kitchen.

"Where you goin'?"

But she doesn't answer me. Just walks over to the front door, looks at me, and then twists the deadbolt.

"Oh." Is that a...

But while I'm thinking this, she's already moved over to the large front windows and is closing the plantation shutters.

"Well..."

Then Rosie Harlow turns to me, cocking a hip. "Amon Parrish, would you like to have dessert first?"

My mouth is open, a little bit in confusion, but more in surprise. "I'm... not sure if that's a real offer of dessert or—"

"It's the other kind."

I get up from the table, walk over to her, slip my hand around her waist, tug her right up to my chest, and let her fall back in my arms a little so she's looking up at me. Her breathing has hitched up a notch and her eyes are stuck on mine, like she's waiting for what comes next.

Which is a kiss. Our first kiss. Because when a woman you're pulling out all the stops for interrupts dinner to offer you dessert, a discussion is not necessary.

But just as I lean down to do this, Rosie says, "Small-town woman with shining gray eyes and a personality to match who also loves dogs is seeking a handsome man to make her swoon over hamburgers and fried chicken while he promises to take her son buck hunting in the fall. She is a bit dramatic, dresses like a teenager, and is perpetually optimistic. He kisses like a prince, fucks like a villain, and she wants him to take her right now because he said all the right things at the dinner table and deserves an extra-special helpin' of dessert for his efforts."

It is in this moment that happiness and I truly meet. She's not only pretty—she's clever, and fun, and made of sunshine.

I lean in, our lips barely touching, and whisper, "Desperately seeking you, Rosie Harlow." Then I kiss her. Slow and gentle at first, but it quickly escalates into something urgent and hard. Our mouths open, tongues searching. I reach under her ass and pick her up, gripping her thighs as I carry her over to the wall and press her against it.

Rosie laughs into my neck when I do this. But when I drop her legs, pop the button on her shorts, and start tugging them over her hips, she gasps, wide gray eyes looking up at me in either surprise or delight, then begins helping me out by shoving 'em down until they fall to the floor at her feet.

I reach under her knees and hitch her up again so her thighs are wrapped around my hips and use the wall to steady us as I press my hard-on between her legs.

We kiss again as her hand pushes between us, slips down to the button on my jeans and pops it open. A moment later she's pulling me out and running her fisted hand up and down my rock-hard shaft.

"I want to be inside you right now, Rosie." My words come out gruff and rough in a rumble, like thunder.

"Well, let me just help you with that, Amon." Rosie's cooing reply is sexy and smooth, like an echo crossin' water.

I hold her up with one hand, using the other one to push her panties aside as she guides my dick inside her. She's slick, and wet, and warm and she sighs out a breath like she's been holding it for years, waiting for this moment, just to let it out.

Everything that I've ever wanted out of life comes true in this moment. Because a feeling of utter completeness floods through my body as we move together. Breath hitchin' up, eyes locked in the moment, desperate to be even closer to each other like what's building between us might fade into a fairy tale if we don't become one.

I slow down a little, pushing harder and deeper inside her, and this makes her moan and close her eyes. But her mouth is open and her lips are teasing me, so I kiss her again as she throws her head back, wriggling her hips.

When she comes I'm ready too, but I hold it back until she's done because I don't want to miss a single moment of that plump mouth as it twists in bliss. She goes stiff and her head lolls back, revealing her throat. Her hips thrust forward and the whining and whimpering coming out of her mouth makes me want to explode inside her while she's coming all over my cock.

But I hold it in and go slow so she can enjoy herself to the fullest.

Just as she's about to wind down I bring my hand up, press my palm right up against her neck so my thumb is on her jawline, and I lean into her ear so I can give her a little boost and get her across that finish line one more time.

"Next time... I'll take you from behind, Rosie Harlow." I barely recognize my own voice, it's so husky and filled with lust. She must not either because her eyes slowly open—just halfway though. Like she's not quite finished, but at the same time, she can't help but pay closer attention to what I'm saying. "Next time I'm gonna blow your fuckin' mind, Rosie Harlow. Next time, you sweet peach, I will make you beg for it. But tonight... you get this."

And just as I say these last few words, I start fucking her. Like *really* fucking her. My head pressed into her shoulder, my arms straining as I grip her ass and hold her steady, and then I pull out, drop her, making her crouch in front of me, and I grin as she tilts her head up with wide, surprised eyes. Wondering what I'll do next.

Everyone knows what comes next and, if I'm being honest, I quite like the facial.

But you don't give a ray of sunshine a facial the very first time you fuck. I would not disrespect Rosie that way. Instead I bend down, spread her legs open, and look her right in the eyes as I come, squirting it all over her beautiful pussy.

I think she moans a little, but honestly, it's rather difficult to pay attention when I'm in the middle of raptured delight.

We both stay like this for a moment. Replaying what just happened.

Then, when I'm done experiencing my moment, I stand up and offer her my hand.

She blows out a breath and with it comes a smile. She accepts my hand and stands up in front of me. Her hair is all askew, looking very much just-fucked, and her halter top is all sideways. I look down at it, then up to meet her gaze. "Next time, I'm gonna play with those tits too."

Rosie blinks at me but doesn't say nothing.

I put myself back together, go into the kitchen, tear off a paper towel, run it under some warm water, and then take it over to her and start cleaning her up, wiping down her stomach and inner thighs as well as her pussy because I wasn't very careful with the aim.

When I'm done, I crouch down, pick up her shorts, and hold them up.

Rosie bites her lip, trying to hide a smile, I think. Then places her hands on my shoulders and steps back into her shorts.

I pull them up her legs, fasten the button, and then lean in and kiss her soft and slow, whisperin', "You are delicious. I'm gonna have myself two helpings of dessert next time."

Then I turn and head to the door.

I would like to spend the night, but I know the limits. There's no way that's even on the menu tonight. And as I'm walking down the path to my truck, the reason why comes jogging up the street.

Cross waves, cutting across the grass towards his front door. "Bye, Amon!"

I salute him. "See ya next time, kid." Then I get in my truck and smile like a fucking fourteen-year-old boy all the way back to the compound.

ROSIE

*S*mall-town woman *with shining gray eyes and a personality to match who also loves dogs is seeking a handsome man to make her swoon over hamburgers and fried chicken while he promises to take her son buck hunting in the fall. She is a bit dramatic, dresses like a teenager, and is perpetually optimistic. He kisses like a prince, fucks like a villain, and she wants him to take her right now because he said all the right things at the dinner table and deserves an extra-special helpin' of dessert for his efforts.*

IT'S GOOD. I am not a bad copywriter by any means. But there's a lot of room for improvement. I mean, 'kisses like a prince and fucks like a villain' is pretty prime, but the rest can use some work.

It's Tuesday morning and I'm sitting inside my Bishop printshop wearing my favorite pretty dress as I chew on the end of a fountain pen, trying to come up with some enticing words.

My mind, however, is still stuck on the sex last night.

Amon Parrish was everything I thought he'd be and more. He was forceful, and dirty, and made me a little nervous if I'm being honest. But not in a bad way. More of a breathless way. The wall fuck on the first time?

It makes a lot of sense with certain guys. The alpha type. Which Amon definitely is—in his own way, at least. But he's not typical. I mean, the James Dean date definitely says alpha but would the alpha type put on the Colonial costume?

I don't think so. Amon isn't typical and every time I think about last night and how he just put me on my knees like that—oh, mah God. I fan myself with my vintage-looking paper because just thinkin' about it gets me all hot and bothered. And if he were to walk through this door right now, I'd sweep my arm across the set-up table and scatter all the printing blocks to the four corners of the room so we'd have a nice solid place to have a fuck.

Of course, a dress like this one doesn't lend itself to a lunchtime quickie and my mind starts wandering to how Amon might even find my sweet spot though all these underlayers, so my lewd daydream stalls. But still, it's a nice fantasy and one day I would like for him to give it a try.

Then I remember what he promised at the end. *I'll take you from behind, Rosie Harlow.*

So then I picture him pushing me forward over the table, and hiking up all my many layers of skirts, and pulling down my drawers and... oh, yeah. I fan myself again. That's a much easier scenario to imagine.

My eyes wander up to the clock, find that it is already eleven-thirty, and I snap out of it. "Focus, Rosie. If you don't get this ad written today, you're not gonna get this printed up tomorrow."

So I push my lust for Amon Parrish aside and concentrate on my response to his personal ad.

Gray-eyed girl is desperately seeking rugged and worldly man who kisses like a prince and fucks like a villain. He wants to spank me like a master, fondle me like a toy, and take me from behind.

I snicker as I read that first part over again. Of course I'm not gonna print this. I'm gonna use the dull one I came up with first. I still have to take out 'fucks like a villain' and all mentions of dessert. I don't want to piss off Jim Bob and get my insert revoked. So it will probably just end with, 'Kisses like a prince, plays hard like the Devil, and repents like a sinner in the Revival tent on Sundays.'

This will be my public ad and Jim Bob will *loooove* that last part. "All publicity is good publicity, Rosie," he used to tell me back when I first started getting cast as the plot twister. "The scandal is the lifeblood of good entertainment and good entertainment creates the building blocks of success."

Which may or may not be true, but it doesn't matter.

Now that I've got that ad settled, I go back to this one here, which will remain private. This is for Amon's eyes only because we got ourselves a little thing going on here and I like it. He's playing along with my little fantasy life and being a very good sport about it, so I want to play back, even if it's just a little seemingly impromptu speech as we're lusting for each other.

I chew on my pen for another moment, trying to think up the next part. Then smirk as the words come pouring out...

He is a wicked scamp with a pioneer spirit who spends his days dreaming about all the different ways he might press my pleasure button.

I start snickerin'. 'Pleasure button' is rather good, I think.

It's got a trashy novel vibe to it, which is exactly what I'm going for.

My eyes shift up to the clock again and I realize I've only got ten minutes before I have to change and get on down to the Bishop Inn to work. *Come on, Rosie! Focus!*

She is willing, and obedient, and loyal. And she will writhe, and moan, and scream out in ecstasy at his simple touch because this will be all it takes to light her up. If this sounds like you, please respond in the next issue so we can continue our correspondence.

I giggle as I read it again. I need to memorize this so I'm ready the next time we're together. I'm gonna recite it and get him all bothered so he's got no choice but to follow through with those promises he made before he left last night.

Then I put it aside, straighten up my desk, grab my bag and my parasol, and leave, locking up behind me. It's unbecoming of a woman to rush through the streets of eighteenth-century downtown Bishop, but I get to my little cottage as fast as I can. There is really no shortcut in taking these dresses off, it's always a good twenty-minute process because you've got to hang everything up as you go or it just leaves a mess.

But thirty minutes later I'm changed into my shorts and halter top. This top is made of suede and has fringe hanging down my bare belly, ticklin' it to no end. Which does drive me a little crazy, but I'm the kind of woman who doesn't mind small annoyances like that if it's for the sake of fashion. Besides, this top matches my suede clogs—which are thick, and chunky, and have wooden soles.

Now that I am not dressed like a prim and proper

Colonial woman, I can rush through the streets without making a spectacle of myself and I land at the Bishop Inn promptly at twelve-thirty, right in the middle of the lunch rush when Bryn is in her worst mood and I am nothing but a gift from God when Jessica looks up from her hostess podium and nods her head in the direction of the kitchen. "You're in the kitchen, Rosie."

I wave as I pass. "I'm on it." I'm expecting Bryn to be cussing out loud when I get to the saloon door—dirty dishes everywhere, and an atmosphere of chaos. Like it usually is. But instead, I hear laughter. Bryn's laughter.

When was the last time I heard Bryn laugh?

I can't remember. She's always sour and focused.

But then I hear another laugh and this one I recognize. He brings joy everywhere he goes.

I push through the door and there he is.

Amon Parrish. Wearing light-green rubber gloves and up to his elbows in suds.

"What are you doin' here?"

Bryn and Amon stop their joke to look over their shoulders at me.

"There you are," Amon says.

"Here I am," both delighted and surprised. "But…"—I make a little motion between the two of them with my pointer finger—"why are you doin' my washin' up?"

"He came to take your shift," Bryn answers. "I swear, Amon Parrish, I had no idea what a romantic jerk you were. You've shattered all my preconceived notions that had been living in my head rent-free since you were ten years old and let two dozen frogs loose inside the Revival tent to mimic a biblical swarm."

I chuckle because I remember that day. What a sight. Frogs jumping everywhere, tourists screaming, Jim Bob losing his mind, and it was Collin's father who was preaching that day. He grabbed Amon up by the collar and threw him out with a swift kick to his backside.

If I remember correctly, Amon was laughing so hard, he didn't even feel it.

Amon pulls the plug on the suds, takes off his gloves, and hangs them up on a hook. "There. All done. Now you're free."

"I didn't realize the two of you were serious, Rosie!" Bryn is grinning at me from over her shoulder as she pushes some vegetables around on the grill. "You better dump whatever out-of-town rascal you're dating and keep him. Because if you don't"—Bryn pauses to wink at Amon—"I might steal him."

She's joking, I know this. But she's also not. She's telling me that I had better take this seriously because he's not messing around. When a man shows up to take your shift washing dishes for the sole purpose of freeing up your time so you can spend your afternoon with him, well... that's a whole other level of romance that goes above and beyond fucking a girl up against a wall.

Amon is looking at me when these words come out of Bryn's mouth. He winks. "Sorry, Bryn, but she already gave in to the idea that this is goin' somewhere. Better luck next time."

Which makes Bryn the Buzzkill practically cackle, she's that tickled by this new development between Amon and I. "Get out of here, you crazy kids!" Then she shakes her head and starts tossing her grilled vegetables.

Amon offers me his hand and I nearly blush when I take it. "My God, Amon Parrish. You're something else."

"Oh, I've got layers, Rosie Harlow. You've got no idea just how many."

His hand is warm, but not sweaty. So he's not nervous. But I might be. I mean, this is a serious courtin' effort and it's only been a week. As we make our way outside through the back door, and start heading not towards the street where he must be parked and I surely am, but into the maze, I say, "Can I ask you something, Amon?"

"Sure, Rosie. Hit me up." We make the first left in the maze, which is the wrong way to the middle and he and I both know this.

"Why?"

"What?"

"Why me?"

"Why—Rosie? That's a joke, right?"

"No, it's a serious question."

"Well, OK. I can see that I didn't explain myself properly when all this started. And it's probably because I was struck dumb with your many layers. That's my excuse, anyway. So let me start over and say this: Lady, you are cute as fuck. I'm talking... like... buttons, and puppies, and smiling babies kinda cute. So that's number one. Number two is a little bit contradictory, because don't take this the wrong way, but you're kinda slutty at the same time, Rosie."

I nearly come undone with laughter, that's how much this makes me happy.

"Seriously, I don't mean it in a bad way at all. I mean... you're like... every man's dream. You're sweet in a 'cookin' dinner, mothering kids, keeping a home' kinda way. But then you show up to work wearing this tantalizing halter top and last night you told me I kiss like a prince and fuck like a villain, and damn, Rosie. I mean… that right there was enough to up my interest level by a thousand. And the best part is that right now you're wearing clothes that could be removed in a matter of seconds and an hour ago you were covered neck to toe in a dress that might take me the better part of an afternoon to get off you. Don't even get me started about the diner uniform because I've had a thing for pink diner dresses since I was twelve."

I laugh and slap his arm playfully. "That's sick."

"You don't need to tell me. But listen, it all just came full circle last week when I caught you coming out of your little shop. I mean, one minute I'm just picking up some soup bones for my dogs and the next I'm caught in *Charlotte's Web*."

"Well, now I've heard it all. I've lived here my whole life and I'm pretty fluent in colorful analogies, but I'm afraid you're gonna have to explain *Charlotte's Web*."

"Ya caught me in your web, Rosie. And it's all sexy and shit. But it's sweet too. Like a fourth-grade chapter book."

I just shake my head. "How did you get along in the outside world with all these colorful comparisons, Amon? Because I'm trying to picture you in the marines talking about fourth-grade chapter books."

"Well, funny you should ask. Because I wasn't ever the wordsmith the way some people are around here. Collin, for instance, but Lowyn too. She's always got something cute to say. And you, of course. 'Kiss like a prince, fuck like a villain.' I don't think I'll ever get over that. But I never talked like this until you and I met up. I gave up the accent long before Collin did and I never did have his vocabulary. That's why Charlie Beaufort, our DC contact, liked him better than me. But here in this place, it came rushing back the moment I saw you in that dress outside your print shop. I mean, where else in the world can I date a woman like you? Nowhere, Rosie. You're one in a billion. And that's my long, winding answer to your 'why me' question. You're just one in a billion."

"Wow. I don't even know what to say to that, Amon." I look up at him, feeling slightly shy as our eyes meet. "But I would like to go on record here that I feel..." I let out a breath because I was gonna say 'the same' or similar, but it's not enough. "I feel... like I just stepped into a fairy tale and I'm like... the star of the show. And I don't really know what to think about that. No man has ever said things like this to me."

"Well, I would also like to go on record here and say that I have not said these things to any other woman. And I know it's kinda abrupt and seemingly comin' out of nowhere. But I think that's just how love works for some people. Sometimes you get caught in the storm and there's no way to stop the lightning strike. You just get struck, ya know?"

I smile up at him, marveling at how this gorgeous, charming, honest, protective, and romantic man has become mine. "Yeah," I say. "Sometimes you just get struck."

"So, hey. I'm gonna be at the Revival this Sunday working security."

"You are? Well, how'd that happen? I thought you boys were washing your hands of the Revival for good?"

Amon shrugs. "Eh. Hatin' the Revival is Collin's thing. I

actually don't mind it. I just wanted you to know I'll be there."

"This Sunday. That's Fourth of July."

"Yep. It's a big one, I hear."

"Oh, it's huge. It's as big as Christmas Eve. Lots of dancing, and a big garden party, and there's a massive rumble with the Revenant bikers."

"A rumble, you say?" When I glance up at Amon he's got one eyebrow raised in surprise.

"Yep. Oh, how the tourists love the fuckin' bikers. They come and crash the garden party and tear up the grass. Oh!" I look at Amon. "So that's why Jim Bob wants you there. You're gonna be a gangster and there's gonna be a shootout. There's almost always a shootout. Sometimes it's a knife fight, but mostly people like the shootouts."

Amon gives me another one of those winks of his. "Yeah, that must be it." But he's got a funny smirk on his face. "Anyway. Here we are."

We stop walking and I notice that we have ended up at a dead end under the big sugar maple on the edge of the maze and there's a bench here. Nice and shady too. "I don't think I've ever seen this bench. Now how can that be? I've walked this maze hundreds of times."

"Because you gotta take a wrong turn, Rosie. That's the only way to find this dead end. And most people don't like to take wrong turns." He points to the bench. "You wanna sit? Or do you have people to see and places to be?"

I let out a breath. Again. And once again I wonder just how I got here in the span of a week. "Oh, Amon. I've got all the time in the world for you."

And this makes him happy so we sit, and talk, and kiss a

little. But I'm distracted because I'm thinking about what my next move is. Not to impress him, or anything. I just like this game because there doesn't seem to be any risk. He wants to be mine and I want to be his, so why not keep playing, ya know? Why not keep this going a little longer and stretch it out for as long as possible?

So I come up with a plan. I'm gonna print up two copies of the *Bishop Busybody* this week. One for the masses and one just for Amon Parrish. A bonafide version of my slutty side.

If he can make me all hot and bothered by being spontaneously creative, then so can I.

AMON

It's Wednesday morning, a seemingly ordinary day in late June, and I couldn't be more excited about it if I tried. I'm standing on my porch sipping coffee, just looking out over the misty rolling lawn of the Edge Security compound, watching the men do their early-morning PT. The rhythmic thumping of boots hitting the ground in unison is a sound I will never grow tired of. There's something comforting in it.

We're not a boot camp, but then again, we kinda are. It was Ryan's idea to have mandatory PT at five a.m. every morning. Collin wasn't impressed and Nash didn't really have an opinion on it either. But I agreed with Ryan. PT is a good idea for men like this. Most of them came to us in pretty good shape. I mean, nearly all of them needed a little kick in the ass to be back in optimal condition, but only a couple were on the washed-out side.

At first, they were fairly lazy when it came to morning PT. Lots of complaints.

But on day two, the cadences started. And we got ourselves a good caller. Big shaved-head tattooed guy named Grinder who kinda took it upon himself to be leader. There were scuffles over who would unofficially be in charge when it all started, but while Grinder's smugness and no-nonsense attitude can be a little off-putting, he's actually very fair. And most men respect fair.

So he calls and they respond, and not a single one of them, not even the washed-up fucks, wants to miss PT every morning. It's fun. Sometimes I even have the urge to join in. But we really are leadership and it would mess with their routine. So we stay out of it. Because these aren't new recruits—these are experienced men. Men who have seen things, and done things, and have the nightmares to prove it.

Grinder and his number one—skinny guy, former SEAL sniper called York who lost his mind several years back, but found it again a couple years later—have a whole course set up that they run every morning that starts at the top of the driveway, comes all the way back here to my house, loops through the woods behind the kennel, and comes out on the other side of the church-slash-munitions depot. They even have a ruck course that goes deep into the hills that they do at least once a week.

A month of this has turned these once-lost men into serious, focused, downright dangerous members of the Edge team.

Of course, it's really the dogs that did that.

God, that was a good idea. I mean, if they could sleep with their canine partner every night, they would. But they can't. The dogs stay in the kennel because they are not pets, they are actually employees.

A screen door squeaks on my left and I look over and find Collin coming out holding his own cup of coffee. He looks over at me and smiles, nodding his head to the group as they pass our houses. "Can you believe this shit?"

I chuckle and watch the men as they disappear behind the kennel. But no, I actually can't. It was a risky idea, what we're doing. Taking these men who are all sorts of fucked up in the head and giving them a second chance. I mean, there are second chances and then there are second chances.

This one in particular involves a whole lot of weapons.

Is it a mistake?

I guess only time can tell that. But they're less dangerous here with us than they would be out there with no one. That's how we see it. I mean, once you teach a man how to work a rocket launcher, kill someone with a knife, survive in the wild, and sweep an urban center for enemies, the thing is pretty much done, ya know? You can't make him unlearn those things. So why not redirect all those skills into something profitable? Both for us and them.

Maybe it's a good idea, maybe it's not. But it sounded just dandy to Charlie Beaufort and I guess that's all that matters.

Collin comes down off his porch and heads my way. "What are you up to today, Amon?"

I grin like a fuckin' schoolboy. "Oh, I got a lunch date with Rosie." I side-eye Collin as he stops in front of my steps. "She doesn't know it yet, but it's gonna be fun."

"The two of you gettin' serious then?" He's got one eyebrow cocked.

I nod, slowly, looking him in the eyes. "Yep. It's a fact."

"Well, good. I like Rosie. Hell, everyone likes Rosie. Speaking of, did you send in for some kind of forensics?"

"Yeah. Why?"

"Oh, well, I got an email from Penny Rider in DC that

they're sending it out by courier and it'll be here this afternoon."

"Well, fuck, that was fast. I only sent it in a few days ago."

"What's this all about? Somethin's going on with Rosie, obviously. Because Penny attached a copy of your request so I read it. Sorry to pry, but blame Penny for that. If she didn't want me to read it, then it shouldn't have landed in my inbox."

"She probably thought it was Edge business. But whatever, I don't care if you know. Rosie's been gettin' weird letters and this man who is sending the letters claims to be Cross's father."

"No shit?"

"Yeah. I sent the letters into forensics before she figured out who it was, so it's probably all moot now, but whatever. All information is good information."

"She's got herself a stalker?" Collin looks worried. "Is it gonna turn serious?"

I shrug. "Dunno. Maybe, maybe not. But I got it all under control now, so don't worry." Then I grin. "Because I'm not worried."

Collin nods. "OK. Well, you have a good lunch date." Then he chuckles and takes off in the direction of Ryan's house, which also acts as Edge Security's main office.

"Roger that, Sarge. I will."

Collin shoots me a dirty look over his shoulder. He hates being called Sarge. But doesn't stop and start a fight.

Then I head over towards the kennel to keep myself busy until my big date at noon.

WHEN I WALK **into the Bishop Busybody** I nearly lose my breath at the sight of Rosie Harlow. She's wearing that same dress I first saw her in last week. It's pink, and cream, and has little flowers all over it. There seem to be many layers, and this is what's so sexy about it.

Also the whole reason I'm here.

Well, maybe not the whole reason, but it's a good part of it.

"Amon?" Rosie's face is flushed and she seems very surprised to see me. "What are you doin' here?" She starts hurriedly shuffling papers. Obviously, she's been printing because there's a little smudge of ink on her nose.

"Surprise."

Her eyebrows go up. "We're goin' to lunch or something?"

"Well, we can certainly do that. But I'm really just here to walk you home." My eyes might—involuntarily, of course—slide down her body and come back up.

She's grinnin' now. "You want to walk me home?" She's cocking an eyebrow as well, which implies she gets my meaning.

"I most certainly do. I mean, you can't be walking around unescorted. What are your plans for this afternoon?"

"Well"—she looks down at her mess of papers on the table, then starts sorting them—"I have to go to the copy shop and print off this week's edition, then come back here and stuff some into these envelopes and then take the rest of them with me for the Revival inserts."

I take Rosie's hand and do a little bow here. "Allow me to escort you to the print shop then, good lady." Then bring her hand up to my mouth—lookin' straight into those thunderstorm eyes of hers as my lips graze across her knuckles.

She gets all flustered at my flirting and goes red. "All right," she says. Which isn't much of a verbal response to my gesture, but I know I'm really startin' to get a hold of her heart and it's overwhelming her a bit. Getting her all flustered and shit.

So I say, "Come on then. To the printer we go."

Rosie makes a mad grab at all her paperwork on the table and stuffs it into a leather messenger bag. Then, when I hold the crook of my arm out for her, she latches on to me and we leave to run errands as a team.

IT IS NOT **a quick thing** to print and stuff seventy-three envelopes. Rosie and I do this and it goes by fast because we have a nice, easy conversation while we work. Finally, everything is done and it's time to leave.

I take her messenger bag stuffed with this week's edition of the *Busybody* and once outside, I wait for her to lock up and then offer her my arm when she turns.

"Amon." She huffs a little. But she's smiling too, so it's the good kind. "You don't have to do this, ya know."

"Do what?" I lead her down the front walk and open the gate.

"Court me this... hard, I guess. I mean, you're really pullin' out all the stops. A girl could get used to this, ya know."

We scoot through the gate and turn right towards Goosebeak Alley. "You mean like... if I do this now, during our courting, then when I stop, after we settle down, you're gonna resent me?"

She giggles. "Wow. You just assumed a whole lot there, buddy."

"I really did. But it's what you mean though, right?"

"I suppose it is. I'd like to see the real you. The everyday Amon Parrish."

"What if this is the real me?"

"Come on now. You live on a compound overflowing with dangerous men. This is not everyday you."

"Well, I like doing stuff like this. And if you're asking to move in with me, the answer is yes. Come on over. I've got a nice house and room for more."

She smiles and shakes her head as we head down the alley where all the women are out in their backyards doing their Bishop backyard stuff. Roosters are crowing, pigs are snorting, and there's even a couple of moos.

Then we are at her front porch so we stop and look at each other. I know she's about to say goodbye, so I interrupt and just say what I came for. "Can I come in?"

Rosie's eyebrows go up. "You want to come in? Well, it's

really not a place to host people, Amon. It's just a dressing room."

"Right. Where people undress as well, correct?"

Her face goes pink and I swear, it's so fuckin' cute, my dick jumps in my pants. "You want to... oh!" Again, she blushes, her face almost red now. "Well... all right. OK. Come on in."

There are no fewer than seven backyard busybodies watching us on both sides of the alley. Some peeking over clothing lines, some looking through fences, and two just standing right there in the alley holding baskets of eggs with their mouths open.

But I just salute them as I turn and follow Rosie to the door.

Inside it's cool and comfortable and there are so many feminine, womanly things around, I don't know what to look at first. Her elaborate gowns take up most of the space, since it's very small in here. And I look at each one, studying details. Then I walk over to the vanity where she must do her makeup or something, and pick up a fancy hairbrush.

I can see Rosie in the mirror behind me and our eyes meet. Then I look down at the chaise in the middle of the room covered in light-blue velvet. I turn and look at her straight on. "So."

"So." She looks a little bit uncomfortable.

"Do you want me to leave?"

Her head is shaking before I even finish. "No."

I take two steps in her direction but that's all it takes to have us practically pressed together. And then I'm looking down, and she's got her head turned up, and there is only one way this ends.

With that dress on the floor and us fucking on that chaise.

"What do I take off first, Rosie? Tell me how to do it."

She bites her lip, trying to stifle a grin. "Well… the stomacher comes first." She points to a light pink triangle section of stiff fabric that covers her front. "It's got hooks on both sides and you do it like—"

She begins to unhook the top left side, but I gently push her hands away. "That's my job. You just get to watch." I mean this literally and nod my head at the mirror.

Rosie's breath comes out in a rush, but she doesn't say anything.

I take a step closer, which shouldn't actually be possible, so we are right up against each other. She's breathing a little faster now and this makes her breasts even more tantalizing, even though this dress wasn't designed to be sexy and absolutely does not show cleavage. But that's what makes it so alluring. It's all left to the imagination.

The hooks holding this center piece in place are tiny, so I might fumble a little bit. But after a few moments I get the hang of it and soon this piece is free and I drop it on the ground. I'm not trying to disrespect her dress. I just kinda like the idea of taking everything off this woman and leaving it in piles all around us.

"Now what?" I ask. She takes a breath, and this time, with the stomacher thing gone, it's very sexy. Because even though I can't see those breasts yet, the cleavage has made an appearance. "This part?" I reach up to one of the little bows on either side of her clavicles and pull, letting the lace fall free, then do the same on the other side. But that doesn't actually remove anything because they're only the delicate shoulder straps of another stiff undergarment that laces in front and looks likes a corset.

Rosie points to it. "This is the stay."

"The stay? Well, it needs to go." I untie it, then start unlacing it until it completely opens up But those breasts of hers are still covered by yet another layer. Some kind of undershirt.

But over that shirt is the actual dress. Which is not a dress like how I know a dress to be, but more of a jacket-skirt combination. It's very tight on her arms so I have to tug on one sleeve—which only reaches her elbows—while she pulls her arm out. We do that again on the other side and finally, another piece of clothing falls to the floor at her feet and the stay drops with it.

Things are clearer now. The only things in my way are the underskirts and the undershirt. I grab the skirt and pull the elastic over her hips, letting it too fall to the floor. But surprise, surprise, she's wearing loose undershorts as well as the undershirt, both of which go down to her knees.

I look up, meet her gaze, but can't hold it because her nipples are poking up against the soft cotton fabric of her shift and all I want to do is look at them, and reach for them, and fondle them. She's nearly naked and this whole uncovering thing we're doing is driving me wild, and making me hard, and I'm so ready to fuck this woman. But I force myself to stay on task. Because this final reveal is the best part now.

Rosie is biting her lip when those gray eyes of hers land on mine. She's nervous. Maybe a little embarrassed. It's an awfully vulnerable position to be in. But she's not gonna stop me. She wants me to keep going.

I reach down, tugging on the elastic of her shorts, pressing myself up against her. Grinding a little. And then I bend down and take those shorts with me.

She's practically panting now. Her breath coming in short, soft gasps. The next thing I feel are her hands on my shoulders as she steps out of her shorts the same way she did last night. I push them into the considerable pile of clothing at her feet and look up at her as I lift her shirt, exposing her pussy, and lean in to kiss it.

Everything about her goes soft in this moment. Everything but her hands, which grip my shoulders tighter. I push her back a little, so she bumps into the chaise, and then she's sitting and I'm opening her legs up, and all I see is her glistening, wet pussy as I slip my tongue into her soft folds.

She grips my hair and then it's on. Erotic undressing over, now it's time to get busy.

I slip a finger inside her and this immediately has Rosie writhing. Her knees come up and open wider, giving me more access.

Her shirt is still on, but I'm gonna leave it that way because I've got plans for that shirt later. Right now, I just concentrate on eating her. Licking, and kissing, and making her moan as I pump my fingers in and out, all the while flicking my tongue back and forth against her little button.

She comes. And it's a little bit loud. Like if those backyard ladies are in any way trying to listen in, well, they just got an earful. Rosie's thighs are shaking and trembling as her back arches and this orgasm goes on for a full ten seconds. All the while, she's letting me and everyone else along this alley know that she's having a very good time.

I stand up, take off my shirt, throw it into the pile of clothes, and then unbuckle my belt. The jingle of it pulls Rosie out of her post-coital bliss and she looks up at me with just-fucked eyes. I push my pants down, letting my hard cock fly out, and then, without me even having to ask for it, she slips down onto her knees and wraps her hands around my shaft. Squeezing me hard until I close my eyes and grit my teeth.

The next thing I know, her soft lips are caressing the tip of my cock and her hot breath is about to drive me crazy. She swirls her tongue around my tip and I have an urge to grab her by the hair and push myself deep into her throat, but I don't. Maybe one day the sex will get rough like that, but then again, maybe it won't. When you're serious about a woman, right here in the middle of things isn't really the time to find out if she likes to swallow. Not if you wanna see her again. And I do.

The blowjob is meant to be an appetizer, so I enjoy it for a few minutes, then pull away and offer her my hand. She looks up at me, wiping her mouth, and accepts my hand, allowing me to help her up.

And when our eyes lock, for some reason I'm thinking about that day back in high school when she was standing in the cafeteria all swollen with baby, and that look of horror on her face when her water broke. The fear. The absolute terror.

But it hits me now why it bothered me so much at the time and why I'm still thinking about it to this day. It was because she was alone. There was a circle of emptiness surrounding her. It was a small circle and it only lasted for a few seconds. But it was there and it was real. Like her longing for... whatever, or whoever, was making a hole and, in that moment, it got a hold of her and took over.

I bring my hands up to her face and place them flat against her cheeks. "If I had one wish, Rosie Harlow, I would make it so that you were never alone. So that you were never unhappy. So that you were never scared. I would be there for you. Every single time."

Her immediate response is a smile. But she's confused, I think, about where this is coming from and why it's comin' out right now. She brings her hands up to cover mine, never breaking eye contact. "Well, that sounds like a dream, Amon Parrish. But if I never knew sadness, or loneliness, or fear then how would I know that you are my comfort, and company, and courage?"

That mouth of hers. The words that spill out drive me almost as crazy as her naked body standing in front of me. "You can't have one without the other, can ya?"

She presses her lips together and gives her head a tiny shake. "No. Sad, isn't it? But it's the absolute definition of humanity to swing like a pendulum from one emotion to the next."

I see her again, standing in that cafeteria. Just a few moments after her water broke when everyone rushed to her aid. Everyone but me, maybe.

It was a good day, it was a bad day.

But really, it was just like any other day. Because that's what days are. Always some good, always some bad.

My body presses forward, leaning into her, setting her off balance. Her hands drop from mine so she can catch herself when she sits down on the chaise in the middle of the room. Then I sit next to her, leaning back against a decorative rolled pillow, and pull her on top of me.

She straddles my hips and when I reach up and pull out a pin, her long brown hair falls out of place and hangs down over her shoulders, tickling my chest as she leans forward just enough to slip me inside her.

We begin to move together, her smiling eyes gazing into mine. And it goes so slow. It's something altogether different. This time is so separate from any other time, it's not even sex.

And lovemaking isn't good enough.

This time it's heaven.

And I can't help but wonder if it's luck, or skill, or both that got me through the last twelve years. Because I can easily count to twenty and each number would represent a time I should've been killed.

Because Rosie Harlow shouldn't be single. Someone should've made her theirs a long, long time ago.

But she's not theirs, she's mine.

And this makes me want to buy into it. The whole notion of what goes on inside that Revival tent. Not the carnival sideshow or the lies Disciple tells ad nauseam. But the rumble and the glory and the echo on the water.

Rosie and I are that echo, I think.

Something distant from those people we were, but also related.

Not a passing, or a coming, but an arrival. Which is something very different from either of the aforementioned things because an arrival is something new. Almost expected, but not really. Something you didn't know you were waiting for.

I could've gone to her that day in the cafeteria. I could've acted. I probably could've made her mine right then and there.

But just like Collin and Lowyn, we weren't the people we'd become. We needed these twelve years to grow and realize what's important so we could come back together when the time was right.

Rosie was the very first person I saw when I got back.

Let it be a sign, the call to Revival says.

So I do.

I let her guide me.

She is my sign.

WE LINGERED *in the cottage* for another hour, at least. But eventually we pulled ourselves together and I hung up her dress as she put her everyday clothes back on. We took her envelopes to the post office and then I walked her to her car, made her wait until I got my truck, and I followed her all the way back to Disciple, dropping her off at McBooms.

We had a nice kiss goodbye from my truck window and it felt a little bit like high school. But I'm still smiling about that kiss when I pull into Edge and stop at Ryan's house before going home to see if my forensics came back from DC.

There's no one inside the office so I look around until I find one of those rugged, white mailers that Penny Rider uses to deliver things. I take it, get back in my truck, and go home.

There's no one around, but when I get out, I can hear shooting from one end of the woods and dogs barking in the distance coming from the other. Range practice and tracking today, I guess.

I'll go find them in a minute, but first I take a seat on my porch step and cut the envelope open with my pocketknife. There is a folder and inside the folder is a small stack of papers. Maybe twenty pages.

Ever-efficient Penny has written me a cover letter, so I read it because her summaries are always short and informative.

DEAR AMON,

I RAN *the tests you asked for and did a complete background check for one Erol Cross, West Virginia. It's not much to go on, and I found seven matches. Only three fit the profile, but only one was seventeen years old when you were a senior in high school. He's listed below. But I won't bury the lede, he's dead. He died that same year in the springtime. All the details are inside. There's a headstone in Pebble Falls if you care to check it out. I've included a map and directions from Edge Security.*

DEAD. I pause to consider this. Then who the hell is sending Rosie those creepy letters? I look back down at the paper and continue reading.

. . .

WE DID FIND prints on those letters, but unfortunately, none of them matched the set obtained from the West Virginia Motor Vehicle records for one Erol Cross. Which, of course, makes sense, because he is dead and dead people don't write letters. The prints belonged to you and one Rosie Harlow, from Disciple, West Virginia, which I assume is not what you were looking for.

The ink analysis will take weeks to be conclusive, but preliminary results indicate it's the most popular printshop ink on the market at the moment.

The paper is a little bit unusual as it is not standard copy paper, but a high-quality offset paper used in book printing. Which makes sense because it was a worksheet, but there are no ragged edges to indicate it was torn from a workbook.

Again, this paper is very common in printshops. Hundreds of millions of pages are probably printed every year. It comes up in almost every paper analysis I manage because all the military printshops use it.

My conclusion is that these papers were professionally printed, but as to where and when, there is no quick way to find that out.

Please let me know if you would like me to continue the analysis and I will do my best to get you the information you are looking for.

Thanks for your continued business and talk soon,

PENNY

. . .

WELL, shit. That didn't get me anywhere. In fact, I'm in the hole because this man is dead. I flip through the paperwork, just giving it all a cursory glance, then shove it back in the envelope. I rub my hands over my face, taking a breath. Because Rosie doesn't know he's dead. And no matter how much she says she's over him, this Erol guy is Cross's father.

I take out my phone, ready to call her and get it over with, but just as I do that King and Mercy come bounding out of the woods, barking and nipping each other's heels.

Both dogs stop what they are doing when I whistle. Then I give them the hand signal for sit—which they do— and walk over there. Because obviously people are coming back and these two got ahead of themselves.

Sure enough, a few seconds later Collin comes walking out of the woods, laughing and smiling. But I go tense and get hot. Because all that laughing and smiling is directed at that fuckin' inspector, Sawyer Martin.

Collin looks up from his conversation, catching my eye, and the smile drops. "Amon. When did you get back?"

"Just now." I glare at him. "Were you two out in the woods working the dogs?"

"Oh, yes," Sawyer says. "I like dogs. And I needed to check off a few boxes about them for my inspection, so Collin here gave me a little demonstration this afternoon."

I'm still lookin' at Collin. "Did he now?"

"It was great." Sawyer actually claps Collin on the back like they're old buddies or something. "Thanks. I got what I needed. In fact"—Sawyer looks at me and I have no choice but to tear my glare away from Collin so I can direct it at him—"you'll probably be happy to hear that I'm leaving tonight."

"So soon?" I deadpan.

Sawyer just smiles. "It was nice to meet you both." Then he nods his head a little, and walks off up the driveway, leaving Collin and I alone.

When he's a far enough distance away I return my glare to my best friend. "What did he want to know about the dogs?"

"He just wanted to see what they could do."

"Don't you feel that kind of thing should remain a proprietary secret, Collin?"

Collin is not the least bit chilled at my reaction even though I'm sending ice vibes. "I'm not an idiot, Amon. And anyway, he asked me this morning about a dog demo, and I said yes, of course. But I told him after lunch because I was busy. And then I set a trail that led right to the old mine."

A smile creeps up my face. "You did?"

"I did. So, of course, when I set Mercy and King on track they took us right there."

I laugh a little. "What did he do?"

"Oh, he was all kinds of flustered. Couldn't get out of there fast enough. Started thanking me for the demo and then, as you just heard, we got back here and there he goes."

And sure enough, when I look down the driveway I see Sawyer getting into his little silver government car. He backs up so fast, his tires spit gravel.

Collin and I both chuckle. I say, "Good riddance."

Collin agrees. "And goodbye. I don't know what he was all about, but he's done now and I doubt he'll be back."

"But we still don't know what he was really looking for."

"My guess is that this property is part of whatever's

going on with Blackberry Hill. They've got tunnels. We know that, even if we haven't seen them."

"And this property has an old mine," I add, making Collin nod his head.

"There's an entrance," Collin says. "It's all connected. I think that's why Charlie told you about this place. He had some suspicions and even if he didn't want us to know about it, he trusted his relationship to me enough to put it in my hands until such time he could make use of it. That's my guess anyway."

"What should we do about this, Col? Move?"

"Move?" He laughs. "Hell no. We've got a doorway, Amon. A front fuckin' door right into their secret business. This is a blessing. A gift that Charlie Beaufort never meant for us to receive."

"Won't this just piss them off, though?"

"Of course it will. But there are no cameras up there, so they don't know we know."

"How can we be sure?"

"Because I had it swept last night. I sent Grinder and York into the woods on the pretense that they were setting up the course they were running this morning. But they were really just sweeping a perimeter around the mine for wi-fi and radio frequencies."

"Yeah, but those detectors are rinky-dink, Collin."

Collin puts up his hand. "No. You don't understand. They weren't using some phone app, Amon. After you told me the forensics you had Penny do, I sent a request to her for some augmented reality visors that indicted any and all types of electromagnetic waves across all spectrums and they were delivered yesterday afternoon. There are no cameras or microphones up there. My guess is that this place was decommissioned decades ago, Charlie knew about it, told us about it, and now he's hedging his bets on just how loyal we might be so he sent this Sawyer guy in to figure us out."

"Hmm," I say. "Sawyer was here to see if we were using that mine or had suspicions about it."

"That's my guess."

"Do you think he bought it?" I nod my head down the driveway, but the inspector is already gone.

"Fuck no, he didn't buy it. But he was nervous enough to get the hell out of here. I doubt he'll be back. And anyway, we haven't disturbed that place. He's got nothing to say about it."

"What are you gonna tell Charlie?"

Collin scoffs. "I'm not tellin' Charlie nothing. It's none of his damn business what we do up here. And as far as I'm concerned, what lies below our property is ours to do with what we please."

"But do you think there's tunnels that lead directly to Blackberry Hill? I mean, they did infiltrate us."

"That's because you *hired* them, Amon." He gives me a scornful look. "Which I advised you against, but you didn't listen."

"I know. It was a mistake."

"Doesn't matter. And anyway, it's the kinda thing that falls under an 'earlier the better' kinda heading, ya know? But I think if there were direct tunnels to Blackberry Hill and they knew about them, then this property wouldn't have been for sale in the first place and we wouldn't even be here."

"It's Trinity County, though. Which means all the land is private, open to residents only. Blackberry Hill…" I think for a moment, puttin' some pieces together. "I suppose Ike could've bought it, but no outsider could."

"And Ike's not technically an insider, is he?"

"No. He's not. But we are. And Charlie used us to get this property not figuring that you'd stumble upon that boneyard and blow everyone's cover up there on the hill. But you did and now they're all panicking."

"That's my guess."

"What are we gonna do about it?"

Collin laughs. "We're gonna use it, Amon. We're gonna blow that mine open and take what's ours, that's what we're gonna do about it." He winks at me. "Ryan's locked and loaded. We start blasting tomorrow at dawn."

Then he gives me a little salute and starts walking up the driveway.

But I see it just before he turns.

That little glint in his eyes.

That little gleam.

A sparkle, almost.

And when he starts whistlin' 'Ring Around the Rosie,' that's when I know… *he's back.*

I didn't know Collin well before we joined the marines together, but that's not the Collin I'm referring to. I'm talking about the Collin I served with. The Collin who had my six, and the six of many others, over the past decade. The Collin who started a secret black-ops military at the request of Charlie Beaufort and under the direct orders of more five-star generals than I can count. The Collin whose name never even came up in official testimony during the congressional hearings. The Collin who didn't spend a day in prison and made sure the rest of us didn't either.

That's the Collin walking up the Edge driveway right now.

It was a close call, that possible prison sentence. We could've been charged with sedition. So *that* Collin took a little vacation while everything cooled down and we came home to start over.

But Edge Security just added one decommissioned underground military base to the long list of weapons in our arsenal, so I guess things might be heatin' back up.

And even though I really couldn't say I've missed it, I do get a weird sense of satisfaction over this revelation.

"*Rosie? Hello?* Earth to Rosie?"

I turn towards Lowyn and smile. "What?"

"Did you hear me? I'll be pickin' next week. I asked if you're still good to mind the store while I'm gone."

"Oh, sure. Yes." I close my eyes and shake my head a little to clear it, and when I open them again Lowyn is smirkin' at me. "What?" I ask her.

"You."

"Me what?"

She tsks her tongue. "You're swoonin'. This is about Amon, I gather?"

Despite my best efforts to rein in my happiness, it simply can't be done. So I smile even bigger. "I'm fallin' for him, Lowyn. Like off a fuckin' cliff fallin' for him. Do you know what he did yesterday?"

"I can't even begin to imagine. Tell me. I'm dying for details."

"He came to my printshop in Bishop and walked me home to my cottage." I'm sitting at the front counter on a stool, and just saying this out loud makes my whole body weak. So I prop my elbow up on the glass counter and slide my chin into my palm with a sigh.

"To the cottage, you say?" Lowyn raises an eyebrow at

me. "The one where you take off your Bishop clothes and change into Disciple ones? That cottage?"

"The very same." I'm smirking now too.

"And?" Lowyn is rolling her hand at me to keep going. "Tell me what happened!"

"He happened, that's what happened."

Lowyn comes over to the counter and stands in front of me with both hands flat on the glass. "Rosie Harlow. I want details! This is the first time you've ever dated a man I knew. And boy, talk about goin' for the golden ring! Amon Parrish is kind of a dream, isn't he?"

I click my tongue. "Let me tell you, what he did to me yesterday felt pretty dreamy. Let's just say that his mouth is very talented."

Lowyn giggles. "Is he dirty?"

"Dirty how?"

She shrugs up one shoulder. "You know. Like... does he talk dirty to you and get you all down on your knees and stuff?"

"Well"—I aim a pointed look at her—"I was on my knees for a time. But only after his face was between my legs."

"Keep going."

"But... he didn't talk dirty to me. He said really sweet things. And then we did the ultra-slow fuck."

"Were you on top?"

I grin. "I was."

"Yeah," Lowyn sighs. "The ultra-slow is fun on top. But he doesn't talk dirty to you?"

"Dirty how, Lowyn? I mean, clearly you have something in mind, so give me an example."

"You know, like..." Her eyes roll up like she's thinking.

"Like… asking you questions. 'Do you want me to do this or do you want me to do that?'"

"Well, don't leave out the good parts, Low. What did he want you to do? Because obviously, we are talking about Collin!"

Her eyes dart around, looking for teenagers. They're on the other side of the showroom, so then she leans forward and says, "You know. 'Do you want me inside you, Lowyn? Do you want me to lick you, Lowyn?'"

My hand automatically reaches for a pad of paper next to the cash register and I start fanning myself. "Lord, that's hot."

Lowyn winks at me. "Isn't it?"

"Well, Amon hasn't gotten there yet. He's just…" I roll my eyes up and swoon again just thinking about how he's pulling out all the stops for me. "'Dreamy' really is the right word. He's sweet, Lowyn. He says romantic things."

"Like what?"

"He said that if he had one wish, he would wish that I was never alone, or unhappy, or scared."

"Aww," Lowyn coos. "That is sweet. Collin recited the Revival wedding vows to me once."

My eyes light up. "Well, that counts, my friend. That counts."

"I think so too." Now it's her turn to sigh. "You do realize that we're automatic best friends now, Rosie. Right? Because if Amon and Collin are besties, then it's practically the rule."

"It is, Lowyn. And we are."

"And you know what that means?"

"A double wedding?"

She laughs. "I hadn't gotten that far yet, but maybe. I was gonna say that we're sisters now."

"Mmmm," I hum. "I've never had a sister, so this is an upgrade. And you know what else?"

"Tell me."

"Amon has four sisters. And you have one, aside from me. So that makes seven of us. Seven sisters. I like the sound of this."

"It's quite the extended family we're gathering, isn't it?"

I nod. "It is. I love my family. They're very good people. My mama and daddy stood by me when I got pregnant in high school, as did all my brothers. But you know what I've figured out, Low?"

"What, Rosie?"

"That you can't have too much family. You just can't. There can never be too many people who care about you."

She reaches across the glass and takes hold of both my hands. "I can't wait to spend the rest of my friend-life with you, Rosie. We're family forever now." Then she gives my hands a squeeze, lets go, and starts walking towards the break room. "I'm gonna work on my schedule for next week. Let me know if you need anything."

"I will, Low. I will."

And if I did need something, she would be there. I've always thought I could depend on Lowyn McBride, but now I know it for sure.

We're family.

And that's that.

LOWYN LEAVES **around** noon and not more than five minutes go by before the teenage boys show up to join the girls. The next thing I know, the jukebox is jumping and they're all bouncing around in the middle of the store like this is someone's basement rumpus room instead of a business.

But I hate to break it up. It looks fun, actually. So I let it go.

Cross comes by about an hour later, a couple of his friends tagging along. Cell phones are pulled out, messages are sent, and the next thing I know, McBooms is having a party.

I might dress like a teenager, but I'm an adult. I am *not* the cool mom. Cross and I are not friends, he is my son. I don't believe in that sort of thing, I believe in parenting. I am one hundred percent mama bear. But I don't really mind that they're all here, kinda sorta taking advantage of Lowyn and me, because I like knowing where they are. I like knowing that they're all safe.

So I don't say anything when all the chairs have a teenage butt in them and all the rugs are getting cut with dance moves. I don't even mind when Leland Bowers shows up with seven pizza boxes and all the kids dig in their pockets to pay for it. They come up five dollars short, but I pitch in and take my two pieces back to my counter and just watch pretty much every kid over the age of ten have a good time in McBooms.

The funny thing is, I don't think Lowyn would mind

either. I mean, they're not destroying nothing and rarely do we have walk-in customers on Thursdays. This is what small-town life is for. You don't get all the bells and whistles of the city. You don't get bright lights or crowded streets filled with possibilities.

You get a spontaneous afternoon party at the local semi-famous vintage thrift store where no one's gonna yell at ya, and no one's gonna hurt ya, and everybody's gonna be themselves and have a good time because there isn't a single strange face for miles in any direction.

This is why I fought so hard to stay in Disciple and be the only single mom in town back when I was fifteen.

It's worth it.

This is the best gift I could've given my son.

And sure, one day he might leave. One day, he probably *will* leave. But that's years away, so I don't have to think too hard about it. And anyway, if he did leave, I think he would come back.

Collin and Amon did.

I swivel in my stool and look out the window so I can daydream about Amon a little bit before I shut the party down and close up. He said some pretty nice things to me this morning. I think he made his intentions perfectly clear and it's exciting. I stare at the backwards varsity letters that spell 'McBooms' on the front window and have a revelation.

My luck has changed. I don't think I realized it until just this very moment. I mean, a few months ago Cross and I were renting a doublewide situated in a vacant lot across the alley from the bakery. And then, one day, Lowyn McBride asked if I would like to live in her cute-as-fuck little house that looks like it belongs on the glossy pages of a lifestyle magazine.

Then Jim Bob said I could put my little lonely-hearts publication inside the *Revival News*, which got me ten new regular subscribers over the next few weeks.

And then Amon Parrish appeared outside my little print shop pulling a wagon of bones and the next thing I knew, I had myself a love interest.

It's so weird how life can turn on a dime like that.

Everything has changed.

Hmm. One of my eyebrows goes up because there's a connection to this turn of luck and it starts and ends with Amon Parrish. He came back into town and suddenly, life is better.

And for some reason this thought leads to the call of Revival. And I think… maybe it really is a call? And maybe people really do answer that call?

Let it be a sign. That's how the call ends.

Let it be a sign.

This is my sign.

AT SIX O'CLOCK ALL THE kids are kicked out and I lock up. Cross waits for me, sitting on the very stool where I spent my afternoon daydreaming. And when I'm all done, we walk out the back together, drive the few blocks home, and go inside.

"What's for dinner tonight?"

"Hamburger mac." I watch Cross's face as I say this because hamburger mac has been his favorite since he was two. Is he growin' out of it? Is it kind of embarrassing to love hamburger mac when you're twelve and heading into junior high this fall?

I wait for the disagreeing scowl. The one he's been practicing for the better part of six months now. The one that comes with the attitude that parents are the stupidest people on earth.

But to my delight he smiles. "Yum. I love hamburger mac. I'm so hungry. When will it be done?" His eyes dart over to the kitchen like he's expecting it to be cooking on the stove. And even though he knows better—even though he knows that we just walked through that door and into this house together—his little boy brain still expects there to be food cooking on the stove just because he's hungry.

Some mamas might get frustrated at their son's utter and complete lack of situational awareness. But not me. No, sir. I love that my boy thinks my superpowers are limitless.

So I smile as he frowns at me, which irritates him. "Why are you just standing there? I'm starving."

I turn my back before I laugh so he doesn't see me.

Now, again, some mamas might take offense to his unreasonable expectations. Mostly for the fact that he is a boy expecting his mama to serve him.

But that's my job. For now, anyway. I'm not in a hurry to give this up. We're on the cusp here. He's gonna be gone soon enough and I will never get these years back. With each day that passes the number of times that my son will look to me to meet all his needs dwindles.

And if I think about it too hard, I'll cry.

So I don't think about it at all. I just go into the kitchen, tie on an apron, and rustle this boy up some hamburger mac. Cross goes into his room and I don't hear a peep out of him until dinner's ready and I go knocking on the door.

"What?" he calls back. And he sounds irritated. Which baffles me a little because wasn't he just starving to death?

"What? Dinner's ready, that's what. Get your butt out here." I go to open the door, but I find it locked. "Cross Harlow! Why on earth are you locking me out of your room?"

"I'm doing something."

"You're doin' what, exactly, that you need to talk to your mama this way? Especially since I just rustled you up some dinner."

I hear him sigh on the other side of the door. The lock disengages and there he is, peeking at me through a crack in the door. "I'll be right there." His voice is calmer now. "You don't have to wait at the door like I'm a baby."

I put up both my hands in surrender. "Fine. You're a grown-up." Then I turn and walk back to the kitchen.

I guess I should get used to this because twelve leads to thirteen and from there, his childhood is pretty much over. I don't like it, but there's nothing I can do to stop it. As a teenager, I had it easy because I am the youngest of five. Four brothers came up in our house before me so my mama and daddy had lots of practice by the time I turned sour.

They let me be, mostly. Which, in retrospect, might've been a mistake.

Except I cannot call my son a mistake.

And just as I think that, he appears, smiling and hungry. Like our little interaction never happened.

TWENTY MINUTES *later* Cross's bowl is clean and it's not even dark yet. So of course he wants to go back outside and squeeze in every bit of summertime he can.

Which I do not object to. But I call out the rules from the front porch as he takes off running down the street anyway. "Cross Harlow! You be home when those streetlights come on!"

There's a faint, "I will," response as he turns the corner, heading up the hill towards the Revival ground. That's where the kids mostly hang out because there's a private park in the back of the tent, right near the river, where no tourists can go but every kid in Disciple is welcome.

I go back inside, sighing. Then clean up the kitchen, take off my apron, and decide that I deserve a long, hot bath to cap off such a fine day.

Even though I've lived here in Lowyn's house for a couple months now, I still get a little flutter of excitement as I climb the stairs because this place is truly something out of a catalogue. And I can't help but think about that as I enter the room. And then, of course, I have to count my blessings because there is such a thing as too blessed, and when this happens, that's when karma catches up.

This sentence is literally still playing in my head when I spot it on the bed.

At first, I can't make sense of what I'm seeing. And then, after I fully comprehend what it is, I can't remember if it's supposed to be here or not.

Because it's a thing that is both familiar and out of place at the same time, so my brain is muddled for a good ten seconds before it finally puts all the pieces together.

My stomach sinks. It's that hollowed-out kind of sinking stomach that comes with terrible news. And this *is* terrible news because on my bed, propped up right against my pillow, is a piece of paper and on that piece of paper is a crossword puzzle.

I look around real slow. Like whoever left this here might still be close.

Then I take out my phone, snap a picture, and run my ass back down those stairs and right out on to the porch, the whole time looking for Amon's contact in my phone. I keep walking when I get outside, all the way out to the sidewalk. Then I stand there, staring at this too-cute fairytale house, and nearly come undone when Amon answers.

"Hey, Rosie, what—"

But I interrupt him. "Someone was in my house, Amon! Someone was here and left me a crossword puzzle on my pillow!"

"Where are you?"

"Outside. On the sidewalk."

"Where's Cross?"

"Revival Park, I think. He went that direction about ten minutes ago."

"Walk up there and get him and I'll meet you at the Revival tent in twenty minutes."

The call drops and I take a deep breath.

Erol. It had to have been him. And if he was in my house, then he's... *here*.

Suddenly, I have an urgent need to find my son, so I start running up the hill towards the Revival grounds. I fly through the gates, calling out polite hellos as people greet me, and make my way all the way back to the park where I can see a group of kids hanging out by the river.

I scan the crowd, but I don't see Cross. I'm about to lose my mind and start yelling his name like a crazy woman when the gang of kids breaks up and there he is in the middle, smiling and laughing like he hasn't got a care in the world.

My breath comes out in a rush and my whole body relaxes.

He's safe. And I'm safe. And Amon is coming here to make sure we stay that way.

AMON

The drive into Disciple feels like it takes years even though I'm pushing ninety in the truck the whole way and it actually only takes twelve minutes. Of course I have to slow down when I get to town and since it's Thursday night in the summertime, Disciple is crawling with locals doing last-minute things before the weekend starts tomorrow.

Except on very rare occasions, there's no Revival on Friday. But that's when the tourists start coming in if they're from outside the local area. And most are, but not all. We've always had quite a few regulars who come in from Charleston each weekend like clockwork. Like the Revival is their actual church or something.

So Thursday nights are busy around here and though it is mostly a local thing, there's always a couple dozen strangers milling around the edges of the grounds eating dinner or getting ice cream or whatever.

There is no chance of finding a parking spot so I just go to Rosie's house and park my truck in her driveway. I don't go check things out inside. That can wait until I know they are safe. Instead, I walk up the hill to the Revival grounds and see her waiting, panicked look on her face, with an arm wrapped around Cross's shoulder. He's nearly as tall as she is, I notice. Which is kinda cute, even though the occasion for me being here is anything but.

"Rosie. You OK?"

She presses her lips together and nods, then makes a little eyeball motion towards Cross, like she hasn't said anything to him and she doesn't want me to either.

I respect her wishes and give Cross a playful punch. "What's up, partner?"

He makes a face. "Absolutely nothin', since my *mother*"—he stresses this word and gives Rosie the stink-eye—"came up to the park and pulled me away from my friends like she's a crazy person."

"Well, that's because we've got a surprise for you."

Cross shoots me a suspicious look and his question comes out tentative. "What kind of surprise?"

"You have won yourself a… a… a weekend kinda… camp-like… package deal thing up at my compound." I smile. That was smooth. "Yeah. You won. And you get to work the dogs, and shoot on the range, and stay at my house tonight."

His whole face lights up. "Really?" He looks at his mother. "Did you do this?"

"She sure did," I interrupt. "She wasn't gonna tell you about it unless you won, but of course you did! So… yeah. Now we're telling you about it." I make one of those all-teeth smiles at him. "Come on, let's go pack you a bag and hit the road so you can help me say goodnight to the dogs."

"Well, all right!" Cross pumps a fist in the air. "Finally, something cool happens." Then he takes off running.

Before Rosie can object, I put my fingers in my mouth and crack out a sharp whistle. "Cross Harlow, you were not dismissed. Get your ass back here and stand at attention until you are."

Cross has turned, his face about to morph into an expression of defiance, but he's a Revival boy and he's been playing his part in the show since he was born. So instead, he switches into 'performer' mode and straightens his back and snaps off a salute. "Yes, sir."

Rosie chuckles but I keep a stern face as I bark commands at her boy. "You will walk exactly five paces in front of us and stay in our line of sight the entire way home. Do you understand me?"

"Yes, sir." He says it all seriously, but when he turns to start walking, I catch a smile.

We give him five paces and then we take off as well, whispering a little, so as not to catch anyone's attention with the subject matter of our conversation. "Where was it?" I ask.

"On my bed. A puzzle, just like the others, but a crossword this time. Which worries me because the cross is in that puzzle by default. It was Erol. He was in my house, Amon." Her voice is a little shaky, and I don't blame her. It's a frightening thing to think you're safe, only to realize—way after the fact—that you aren't.

It's not the right time to tell her that it's not Erol. I'll break that to her later, once she's settled.

"We don't have to stay at your place, though, Amon. It's not that big of a deal."

"A strange man was in your house, Rosie. And not to be a dick here, or dramatic or whatever, but this is the very same house where Olive Creed was nearly kidnapped when she was a girl and where Collin Creed blew that man's head off. So. Yeah. It's kind of a big fuckin' deal."

"Oh. Well, I had kinda forgotten about the history of the house, but thanks for reminding me."

I chuckle. "I'm not trying to scare you or nothing, Rosie, but it's much better to be too cautious than it is to be indifferent. I've learned that the hard way, take my word on it. So the two of you are gonna pack a bag and stay with me until I feel it's safe."

She's got a hold of my upper arm with both hands and when these words come out, she hugs it a little, pressing her cheek up against my shoulder.

When we get to her house, I tell her and Cross to wait outside while I go in and check things. Inside, I pull my sidearm and check the first floor, then go upstairs and check there too.

The puzzle is propped up against Rosie's pillow. A crossword, just like she said.

After checking the bathroom and closet, I go back outside and wave Rosie and Cross inside.

"What's goin' on?" Cross asks.

Rosie would probably like me to lie to him, but I'm not gonna. "There was a break-in, Cross, and your mom called me so I could check it out. So I did. And the house is safe now."

"A break-in?" Cross's eyes go wide as he looks to his mother. "What the fuck?"

"Cross! Mind your mouth!"

"A break-in?" he says again, ignoring Rosie's admonishment and looking up at me instead. "Who the hell in their right mind would break into a house in Disciple, West Virginia?"

His innocence is adorable. But he's only half wrong because the answer to his question is—a stranger. That's who would break into this house. A stranger. Someone not from here.

And then a wave of déjà vu hits me and I'm in high school again, the day after Collin shot that man in his house who was trying to kidnap his baby sister.

Collin was one of those good kids, as are most Disciple boys, except for me, of course. But something hit me sideways that morning. Deep, too. Because it was a realization that I didn't know Collin Creed. We had grown up together, played sports together when I was very young and into that. He was never in the children's choir, of course, because he was always on stage, behind his daddy. But I was in the choir until I was eleven, so I was on stage too, and we were friendly.

Collin was never small, or passive, or weak, but he was never aggressive either. Even on the football field, everything about how he caught that ball was about job performance and had nothing to do with ego.

And that morning, when I found out he had killed a would-be kidnapper, everything I knew about Collin Creed reset to zero.

I am thinking about all this because Cross's attitude about this intruder has me rethinking my opinions about him as well. If he was home and someone came in, threatening him or his mother, and he had the chance to get a shotgun—or a rifle, as it was in Collin's case—he'd take that shot too. I know he would.

"Pack a bag, Cross." I say this the way I would say anything to Collin, or Ryan, or Nash. "You've got five minutes."

He wants to say more. He wants to demand answers from me. But he recognizes this tone of voice and instead presses his lips together and gives me a small nod, then retreats to his bedroom.

"You too, Rosie. Go pack something."

"For how long, Amon?"

I smile at her. "A long weekend."

"Should I bring my Revival costumes then?"

"Sure. Bring 'em."

She nods as well, then disappears upstairs while I walk out onto the front porch and stare across the street, listening to the river down below in the valley.

Someone came in this house.

Someone was in her bedroom.

And it wasn't Erol Cross, so who the hell is stalking my woman?

I think about that the whole way back to the compound. Cross wants to listen to the radio, and there's a station that runs out of Revenant that plays oldies—which, for reasons unknown to me, seems to be all the rage around here at the moment—so we listen to that instead of trying to have a conversation. It's useless to pretend that this is anything but what it actually is, so we don't even bother trying.

It's dark by the time I pull into the compound, but nights out here don't end with the sunset. The dining hall is lit up bright as I pass and there are dozens of men wandering about. Some have fires going in the various pits, some are sitting on the church steps, just talking, and some sitting at picnic tables, cleaning their weapons.

My eyes track up to the rear-view mirror and I catch Cross practically pressing his nose to the window, trying to take it all in.

I park in front of my house and spy Lowyn and Collin sitting on their porch steps, talking.

Lowyn gets up first when she realizes who's getting out of my truck. "Rosie!" she says. "What's goin' on?"

"Well..." Rosie looks to me, wondering what to say.

I look at Collin. "Someone broke into Rosie's house earlier today."

"What?" He looks at Rosie, then Cross, then back at Rosie. "Are you all right?"

She nods. "I'm fine. We weren't home at the time. I just..." She looks at Lowyn. "Someone's been sending me weird letters. With puzzles inside."

"*What?*" Cross says. Because of course he hasn't heard about this yet.

"Let me get them settled and then I'll be back," I tell Collin.

He nods and pulls Lowyn a little closer. And of course he does. Because, like me, right now Collin Creed and Lowyn McBride are picturing that night twelve years ago when that man tried to kidnap Olive and Collin killed him for his troubles.

Lowyn was there. She saw the whole thing. And I bet, all this time that she's been living in that house—remodeling and redecorating it so there was almost no trace of what happened that night—she's been telling herself it would never happen again.

And now it has.

No one was there and no one got hurt, but that hardly matters.

Someone came into that house uninvited. *Again.*

"Wow," **Cross says**. He stops in the middle of my living room and looks around. "Your place is cool, Amon. Where's my bedroom?"

I'm looking at Rosie when this comes out of his mouth and she blushes a little. "Cross. Don't be silly, you don't have a bedroom here."

"You take that first room in the hallway right there, Cross. That's your room."

"Thanks, Amon!"

He goes off to explore and Rosie turns to me. "Your place is... not what I expected."

I look around, taking it in with new eyes. "Well, most of this was Lowyn. When we bought the compound, everything was a mess and needed reno. But my kitchen was this cool-as-fuck turquoise and black color. It even had black velvet wallpaper."

Rosie makes a face.

"Cool, right?" I know she's not thinking 'cool,' she's thinking 'gross,' but I'm playing with her. "So I told Low that I wanted to keep that vibe. And this is how it turned out."

I grin and spread my arms wide, completely ignoring that this house has 'man' written all over it. It's nice though. Lowyn is partial to mid-century modern, and what do I know about decorating? I picked things from the samples she showed me. None of the mid-century modern furniture is actually vintage, that's just not my style. But I do like me some tapered legs and soft curves.

"Turquoise ceilings are... a... *bold* choice." Rosie laughs. "But it looks good."

"That was Lowyn. Again. Because I tried to paint the walls black, and she pitched a fit. So she met me halfway with black baseboards and crown molding, but the walls had to be gray."

"Black walls." Rosie shakes her head and tsks her tongue. "Thank God for Lowyn." Then she turns to me. "It's actually quite nice. You've got style, Amon. Who knew?" She grins, shooting me a side-eye. "Where do I sleep?"

"Well... I do have another spare room. Or"—I shrug—"you could stay upstairs with me."

"She'll stay with you," Cross calls from his room. Then he peeks his head out. "She's gonna say, 'I'll take the spare room.'" He says this last part mimicking his mama's voice. "But don't let her, Amon. She'll boss you all over the place if you let her. Better to take control now." Then he retreats back into the room and closes the door.

"Oh, my God. My son. Please excuse him."

I ignore that and stay on point. "Spare room or upstairs?"

Her eyes roll up to the ceiling, then she looks at me. "Well, I at least want to see it or I might die of curiosity before morning."

I grab her shoulders and point her in the direction of the stairs. Then I follow her up, but hold back at the top so I get a good look at her as she learns something new about me.

Rosie's bedroom is all vintage cottage core, mostly because that's how Lowyn had it decorated when she left. But my bedroom, much like the downstairs, says upscale man cave.

The turquoise and black theme continues, but this time it's reversed. Black ceilings and turquoise trim with dark gray walls. Like the downstairs, the furniture is new mid-century modern.

Rosie walks forward, the tips of her fingers tracing the gleaming brass bedframe as she passes. It's a modern and masculine take on the canopy that looks like an open cube. It was custom-made by someone Lowyn knows down in Kentucky and she thought of me when she saw it.

"It's king-size," I tell Rosie. "So there's plenty of room for you."

She turns, letting out a breath at the same time. "Black velvet, huh?" She nods her head to the bedding—which is, in fact, silk velvet. But it's about two shades lighter than true black.

I shrug. "I was pretty keen on the idea and bedding is

easy to change. Though, if you take a moment to touch it, I doubt you'll hate it."

She bites her lip as she bends over to run that fingertip down the velvet comforter. "It's very soft." Then she straightens up and looks around, turning in a slow circle until she's facing me again. "Skulls?"

She's referring to my theme. Which is, indeed, skulls. The pictures on the wall, the pillows on the bed, and the lamps on the bedside tables—gold ones, also made of gleaming brass and which look a little bit like candlesticks with skulls at the base. "What can I say? It's kinda my style."

"Well, it's a bit disturbing. But in a classy way."

"Thanks." Then I turn in a slow circle, taking it all in as well. When I meet Rosie's eyes, I say, "I like it. But everything can be changed if you don't."

"It's your bedroom, Amon. Why would you care if I like it?"

There are only a few steps between us, so I erase that distance and wrap my arms around her waist, tugging her close to me. "Because I want you. It's as simple as that."

Her breasts heave as she takes in a deep breath. "How do you know?"

"That I want you? Come on, Rosie. Everyone wants you."

She nearly snorts. "That's simply not true. Or why would I still be single?"

"Well, that's obvious, of course. You're still single because I just got back. You and I were meant to be. It's just… well, the last time I saw you, that boy of yours was in your belly and I was on my way to the marines. The world wasn't ready for us."

"And twelve years later, it is?"

261

"More than ready. It's dying for us to get serious."

She lets out another breath, pulling back, making me let go of her. Then she turns and takes a seat on the bed. I watch, grinning, as she traces her fingertips over the silk comforter. Then grabs a fistful of it as she looks up at me. "It really is soft."

I sit down beside her, then flop back onto the bed, looking up at the open top of the bedframe. "Rosie, you will sleep naked every night in this bed just to feel this silky velvet across your body, that's how soft it is."

She flops back with me, our shoulders touching. "Is that how you sleep?"

I turn my head and grin at her. "So. Guest room? Or my room?"

"Your room!" Cross calls from downstairs.

Rosie sits up. "Cross Harlow! You better not be eavesdropping! That's rude!"

"Just tell the man you're sleeping upstairs. Can I go outside and check out the dogs?"

I say, "Sure," just as Rosie says, "No!" And we look at each other.

"*Moooom!*"

"It's safe out there, Rosie. Collin and I have put together a little army that every nation on the planet would die for. No one is gonna get him here."

She closes her eyes, then opens them again. "OK," she calls down. "But stay close to this house. And do not go in those woods!"

Cross grumbles. "Why in the world would I go into the woods in the middle of the night?" Then we hear the slapping of a screen door as he leaves.

Rosie looks at me, shaking her head. "Sometimes he's a handful."

Which makes me laugh. "Rosie, think back to when I was twelve and picture what I was getting up to. Cross is an angel compared to me."

She chuckles. "Well, I didn't know you then. I would've been only ten." She side-eyes me. "But I did follow your antics and I do believe that was the summer that you set off firecrackers in the tent during Revival."

I laugh just thinking about it. "Oh, those days were fun."

"You must've exasperated your parents to no end."

"Well, yeah. They did get pretty tired of Jim Bob demoting them over my chronic unruliness. But they were very good sports about it in the grand scheme of things. Probably because they had pinned their hopes and dreams on the sisters coming up behind me." I wink. "It was a good hedge, that bet. Speaking of, do you hang out with any of my sisters? I haven't had time to ask them."

"Not really. Eden is four years younger than me, which would put her at eleven that year I became an adult. And the rest are even further apart. But of course I know them, like I know everyone else in this town."

"We've got a bowling thing going with them on Fridays and that's tomorrow. Collin and Lowyn will be there. Nash and Ryan too. Plus a few of the incorrigible assholes outside. Should we make a date of it? Cross could come as well."

"Our first Disciple date." She looks up at me, those gray eyes bright and shining. "Sounds fun, so yes. I would love that. But as far as tonight goes, I'm gonna stay downstairs with Cross. I just feel like sharing a bedroom should be more intentional, and not based on fear."

"Are you afraid?"

"No. But the whole reason I'm here is because my ex is stalking me. And I don't want to combine the two things to the point where they are inseparable."

Even though we've already had sex twice now, she's right. Sharing a bedroom is a step above. Especially with a kid in the mix. "That sounds fair. But if you don't mind, I think I will sleep on the couch then."

"Why?"

"It's just my nature. To put myself between you and the door. And in my world, a door equals danger. Even here on the Edge compound." I put up a hand. "Not literally, Rosie. No one is coming through that door. It's just training. Ingrained and all that, ya know?"

"Well, truth be told, I would actually feel safer with you on that couch between me and that door, so thank you very much."

I stand up and offer her my hand. "Come on, I'll show you the room."

She takes my hand and we go downstairs. She likes the room—which carries on the same color scheme, but in a more muted way. Light gray instead of black and a swimming-pool blue color instead of turquoise.

Rosie smiles when we enter. "Lowyn did this room, didn't she?"

"Lowyn did all the rooms, but she took a particular interest in this one because I said she could do it any way she wanted."

Rosie smiles and starts talking about Lowyn and their

friendship. But my mind is wandering to what I meant to do tonight, and didn't.

Which is tell her that Erol is dead.

But I can't. Not tonight. Erol, at least, is someone she knows. He's the father of her son. He has a reason to stalk her.

A stranger using Erol's name and sending her puzzles that allude to her boy?

That's something else altogether.

CROSS IS **outside sitting** on Collin's porch petting Mercy as he and Lowyn discuss the finer points of oldies music when Rosie and I join them. When Rosie ushers Cross back over to my house and Lowyn goes inside, I corner Collin so we can have a word.

He raises an eyebrow at me. "What's up?"

I check one last time, just to make sure no one is listening, then lean in. "Remember that forensics thing I told you about?"

"The one you sent Penny?"

"The very one. Well, I got it back and it's not Rosie's ex."

"It's not? Is she sure?"

"Oh, she's sure. He's dead, Collin."

"Well, that's definitely a certainty. It also elevates this little mystery to a new level."

"Especially after finding a puzzle in her bedroom tonight. Whoever this stalker is, he's serious."

"And scary." Collin looks off in the distance like he's thinking, and I can only imagine that once again he's picturing that night twelve years ago. He looks at me again. "What should we do?"

"First of all"—I point at him—"I like that 'we' tag you just put on this problem. And second, I dunno. I think we have to start with a more thorough background check."

"On who though?"

"Erol Cross, of course."

"But if the man's dead—"

"*Is* the man dead?"

"If Penny says he is, then I can't see a way around it, Amon. She's in a class of her own when it comes to this kind of thing."

"She ran the ink, fingerprints, and paper through all the databases and came up with nothing. But there's something not right about it."

Collin's eyes narrow. "Not right about what? Penny?"

"No. Just..." But I can't explain what I'm feeling. "About this whole stalker thing. I feel like I'm missing something."

Collin blows out a breath. "Yeah. I hate that feeling."

"It's not that I don't trust Penny," I add. "It's just... well, these days anything can be faked, ya know?"

This makes Collin chuckle. "If people only knew how easy it was to create somethin' from nothin' in this day and age, they'd never trust a single thing they read or see again. All the world's a stage, after all."

"Yeah. That's the thing. This whole stalking thing, with the worksheets and whatnot, it all feels very... staged."

"You think it's fake?" Collin asks.

"I'm not sure. It just feels *off*."

"Well, if it makes you feel any better, I think Rosie's about as safe as one can be. You've done all the right things. She's staying here on the compound now and she never leaves Trinity County. If anyone tried to mess with Rosie someone would be there, even if you weren't. Everyone knows Rosie. But if you're worried, then..." He shrugs. "Hell, just keep her with you. It's a hard job, monopolizing a woman's time. But someone's gotta do it."

I chuckle. "Yeah, all right."

Collin nudges me. "We'll figure it out, Amon. And she'll be OK. Just... keep her close."

*T*he *next morning* when Cross and I wake up, Amon is already gone. I figure he's outside doing work stuff, so I dress in my Friday costume, pack a change of clothes for after the Revival, and serve Cross a bowl of cereal.

Neary all my weekends from Easter to Christmas Eve are monopolized by the Revival. Once the fall rolls around, it dies down to a monthly thing instead of a weekly. So that's nice. But in the summer, there is almost no chance of gettin' away from the Revival. There's no tent action on Fridays, but there's always a crowd going through the shops on the grounds or just hanging around in town, so Friday's are a costume day.

I don't have any serious parts to play today—or any other day this weekend, since I'm generally a 'filler' character—but MacyLynn and I have to sit in the tea party tent and entertain guests with gossip. On the weekends she mostly runs the funnel cake tent but her granny does it on Fridays, so nearly every week we're partners in crime.

I'm sitting on the porch having coffee when Amon comes back, jingling his truck keys and smiling like a boy. "I like that dress."

I stand up and smooth out some wrinkles. "This old

thing?" Then I bat my eyelashes at him and do a twirl to properly show off this outfit.

It's not an old dress, it's actually rather new, since the one I've been wearing on Fridays all season got a tear in the sleeve and MacyLynn's twin sister, MaisieLee, hasn't had a chance to fix it yet.

Disciple's weekend fashion is just as fictional as the Revival itself—a blend of Twenties high-society, summer garden-party, and a dash of flapper thrown in for good measure. My dress today is made of pale blue silk velvet and tea-stained lace in the vein of 'robe de style.' Which means a fitted bodice with dropped waist, as was common in the era, but with a full skirt that looks especially nice when twirlin'.

This particular skirt is adorned with silk flowers and glass-beaded stems, giving it a bit of weight. And the lace acts not only as a sort of outer petticoat, but as a shawl too. It is a gorgeous example of MaisieLee's talent.

When my twirling ends, Amon is grinning at me so hard, I burst out laughing myself. "I'm being silly, aren't I?"

"Rosie, your silliness is an absolute delight and a big part of the reason why the whole world loves you. So don't ever stop on my account."

I blush. I can feel it. And it's a very nice compliment, but there's a little part inside me that wants to object. To tell him that the world doesn't love me. Because I was a teenage mom who had big dreams. Who thought she could break the rules and buck the system and still come out shiny and new on the other side.

And while I would not call myself used up in any sense of the word, my place in the world changed the day Cross was born and even though I held out hope for a few years that I could push it back into some semblance of what I was, it's just not true.

That girl before Cross is gone and she's never coming back.

This whole time I've been thinking, Amon has been watching me carefully. Like I'm a painting in a museum that must be deciphered. He can feel these doubts inside me—which have nothing to do with him—and he's not sure how to approach it.

So I take over. "Can you drop Cross and me in town?"

Cross pushes his way through the screen door. "Town? I don't wanna go into town. I wanna hang out here, Ma. Can I?"

"It's not up to me, Cross. It's up to Amon. And I'm sure he's busy today and not in the mood to babysit you."

"Actually, I've gotta go into town too, Cross. To talk to Jim Bob about something."

Cross makes a face. "Well, what am I supposed to do while you guys are busy?"

I roll my eyes at my son. "Same thing you do every day while I'm working. Hang out with those friends of yours."

"Actually…" Amon hedges. "Maybe it's better if he does stay here. Collin's gonna be here all day." He looks at Cross. "You can hang out with Collin. I won't be long. Then we'll… I dunno. Go shoot some targets on the range."

This delights Cross to no end. "Deal." Then he takes off down the porch steps, jogging his way up the driveway where Collin is barking out orders to these men of his.

"Are you sure he won't be in the way?"

"Shit, Ryan will put him to work digging ditches, probably. He'll regret this decision by lunchtime."

I chuckle. "You're good with him. I appreciate that because I know you don't have to be."

"I like kids, Rosie. And while it's probably too soon have that conversation, I might as well put it out there." He throws me a weighty look. "I like them. And I *would* like them."

"I see." But though my words come out innocuous, inside I'm sighin'. Because I would love a big family like the one I came from and Amon Parrish would be a perfect father in my opinion.

"Like I said"—he winks—"too early. Come on, let's go to town."

THE RAIN STARTS JUST as we get to Disciple and Amon parks in a covered spot marked for security just outside the east gate.

We both get out. "I'll check in with you after I'm done with Jim Bob. If you go anywhere else but here"—he points to the ground—"you text me, OK?"

With all the excitement of seeing Amon's house, and choosing where to sleep, and chatting with Collin and Lowyn, it was easy to put aside the real reason why Cross and I were out on the Edge compound to begin with. But after he says these words, it all comes back.

I look around. "You don't think he's here, do you?"

"Who?" Amon looks confused for a moment. "Oh. Erol,

you mean? No, he's not here."

"How can you be sure?"

Amon blows out a breath, then takes my arm and leads me over to a more private area under a large sugar maple. "I was gonna tell you this last night, but... whatever. I didn't. And I don't really wanna tell you now because it's not fair. But it's always gonna be the wrong time and the sooner you know this, the better."

"Wrong time for what?"

"To tell you that Erol Cross is dead, Rosie. He didn't go missing twelve years ago. He died."

For a moment, these words don't make any sense and I just blink at him.

"Rosie? Did you hear me?"

I nod my head because I did. But... "Dead?"

Amon presses his lips together and nods his head as well.

My sight narrows down into a little tunnel surrounded by hazy grayness and then it's like time flies backwards and I'm that scared teenager standing in the cafeteria at Trinity High, looking down at the puddle of water at my feet.

Erol had been missing for weeks at that point. So I had kinda gotten over the initial shock of... well, abandonment, I suppose, and was well into panic territory. What was I gonna do with this baby, how was I gonna live, what would people think of me?

And then—

My foggy vision clears and suddenly I'm looking straight into Amon's blue eyes. But he's not a grown man like he is now, he's a teenager, like me. He was the first person I saw when I looked up from the puddle. It was like we were the only two people in the world for a second there. Just him and me. And I just remember staring at him, and him staring back, and then a sense of peace flooded through me and suddenly I knew what to do.

You will just do your best, Rosie. And it came to me in Amon's voice for some reason. Probably because he and I were looking at each other. A moment later people rushed in, the contractions started, and all I knew was pain and I forgot all about that moment when I heard his voice in my head.

But I remember now.

"It was you," I say.

Amon's brow furrows. "What?"

"I was looking right at you that day when my water broke in the cafeteria."

He lets out a huff of breath. "Yeah. I was walking by and you had a weird look on your face and then your water broke and—"

"I heard your voice in my head, Amon."

He makes a face of confusion. "What?"

"I looked at you and you looked at me and then... I knew it was gonna be OK. Because all I could do was my best. And that would be enough. And this bit of comfort came to me as your voice in my head. You helped me that day. You truly did."

"But I didn't do nothing, Rosie. I just stood there. I was closest to you and I wanted to go over to you and help in some way, but—"

"But then a crowd of people rushed in and blocked you out."

"Yeah. And they took you away in someone's car, I think."

I laugh out loud. "Mr. Damian drove me to the hospital. I had forgotten about that."

"Tenth-grade English?"

I nod. "He was the last teacher to come over and someone pointed to him and yelled, 'Get your car! You're taking her to the hospital!' I screamed the whole way there and he just kept mutterin', 'I don't get paid enough to do this. I just don't get paid enough to do this.'"

Amon laughs again. His smile is bright.

But I sigh and shrug my shoulders. "Even though I can laugh about it now, I was horrified, and scared, and sad all in the same breath. And then, after Cross was born, I was all those things, plus happy too. And it made no sense at all, Amon. But there, in my head, were those words that you never said, but found their way to me anyway. *You will just do your best*. And that's all I did. That's all I've been doing this whole time, and now…"

I look away because I'm gonna have one of those cries. The ugly kind. Which I don't normally partake in, but nonetheless I can feel the lump in my throat and the grimace on my face as I try to hold it in.

Amon pulls me into a hug and I rest my cheek on his shoulder until I've got it back under control. Then I sniff real big and push back. "I'm not really crying about Erol." I wipe my eyes, but the tears are big and ploppy, so it doesn't do much good. "I'm just… sad, I guess. Because even though I tried to tell myself he was dead. That was the only way he'd abandon me like that, I never really believed it. I always had that little bit of hope, ya know? And then, these letters came and—"

"It stirred up all kinds of feelings, didn't it?"

"Yeah. It didn't give me hope, I am not interested in Erol. At all. But finding that note from him, well, it made me unconsciously reflect on how I might've jumped the gun back when I was young and it's just kinda hittin' me right now. How nothing about Erol's disappearance made any sense and how I just wrote him out of my life and moved on. I feel a little ashamed about this."

Amon pushes me back, holding me an arm's length away. "Ashamed? No. Why would you feel ashamed?"

"Because I just assumed the worst. That he got scared and bailed out. And it turns out he didn't bail. He didn't leave me. I, in fact, left him. I didn't even try and find him. I didn't even call hospitals or anything, Amon."

"You were fifteen, Rosie. And nine months pregnant. You had more than enough on your mind at the time. Maybe you should come with me today. I'll go talk to Jim Bob and—"

"No." I put up my hand to stop him. "I don't wanna go. Revival is the most consistent thing in my life. I'm surrounded by family and friends, there's nothing but uplifting messages, and it's almost too pretty to be real. I can't think of a better way to work out this sadness than to be here."

Amon places a hand on my cheek and looks me straight in the eyes. "You did everything right, Rosie." Then he leans in and presses his lips to mine. I keep my eyes open and so does he. Right until the very last moment and then I close them and let peace wash over me as this man claims my mouth like I belong to him.

Like this is was exactly how my life was meant to turn out.

When we pull back from the kiss we stay close. Pressing our foreheads together. I would like to linger in this moment forever. Just stay right here and let time stop.

Keep my boy, a boy.

Keep this new love, new.

Keep this life perfect.

But aside from being impractical, not to mention impossible, I don't want to stop things here. There's too much to look forward to. As much as I lament the growin' up of my boy, I'm looking forward to it too. I want to see the man he becomes. I want him to fall in love and have his own family.

And this moment right here can't even begin to compare to the ones coming my way if I just keep going.

Amon holds my face in his hands, looking me straight in the eyes. "You OK?"

I press my lips together and nod. "I am. I promise."

"All right. I'll pick you up at six and we'll go bowling. I'll have Cross with me. Don't worry about him."

I place my hand on his cheek now. "If he's with you, there's absolutely nothing to worry about."

Then I leave him in the east gate parking lot and make my way to the garden tent to get ready for a day of tea parties.

*WHEN MY DAY **ends*** at six o'clock, after I change into my cut-offs and halter top, I find Amon and Cross waiting for me at the east gate. Seeing them together like this is something new. And by that, I mean a man with my child, picking me up from work like we're some kind of family.

That has never happened to me before. Most of my dating life was fake. I told these tales to fit in with my twenty-something friends who were all focused on growing into adulthood, and starting their lives, and finding husbands.

And none of that applied to me. Did I want a husband? Well, sure. But finding one when you've already got a kid isn't as easy as it sounds. Even if you're a cute and perky Valerie Bertinelli twin. I tried to date after Cross was born, but none of the boys from school were interested in me. It scared them to think about babies, I think. And why wouldn't it? I mean, it scared me too.

So once I turned eighteen, and got my Revival trust, I bought a car. I would drive down to Fayetteville and hang out in the pool hall there. Plenty of men were interested, but that was the whole problem. They were men, not boys. And even though I had a baby, I didn't feel like a woman yet. I was looking for a sweetheart, not a one-night stand.

So I stopped really trying long before I was even old enough to legally drink. That's when I started making the boyfriends up. There was a smattering of real dates too. Every now and then I'd get lonely and give it another go. But it was the same thing over and over. They liked me, but they didn't want my baggage.

That's when I decided that free time was my enemy and started taking part-time jobs all over Trinity County. Cross and I lived in that doublewide behind the bakery because there are hardly ever any houses up for sale or rent in Disciple and I was dead set on stayin' inside the town limits. But I'm not poor. I've never lacked for anything I truly wanted, and neither has Cross. Every January first I get my profit share from the Revival, so money is a constant in my life. Something I can count on.

Plus I had my Revival trust, which was saved up in a bank account for me for when I reached legal age. There was a time, back then in my early twenties, when I had nearly a hundred thousand dollars in the bank. I had so much money it started to freak me out, so I took most of it and put it in a second trust for Cross so nothing bad could happen to it.

I just kept working, though. And the years just kept passing, and that bank account of mine got too big again. That's when I opened up the *Bishop Busybody*. I spend a lot of money on that place. On the dresses, and the cottage, and the store.

But as I told Amon that first day we bumped into each other, time is something you make for things you like doing. And for some stupid reason, I fancy myself an eighteenth-century printer. Plus, those dresses are just plain fun.

All my wandering thoughts come full circle when I come up to Amon and Cross and my son is bursting with words, trying to say them all at once to tell me about his day.

Something about shooting, and dogs, and body armor, and I'm pretty sure there was mention of a grenade in there, but he's talking so fast I miss the context. And by the time my brain catches up, he's on to something else about a church basement full of guns.

This is when Amon says, "Your mama don't wanna hear about any of that, Cross." And then his eyes lock with mine and brighten. "Let's hear about your day, Rosie." And he offers me his arm.

So the three of us walk down the hill towards the bowling alley, with me filling him in on all my tea-party details, and Cross jogging ahead, then waiting for us, then jogging ahead again And it's... good. It's really good, and it feels amazing to have someone to share my day with who not only likes me, but my son as well.

And this is when I realize that my life has *finally* started. Twelve years ago I put it on hold—accidentally or not, it was on hold. And now it's going somewhere.

I am no longer desperately seeking anyone.

Because I found my someone and his name is Amon Parrish.

osie is quiet as we walk. Even after we get to the bowling alley and sort out the shoes, and the balls, and the lane, she is still quiet.

But she's not frowning. She's actually smiling pretty big because that whole time Cross was jabbering about his day she took great pleasure in listening to him. I think she likes the idea of him and I hanging out.

Now Cross is preoccupied with my sisters. Halo in particular, since at sixteen she is closest in age. But they are all friendly girls. And anyway, everyone in Disciple loves Cross Harlow because he's perpetually in a good mood, doesn't get in much trouble, and his mother is Rosie, who is kind of a legend in this town for more than one reason. So there is no awkwardness between the five of them.

Even though I understand why Rosie has been quiet, I feel the need to ask about it because I did break the news that her son's father is dead just a couple days after she came to terms with the idea that he might still be alive and all of this feels very much like my fault. "Everything OK?"

Rosie is sitting on the bench behind the score table, watching all the bowling action. But she looks up at me now. "More than OK. Why do you ask?"

"You're just quiet."

"It's a happy quiet."

I sit down next to her, leaning back so I can stretch my arm out just behind her shoulder. "I figured it might be, but thought I'd inquire just to make sure."

She gives me a sideways look, her eyes grinning. "That was smooth."

We both laugh because it really was a teenage-boy move. "I do my best."

She leans back now so that the side of her head leans on my shoulder, and lets out a long sigh. "Like I said this morning when you told me, it feels a little like shame, Amon. It's just this sick feeling inside me that I... behaved badly." She straightens up so she can look at me. "That's what it is. Not looking for him after Cross was born—just giving up like that and accepting things—has always felt like a low moment in my life. Like I failed to live up to my own expectations. It might even be part of my condition."

My eyebrow goes up. "Your... condition?"

"That's just what I call the loneliness in my head. That's why I work so many jobs, ya know? It's why I write fictional desperately-seeking-somebodies, and fuss over those dresses, and keep the cottage and printshop. It's a way to block out the fact that I lost the game of love."

"You didn't lose."

She smiles. "Well, I know that now. But this is a brand-new thing, Amon. Two weeks, that's all. The other twelve years are still up here." She taps her head with a pale pink fingernail. "And the funny thing is, I don't think I understood that I was sad all this time." She squints her eyes at me, shaking her head a little. "It's a weird feeling to realize you've been something for such a long time, you didn't know how to be any other way."

I stare off in the distance, focusing on the people all down the alleys as they throw their balls, and laugh, and have a good time. But I have a realization myself. That if I had gone to Rosie that day in the cafeteria, I'd have fallen in love with her. I would've driven her to the hospital instead of Mr. What's-his-name from tenth-grade English and I would've been there when Cross was born. I would not have left. And even though I have regrets about a lot of things that I did instead, it was all necessary to get right here to this actual moment. Because there was a craving inside me when I was eighteen. A craving to see more, and do everything, and live a less perfect life than the one staged here in Disciple. And if I had stayed, that craving would've never gone away.

That craving would've ruined everything.

"Well." I sigh and look down at Rosie. "It's a brand-new start then, isn't it?"

She nods, snuggling her face up into my neck. "It sure is. A very nice one at that."

Suddenly Cross comes bounding over and sits on the other side of me. "We're staying the night at your house tonight, right?"

Rosie and I haven't discussed the details, but there's really nothing to discuss. Not until we figure out this stalker situation. So I answer him before she does. "Yep. You're staying."

"Good," Cross says. "I love it out there. I like your men, too. They're cool. I wanna be just like them."

I would like to point out that all my men, as he puts it, are permanently scarred from all the terrible shit they did in the military, and Edge Security is their last and final chance. But that's something the boy doesn't yet need to know.

Sensing my hesitation, Cross says, "I should train with them. Every day for the rest of the summer. What do you think? Can I do that?"

"Cross," Rosie starts, "you are a boy. Your job is to play all summer so you're good and rested for the next school year."

"I'm not a boy." Cross's words come out angry. "Stop saying that. And what good are summer breaks if you can't do something important? I want to do something important. I want to *be* someone important. And if this is not the perfect time, then when is?" He looks at me now. "You know what I'm talking about, Amon."

And there it is. He's me, all over again, craving something bigger than what he has because he needs to know what he's missing. He's gonna leave, I can see it coming. But not yet. He's only twelve. We've got time. So I make him a pacifying promise. "We'll shoot some more, Cross. Don't worry. And we'll go huntin' in the fall."

Cross stands up, his fists clenched like he's frustrated to no end. "Not *just* that. I want to do all of it. I want to be like them. I want my own tactical gear, and I wanna learn how to work the dogs, and I wanna do *all* of it. This is the perfect time." He looks at his mother with pleading eyes. "Why are you always treating me like a baby? I'm gonna leave, you know. As soon as I turn eighteen, I'm joining the marines too."

Then he stomps off towards the arcade near the bar.

Rosie stands up to go after him, but I grab her hand. "Let him go, Rosie. You'll just make him angrier if you corner him in public. He'll get embarrassed and then he'll say things he doesn't mean."

She sighs. "What was that about? That threat to join the marines? Because it didn't look like embarrassment to me, Amon."

"No. He's dead set on being a badass, I guess. And if that's how he sees his future, then nothing you say about it will make a difference."

"So I should what? Fit him with tactical gear? Hand him a high-powered rifle and send him to survival camp or something?"

"Let him stay on the compound. I'll be there. I'll watch out for him and when I can't, Collin will. It's the safest place, really."

"I don't mind that part. It's the threats. That's what I don't like. He acts like I'm his enemy."

"Well, you're his mother. A boy needs space from his mother if he is to grow into a man."

"Why?" She collapses down next to me. "Why does it have to be that way? Because I don't think it's fair. He's twelve, Amon. I should have him to myself for a few more years, if you ask me."

I put my arm around her and give her a squeeze. "Well, then. It is now my mission to make sure you get those years. Don't worry, I'll talk to him."

She lets out a long breath. "Thank you. I know you don't have to do this, that he isn't your responsibility—"

"Just stop."

She looks up at me and smiles. "Are you my one, Amon Parrish? Is that what you're trying to say?"

"Rosie, you're like an ironic spring morning when the

flowers are popping from the black dirt while the snow falls all around them. It's a special kind of morning that only happens every now and then. The kind you can't replicate because it shouldn't be happening at all. There is no one else on this earth quite like you. And if you'll have me, I'm here for the duration."

Her eyes go dreamy, like she's swoonin'. Then she settles back into my shoulder with a sigh. "Has anyone ever told you that you say all the right things at just the right time?"

"Once or twice, maybe. But they were lawyers and I was sitting in front of a panel of angry congressmen in DC."

She snickers. "That is probably a story I need to know more about."

"Eventually," I say. "But it's over, Rosie. All that's over and now that I'm home, and with you, I'm never leaving again."

CROSS IS STILL **angry** and Rosie is still upset on the ride back to the compound and I feel like I need to say something here. Like I should explain Rosie's point of view to Cross because I actually agree with her.

Twelve is too young. I mean, if he were some martial arts phenom and had been into it his whole life with some kind of big goal, like the world championships or something, then maybe. If he had put in all that effort it would be criminal not to support him, but a trajectory like that when you're young carries a whole lot of risks. So even then, the answer would not be an automatic 'yes.'

But that's not how this is playing out at all. Cross has big dreams, but all he's done about it so far is whine and complain about how his mother treats him like a kid.

Which is fair because she does treat him like a kid, but that's because he *is* a kid.

I guess, if I was his father, I'd sit him down and give him the hard truth. The whole you-haven't-earned-this speech. I got that speech from my father right about his age too. I wanted the same thing. That's why I joined the military practically the moment I turned eighteen.

But my father was gentle with his speech and I think that was the right approach. He was trying to blend encouragement with independence. And when I left Disciple, they were proud of me. They supported me one hundred percent.

I think this is the right way forward with Cross as well and I think I should maybe have a talk with him before bed. It's no good going to sleep angry because you just wake up the same way.

So after we pull into the Edge compound and I park the truck in front of my house, I tell Rosie, "Go inside. We'll be there in a minute."

She wants to ask what this is about, but she must read my face and decide to hold her tongue because she just nods and then does as I ask.

Cross hangs back as the lights inside flick on, perhaps sensing that he and I are gonna have a talk, or maybe he's just sulking. But either way, we're gonna get this all out in the open now.

"Have a seat, Cross." I point to the porch steps.

He lets out a long sigh, but sits.

I sit next to him, propping my elbows on my knees as we both stare out at the compound. There are still plenty of people around even though it's near midnight. The guys always get the weekends off, so this night will stay alive a little longer than most.

"Well," Cross says, "are you gonna have a talk with me or what?"

"I am," I say, leaning back, resting my elbows on the step behind me.

"Because you think I'm acting like a jerk, don't you?"

"A jerk?" I turn my head to the right to look at him. "No. You're not acting like a jerk. You're acting like…" I sigh because it's the wrong thing to say to a boy this age. But it's also the truth, and the truth wins out. "You're acting like a kid, Cross. That's why your mama's treating you like one."

"How do you mean?" His voice cracks and goes shrill. "I'm not! I'm just trying to tell her how I feel about things and she's not listening! She still thinks I'm a baby."

"Cross, I hate to break it to you, but she's always gonna see you as her baby. She's your mother. And the point I'm making here is that this isn't about her, this is about you, son. If you want to be a grown-up, you gotta act like one. Stop blaming your mother for holding you back when you're not doing nothin' to take a step forward."

"What do you mean?" His eyes are making this shocked expression.

"If you had been taking martial arts classes all your life and then your mama was trying to forbid you from fighting in some big championship, then I'd be having this talk with her instead of you. But what are you good at, Cross? What are you doing to better yourself and carve your own destiny? Because kids with goals have commitment. What are you committed to?"

He blinks at me. "What?"

"Are you in the shootin' club?"

"Well… no."

"Why not?"

He huffs, giving himself time to think up an answer. "They're all about hunting. And hunting is fine, but that's not what I want."

"You want to be dangerous."

"Like you!" He stands up, his hands out in a pleading gesture. "I just wanna be like you, Amon."

"OK. It's a start. But wanting something and getting something are two different things."

"Well, how am I supposed to get what I want if you guys won't let me do what I want?"

"You gotta change our minds, I guess."

He's mad again now, because his words come out growly. "And how am I supposed to do that?"

"Show me you're committed. Get up early and go into the kennel and help the men take care of the dogs. Get up early and come out here, and when those men run by, fall in behind them. And then keep up." I wink here. "That's how you carve your way, Cross. You make it happen."

He sighs and turns his back to me, staring out at the camp. After a few minutes of silence, he turns back. "Fine. Then that's what I'll do."

He doesn't wait for my reaction or my approval, he just walks up the steps and goes inside.

I let out a breath and smile.

It was a good talk.

So I go inside as well, but Cross closed his door and the room that Rosie slept in last night is dark and empty. When I look upstairs, there's a light on. And when I go up, she's in my bed.

She waves her fingers at me in a flirty way. "Hi."

I wave back, checking her out. "Hi."

"Did you have a nice talk?"

I nod. "I think we did." And then I take my shirt off, kick my boots off and take my pants off as I cross the room and get in bed next to her. She's wearing one of my t-shirts.

She points to it. "I found it in your closet. I hope you don't mind."

"I don't mind at all." But as I'm saying that, I'm reaching for the light on the nightstand. And then I'm settled in next to Rosie, her face buried in my neck.

She sighs. Tired, I think. And the next thing I know she's sleeping.

But I don't sleep. Not right away. I play with her hair a little and enjoy this. Because it's the start of something. Maybe she goes back to Lowyn's house in town, or maybe she stays here forever.

It doesn't matter.

One way or the other, we're really together now.

I *wake up suddenly* to the sound of my boy shouting. My eyes fly open and then... confusion. It takes me whole moments to figure out where I am.

And then I smile.

Downstairs a screen door slaps and feet go thudding down porch stairs. I sit up, looking around at Amon's room, then look down at the t-shirt I put on last night for bed.

It smells like him and Amon Parrish smells like love, and loyalty, and protection, so this is quite a nice smell in my eyes.

I thought we might have a little fun time last night. I wasn't convinced it was appropriate, but I was thinkin' about it. Except I must've fell asleep because the last thing I remember is resting my head on Amon's shoulder.

It's amazing how much this man settles me.

I turn to the sound of boots on stairs and then there he is, holding a tray of food. I push some wild hair out of my eyes and grin at him like a fool as he comes over to the bed.

"Hungry?"

I sit up and scoot back as he places the tray over my lap. Then I look up at him with adoration. "Breakfast in bed, Amon? You're spoilin' me. You do this often enough and I'll come to expect it, so you better watch out."

He smiles through his response. "I like 'em spoiled, Rosie. So it's just fine by me if you get used to it."

I think I must blush seventeen shades of red at this bit of courting.

"Oh. Before I forget, Cross said something about not having a job at the Revival anymore. What's that about?"

I feel sad for a moment and pout my lips. "He grew up."

"What?" Amon sits down on the bed next to me.

"Yeah. He grew up and got kicked out of the children's choir last weekend because his voice is breaking. He was working with my brothers last weekend, so he'll probably do that today." Just as these last few words come out of my mouth, Amon starts making a weird face. "What?"

"Well"—he puts up a hand—"don't get mad at me, but when he told me he didn't have a job I said he could hang out here today. With the guys. It's just fun stuff because it's the weekend. No guns." He pauses, then adds, "I don't think, anyway."

"Amon Parrish," I admonish him. "You know better than anyone that boys can't play hooky from the Revival. It's duty. He should go work the tent with all the Harlow men."

"It's one day, Rosie. Ryan's gonna be here. There ain't nothing worse than a bored boy and that's what he'll be if you make him go in today. Besides, it's probably the only free Saturday he'll get all season. Tell Jim Bob and your brothers that he's sick. Let him have a day with the men. It'll be good for him."

I know Amon's right. Especially since Cross has been pitching a fit all week about being grown up. This will be a compromise. Something he will appreciate. "OK. He can stay." Amon smiles. I hold up a finger. "But he can't stay tomorrow. It's Fourth of July. It's a big show and even if he doesn't have a part, he won't want to miss it."

"Deal. Today he stays, tomorrow he goes. Now"—Amon stands and grins at me—"I've got to get changed."

"Why?" I waggle my eyebrows at him. "What you're wearing looks pretty good to me."

"I mean, into my costume."

I suck in a big breath of air. "Oh, I forgot. You're working the Revival this weekend. And you're wearing a costume? Is this another date?"

He bends down and kisses me as an answer, his hand coming up to my cheek, his mouth opening to slip me some tongue. And we linger in this kiss for a good fifteen seconds. When he pulls back I'm ready to melt, that's how wound up I am.

Amon points at me. "Save that thought for tonight. I might have another reason why Cross is staying here today."

My eyebrows shoot up. "Is that so?"

"Indeed. Eat, get dressed, and I'll meet you downstairs. I gotta go check on some things."

Then he turns and hits the stairs. I stay there in bed, mind racing but unable to move until the screen door slaps for a second time.

Then I pinch myself. Because this feels like a fairy tale ending and for once, I feel like I'm playing the starring role.

ONE NICE THING about dating the security guy for Revival is he gets to park his truck right up next to the tent. I don't mind walking up the hill and I've been doing it all my life, but when you're wearing a fancy garden-party dress with fancy-fancy shoes it's nice to get a ride all the way up to the entrance.

It's also a bit weird to be entering the grounds without my son. "Maybe I should text him?" I'm reaching for my phone when Amon puts a hand on my shoulder.

"He's fine, Rosie. I'm telling you, these men are trustworthy. In fact, he's so fine I made plans for us tonight."

I look over at him, confused. "Are we going bowling again?"

Amon scoffs. "It was fun, but no. I'll tell ya later. Come on, we've got jobs to do."

So we get out and he takes my hand, holding it like we're teenagers in love, and we walk through the security entrance like this.

But as soon as we do this, all the people around us start whispering, covering up their mouths with their hands as they eye us.

"What's going on here?" I ask, waving my finger at the crowd.

Amon shakes his head. "No clue. But they are acting weird, aren't they?"

I spot April Lavar and call out. "April. Come over here."

She giggles with Taylor Hill, and they both fall into a fit of laughter.

"April!" I bark.

She turns to me, still giggling, and comes over.

"What is going on here, April? Why is everyone staring at us?"

"Oh, my God. Did you..." She looks at me. She looks at Amon. She looks back at me. "Oh. My God. It was an accident, wasn't it? The two of you have some secret role-playing thing going, don't ya?"

I'm so confused. Because on the one hand, we kinda do, and on the other... I gasp. April laughs harder, holding up this week's *Busybody* insert. "Oh, no!" In all the excitement on Wednesday when Amon came into my printshop, I had the wrong Busybody printed up!

The one that's been inserted into the *Revival News* is the dirty one I wrote for Amon's eyes only. I look at him with a grimace on my face. "I'm might die of embarrassment right here on this spot."

"What's going on? I don't get it?" When he remembers our flirty written correspondence, Amon's eyes start smiling. "Is that your reply to Rugged and Handsome? Give it here, April. Let me read it."

I prepare myself as Amon's eyes glide down the paper and then a guffaw comes flying out of his mouth. Those wild eyes of his are dancing when they meet mine.

April sighs. Holding her hand over her heart. "'Kisses like a prince and fucks like a villain!'" Then she bends over laughing. "Jim Bob is gonna pitch a fit!"

And this is true. He's going to kill me.

As soon as I think that I hear him. "Rosie Harlow! Where are you!"

Amon takes my hand, pulling me deeper into the tent grounds, and we run all the way over to the tea-party tent. When we stop, we're out of breath. "Hide in here until

Revival's over," he says. "I'll handle Jim Bob." Then Amon leans in and growls, "I'm gonna spank you like a master, fondle you like a toy, and take you from behind tonight, Rosie Harlow. So you get ready for it."

Then he spins me around, slaps my ass, and gives it a teasing pinch before turning his back and walking back to security.

I swear I can hear him cackling until he disappears around the funnel cake tent.

THERE IS **no tea party** before the Revival, but it's the general meetin' place for us tea-party gals if we get here early enough. So when I turn and walk in I see MacyLynn and MaisieLee Roberts doin' their best to hold back their smirks. Behind them Lettie Gainer is waggling a finger at me. The twins are my age, but Lettie is a good ten years older than us and she's the big boss of the tea party tent.

I put a hand up. "I don't wanna hear it. I really don't wanna hear it."

"Oh, come on, Rosie!" MaisieLee hooks her arm in mine and leads me over to a table. "'Fucks like a villain!' You can't tease a whole town with a detail like that without spilling some tea!"

"That's enough!" Lettie kinda roars this. "There will be no discussion of *Ms.*"—she practically buzzes my title out, emphasizing that 'z' sound for many seconds longer than she should—"Harlow's private life in the tea party tent!"

Lettie narrows her gaze on me. "You should be ashamed of yourself, printing those words and smearing the good name of the *Revival News* like that."

"Obviously, it was an accident, Lettie. For fuck's sake. Why the hell would I incite Jim Bob's temper on purpose? I made two editions this week, one for Amon's private eyes only and one for public consumption. They just got mixed up, is all. I was…" I blow out a breath. "Distracted."

MaisieLee points at me, her eyes dancing with wild abandon. "You fucked him in the print shop, didn't you?"

Lettie is just about to blow her top when the call to Revival sounds and the twins laugh as they pull me up from my chair and drag me towards the tent, far, far away from Lettie Gainer's wrath.

THE REVIVAL IS a mess of whispers about my private life, but I think the tourists kind of enjoy the drama. Jim Bob makes my great-aunt Ester stand at the entrance of the tent with her hand out, trying to collect the papers, promising free tea cakes if they hand them over.

Almost no one does, so after a couple of minutes she gives up and Jim Bob calms down, and Pastor Simon pushes his glasses up his nose, and the Revival begins.

But I'm surrounded by Disciple girls and they do nothing but jab me for details the whole service. I even miss my faintin' cue, I'm so distracted.

My afternoon at the tea party tent goes much the same, but again, the guests eat it up. It's really only Lettie who's put out. So far I have avoided Jim Bob, but I'll have to pay the piper eventually, that's for sure.

Still, it is kinda fun. Especially since Cross isn't here to see any of it. And I'm glad that my relationship with Amon is so public now.

At four o'clock, Amon appears at the tea party tent, whisperin' something into Lettie's ear. She scowls at him, then me, but then just shrugs.

Amon comes over my way. "Let's go. We're outta here."

"What do you mean? We've got one more party before quittin' time."

"No, we don't." Amon's eyes are filled with mischief. "We've got a date."

"We've been driving a long time, Amon."

I side-eye my date, grinning. "We have."

"Are you gonna tell me where we're going? And why didn't you let me change?"

"Don't worry. I packed you an overnight bag."

Even in the approaching darkness her face lights up. "You packed a bag for me?"

"I sure did. And look, here we are." I slow the truck down and turn right onto a long driveway that leads through the hills of Virginia.

Rosie nearly misses the sign, so she turns in her seat to catch a final glimpse of it. Then she looks at me. "The Dixie Yonder? Isn't that the fancy-fancy place where Clover Bradley works?"

"It sure is."

She leans back in her seat and crosses her arms, but she's smiling. "An out-of-town, overnight date."

"It's a big step, isn't it?"

She giggles. "Baby steps are overrated."

"Agreed."

I park the truck, text Clover, and we get out. She appears just as I'm slipping two bags out of the back of the truck.

"Rosie Harlow!" Clover exclaims. "I haven't seen you in years!" They hug and chat, and ignore me for a good three minutes. But finally Clover turns to me. "And Amon Parrish. My, my, my. The boys are back in town, aren't they?" She winks at Rosie. "And it appears that you and Lowyn have snatched them both up lickety-split." Clover gives me a playful punch in the arm. "Who's left for me, Amon?"

"Nice to see you again, Clover. And I figure a pretty girl like you has her hands full of handsome men up here in the big city."

"Big city." She nearly snorts. "You're hilarious." Then she hooks her arm into Rosie's and tugs her towards a path that leads into the trees. "Come on now. Your love shack is a-waitin'." She winks at me over her shoulder and I just smile and follow.

The cottage is everything a woman might want for a romantic night away. It's an outbuilding from days gone by. Some kind of carriage house, maybe. Made of brick that's been painted white and dotted with shuttered windows, it's something right out of a fairytale.

Clover opens the door, revealing a warm and inviting room lit up with candles. "You two have yourselves a real good time now." Then she squeezes Rosie's arm and turns away, walking back the way we came.

I pan a hand to the door, inviting Rosie in, and even in the rapidly fading light I can see her blush. Her garden-party dress is a soft white color and my security outfit is a tan suit, so we look like a power couple straight out of the pages of *Gatsby*.

As she walks through the door, her arm brushes up against my chest and I feel a powerful hunger to rip her clothes off and stick her on top of me.

But I take a breath. There's no need to rush. We've got all night and the date doesn't stop there.

The door closes with a soft click behind me as I come inside the cottage and Rosie turns to face me. Her breasts heave as she sucks in a deep breath and then she lets it out real slow.

My eyes are locked on hers and we stare at each other for a few moments. Then I say, "This isn't gonna be quick."

Which makes her laugh, and relax, and then she's smiling. "Good. I was countin' on it taking all night."

And now I'm grinning, but also taking off my jacket. I toss it in the direction of an antique chair and take a step forward as I unbutton my vest. She's watching my fingertips as one by one the buttons come undone. Then I toss that aside as well.

I'm only a couple of paces from her now and she's startin' to fidget. Like she's not sure what to do. "Just watch," I say. "That's your job right now, Rosie Gray Eyes. Just watch." And as I say that, I unbutton my shirt. Again, her gaze falls to my fingertips and I swear, she leans forward a little, trying to get a better look at my chest in the moment before I open the shirt up and slip it down my arms.

Now I'm only wearing pants and shoes and this is when I close the distance between us. I take her hands, place one of them over my hard cock and bring the other up to my lips so I can kiss her fingers.

We're staring at each other as all this happens and then she leans in, her hand on my dick, squeezing it and playin' with it. At the same time, I place her other hand on my cheek. She holds me like that, gazing into my eyes as she grips my cock.

Now that her hands are busy and mine are free, I unbuckle my belt, unbutton the pants, and push them down my hips just enough to let my long, thick cock spring out.

Her hand repositions, gripping my shaft. She starts jerking me off and I find a growl rumbling up from my chest.

"I want you so bad," I say, looking right into those gray eyes.

"Then take me. I'm yours, Amon. All yours."

I lean in and kiss her. Soft at first, like a dainty appetizer. But when I reach down and help her jerk me off—making her grip me harder and move faster—the kiss turns into something more akin to an insatiable hunger.

I pull back, turn her around so she's facing the end of the bed, and then I place my hand on her back, right between her shoulder blades. Here I am gentle, and I don't push. Because I don't want her to do anything she's not ready for.

But she's ready. Because she bends over without me even saying a single word of encouragement or pressing down on her back in the slightest.

She's ready.

And once she's settled face down on the mattress, I'm ready too.

I grab the silky hem of her garden-party dress and slowly drag it up her thighs. She's wearing nylons. The kind with garters, of course. And this is so fuckin' sexy, I take a step back and just look at her. Those creamy thighs. The way the elastic of the hose is tight around her leg and how it cuts into the skin just the slightest bit.

Her panties are white, as are the garters. And they are silky. I slip my fingers between her legs, massaging her until those pretty panties are all wet and she lets out a moan.

Then I push them aside and push my finger into all that slick juice.

I lean in, rubbing my cock on her hip as I finger her. She's breathing hard, her hands balled up into fists as they grip the comforter on the bed.

I pull her panties down, just enough to expose her ass cheeks, and then I slap them. Once on each side. A loud crack sounds off twice in nearly the same moment and Rosie lets out a gasp. And when I look down, her cheeks are bright red with my handprints.

"Sometimes even a good girl needs a good spankin'."

She laughs a little, trying to look over her shoulder so she can find my eyes. I lean down, covering her, grinding my cock into her ass, and press my mouth against her shoulder, giving it a little bite.

Another gasp, but this time it's more of a hiss.

But she doesn't tell me to stop. In fact, when she turns her head so we're eye to eye, she says, "Do it again."

"Which part? The spankin' or the bitin'?"

"Both." And then she spreads her legs wider, and stretches her arms up the bed, and arches her back.

Daring me? Teasing me?

Doesn't matter. All I see is an invitation.

I take a step back, lift her skirt back up to reveal her ass, place both my hands on her hips and bend down. Dragging her panties down with me.

Her legs are spread too wide to take them all the way down to her knees, but I like 'em half on, half off. It's sexy.

I lean in, bite her ass cheek—hard. Hard enough to make her hiss again—and then spread her cheeks and give her a lick.

She about loses her mind right here. She starts wiggling and fussing. But I was counting on that and I give her a quick slap across her left cheek. Her round ass was beginning to pale after the last one, but now it brightens up all red again.

I slap the other side, evening things up. And then slip my fingers between her legs and fuck her until she's panting, and writhing, and begging for my dick.

"Fuck me," she's saying. "Fuck me."

And I'm tellin' her, "I am, Rosie. I am." But she wants my cock.

And this is what she tells me next. "I want your dick, Amon. I want you inside."

"And I want you to come all over my fingers, Rosie. Then, and only then, will you get the cock."

She wriggles. Hard enough that I have to step back and let her move. Her hands are still bound as she turns to face me, but she hops up on the bed and then opens her legs for me. "If that's how you want it, then that's how I want it." She nods her head to her open legs and then she lowers herself back onto the bed.

I smile at her audacity. And I am happy to oblige. My hands find their way between her knees, opening them up wider. Then I reach for those silky panties and rip them right down the middle.

Her pussy is manicured and pretty. It's glistening with her desire and her little button is all swollen and engorged with blood, ready for my lips to grab it and suck.

I lean down and the moment I start licking her, she goes wild. Her hands gripping my hair, her legs clamping against my head, and her back arching up. She is moaning, and panting, and acting like a wild woman.

I suck on those juices, licking her and lapping at her like I'm eating ice cream.

Her orgasm is nearly immediate and I watch her face— eyes closed tightly—as she clenches her teeth and lifts her chin up as the wave of pleasure floods her body.

When she's done, she lets out a long breath and opens her eyes back up. Smiling at me.

I stand up, pump my dick a few times, then grab her hips and pull her towards me. My dick slides inside her, the walls of her pussy gripping me tight, and then I fuck her.

Hard, thrusting into her. Then soft, leaning down on top of her so I can bite her nipples as I squeeze her breasts.

I fuck her until she's whining, and moaning, and sweaty, and spent.

And then I fuck her some more. Pulling out at the last minute so I can come all over her thighs.

I stare at her, catching my breath, and then I get a towel from the bathroom, make it all warm, and clean her up. When that's done, I bend down and release her garters, pulling the ripped panties away from her body, and then I stand her up and take off her dress and bra.

She undresses me too, telling me to sit down in the nearest chair as she takes off my shoes and socks. Then she offers me her hand, stands me up, and slides my pants down.

When we're both naked, she grabs me by the cock, gives it a nice tug, and leads me over to the bed. We get in, and I pull her on top of me, and we have a nice slow fuck with lots of kissing.

This time the climax is more subdued. Quieter, for sure. But nicer too. Because she lets me come inside her this time and when we're both done, she slides off to the side and we just fall asleep in each other's arms.

ROSIE

*I*n the morning Amon pulls me into the shower. It's early, like way too early. Four a.m. early. But it's Sunday. Revival day. And not just any Revival day, but Fourth of July Revival day. Which means we gotta be back in Disciple by eight so I can be ready for the show.

While we're in the shower I feel this urgency to hurry. But he's soaping me up, and caressing those bubbles all up and down my body, and I just don't have the willpower to make him stop. So when he pushes me up against the wall and presses his cock into my ass, I don't even think about telling him no.

Last night was glorious. And I want to be with this man forever and ever. And let him take me any way he wants. *Any way* he wants. Because after last night I know something new about him. I know that he will make the sex exciting, and he will make me nervous—but he will not hurt me. Ever.

Amon Parrish might be a dangerous man to some, but he's not to me.

I FALL ASLEEP AS SOON as we get on the highway, and I stay asleep until we come to a stop and Amon is gently pushing on my shoulder.

"Wake up, Rosie. We're home."

I look up, wondering which home, and see that we are idling in front of Lowyn's house in town. I let out a sigh, desperately wishing there was no Revival today, but that's when I see the porch is covered in boxes. "What's that?" I ask, pushing wild hair out of my eyes with one hand and pointing to the porch with the other.

Amon has a scheming glint in his eye when I look at him. And he's grinning like a fool. "That, dear Rosie, is a costume change."

I gasp. Loud. And my eyes go wide. "What?"

"A costume change."

I look around, confused. "Well... Lowyn doesn't live here. I live here."

Amon laughs. "I know. That's why the boxes are on the porch."

I point to myself, blinking and still confused. "Those boxes are for *me*?"

"Of course they are. Why do you say it like that?"

"Because... well"—I take a deep breath—"I'm not a star. I'm a side character. I've never had a starring role in my life. And side characters don't need costume changes."

Amon pulls the truck into my driveway and shuts it off. Then he reaches for me. "Oh, Rosie. There has never been a woman more deserving of a starring role than you."

"You did this?" I laugh. "This is a date, isn't it?"

"It's a date. I asked Jim Bob to make it happen."

I squint a little. "In return for what?"

"For me coming back to the Revival."

"And you agreed!"

"Why wouldn't I? It's not a hardship, that's for sure. I mean, I'll be spending every weekend with you. And"—he opens his door—"we're the stars of the show. So how fun is that?"

I'm still processing this as he closes the door and walks around to my side to open mine. "But"—he waves his hand, inviting me to step out. I get out—"but Grimm and Taylor are the stars. There's a great big story going with the two of them. And she's pregnant and he's..."

I stop.

Amon laughs.

"Oh, my God. Jim Bob did *not* write a trampy single mother into the Revival!"

Amon's still laughing. "Well, I don't know. He didn't tell me, but knowing Jim Bob, and after what he did to Collin—"

"I'm a trampy single mother! Oh, Taylor was so pissed off about this role. She hates Grimm already, and this—well, let's just say that Jim Bob plays up everybody's bad side. He was getting all hot about it. So does that mean I have to hate you and be pregnant with your baby?"

Amon could not smile any bigger. "I doubt that, Rosie. But the only way to know for sure is to open all those packages and read the new script."

I look at the porch again. There are so many boxes. Not crappy cardboard boxes, either. But really nice shiny, glossy boxes with satin ribbons. And at least one of them is very big.

"Come on." Amon takes my hand. "It's already seven-thirty. We need to get dressed. We've got a big day coming."

There are at least a dozen packages that we take inside and Amon places them in two piles. One for me and one for him. The huge box is in my pile.

I bite my lip, nearly bursting out of my skin with anticipation as I kneel down next to it and tug on that gorgeous satin ribbon the color of sparkling champagne.

It's a dress, obviously. But the box is big enough to hold a ball gown. I lift off the lid, pull the pretty tissue paper aside and nearly fall over backwards in shock.

I look at Amon, my mouth open.

He chuckles. "Take it out! Look at it! I wanna see it!"

"No, Amon. You don't understand."

"Understand what?"

"This"—I point to the dress in the box—"this is not just any dress. This is *the* wedding dress."

"*The* wedding dress?"

"*The* wedding dress. I'm getting married today!" I lift the dress out of the box and jump to my feet. Then I hold the dress up against my body. I look down at it, taking in all the details.

Every single bride in the Revival wears this dress. It's a long full skirt made of several layers of hand-beaded tulle and the bodice has a plunge neckline.

But every time we have a wedding in the show, MaisieLee adds a custom detail and the bodice has been completely covered in beads in a geometric chevron pattern.

I look over at Amon, my expression all serious. "Now, listen. If you're not the groom, I'm not playing. So open those boxes and let's make sure because you know how much Jim Bob likes to stir the pot."

Amon kinda scoffs. "Oh, I would kill that fucker if he pulled that on me." But we both know Jim Bob likes the drama and if this murder scene happened inside Revival grounds, he'd die happy. So Amon grabs his biggest box and pulls on his satin ribbon. We both lean in, holding our breath as he takes the lid off and pulls the tissue paper aside.

"A suit." And he says these two words with relief.

"A very nice suit," I add. Made out of very fine cream-colored linen.

Amon takes out all three pieces. Trousers, a vest, and a coat.

But there are a ton of boxes to open and we set about doing this like we are kids on Christmas morning, tearing them open and throwing the packages aside.

By the time we're done he's got a shirt, a tie, cufflinks, a hat, shoes, socks, and braces.

And I've got a bouquet, a Juliet cap wedding veil, several strings of pearls in varying lengths, fancy new lingerie, and shoes.

The dress might be the same, but the accessories are all new. If you're a bride in the Revival, you get to keep the accessories. And mine are lovely. The bouquet isn't real flowers, but silk ones. They are tiny pink and cream rosebuds set in a mound and surrounded by beads. The center of each flower has a delicate pearl and there are strands of silver, white, and gold pearls hanging from it.

I hold the bouquet to my chest, knowing I can keep it forever. Amon is smiling at me when I look over at him. "It's stupid, right? To be this excited about a fake wedding?"

He comes over to me, placing his hands on my hips, looking down at me like I might really be his bride. "It's not stupid, Rosie. And it's only as fake as we let it be. I mean, Simon is a real preacher. If we say the vows and mean them, then is it fake?"

I was holding my breath for that and now it comes out in a rush. "I don't know."

He leans down and kisses me. "Come on, let's get ready. I've never been so excited to get to a Revival in all my life."

"Wait! What about Cross? Oh, my God, we have to go get him or he'll miss it!"

"Nah. You're crazy. Collin's bringing him. Lowyn's coming too."

"You knew this was a wedding?"

"I didn't. But I got a text from Collin this morning before we left the Dixie Yonder and he said he and Lowyn would be there and bring Cross."

I relax and my whole body gets warm. It's not real. Amon never asked me to marry him and anyway, it's just a show. But I agree, it's as real as we make it. And maybe we won't be signing no marriage license when we're done, but I'm sold on this man. I'm in.

AMON **and I are barely dressed** and ready when the call to Revival sounds. And then, a moment later, he's got my hand and he's leading me out the door. As soon as we get outside a horn honks and I about lose my mind when I see Collin and Lowyn sitting in Old Man Hunt's 1933 Rolls Royce Phantom II.

Again, this is the car we always use for special scenes like this so it shouldn't feel special. But it does. Because all of this fuss is being made over Amon and me. And I have never ridden in the Phantom as the star, only as a friend of the star.

Amon laughs. "Well, this looks familiar."

Collin winks at him. "Doesn't it though?"

Amon looks around. "Where's Ryan and Nash? They didn't wanna come?"

"I told them about the little problem with the mine," Collin says. "And Ryan's eager to tear that thing apart. So he's on that today and Nash is helping."

"Perfect." Then Amon opens the back door of the car and beckons me to get in with a flourish of his hand. "Your chariot, my bride."

"Oh, Rosie!" Lowyn exclaims. "You look amazing in the dress. A Revival wedding. We haven't had one of these in years!" She winks at me. "I'm jealous."

I get in the car and scoot over to make room for Amon, but I wink at Lowyn. "Now you know how I felt when you had your big day."

Lowyn lets out one of those blissful sighs, like she's picturing her big day right now. "What a lovely time we had. Didn't we, Collin?"

I catch a side view of Collin smirking as he looks back at Amon. "I hope you've got your dancin' shoes on."

Amon just puts his arm around me and tugs me a little

closer to him, whisperin' in my ear, "This is gonna be a great day."

"Oh! Where's Cross?"

"I dropped him off earlier," Collin says. "He needed a costume. But don't worry, he'll be there, Rosie. He wouldn't miss it for the world."

"I hope he hasn't been giving you any trouble out at the compound," I say.

Lowyn turns in her seat to look at me. "Oh, he's such a nice boy. And he's been outside the whole time, doing things with the men and the dogs. I think he really likes it out there, Rosie."

I let out a sigh of relief. "I imagine he does."

The next thing I know we're pulling into the special parking space outside of the security tent and everything starts happening at once.

All my girls are waiting for me, and they rush the car. April, Taylor—who is probably extra relieved that she is not the bride today—MaisieLee, MacyLynn, Bryn, and all of Amon's sisters, Eden, Angel, Vangie, and Halo.

On the men's side it's Grimm—also probably relieved that he is not the groom—Ethan Sardis, Jacob Wonder, Cross, and all my brothers, Pate, Rush, Ash, and Lecter.

Amon grabs hold of my hand just as the girls open my door and start tugging on me and his men open his door and start tugging on him. But Amon and I lock eyes and hold tight to each other for as long as we can.

Then we break apart, laughing. And we are ushered into our respective spaces for some pre-wedding antics.

Revival weddings are a big deal and if you're lucky enough to be a guest at one, then you get all the bells and whistles that come with it. This includes the reception, of course, but also the bride and groom parties. Which is just a little celebration before the main event so all the ladies can see my dress up close and all the men can toast Amon while gently chiding him on the new ball and chain.

The bride's tent is nearly overflowing with people—mostly out-of-town guests. But I don't mind. I've never been the center of attention at any Revival show for more than a few seconds. I do typically get cast as a scene starter, so I do have my moments, but that's just it. They are literally moments. Just enough time to say something like, "There he is! That's Collin Creed, the murderer!"

So I've made people gasp probably hundreds of times at this point. But these gasps were not about me. The focus was on the other person.

But right now, everyone in this tent is looking at me with sparkling eyes and shining smiles. Me. This whole day is about me.

And Amon Parrish made it happen.

"Look!" April is shoving the *Revival News* in my face. "You guys are on the front page!"

My eyes are dartin' all over that page for a few seconds, trying to take it all in. *The Harlow Parrish Wedding*, the headline says. And it's got pictures of us—both of which were taken during Collin and Lowyn's big Revival party so we look extra special cute. There's a whole fake story to go with it that I don't have time to read, but I will be framing this page and puttin' it up on a wall somewhere so I can look at it daily. My mouth drops open and I just shake my head as I look at April. "Who? How? Jim Bob was pissed about yesterday!"

"Apparently not, because this is quite special. You're gonna have to frame it," Lowyn says. Like she's reading my mind. "Put it up on the wall and save it forever. Because this is your day, Rosie. It's not fake." She presses her lips together and shakes her head. "No, ma'am. This is real."

She hands me the paper and then I am pushed toward a chair and told to sit while they fuss over me, touching up my make-up and tucking stray bits of hair into my Juliet cap.

This is when the dream catches up to me. Not in the bad way, like you're delusional and you suddenly wake up, but in the good way when you realize there's more to this world and to this life than you thought. Because when I look at this fake article on the front page of this fake newspaper, I see so clearly how I ended up with a fake life filled with costumes and acting parts.

It's in my blood.

I'm just... a performer.

And the fact that there is a word for me—'performer'—it matters. It makes a difference. It means I'm not weird. It means I'm... artistic. Or something. I'm creative.

Lowyn purses her lips and says, "Pucker up, Rosie. Let me see if you're glossy enough."

To which I say, "Do you think I could write things like this?" while holding up the paper.

"What?" Lowyn looks a little startled. "What do you mean? Like articles?"

"No." I get frustrated for a moment because I'm still trying to sort out what I mean. "Like... stories."

Lowyn's eyebrows go up. "Fiction?"

I snap my fingers and point at her. "Yes. That. Do you think I could write fiction?"

She makes a look of confusion. "Well... don't you? I mean, isn't that what the *Busybody* is?"

I lean back in my chair. "Yes. It is. But I mean... like *books*." My voice goes low for that last word. Almost a whisper. Like I'm embarrassed to say it or maybe ashamed to think that maybe I could do something as big as writing a book.

"Books?" Lowyn looks a little taken aback.

Which doesn't bode well. So I brace for it. I mean, I am a high school dropout, even if I did get that GED. I put up a hand. "Never mind. It's a dumb idea. Single-mother high-school dropouts don't become authors. That's stupid."

"Now hold on here." Lowyn stands up and puts her hands on her hips. "You can do anything you put your mind to, Rosie Harlow. I mean, look at you. You run a printing press, you raised a very nice boy, you manage a semi-famous vintage store, and you still find time to help Bryn out during the lunch rush at the inn two days a week. If you think you can write a book, well, that book is as good as written." Then she nods her head and smiles at me, like the whole matter is settled. "Now let's get you fake-married so we can move on to the fake party. I've got my dancing shoes on and I might even have a drink to celebrate your fake happily ever after."

Which makes me, and all the girls around me, laugh.

But as I get up and let them hustle and bustle me out of the bride's tent and over towards the Revival tent, I have to wonder just how fake this is.

Not just the marriage, either. But all of it. The tents, the show, the characters. And the funny thing is, we don't ever use fake names when we play out these fake stories. We always use our own names.

Maybe that's why I'm having a clash of realities right now?

Maybe this is just... who we are?

"I think we're circus people." I say this right out loud and April and Bryn are the closest to me.

Both of them laugh. "Oh, for sure," April says. "We might not be taming lions or flyin' on a trapeze, but we nailed it with the big tent."

All the girls start laughing. And then someone is talking about the last wedding we had for the Revival, which starred Lettie Gainer and Tommy Masters, the tractor mechanic down on Fourth and Rowan. There were bloodhounds involved in that and no one can quite remember why, so the conversation shifts as they try to recall details.

But I'm too stuck on my present to worry about anybody else's past.

As we approach the tent my father steps out. He's wearing a suit in the style of the Revival, a light brown instead of cream like Amon's. And he's smiling at me.

All my girls part and go their separate ways so when I stop it's just me and him. "Hi, Daddy."

He doesn't say anything at first. Just stands there, grinning. Then he takes both my hands, leans in, and kisses me on the cheek.

Which makes me blush and kinda giggle. "Thank you, Daddy. That was nice."

"My girl. I just can't get over it." He shakes his head. "You look just like your mother on the day I stood inside this same tent, in front of these same people, and said the same vows you're about to say with Amon. It's just… slipped by me, I think."

I huff a little. "Daddy. It's a show. Amon and I aren't getting real-married. It's just a date he set up with Jim Bob as part of our courtin'."

But my daddy is shaking his head no all the while I'm saying that. "That might be the official reason for this wedding, but it's not fake, is it? It's real."

I chuckle. "Well, maybe."

"No maybe. He's your one, isn't he, Rosie?"

I sigh, then look past his shoulder where I can see Amon standing on the stage in front of Pastor Simon. He's watching me and my daddy, squinting his eyes a little like he's not sure what we're gettin' up to.

I look at my daddy again and nod. "I think he is. Yes. But we've only been at this a couple of weeks now, so this isn't the real wedding no matter how real it looks. I won't accept it."

Which makes my daddy laugh right out loud. "As you shouldn't, Rosie. As you shouldn't. Because your mother will never forgive me if I don't spring for the biggest private Revival wedding this town has ever seen. That woman gave birth to five children and only one of them came out a girl. You're gonna give her every one of her mother-daughter milestones, even if they happen out of order. Now." He looks me up and down and I can just tell that he's proud as punch of me. "Let's get you fake-married."

Then he offers me his arm, and I hook mine in his, and the music starts. My daddy starts forward but I can't seem to move. Everything catches up to me in this one moment and I'm suddenly confused. All my surety leaves me and even though I've been to dozens of Revival weddings and I've played my part for each and every one knowing it's just a show, I can't quite come to terms with what is happening.

We're a little behind the music now, but still my feet won't move and people are starting to whisper. Then a head pops out to the side of the aisle from the front row and I hear that voice. The one I know better than my own, the one I love the most, and the hardest, and the deepest. My son says, loud enough for everyone to hear, "You got this, Mom!"

There's a smattering of applause and a couple of encouraging whistles. So I take a deep breath. And he's right, I do have this. And the moment my daddy and I take that first step and start our walk up the sawdust aisle, everything about Revival stops being fake.

Maybe it's a dream. Maybe it's a lie. Maybe it's just a fuckin' circus.

But no one can deny that this really and truly is happening.

I'm watching Amon's face the whole time and he's wearing a look that I don't quite have the right word for. Happy doesn't even come close.

He looks like a man in love.

And the moment I realize this, I blush. Hard and hot.

Amon sees it, because he chuckles and his smile gets bigger.

The next thing I know, the walk is over, and my daddy is kissing my cheek and then Amon offers me his hand.

I take it and we face each other. This is when I glance

over to the bride's section and see my mama and she's crying her eyes out. My brother, Ash, has his arm around her shoulder and he's hugging her, but still looking at me, and suddenly I realize... not one damn thing about this wedding is fake. Hell, not one damn thing about this town is fake, either.

Disciple might not be your average town in Appalachia, but it's still very much real.

By the time I look back at Amon, Simon is already talking. And the next thing I know, Amon is staring at me with those blue eyes of his and his mouth is moving and the loveliest words are spillin' out. These words being in the Revival wedding vow, of course.

"When the trying times come," Amon Parrish tells me, "we will hold hands. And when the heavy times come, we will walk them together. And when the depressing times come, and you feel the burden of life to be so vast and wide that you feel forsaken, I will be there to carry you. No matter how long it takes or how far we must travel, no matter how many miles it be, I will carry you, Rosie Harlow. I will carry you."

To which I reply, "I know you will, Amon Parrish. I know you will."

And that's all there is to a wedding vow here in Disciple. He promises to carry me and I promise to trust him to do that.

"Amon," Pastor Simon says, "you may kiss your bride."

I *kiss Rosie Harlow* like she really is my wife. Because in my eyes, we did get married. It's a done deal. Oh, we'll be doin' it again, for sure. And it'll be a lot bigger than this. It'll happen on a Wednesday, not a Sunday, and there won't be a single stranger in the crowd.

But I'll happily take this day as a placeholder for that one.

Our kiss lasts just long enough for people to start laughing and clapping. Then, with a lot of reluctance, we pull apart. But not completely apart. I lean down a little so my forehead touches the top of her head and I whisper, just loud enough for Rosie to hear, "Mrs. Parrish, I do believe you are my wife."

Which makes her eyes smile.

But then it's over. There's more to a Revival wedding than the actual wedding. The party is the main attraction. And that starts now.

I take her hand. "Shall we?"

She nods as she puts her hand in mine. And then we run down the aisle, stopping at the edge of the sawdust so we can turn and she can throw the bouquet.

My sisters are wild for catching bouquets. I'm a hundred percent sure there is money on this toss, because they practically break out in a fight. There's actually a moment when Vangie is on top of Halo, but then someone pulls her off and Halo stands up, bouquet in hand, arms stretched high, grinning like a winner.

Everyone claps.

And then I lead Rosie over to Old Man Hunt's 1933 Rolls Royce Phantom II—which is the only vehicle ever allowed to operate on Revival grounds during a show—and we get in. Our chauffeur is Old Man Hunt himself. He looks back at us and tips his hat. Then we roll, goin' about five miles an hour down the dirt road between storefront tents, and all the Disciple children jog along beside us.

We end up at the tea party tent—which has been transformed into the wedding reception tent—and we get out and stand at the front like every dutiful bride and groom, greetin' people as they pass by.

There are several hundred people here today so we stand there a good hour saying hello, but once that's done, the band starts playing—a bluegrass band, of course—and we have our first dance to the tune of 'Can the Circle Be Unbroken,' which is neither slow nor fast. But since every child in Disciple takes dancin' classes from the age of three to twelve, I break into a nice little flatfoot dance, which is something halfway between clogging and tapping.

Rosie knows more steps than I do, so she doesn't even blink at my choice. And pretty soon the whole tent is clapping along. But as soon as that song ends, our first dance officially over, there is a mad rush for the dance floor and we spend the next couple of hours jigging around elbow to elbow, even breaking into a few more formal square dances every now and then.

It's a party and everyone's having fun. But eventually, six

o'clock comes and this means that the Revival is officially over and all the guests who are not performers need to go.

So the festivities wind down and Rosie and I stand at the front gate like a good bride and groom and thank everyone for coming.

It takes a while for the grounds to be cleared out, but eventually it quiets down and we walk, hand in hand, to the park by the river in the back of the grounds where everyone is hanging out for the fireworks show.

The tourists are welcome to stay in town for this part of the show, and most of them do. But it's been a long day for us and that's why the park is here. It's a place for us, the townspeople and performers in this show we call the Revival, to be alone.

"That was nice," Rosie says.

And I just smile. "Rosie, I can't remember the last time I had this much fun. I mean, when Collin and Lowyn had their fun day, it was pretty cool. Especially since I was newly home again. But today beats that out hands down. I think I owe Jim Bob a pretty big favor to make up for this."

"So you really did plan all this as a date?"

When I look down at her, her eyes are wide. "I really did."

"And now what? I mean…" She shrugs up one shoulder. "We've done all the towns now. You've visited me—in costume—at every single one."

"Well… if you don't have a next step in mind, then I'll just tell you what I'm thinking. I'm thinking you and Cross move in with me and we do this day all over again at some point in the future. Only this time, we do it legal."

She lets go of my hand so she can grip my arm, and then

she hugs it, leaning her head on my shoulder. "I think that's a pretty good idea."

"Even the movin' in part? I figured that'd be a stickin' point with you since you're so... you know, independent."

"Well, if that were my house and not Lowyn's I might tell you to move in with me. But it's not. And that house of yours really is yours. So I think that's where we belong."

"That's good—"

"Hey." Rosie interrupts me, looking around. "Where's Cross?"

I look around as well. "Hmm. Must be with those friends of his."

"No." Rosie is looking at a group of kids off to the left, all about Cross's age. "Those are his friends right there." She puts a hand on my shoulder. "Hold that thought about the shacking up." We both chuckle. "I'm just gonna go ask them where he is. BRB."

I wait, watching as she walks away, appreciating her back view. Even this late in the day, she looks gorgeous in that dress. I'm just starting to daydream about how I might take it off her when we get home when she reaches the group of kids, all of whom stand at attention. There is some nodding, then some head shaking. Every one of them begins looking around.

And watching this, even unable to hear what they are saying, I know something is wrong and my stomach clenches up with dread.

"Cross!" Rosie starts calling for him. The sound is distant from here, but still plenty loud and I can hear the restrained panic in her voice. "Cross!"

Then she's rushing in my direction and I'm meeting her halfway. "What's wrong?"

"He's missing, Amon. Cross is missing. His friends haven't seen him since the wedding ended."

"What?" Now I look around too. "But that was like six hours ago." I walk over to the kids, who are still standing at attention. "When was the last time you saw Cross? And I want specifics."

They all start talking at once, but they're all saying the same thing so I don't bother telling them to go one at a time. "The last time we saw him," a tall boy with freckles says, "was inside the church. Right about the time your sisters were fighting for the bouquet."

I turn back to Rosie and she's about to scream. "Don't panic."

"Don't panic! What the hell was I thinking? I have a stalker pretending to be my son's father and I didn't have eyes on him today! I just…" She scoffs. "I just went about my day, pretending to get married, and now my son is missing! So do not tell me not to panic, Amon Parrish! I am not overreacting!"

"No, that's not what I meant, Rosie."

"Cross!" She's not listening to me. In fact, she starts running off, back to the Revival grounds.

I realize in this same moment that it's gotten dark. Not just twilight, but actual dark, and this is the signal for the fireworks to start. The shrieking whistles of the launch followed by the booming of light and sizzle of burning explosives overpowers her desperate calls. And this makes her panic for real. She stops in place, bending over as she yells his name.

People come running, realizing that something is wrong, and I'm just... stuck here.

Again.

Just like I was in the cafeteria that day.

Unable to do anything but watch.

Two hours later there is still no sign of Cross. We're sitting out on Rosie's porch, watching people walk by and listening as they all call Cross's name.

Rosie is beyond comforting. Even now, sitting on the front steps, she is on edge. Leaning forward, unable to relax.

I rub her back, but she stiffens. "Don't. I don't want to be touched right now, Amon. My boy is missing."

The only reason she came home was to change out of her dress, so now she's wearing her typical summer outfit of shorts and a tank top. The only reason she's here and not out there yelling with the rest of them is because Abel Bettington, the police chief, told her Cross might try and call the landline so someone needed to be there to answer.

It's actually a very good point because the landline is harder to trace. Though Collin is already on that and it won't be that way for long. He's also called in our whole company of men to help with the search, but we both know we're not gonna find Cross.

Not like that.

The hours tick off, people start to go home. And a little bit past midnight, Abel comes.

We both stand up, Rosie wringing her hands as she waits to see what he's got to say.

Abel takes off his hat before he speaks to her. "Rosie, we're all going home now and we'll pick it up when it gets light out."

"No!" She stays this emphatically. "If you guys go home, I'll go looking."

Abel shakes his head. "He's not *here*, Rosie. We've been through the whole town. We've searched every house, we've been up in the woods. Whoever took him took him *away*."

She's about to lay in to him, but I step in front of her. "Thanks, Abel. Collin will probably keep our guys stationed around town just in case, if that's all right."

Probably, normally, this would not be all right. But Abel's in no position to argue. So he just nods at me and looks to Rosie. "I'll be here at first light. We'll call in the Feds, we'll do whatever it takes, Rosie. I promise."

There will be no Feds. Edge Security is gonna handle this. But none of us are in any mood to hammer out specifics, so I let it go and Abel turns and walks back the way he came.

"Come on. We should go inside and get some rest too." I take Rosie's hand, but she shakes me off.

"*No*, Amon. I'm staying right here on this porch. I'm not going inside and sleeping. Not while my son is missing." She's not looking at me when she says this. And there's a moment of silence after she finishes. But then I hear her whisper, "Erol. This is Erol." She turns to me now, eyes wide and red. "He took him. He came here to take him and he's done. And he's gonna get away with it, too. Because he knows how to disappear. He's done it before. How hard could it be? I'm never gonna see my son again, Amon. Never."

She and I stare at each other for a few moments. And I want to tell her that it's not Erol. Because Erol is dead.

But I know better than most that dead men don't always stay that way. Not because of anything supernatural, but because there are really two levels to this world we live in.

Two totally different realities. There are people who live in this one, the one we're in. The one that has rules and regulations. The one that has congressional hearings. The one that has consequences.

And then there's the world underneath. The black one. The secret one. The one run by men like Charlie Beaufort and filled with others like Collin Creed.

And me.

I lived in that other world for nearly a decade before it came apart at the seams, so I know it's there. And I know that when a man goes missing and comes back dead when you run a background check a dozen years later, it's just paperwork.

That's all it is. Just paperwork.

I *SPEND THE NIGHT SITTIN'* on the porch steps, leaning my head against the railing as Rosie sits in the glider behind me.

She stays up for a good while, but when I look over my shoulder around four a.m., I find her slumped over and sleeping.

Erol is not dead. This has to be him. What other reason could there be to take this boy?

I stand up, debate with myself on the pros and cons of trying to rouse Rosie and get her up to bed, and decide to let her be. She's exhausted, scared, and sad. The last thing she needs is for me to interrupt her sleep.

But I need to stay awake and my eyes are getting heavy, so I quietly go inside, being careful not to let the screen door slap, and rustle up myself a cup of coffee.

I check on Rosie, find her still sleeping, and then decide to take a look in Cross's bedroom for clues because I suddenly realize that's something we forgot to do. Rosie was convinced it was Erol right away, so it's not like we started thinking he was a runaway and needed secret information he might've been hoarding.

Clearly, this was a kidnapping.

Or was it?

So I go into the room, flick on the light, and find a twelve-year-old boy's room. There's a messy stack of homework on the desk, clothes everywhere, unmade bed, and it smells like a locker room.

My nose crinkles up in protest, and I'm just about to turn around and flick the light back off because this room is really none of my business when I spy something familiar yet out of place on the desk.

I reach for the paper and realize it's the first puzzle Erol sent to Rosie. The one she never showed me because it's been here at the house the whole time. This one is an extreme dot-to-dot puzzle. It doesn't have numbers, but letters in what looks to be a couple of different languages at least.

I don't know any of these languages—none of them are in English—but it doesn't matter because the puzzle has been solved. The dots are connected. And it's not a picture. It's a message.

DEAR ROSIE,

I am not dead.

I need to talk to you.

Meet me our spot by the river. You remember where.

June nineteenth. Six p.m.

I'll explain everything.

THE FIRST PUZZLE was a letter to Rosie asking for a meeting —which she clearly missed because she didn't solve this puzzle, Cross did. My eyes flit across the desk looking for more clues, and sure enough, there's another envelope. This one is not addressed to Rosie, it's addressed to Cross, and there's no postmark. It was hand-delivered. There's also no letter. Whatever was sent, Cross took it with him.

Cross hasn't been here for days, so this letter came in before they came to stay with me. Before Rosie found that letter on her pillow.

She didn't look in Cross's room that night. No one looked in Cross's room that night. He got a letter too, we just didn't know it.

And this explains why he was so happy to come stay at

the compound and why he was so agitated for Friday night bowling, insisting that he was ready to grow up right now and do important things.

What if Erol was spying on us? What if Erol knew that Cross was antsy? What if the letter or puzzle he sent Cross was some kind of invitation?

If Erol Cross is coming up dead in Penny Rider's database, but isn't, in fact, dead, then he's military. He's black ops, just like we were.

Honestly, six months ago I'd have thought this idea to be ridiculous. Even though I was black ops and I know it's real, I would have a hard time thinking lightning might strike twice in the same place. I mean, what are the odds that some random missing boy was never missing at all, he was just recruited?

It's a movie plot.

But after Blackberry Hill, I'm not so sure it's actually that farfetched.

And if a boy of age twelve who is eager to make his way in the world gets an invitation from his missing daddy to join him in some secret something or other, might said boy find this to be a grand opportunity? And might said boy agree to meet this daddy of his to hear more about this exciting offer?

I turn around and blow out a breath.

This is what happened. Erol, sensing I was coming between him and using Rosie to get to his son, went straight to Cross instead.

Because he doesn't need Rosie to agree to anything if Cross wants to see his father. He does, after all, have some rights. Whether he deserves them or not is another story and there might be a fight in court. But if Erol is involved in things like Collin and I were involved in, and he's got the balls to show up like this… well. He's sorted out a deal. He's made plans and gotten them approved. He will fight and he will have powerful people on his side.

He could, in fact, just take Cross and leave Rosie behind.

This would tear Rosie Harlow in half.

She would never agree to it.

If Erol won the right to keep Cross, and he made her an offer to come with them, what would she do?

I huff out some air. Because I know damn well what she would do.

She would leave me so fast, my head would spin.

I FORCE **myself** to wait until seven a.m. before I call Collin. I figure I'll be waking him up, but he answers on the first ring and there's so much noise in the background, he's gotta yell. "Hello!"

"Collin?"

"What? Amon? Hold on a second." He must cover the phone because things get all muffled. And then the horrendous background noise abruptly cuts off. "Sorry," he says, kinda out of breath. "Amon, is that you?"

"Yes, it's me. I got a problem."

"We need to talk."

"I know. My problem—"

"No. I don't mean your problem. We gotta talk about this fuckin' mine."

I'm confused. "Mine? What?"

"*The* mine. The old mine. The one Sawyer was poking around that week?"

"Oh, right. I'd forgotten about that." I wave a hand in the air. "Forget the mine. Forget that asshole too. Cross is missing, Collin. We gotta get back on this."

"Oh, I know. I just sent twenty-five men back to Disciple so they can start searching."

"Right. Well—"

"Amon?"

"Amon?"

I turn and find Rosie standing in the front doorway looking all disheveled and blurry-eyed. I cup my phone with my hand. "Hey. The search is gonna get started soon—"

"They're not gonna find anything."

Despite the fact that I agree with her, I can't let her go down this path. So I say, "You don't know that, Rosie."

"I do. He took him. Erol took him. He's not dead. I don't care what your people say. He's just not. This is all him, I know it. I feel it in my soul."

"Amon!"

Collin is yelling at me so I put the phone back up to my ear. "What? Yeah. I'm here."

"I gotta go. We're opening up the mine. You need to get here."

"I can't, Collin. I gotta stay here with Rosie."

She breezes past me, heading towards her bedroom. "No, you don't, Amon. If Collin needs you, you should go. Because I'm gonna take a shower and go to work."

"Work?" I say this loud because I'm like… what the fuck? "You're not going to work, Rosie! Cross is missing."

She whirls around, angry. "He's not missing. We know who he's with. And he's not coming back until Erol brings him back. I need to get the hell out of this house, so I'm going to work at the diner. Because if I stay here I'm gonna cry my eyes out and lose my mind."

I don't say anything back to that and we just stare at each other for a second. Then she turns and goes up the steps to her bedroom.

"Amon!" Collin is yelling again.

"What? Yeah, I'm here."

"Get here! I'm telling you, you gotta see this."

"Wait!" I say this quickly because I know he's about to hang up.

"What?"

"Did you call Charlie?"

"About the mine? Fuck no."

"Oh, my God. Shut up about that fuckin' mine. The boy, Collin. Cross Harlow. Did you call Charlie and ask him to help us? Because at this point, I'm a hundred percent positive that Erol Cross is connected to this Blackberry Hill shit."

"No, Amon. I didn't call Charlie about Cross."

"Well, could you? Could you at least ask him to help us?"

Collin blows out a breath. "Well, of course. Yeah. But I don't know what he can do, Amon. This kid is not connected to us."

"He's connected to *me*, Collin."

"Well… I get that you and Rosie are kind of a thing. But Charlie Beaufort isn't gonna make waves in his little black-ops boardroom over a missing Disciple boy who is not yours, Amon."

I don't say anything. I know he's right, but I'm pissed about it. And when I'm pissed, it's better that I don't say anything.

Collin knows me well, so he gets this and starts backtracking. "Look, I don't mean it that way. But you know what I had to promise to get that man to help me save Lowyn. You know it was a bad deal, Amon."

"I don't care. I'll make that promise too. Just… call him. Just ask."

After a short pause, Collin relents with a sigh. "Fine. I'll call him right now and call you back."

The call ends and I exhale, then say a little prayer. Which I am not one to do, but it's just an automatic thing when shit starts going sideways. I go outside and pace the porch, wondering how yesterday could've been so fun and we were so happy and now everything is falling apart.

My phone buzzes and I answer. "Yeah."

Collin sighs, so I know it's bad news. "He said no. He's not gonna help. He said there's no scenario in which he could interfere here."

"Not even if I agreed to work for him on his personal projects?"

"He said it was out of the question. That he's replaced you already."

"What about you? You owe him ten hours."

"Yeah, I know. I asked him and he said he's got nothing for me right now. So he's saving me up for a rainy day, Amon. I'm sorry. He can't help. But if you really think this

Erol guy is connected to Blackberry Hill, then you should get up here."

"Why?"

"Because this mine isn't a mine, Amon. It's something else."

Just as he says that, Rosie comes out the door. "I'll call you back, Collin." Then I end the call and turn to Rosie. She's wearing her waitress uniform and her hair is all pulled up in the usual diner style.

She and I look at each other awkwardly for a moment. Then she says, "You can stay here. I'll be back around one." And that's it. She walks right past me and a minute later, she's backing out of the driveway.

I don't know what to do next, but I'm tired and I don't feel like going home because... well, I just have this bad feeling that if I leave here, I'll never come back.

So I go inside, get my coffee, and sit down on the couch to wait for news.

ROSIE

I feel like my life ended last night during those fireworks and what's walking around today is just some shell of what I was.

I am never gonna see my son again. I feel this in my soul.

And I'm floundering this morning at work. I can't take orders right, I can't pour coffee right, and everyone who comes in stops to look at me with pity eyes. Because of course, news travels fast around these parts and everyone in Revenant knows that Cross is missing.

Both Geraldine and Jonesy tell me to go home. It's slow, they don't need me.

But I can't go home. I can't. Not with Cross missing. I can't be in that house without him. So I tell them this and they nod, and look at me with sad eyes, and then Jonesy says, "Amon will get him back. Don't worry. He'll be back, Rosie."

Which does help, I do admit. Because I know that Amon's trying. I heard him this morning on the phone with Collin. It's just… well, maybe I didn't actually hear the conversation, but I can fill in the blanks just from his tone.

Amon said he was one hundred percent positive that my Erol is connected to Blackberry Hill. Just thinking about this makes me sigh because while I don't know the whole story about what happened up there—Lowyn didn't want to talk about it—I got lots of third- and fourth-hand gossip from all kinds of people after it happened.

Secret military bases. Underground tunnels or some such. Aliens. The gossip kinda turned into conspiracy theories at that point and stopped having any value, but while aliens might be a tick too far, underground tunnels actually make sense because there are tons of caves in West Virginia.

People always think they know everything because you go online and you look up caves and it pops up a list with a bunch of pictures. And we think to ourselves, *Well, that's that. Those are my choices for caving.*

But it's not true. For every one cave we know about there are probably a hundred that we don't. We think the internet is God, and it's not. It's just a collection of things that we put there. Like the inventory in Lowyn's shop.

So I would know this underground thing could be true even if my Aunt Ester hadn't told me once, a long time ago, about a girl Jim Bob needed to save up in the hills because she saw something she shouldn't have.

That was Lowyn the first time Ike had her, of course.

And isn't that something those Blackberry Hill people fancy doing? Taking people?

They did try and kidnap Olive.

"Why don't you go take a break, Rosie?"

"What?" I look up, sighing, and find Jonesy lookin' down at me with worry crinkles in his forehead.

"If you won't go home, at least take a break." He nods his head to the back door. "Go on. Go take a walk or something."

My mouth makes to form the word 'no' but I stop myself

from saying it. Because he's right. Being here isn't helping. So I take off my apron and nod my head. "All right. I'll just walk down to the river or something."

Jonesy places a comforting hand on my shoulder as I pass by him.

When I get outside it's bright, but quiet. Weekends around here are loud and long, so Monday mornings are always especially soft and slow. But I can hear the river and it's calling me, so I head across the street towards the teeny-tiny marina. Which is there mostly for atmosphere because Revenant modeled itself after a coastal town for reasons unknown to me. It's been this way my whole life, so probably this decision got made a hundred years ago, at least.

The only reason the town can pull this esthetic off is because the river has this weird bend in it right here where I'm headed. And this bend happens to be wide, relatively speaking. So on this bank it creates a little bay of sorts and this is where there are seven little sailboats tied up to the dock.

I can't recall a single time those boats actually went for a sail, but that's fairly typical when your town is a carnival and they're just props to begin with.

They look pretty, though. This whole part of Revenant is nice. There's a little cluster of shops—a fortune teller, an arcade, a taco place, and a tattoo parlor—and the storefronts all have custom signs with fancy hand lettering. So it comes off cute during the day.

At night, this place is filled with buskers all lit up with glowing neon face makeup and other performers who do things like fire juggling and street dancing.

It's a good time and since it's July fifth, I bet last night was a party.

I make my way over to a picnic table and sit down, leaning my elbows on the old wooden top so I can prop my chin in my hands. I just stare at the water and wonder where it all goes. Where it all comes from, for that matter. How there can be so much water that it just... flows like that.

A shadow appears to my right and when I look up, there is a man sliding his way around the other side of the table. He sits down across from me and waits, saying nothing.

He looks like any other man from these parts with his fair skin and blond hair. But I'd know those blue eyes anywhere.

Erol.

He speaks first. "Aren't you gonna say anything?" And then he has the audacity to smile.

This smile is like a gut punch. Because it's so familiar. I saw this smile in my dreams twelve years ago. Then, last night, I saw it in my nightmares.

I do not say anything.

"No?" He shrugs. "Well, that's fine, I guess." His accent is the same too. His voice, his lips, his mouth. "I've got plenty to say for the both of us, so I guess I'll just get to it."

Still, I say nothing.

"I've got Cross."

I suck in a breath when he says this and I am suddenly filled with so much hate and anger, I break out in a sweat.

"He's fine. In fact, he's better than fine. I didn't take him, ya know. I didn't. I just... made him an offer. One he couldn't refuse, I guess."

It's almost diabolical the way he says these words. All casual and with a smirk on his face.

But as the seconds tick off and I don't reply, this smug look falls and then he's frowning. "I didn't leave you, ya know."

"You lying piece of shit." My words come out angry and low. I nearly growl them out.

"I'm not lying."

"You left me. I was eight months pregnant and you got scared—"

"That's not what happened." He's loud now and he bangs his fist on the table, making me jump.

I lean back, eyes wide, thinking I should probably get up and run.

But then he sucks in a breath and lets it out slow. "That's not what happened, Rosie." His words are softer now. Like he lost control there for a moment, but he's reined it back in. "You can think whatever you want, but this is the first time they let me out to explain."

"Explain *what*, exactly?" I have not wrangled my control back, so these words come out angry and loud.

Suddenly he's reaching for me and I'm so startled by this that he's got a hold of both my hands before I can start pulling away. He doesn't let go when I resist, just holds them tighter like he's afraid I'll run. "Listen to me. I only have a couple of minutes before they turn the cameras back on."

"What? What the hell are you talking about?"

He nods his head up to the street lamps that are positioned every so often along the walkways. "They've got cameras all over this town and if I get made, then I'm done."

"Made for what?"

"I'm..." He stops and takes a breath. "It's gonna sound stupid, but I swear to God, this is the truth, Rosie. So I'm just gonna say it and you can do whatever you want with it. I didn't disappear. Not with you, anyway. You see... I was a runaway when I met you."

I'm so confused. "What?"

"I was on the run. I had escaped." He sighs again. "I mean, 'escape' is a little bit dramatic, but only a little. Because I was born into a family that... well." He nods his head at Revenant. "You get it, right? I mean, you're part of the Trinity too. It's just the public face, of course. So you don't understand what it really is."

I stand up, use every bit of strength in my little hundred- and twenty-pound body, and rip my hands from his grip. Then step out from the inside of the picnic table bench and glare down at him. "What are you talking about?"

He stands up too. "I'm talking about Blackberry Hill. I'm talking about what's underneath Blackberry Hill. I'm from there. I was born there." And then he points to the ground.

Which makes me look at the ground. And while I'm doing that I'm thinking that gossip back when Collin rescued Lowyn from Ike Monroe.

Underground military bases.

I look back up at Erol. "It's real?"

He exhales out a smile. It's a small one, but that just makes it more attractive. "It's real. You have no idea what this place is." He pans a hand in the direction of Revenant behind me. "All of it. Disciple, Bishop, and Revenant. They're just... cover, Rosie. And I was born into Blackberry Hill the same way you were born into Disciple. You grew up playing your part and I grew up playing mine."

I sit back down. Because I don't know what to say and my legs are feelin' weak. Of all the things I imagined happening to this man who used to be the boy I loved, 'underground military base' never even made the top million.

"So, on my seventeenth birthday, I ran away," Erol continues. "I went to New York. I went to Boston. I went all kinds of places. And I figured it was safe. They didn't come get me. So I came back this way, took a job, and met a really pretty girl who just blew my mind. And we fell in love—"

"Stop it!" I yell it. "Just stop. You're a liar."

"I'm not lying."

"You're not lying now, or you weren't lying then? Because you told me you were from Fayetteville! That you were trapping beavers or something."

"Well, what else was I gonna say? That I grew up in an underground military base that literally exists under your feet? That I ran away because I have no choice but to work for them? Because I was born into it? I mean, at least you people out here get a choice. You can leave if you want. You choose to stay, Rosie. I never got that choice. I guess they figured they'd let me run for a year. But only a year. Because on my eighteenth birthday, as you well know, they came for me and took me back."

"You've been underground this whole time? All twelve years of my son's life? And you didn't once think to maybe write a letter?"

"Don't you get it?" He's growling at me now. But I'm not afraid of him, so he can growl all he wants. "I'm not allowed to leave. I'm not allowed to talk to people on the outside.

I'm not allowed to do anything but exist in the little bubble I was born into."

I scoff. "Well, for someone who isn't allowed to do any of that, you sure did find a way to stalk me with letters."

"With puzzles."

I place both my hands over my face and scrub them down my cheeks, trying to pull myself together. When I manage that, I pull them away and look Erol in the eyes. "What do you want me to do in order to get Cross back? Because that's why you're here, right? You want something from me and whatever it is, you knew I'd say no. So you took my son as insurance. And I would just like to be upfront with you here, you are an *evil* son of a bitch, Erol Cross, for using my son like this."

"Come with me."

"What?"

"Come with me, Rosie. Be with me. We can all be together. I talked to them. I worked it out. They love Cross—"

"*What!*"

"They want him to join. You did a good job. And of course he's half mine, so he's half Blackberry Hill, too.'"

"What the hell kind of delusion are you living in, Erol? I'm not going anywhere with you! I want my son back and I want him back right now!" I pound the table with my fist and stand up again. "*Right now!*"

He pulls out a phone and before I can ask what he's doing, he's got it on speaker and it's ringing. The call is picked up on the first ring. "Daddy?"

My heart sinks. And Erol is watching. His eyes are

locked on mine when my son's voice comes through the phone calling him 'Daddy.' I shake my head.

But Erol doesn't care what I'm feeling. "It's me, son. I've got your mama here. She wants to hear all about what you're doin'."

"Oh, Mom! This place is great! Did you know there's a city underground? Right underneath Disciple! It's got everything down here. I love it. And I've got my own gun now!"

"Isn't that great, Rosie?"

Erol and I are still lockin' eyes. And I don't know what to say. What does a woman say when something like this— something so unbelievable, extraordinarily improbable—is happening in real time? What can she say?

"When are you getting here, Ma?"

"When am I getting there?"

"Yeah! Daddy says we're gonna live down here now."

I turn away and the tears are falling down my cheeks before I can stop them.

"All right, Cross. I'll be back soon and I'll see you then. Your mama will come tomorrow, OK?"

"All right, Daddy! See ya tomorrow, Ma!"

The call ends and there's a bit of silence. But then Erol says, "You've got twenty-four hours. That's all the time I could talk them into. I'll call you on your house phone at noon tomorrow and we'll make arrangements."

I don't look at him and my words come out as a whisper. "And if I say no?"

He scoffs behind me. "You're not gonna say no. We both know that."

Then he walks away and all I can do is watch him.

AMON

I'm still sitting on the porch when Rosie pulls into the driveway. I stand up and meet her at the car. "You left work early? It's only ten o'clock."

She doesn't look at me. Just walks right by me. "I'm going upstairs to bed. You should go home, Amon."

"What? No. I'm not going home. I'm staying right here with you. The search has started again—"

Rosie whirls around so fast, I stop talking. "They're not gonna find him, Amon. The search is pointless. He's with Erol. And he's not coming back."

"You don't know that."

"I *do* know it." She's glaring at me. Like I did something wrong. Or… like something happened.

"What aren't you telling me?"

Rosie sucks in a deep breath, then slowly lets it out. "Erol. I saw him. We talked."

"What? Where? When did this happen?"

"Just a little while ago. In Revenant. Jonesy told me to take a walk because I was acting like a zombie, I guess. So I went down to the river and Erol showed up."

"What did he say?"

She shrugs. "He's got Cross. He took him. He even called him on the phone and let me talk to him."

"To Cross? What did he say?" Rosie laughs, but a tear

slips out and starts rolling down her cheek. "Rosie?" I pull her in and give her a hug. "It's OK. It's gonna be OK. We're gonna get him back."

But Rosie is shaking her head. "He doesn't wanna come back, Amon. He's happy this happened. He's happy as can be. Erol got him a gun. His daddy is back in his life and he got him a gun! What more could this boy want?"

"Well... we'll just go get him. Where are they staying?"

"You don't understand, Amon." She stops crying now and wipes the tears off her cheeks. "You don't understand. Erol? He's part of Blackberry Hill. Cross is with *them*."

I turn around and stare at the valley across the street. I *knew* it.

"That's not all, either. It's much worse than that. Because this Blackberry Hill is some kind of secret military thing. There's like... a city underground." I turn back and she points to her feet. "Under us, Amon. There's some kind of secret city underneath us. And we all know that Lowyn saw something up there when she festival-married Ike and that's why she wanted to leave. That's what started that whole thing. So I don't care if you don't believe me, this is real. There's something weird and wrong going on here and my son is now a part of it. Do you know what Erol said? He said Cross is half his. Cross is half Blackberry Hill and he belongs with them. And it's not even a lie."

"Rosie—" I take a step towards her, ready to hug her again.

But she puts up a hand. "Don't. Just... just go home. Because it's over, Amon."

"What's over? Nothing's over."

"We're over." And she says this so seriously, my heart

feels like it just got stabbed with a pitchfork. "We're *over*. Because he said that I can come with them."

"What does that even mean, Rosie?"

"Tomorrow. He said he'll call me at noon tomorrow to get my answer and then he'll pick me up and I can go to Blackberry Hill and be with him and Cross."

"But—"

"Oh, trust me. I would rather stay with you. But this is my *son*, Amon." She shakes her head. "He's my whole life. I cannot choose a man over my son, even if that man is you."

"So you're just… what, gonna go? Gonna give in? That's not the answer, Rosie."

"Then what's the answer? You tell me. What do I do? Because he's got him, Amon. He's got my boy and not only that, my boy *wants* to be there. He's not coming home! That's his daddy. This is like a fairy tale coming true to that kid. His father returns after twelve years and not only that, he's some kind of secret military guy?" Rosie scoffs. "There's no way he's coming back to Disciple. Not now. Not after seeing the secret underground city." Now she laughs. "It's so ridiculous, I can't believe those words just came out of my mouth. But there it is. That's what's happening. And you should leave now because I'm just gonna go upstairs and cry all day and I don't want anyone around while I do that."

Then she pushes past me, walks up the porch steps, throws the door open, goes inside, and slams the door closed behind her.

Then there's a click. The tell-tale click of that door being locked.

My head hangs low and I play back what just happened.

Surely, this is some kind of dream. And if I could only wake up, it will all go away.

But when I look up again, it's not a dream.

It's just a nightmare.

*I LEAVE **Rosie's house*** because there's not much I can do if she doesn't want me there. But I text Collin on the way back to the compound, telling him to call the men home because the search is over.

Cell service is spotty in the hills between Disciple and Edge, so I don't get the return text until I'm actually pulling into the driveway. All he says is, *Come down to the mine.*

That damn mine. I don't give a fuck about the damn mine.

I go into my house and stare at my phone for a good ten minutes before I actually work up the nerve to press that contact.

It rings and Charlie Beaufort answers. "What can I do for you, Amon?"

It's not a congenial 'what can I do for you?' It's nothing like the way he talks to Collin. But that's because I'm not Collin. Charlie respects Collin because he knows what Collin is capable of. He *needs* Collin. Not today, not tomorrow. But there will come a day when Collin is the only man who can get the job done. So Charlie will maintain a relationship with Collin until such a time when Collin is no longer useful.

Me, though? He's got no respect for me. "Hey, Charlie. Yeah. So. I guess you've heard that we've had a little trouble over here with a missing boy?"

"I heard." He sounds bored. "But I don't know why you're calling me about it. I already told Collin we can't get involved in this."

"So you know what it's about though, right? And you know who this kid is? And who his daddy is?"

"I do. But Amon, this call is a waste of time. You're not gonna get any help from me."

"But the underground city? This is real?"

He doesn't say anything, but I can practically hear his anger.

"Because I was just told that it is. That Blackberry Hill isn't some little village in the mountains. It's not a hill at all, is it?"

"Amon, I'm gonna say this once and only once. You should forget you ever heard about that place."

"Should I forget I was up there too? Should I forget the fact that General Forbe rode in with us to save Lowyn McBride from Ike Monroe? Should I forget about him as well? How about Disciple? Should I forget I come from Disciple?" I snicker here. "You know what's funny, Charlie? The way you lied to Collin all those years ago. Talking him up and pretending you had no idea who he was or where he came from."

"Look, I'm sorry it turned out this way, I am. You might not believe it, but it's in the best interest of everybody that you, and Collin, and Ryan, and Nash all stay happy so you can play your parts. And that part is a pretty good gig, if you ask me. I mean, no prison time, right? Your names are in the clear. And we keep you alive, don't we? Every Monday you get that little cooler of fruit drinks, don't ya? You're gonna get one today, in fact. *We* do that for you, Amon. Us. The bad guys. We keep you alive with those drinks."

"Funny. Because the way I remember it, you're the whole reason we needed those drinks in the first place."

"I'm not having this discussion with you, son. I don't owe you a fuckin' thing. And as I said, the only reason you're not in prison, or dead, right now is because I need Collin. But if Collin doesn't play ball, then… one day, I might not need him. So you best remember that, boy. Because one day he might not be enough."

The call ends with three quick beeps.

I fume. I'm talkin' steam coming out my ears kinda fuming.

One day he might not be enough.

That fucker just threatened me.

I shake my head and pace my front room as I plan two dozen ways in which I could kill Charlie Beaufort and get away with it. If I tried a little harder, I could come up with four dozen. And that man talks to me like I am some kind of intellectually-challenged toddler.

"Amon!"

I turn as Collin comes up my porch steps. A moment later he's pulling the screen door open and it's slapping closed behind him. "What the hell did you just say to Charlie?"

"Me?" I point to myself and laugh. "He's got some fuckin' nerve."

"Well, I just got an earful. I'm supposed to take your phone and erase his contact." This sentence starts out serious but by the time it's over Collin is laughing. Even his eyes are smiling.

Which allows me the opportunity to release my anger and tension and chuckle back.

Because it's crazy.

If there is one man on this earth who's on my side, it's Collin Creed.

"Don't call him no more, OK? I swear, he's like a fuckin' child. Calling me up, bitching about you. I'm gonna lose my cool with him next time and we've got a good start here, Amon. We're not gonna need him for much longer, I promise. Six months, tops."

"Well before you just go and dismiss what he just said to me, you should know that he threatened me with those drinks."

"What?" Collin makes a face of confusion.

"The fruity drinks that we stopped drinkin'? Remember them?"

"Oh, by the way. Any side effects presenting?"

"Nah. I feel fine. What about you?"

He shrugs. "I feel good too. Better than fine, actually. So fuck him and his threats with those damn drinks. They're just another bullshit PSYOP, just like everything else about Charlie Beaufort. And anyway, we've got more important things going on out in the woods. You need to come with me right now."

"Don't tell me." I roll my eyes. "It's about that damn mine."

"Ya know, you're the one who got me all interested in

that place. It was you who was all suspicious of Sawyer Martin, remember? This was your thing. If it were up to me, I'd have left it alone." He pauses here to look me in the eyes. Which can be quite disconcerting, because that means I have to stare back, and Collin Creed has the most unnatural-colored eyes I've ever seen. Little bits of turquoise and amber all swirling together in a way that when he's angry makes him come off as not quite human. I think ninety percent of Collin's don't-fuck-with-me factor is because of his eyes. "Let's just say your instincts were spot on the money."

"What do ya mean?"

"It's not a mine, Amon. It's a tunnel. And tunnels go places."

"Where's it go?"

"We haven't gotten that far yet." He claps a hand down on my shoulder. "Come on. You gotta see this."

So we go traipsing into the woods and even though this trail usually takes twenty minutes, it only takes ten. Because while I have been falling in love, Ryan has made a road using all that heavy equipment he made us buy last spring. He's just hopping out of a front loader when Collin and I enter the newly cleared area in front of the old mine.

We walk up to the entrance, which has been cleared and is indeed a tunnel. "Looks like a mine to me," I say.

"It's not a mine." Nash is holding up maps or something. "I've looked into the history of this place, and there was never a mine here."

"Well, what was it?" I ask. "Because clearly it was something."

"According to what I could dig up," Ryan continues, "this

is a natural cave that was used as a munitions depot during the Civil War. Then it was a hideout for some outlaws called the Jesco Harmen Gang at the turn of the nineteenth century, and after that, this whole section was lumbered. There wasn't ever a coal mine here."

"What about the church camp?" I ask.

"Oh, that was real. But it was forty years after the lumbering, so the trees were just starting to get big again."

"All right." I look at Collin. "So what's that have to do with anything?"

"Well, interestingly enough, after the deforesting the US government bought this land in nineteen twenty-one and started digging tunnels for reasons unknown."

"Where'd you dig that info up from?" I ask.

Collin smiles at me. "Penny Rider. She's a history buff, don't ya know. So I called her up this morning and asked her about these parts and she went on for twenty minutes straight mentioning all kinds of places."

"Places like where?"

"Nothing more in Trinity County. But that's the weird part. She name-dropped Dixie Yonder."

"Dixie Yonder? Rosie and I were just there on Saturday night for a little one-on-one time."

"I know," Collin says. "And the reason it's so interesting —aside from the fact that one of our childhood friends is the events coordinator up there—is that it's got its own secret tunnels underneath all that grandeur and the rumor is, they go all the way to Washington, DC."

I whistle and look at our tunnel. "No shit."

"No shit," Collin says.

"So where do our tunnels go?" I look back at Collin to find him smiling.

"Take a guess, Amon. And you only get one."

I point to our little hole in the mountain. "Do not fuckin' tell me this tunnel goes to Blackberry Hill."

"That's what we're thinking," Ryan says. "We blew open that first door you and Collin saw through the rocks a few hours back, but there was nothing but more rocks on the other side so that's what we've been working on this morning. There's one more pile of rubble to get through before we break into the next open space. Give me and the guys a couple of hours and we'll find out for sure where the hell this things leads."

He takes off and goes back to the heavy machinery, starting it up again. So Collin pulls me back into the woods so we can talk. "I think," he says once we get there, "that this is somehow connected to whatever they're doin' in Blackberry Hill."

"Well, if that's the case, why didn't they buy up our compound themselves? Why'd they let us buy it? I mean, this whole thing was Charlie's idea, remember? He's the one who slipped me that listing."

"I don't think Charlie knew about it when he planted that seed in your head."

"How could he not? And why would he send that Sawyer up here to investigate if he didn't?"

"I think maybe he heard his own rumors, but wasn't able to suss out the details."

"Well, I guess it's a good thing that he and Penny don't know each other then, huh?"

Collin laughs. "It almost feels like fate, doesn't it?" But

then his face goes serious. "Listen, I'm sorry about Rosie and Cross. I don't know what's goin' on, but I know you're falling for her. And the boy too."

"I was. I have. But I'm not giving up hope yet. He got in touch with her this morning."

"Who?"

"Cross's daddy. He met her down in Revenant and they had a chat. He's got Cross in Blackberry Hill. But what we saw up there, Collin, that's not what Blackberry Hill is. It's some kind of secret underground base."

"I figured it was all leading in that direction. From the moment those assholes ambushed me up at the boneyard with Mercy, I knew there were tunnels. And Lowyn told me she saw some control room in Ike Monroe's basement when she was up there years back. That's what scared her off and how she got herself mixed up in all that trouble."

"Well, the worst part of all is that Erol got Cross all riled up and excited about joining their secret military bullshit. And, of course, this is every twelve-year-old boy's dream, ya know?"

"He wants to stay, doesn't he?"

I nod. "It gets worse, though. Erol wants Rosie to join them."

Collin makes a face. "What?"

"Yeah. He's using Cross to lure her down there."

"Oh, Amon, that sucks."

"Tell me about it. It's very hard to compete with that kid's father, ya know? I don't believe for a second that Rosie wants to go, or that she still loves Erol. I think she wants to be with me. But given the choice…" I trail off.

"Given the choice between you or her son?" Collin finishes. "She'll choose the boy."

I throw up my hands. "As she should."

"Don't lose hope yet, Amon. We'll figure something out."

"Well, we better do it quick because she's only got twenty-four hours to make up her mind. Then the offer goes away forever."

Collin is just about to open his mouth and say some well-meaning, yet still meaningless, placating words when Nash starts yelling for us to come back to the tunnel. "We got it. We got it open!"

AFTER THIRTY MINUTES OF FUCKIN' around with headlamps and two-way radios, Collin, Nash, Ryan, and I start picking our way through the rubble and squeezing ourselves through cracks and crevices. About a dozen Edge men follow, one of them dragging a rope behind him like breadcrumbs, just in case this cave system tries to get the best of us.

At first, I think there's not gonna be nothing here because every time we get past an obstruction, there's just a dark space ahead. Which leads to another obstruction.

But Ryan keeps muttering, "They don't fill in tunnels like this if there's nothing here. They just don't."

Which makes sense. So we push on. It's gotta be at least

an hour later before we finally break through to a new space and find something interesting.

A door. A very industrial-looking door, which also looks like it's a hundred years old. Collin is reading my mind, I think, because he says, "Well, that makes sense. If the military started using this place in the twenties."

"Yep," Ryan says. "This is it." He looks my way, temporarily blinding me with his headlight before he covers it with his hand. "Now we just gotta get it open." Ryan pulls on the thick steel handle, but it's locked. "Don't worry. I would not come this far into a cave on some Goonies expedition without being prepared." And from his pocket he pulls a bit of C4 explosive.

"Ryan," Nash says. "Are you out of your fuckin' mind? You can't blow a door inside an old abandoned cave! The whole thing will come down around us."

But Ryan is shaking his head. "Nah. If the door is made of steel, then the whole thing is shored up with steel. And besides"—he gets a little glint in his eyes—"I'm like a fuckin' C4 virtuoso." Then he wiggles his fingers at us. "I got the magic touch."

Collin and I look at each other and roll our eyes. But he gives the go-ahead. Because the whole 'shoring up with steel' thing actually makes sense.

"Step back," he says. To us, but also all the guys behind us.

So we retreat all the way back the way we came and give him the go head. Ten minutes later there's a boom and whoop on the radio.

Collin chuckles. "I guess that means he didn't die."

"And got the door open." I chuckle back.

"Oh, my fuckin' God!" Ryan yells through the talkie. "Guys! Get in here!"

We go all the way back in and make our way back to the door. Ryan's head pops out, and he's smiling like he just found his very own Goonies treasure. "You're not gonna believe what I found."

ROSIE

mon leaves after I push him away and lock him out. And, of course, this is expected because that's what I told him to do. Leave me alone. So that's what he does.

But it's not what I want. What I want is someone to tell me it's gonna be OK. That everything is gonna work out, and Cross will come home, and Erol will go back to where he disappeared to, and my life will pick back up with Amon and I falling in love and living happily ever after.

The problem is, if I let Amon stay, he would say all those things. He would make all the promises. And then I would start to believe him because… well, he's Amon Parrish. He's just got that vibe about him. The kind of vibe that comes off as competence. Which, in turn, lends itself to being believed.

But competent as he is, this really isn't about Amon and me. So solving it won't depend on something as simple as competence because Erol Cross is… well, I'm not sure what he is, but he's not a nobody, that I understand. And he's not simple, either. He's complicated and part of something big, and secretive, and mysterious. I mean, if I'm being honest, he comes off as one of those super-soldier spy thriller protagonists. Like he's ten steps ahead of everyone else and the plot only exists so he can play his part in it.

It's the puzzles, I think. What a creepy, yet creative, way to get the attention of the woman you walked out on twelve years ago just as she was about to give birth to your child.

And this is the problem. My child is the whole point of everything at the moment.

Of course Erol was spying on us. He had to be. Because he knew what was on Cross's mind. He understood his longing to grow up and be a part of something important. And then he used it against me.

I don't know how he actually snatched him up or how he got Cross to agree to go with him last night, but it doesn't matter. The timer is a-tickin'.

You've got twenty-four hours, Rosie. That's what he said.

And if I say no? That's what I said.

You're not gonna say no.

This is the part that really kinda pisses me off. This assumption that this man is anything but a stranger to me. That he *knows* me.

He doesn't know me.

Sure, maybe he's been watching. And he knows where I work. All my different jobs. So good for him, I guess. Following me around must've been an eye-opener.

But it don't mean nothin', these facts that he now possesses. Because the actual jobs, or the location thereof, aren't the point of doing them. It's not even the costume. It's not even the fantasy.

See, you put that costume on and you turn into something else. Lots of people like doing this. I mean, they have that damn Confederate reenactment going on all over the South every single fuckin' year. There are whole conventions where people dress up and don't even get me started on Hollywood. That town is nothing but pretend.

It's not the costume, or the implied fantasy that comes with it. Not in my mind, anyway. I can't speak for anyone else who likes to play dress-up, of course.

But for me, it's the story I'm after.

My life is a story—as is everyone's. But I take this storytelling a little more literal than most. That's why I run that stupid printing press every week. Though it's only stupid in an affectionate way, obviously, since I love it. That's why I work in the diner dressed up like Flo from that vintage TV show. That's why I stuck around this town when they all wanted to shame me out.

My life is a story and I'm the writer, and the narrator, and the main character. And Erol Cross can't just follow me around for a few weeks and claim to know my story. Because he doesn't.

And that's what he did. He claimed to know my story. *You're not gonna say no. We both know that.*

Erol Cross thinks he can just swagger his way back into our lives lookin' all Jack fuckin' Reacher and rewrite my story, and I'm just gonna go on record right now and say that's not the case.

It's just not the case.

My story has a big fat copyright sign on it. It belongs to me, and me only. And he can't have it.

But the ownership of my story—absolute as it is— doesn't solve my current problem. Because my current problem is that Cross is in the middle of writing his story as well. And since he's mine, and has lived with me all his life, and has watched me carefully craft my story as he grew—

using costumes, and jobs, and anything else I could get my hands on—well, how could my boy *not* aspire to bigger things?

He does, after all, possess a matching set of 'bold' genes.

And I can respect that. I can. I do.

I see the draw of his secret-spy father. I absolutely get it. Underground cities runnin' military operations? It's a very exciting story. Especially since Cross's story, so far, has consisted of singing old-timey hymns in the children's choir under a big ol' tent.

Which isn't enough for Cross Harlow. It's just not enough.

The sad part of my actualization is that it's coming a couple of days too late.

Yes. This is my true problem. I'm late to the game. It started without me and I'm behind a few points.

But doesn't everybody love an underdog?

Just as I'm thinking these words I glance at the clock and realize that it's dinner time. Seven-thirty. And when I step over to the window and look out, there's nothing to see because the whole town is home right now. Sitting around their table, chatting about their day, and just being a family.

I turn, glancing at my own dinner table. Which is depressing because it's empty. I haven't eaten all day, but I'm not hungry. I just miss my son and want him back.

Noon tomorrow. Sixteen and a half hours until I can see him again.

The roar of a truck pulls my attention back to the window. Amon is here. His truck slides into the driveway next to mine and as he gets out, I walk to the door, open it, and step out onto the porch.

Because I have made up my mind. I know what I have to do.

"Rosie!" Amon rushes up to the porch. He's just about to open his mouth and say something when I put up a hand. A look of confusion crosses his face, but it's enough to make him pause. And this pause is all I need.

"I need you to know something, Amon. And I need you to just… not say anything and let me get it out." Which spurs him into trying to reply, but I push my hand forward, causing him to pause again. "Just hear me out. Because my life has taken a turn here, Amon. In many ways. It's not just you, either. It's Cross—before he was kidnapped—and me, as well. You see, my boy was flashing me all the signs. He was giving me all the warnings. And I was just turning my cheek to him, pretending he's still a child who can be molded into the person I envisioned him to be. But I can't. It is time now for me to let go."

"Are you saying"—Amon's brow is thoroughly crinkled—"that you're not going with Erol?"

"Oh, I'm saying that and much more."

"But… Cross, Rosie. You can't choose me over Cross."

I walk towards him and place my hand on his chest. "I'm not choosing you over him. I'm choosing me."

Amon starts shaking his head. "I don't get it."

"Will you marry me, Amon?"

His smile is so immediate, it lights up my whole life. It is enough to illuminate the darkest black hole. "Did you just ask me to marry you?"

"I did. You see, there's only one way out of this and that's together."

"But what about Cross?"

"Oh, I didn't forget about Cross. This is the selfish part of my proposal because while he might not choose *me* over his exciting secret-spy-thriller daddy, you and me are a whole different story. And that's the best part. We get to write a brand-new story."

He chuckles. "Did you just admit to using me to lure your son back home?"

"I did."

"Well"—he smiles real big—"my answer is yes, of course. I will marry you, Rosie Harlow. And I am happy to be used as bait for a young boy who craves adventure in order to lure him home. But I'm gonna have to say no here, Rosie, you do realize that, right?"

"No? No to which part?"

"You can't ask me to marry you."

"Why the hell not?"

"Because that's my line. As the potential groom, I have one job and this is it." He points to the ground with his finger. "This is it. You stole my line."

"Oh, I see. I got a page ahead of you, didn't I?"

"What?"

"The story we're in. I read ahead."

He places a hand on my cheek and looks down at me like I am the illuminating one. "You can read ahead all you want. I don't mind it a bit. But you don't need to do everything yourself anymore, Rosie. I'm more than happy to do my share."

"Sorry." I giggle a little. "I didn't mean to steal your thunder, I just felt the need to make it clear that I choose you, Amon Parrish. And there isn't a chance in hell that I would even consider surrendering to the whims of one Erol

Cross. He's out of his freaking mind if he thinks he can waltz back into my life with puzzles, and threats, and promises of underground cities thinking I will cower or even be impressed. I am not afraid of him, nor am I dazzled. And he will not outshine me in front of my son. I *am* shining, Amon. I shine. I am bright, and quirky, and a bundle of fun."

Amon takes a step towards me, closing any and all distance between us. He takes my hands in his and looks me right in the eyes. "You shine so bright you make me dizzy. You're a force of nature, Rosie Harlow. You are the definition of joy. You exemplify the idea of life lived to its fullest. You are big fancy dresses, and cheap, pink uniforms, and you play every part with your whole heart. And that's why I love you. And I want *you* to marry *me*."

Without taking his eyes off mine, Amon Parrish slowly lowers himself down onto one knee. And when he looks up at me, he's shining too. "Marry me. Marry me in the Revival tent for real, Rosie. We'll have our own day with no tourists, and we'll have a big sit-down dinner, and you'll get a dress made special that isn't a costume, and everyone will come wearing whatever the hell they want, and not a single person in the tent will be acting, or have a script, or—"

I place two fingers on his lips. "You don't need to convince me. I'm a 'yes.'"

He stands up, smiling as he lets out a long breath. "OK. Good." Then he blinks. "But"—he holds up a finger—"I didn't really come here tonight to propose. You see, I have a way to get Cross back and it's guaranteed to work."

"How?"

"Well, let's go to the Revival tent and then I'll only have to explain it once."

"We're gettin' married right now?"

He laughs. "We can if you want. But I was kinda set on having our boy there as my best man, so how about we table the wedding and just concentrate on the rescue for now?"

And then he pulls me down the porch steps and we get in the truck.

A COUPLE MINUTES later we're standing on the stage inside the tent and the call to Revival is blasting through Disciple. The murmur of people coming out of their houses at dusk rumbles back to us. And then they all start making their way to the tent.

Jim Bob, who lives right across the street in a big ol' white house, is one of the first to arrive. "Why in the red-hot hell is the call to Revival sounding on a Monday night!" His cheeks are all puffed out with anger and his red and white checkered dinner napkin is still hanging from his collar. Jim Bob is a beast on his best day, but he's particularly snarly when he's hungry and we have interrupted his dinner, so to say that he is vexed would be an understatement.

Amon starts talking before Jim Bob can continue his bellowing. "Just hear me out," he says while pushing the air towards Jim Bob with his palm. "There's a good reason for this call." Now he directs his attention to the people who are filing into the tent. "Everyone please take a seat. Rosie and I have something to discuss with y'all."

And then he starts telling them.

AMON

There are one hundred twenty-seven people in Disciple, West Virginia. Sixty-four are male, sixty-three are female, but only eighty-five of that total are over eighteen and only about half of that number are men.

Forty-four grown men, to be exact.

But when you add forty-four to Edge's sixty ex-soldiers —plus me, Collin, Ryan, and Nash—you get one hundred and eight.

It's not quite a company, but that's OK because Collin Creed isn't quite a captain, either. And anyway, it's a good-sized platoon, which fits Master Sergeant Creed's old rank just fine.

When I get done explaining how we're gonna get Cross back, the whole town starts murmuring. Jim Bob takes over, telling people to calm down and take a seat, and doin' all his mayor stuff. Which allows me to step aside and let him have his say.

I already know he's gonna agree to my plan because Collin told me that he's looking for protection. Now, we understand that we do not have all the facts here. And there is something pretty serious going on between the Trinity towns and Blackberry Hill. Probably something dark that comes with undesirable consequences should one stray from the agreed-upon stipulations.

That's why, when we came back, Jim Bob wanted us to run security. Not because he thinks someone's gonna shoot up the Revival or anything as dramatic as that, but because there's paperwork involved here. Contracts and commitments.

And it seems to me that certain people are finished with these contracts and commitments and would like to move on while other certain people are standing in the way of that growth and progression.

So Jim Bob is in.

Most of the town is, as well. But of course they have questions. As they should. Because this isn't some small act of rebellion we're doing here. This is us against the US government.

A secret branch of the US government that they are desperate to keep under wraps, which makes the whole thing even more dangerous.

But... we kinda got them by the balls.

They were sloppy once upon a time. They were using that old mine on our property for something or other, and then... I dunno. Probably funding got cut and they closed it down.

But see, secret projects come with all kinds of sticky consequences. For one, people are desperate to shut up about them 'cause most of the time they're illegal. And for two, once they get forgotten by the small number of people who actually knew about them in the first place, they get forgotten by everyone.

They forgot about our little mine and what they were hiding inside it.

Oh, someone remembered—after the fact. Because

Charlie fuckin' Beaufort sure did get curious about that place. And that's why he sent Sawyer Martin in to check things out.

"What kind of diagrams?" Lecter, Rosie's brother, is asking. "I mean, how is this helpful? And that's my nephew's life you're playing around with, Amon! Rosie?" He looks at her. "Are you on board with this?"

Rosie only knows what I said here in the tent tonight and nothing else because I only wanted to explain once. So my head turns to her, just like everyone else's. We're standing a few paces apart, so she walks over to me and hooks her arm into mine to signal our solidarity. Then she nods. "I am one hundred percent behind this plan and I hope y'all are as well. Because I want my boy back and this is how we're gonna do it."

There's more muttering after that. A few more people start asking Jim Bob about consequences, and he does his best to explain how badly they need us. As in Edge. As in Collin, but me too. I don't have his reputation, but I am most certainly my own force of nature.

Finally, Jim Bob turns to us and nods. "We're in."

I step to the front of the stage again and scan the crowd, giving them all one more serious once-over. "All right, then. Everyone meet out at the Edge compound in thirty minutes. You tell your families to bring one bag and that's it."

They stare at me for a few moments and I think this is when the seriousness of the situation finally sets in. Because Disciple, West Virginia, is about to declare war on the US government.

It's a pretty dumb idea considering they've got all the

weapons one can dream up, plus plenty more we haven't even imagined yet.

But we found our Goonies treasure.

And our treasure is a map.

ROSIE and I arrive back at Edge to a big commotion. Ryan's doing something with a bulldozer, and Nash has got a clipboard and has the men all lined up in formation in front of the mess hall. And Collin is standing on his porch with Lowyn when we pull up, smiling.

We get out and I walk over to his house, just staring up at him. "What the hell are you smiling about?"

He chuckles as Lowyn hops down the steps and hooks her arm into Rosie's, heading into our house so Rosie can collect her things. "I just think it's kinda funny, don't you?"

I smile too. "That they left this place, forgot about it, and then that blowhard Charlie Beaufort practically hand-delivered it right to us a hundred years later?"

"It's fate, Amon."

"Maybe, but"—I nod my head to the driveway, which is filling up with trucks and cars from Disciple—"ruining my life is one thing. Ruining theirs..." I shake my head. "I'm worried."

Collin comes down the steps, nodding as well. "Well, then I guess we should make sure they're all safe. Come on."

BY THE TIME we get to the church, people are already filling it up. Ryan has finished piling dirt up against the sides of the building—which was already reinforced with steel back when we first moved in, but he insisted that a little more dirt never made something less safe. So now the church has a berm of earth all the way around it that goes all the way up to the top of the stained-glass windows.

This is the safe house. It's also got a bunker in the basement, which we did take a good look at when we first got here, but it warranted a second look after we found our treasure in the old mine.

Turns out it wasn't just a bunker. Because with a little sleuthing—and a ground-penetrating radar machine—we found that the tunnels under our property aren't limited to just the old mine. With a little blasting and some concrete removal, we found an entrance. And I'm not talking some little hole in the wall. I'm talking a hallway with lights and everything. Course, we don't know how to turn the lights on yet, but it'll come. This hallway leads to another, which leads to another, and it goes on and on like this until finally, you find yourself standing in the middle of a six-lane highway that spreads out in four directions.

What's going on in the old mine is a whole other kind of special because we found a room down there. An old room sealed up by a steel door. And inside this room was a panel of old computers as well as it's own set of doors that lead other places.

Now, the prevailing wisdom is that the invention of the modern-day computer comes with a date that lands somewhere in the middle of the twentieth century. But that's all lies. That's just when they started *telling* people about modern-day computers, because they were invented much, much earlier and this little room of ours is proof. Because while they do look antique compared to what we have today, it only takes one second of operational time to realize they are, in fact, modern. Relatively speaking, of course.

And once Ryan got the power running, they came right to life, flashing all kinds of old-timey code and shit. But Nash, he's somewhat of a nerd, so he's been our tech guy for years now and was able to finagle his way into a menu—or what passed as one a hundred years ago. Nevertheless, he found the files inside that computer to be quite interesting. Top secret kind of interesting. In other words, information that should've been forgotten about a century back.

There's so much information, it's gonna take months to go through it. But there was something very useful that we could use immediately.

A map. A fuckin' map of every single secret tunnel that the US government ever drilled. Which might be exaggerating things, but only just a touch.

It's what Collin likes to call 'comprehensive,' one of his favorite words. This map shows tunnels under West Virginia. Tunnels under DC. Tunnels under Virginia, North Carolina, Pennsylvania, New York, New Jersey—pretty much tunnels all up and down the eastern seaboard.

All those secret passageways that no one's supposed to know about and we stumbled into the OG documentation for every single square inch.

What are the odds?

It's fate, Amon.

There are whole cities down there. And that was a century ago. I can't even imagine what they've got going on now.

Jim Bob enters the church blowing words like notes comin' out a trumpet. He's complaining and giving orders as he walks up to us. "Do you know what this is gonna turn in to?" He's looking at Collin, not me. "We're gonna be the next Ruby Ridge!"

Collin nods and crosses his arms. "Maybe."

"We're gonna be the next goddamned Waco, Texas, and you're gonna be the charismatic leader they take out with a sniper!"

Collin nods again. "Prolly."

Jim Bob pulls a handkerchief out of his pocket and starts wiping his sweaty brow. "I dunno, Collin. This might be a tick too far."

"It might," Collin agrees. He's not been looking at him thus far, but those unnatural eyes of his migrate over to meet Jim Bob's. And I don't care who you are, it's unnerving, that stare. Jim Bob is a huge man, but even he juts his chin back a little at the attention. "But Jim Bob, we've got no choice. They took a child without permission, and this isn't the first time they've tried this."

Jim Bob and I both sigh at this, because now we're picturing Collin killing that Blackberry Hill man twelve years ago.

"It cannot be tolerated." Collin's eyes are narrowed as he says these words. "And for what it's worth, they can't afford too many eyeballs on this place."

"But what if we can't go home?" Jim Bob's voice is very

quiet now. It's nearly a whisper. "What if you go down there and they got something up their sleeve and we can't ever go home again, Collin? What if this compound of yours is our prison?"

Collin is unconcerned and it comes out in his tone. "There are probably a thousand miles of tunnels under this country, Jim Bob. And we've got ourselves a map. We're not gettin' stuck, trust me on that. And if they try to Waco our asses, we'll just escape out one of our many, many, many backdoors."

"Not only that"—we all turn and notice that Ryan has walked up next to us—"we've got the whole place lit up with cameras, Jim Bob. Shit, we got our own satellites in low orbit. Fifteen of them. We're an elite security company. Do you really think that we didn't fortify our headquarters the first day we got here? This isn't gonna be no Waco. If they attack us, they attack everyone. Because we'll turn this thing into a first-person shooter game and blast it all over the internet so quick, their heads will spin." Ryan lets out a breath because he kinda got himself worked up there for a moment. "It's not gonna be no Waco and we're not getting burned alive or shot to hell. If there's one thing I know to be true about this operation, this is it."

Jim Bob looks at Collin again. He lets out a breath, but then he nods. "All right then, son." He claps Collin on the shoulder. "Let's get this party started."

Collin reaches into his pocket, pulls out his phone, and hands it to me. "You're up, Amon. Make me proud."

I nod, take the phone, and then step outside the church where every single male resident of Disciple, West Virginia, is standing, waiting on orders. They are all armed.

As are the Edge soldiers. And hey, I'm not disparaging the ability of a West Virginia hillbilly to scare the shit out of a person, but these here men of ours are downright bone-chillin' frightful all dressed up in their body armor and packin' heat to the hilt.

One hundred and eight men against the US government. Let's fuckin' go.

I press Charlie Beaufort's contact on Collin Creed's phone and put it on speaker. Charlie picks up first ring. "Collin Creed, my favorite son of a gun. How you doin' this lovely evening?"

"It's not Collin."

There's a long moment of silence on the other end of this line, but I let it hang there like unripe fruit. Finally, Charlie blows out a breath. "Amon, I thought I told you we were done talking."

"You did. At least you said *you* were. But I'm not quite done yet, Charlie. You see, when people steal kids out of Disciple, that act comes with consequences. And I am calling you as a courtesy to let you know those consequences are forthcomin' unless I get my way."

Charlie scoffs here, but doesn't say nothing.

"Now I get it, Charlie. You're a big, important bureaucrat and I'm nothing but a footnote in the history of your long and illustrious career. And I know that your first inclination is gonna be to end this call. But I'm tellin' ya, Charlie, you'd better not do that."

"Or what?" He's angry now. And if he were in this room with us, his whole forehead would be crinkled up and his eyes would be beady.

I hand the phone to Nash. "Hey, Charlie, Nash here.

Welp, here's the deal, buddy. Ya see, that man you sent out to inspect shit? Well, I don't think he found much but he did raise a few red flags around here. Which got us curious about what he was checking on out at that old mine."

"Nash, I'm telling ya, you had better—"

"Charlie," Nash interrupts him, "before you go threatening me, you'd better think long and hard about what I did for you all those years. It's been a while, so I'll give ya a minute." Nash pauses here. Gives me a wink.

"Where's Collin?"

Collin takes the phone from Nash. "I'm right here, Charlie."

"You're gonna allow this to happen? You're just gonna let these boys of yours talk to me this way?"

"See, Charlie, you always did figure that I was in charge here. But I'm not. We're partners. And if Amon wants his boy back, and if Nash wants to do a little sleuthin' on some outdated computers we found in a steel-clad room down in the old mine… well, there's not much I can do about that except join in the fun."

"You're makin' a mistake here, Collin."

"I might be. But I'd just like to remind you that it's one-zero in my favor."

"What? What's that mean?"

"That last man who came into Disciple trying to fuck around and take a child…" Collin scoffs. "Well, let's just say he found out, didn't he?"

"Did you just threaten me?"

"I don't think so. Unless it was you who took Cross Harlow. And if it was, then… yeah. I just threatened you."

He hands the phone to me while Charlie is chewing on

this last bit. "Here's what's gonna happen, Charlie. You're gonna get on the horn and whoever runs your satellites, you're gonna tell them to take a little picture of our compound here. You're gonna see a bunch of men standing outside our church. This picture is just so you know that we're not fucking about and if you try anything stupid, we're gonna have ourselves a war. Because you see, the people of Disciple, West Virginia, won't be tolerating no kidnappin'. And they are all here to make that point clear. And the men of Edge Security are flying the Edge logo like it's a goddamn medieval banner. We have come packin' heat and if you don't have Cross Harlow down in that little underground maze the US government has been hiding for the last hundred years, standing outside door number—" I forgot the door number, so I look at Ryan.

"WDV-907."

"—that's right, door number WDV-907—in one hour, the consequences will be dire."

Charlie's words come out with a sneer. "I don't even have clearance for the tunnel that leads to that door."

"Well, it's a good thing that this exchange doesn't require your presence then, isn't it?"

"What you're asking isn't even possible, Amon. Let's talk this over. I can get the boy. I can have him delivered to you by tomorrow night."

"Charlie? It's Nash here now. And I'm just gonna go ahead and say it plain so there are no misunderstandings. If you don't get that boy down to door WDV-907 in one hour, I'll be sending irrefutable proof that these tunnels exist to the mouthiest, most outspoken and annoying conspiracy theorists on the internet and that shit will be blasted all over the world in a matter of hours. And if you doubt that the world will take this information seriously, mark my word, they will. Because I've hacked into every security camera down in those tunnels in a hundred-mile radius and I've got seventy-five livestreams set to broadcast on every single social network in existence in one hour and one minute."

Everyone within hearing distance of that monologue just kinda chuckles.

Nash hands me the phone back and I take over again. "You get that, Charlie? One hour."

Then I end the call and look at Nash. "Is that true? About the livestreams?"

Nash points to himself. "Do I look like a fuckin' liar?"

I just laugh. "Damn. I forgot how fuckin' ruthless you were, Nash. I thought all that paperwork was turning you soft."

He raises his hand up and I clap it.

Then we all turn to the one hundred and four men of Disciple and Edge who just watched this whole thing go down and find that every single one of them has a hanging jaw.

"Welp." Collin slaps Jim Bob on the back, nearly making him choke. "I just burned a really nice bridge, Jim Bob. You understand what this means, right?"

Jim Bob looks panicked for a minute. Like Collin Creed is about to shake him down like a mobster looking for protection money. But then he pulls himself together and nods. "Collin." He even smiles. "I am happy to announce that Disciple, West Virginia, is gonna hire you full time for Revival security to the tune of..." He hedges here, his eyes dartin' back and forth like he's gonna lowball. But the rational side of him beats down the greedy side of him and he says, "A hundred thousand dollars a week, just like we discussed."

Collin nods, then looks at me and grins. "Looks like this is your lucky day, Amon. We're out from under Charlie's thumb and we can still pay the bills. Now you and Ryan go pick up that boy of yours while the rest of us stay here and keep an eye on things." Then he flashes me a little salute.

I snap off a salute of my own in response and fall in next to Ryan as we take off for the woods.

ONCE WE ENTER the mine it takes about forty minutes to make our way down to the first door. This is the one that leads to the control room with the ancient, but still working, computers. They're all turned off when we enter. "Everything has a shelf life," Nash said earlier. "They work now, but that doesn't mean they'll work tomorrow." So he copied all the files he could find using some kind of hard drive hack, and then we shut them down to preserve whatever life they have left.

This control room isn't the one with the door we're looking for. It's just the starting point. On the other side of this room there's a large open hallway about thirty feet across, and from there, a maze. Not literally, but it might as well be, that's how many choices one has.

Door number WDV-907 is the very first one once you

get out in this hallway. On the other side of this door—according to the map—is a straight-shot tunnel that leads directly to Blackberry Hill. Or whatever's underneath it.

Once we get to this door, Ryan says, "All right, you ready?"

We're both wearing armor and carrying heat. Ryan aims his rifle at the door and stares at it, waiting.

I stare at the door too. Waiting as well.

Our hour is nearly up, and we don't even know if they're coming, so this wait is pure agony.

Then we hear it. Some banging or something on the other side. "They're coming," Ryan whispers.

Sure enough, about thirty seconds later, we catch a faint echo of footsteps. They get louder, approaching. And then someone is fucking with the locking mechanism on the door.

There is no handle on this door. There's no keypad or padlock or anything like that. It looks like a hatch you'd find on a ship. Something that, when locked, can seal one compartment from the next. Which means we can't get past the door. Well, I guess we could if we blew it open, but it's clear that this hatch was built to be some kind of boundary between this station and the one on the other side.

The door opens and I step back in shock at the face I'm lookin' at. But it only takes a second or two for it to click into place. "Sawyer?" I ask. "Or Erol?"

Ryan huffs out some air behind me, but he doesn't say anything because he's busy targeting this man, whoever he is, with the rifle.

"It's either-or, I guess," Sawyer says.

"You're Cross's father?" I ask.

He shrugs. "I am."

"So which name is real?"

"Depends on the day, I suppose."

I try to see past him, but the hatch opening isn't that wide, so I don't see much. But there is a shadow back there.

Sawyer or Erol or whoever he is steps aside just enough to give me a glimpse. I was expecting it to be Cross, but it's not. It's three very big men aiming their heat at us. "Don't mind them," Sawyer says. "They're here for me, not you."

My brow furrows in confusion as I parse these words, but then Sawyer is saying, "Come on, Cross. It's time to go home."

And then there he is. All pouty-faced and pissed off. "This is bullshit," he complains, looking me straight in the eyes. "I wanna stay! You have no right to take me out of here!"

I'm just about to open my mouth when Sawyer bends down a little to see his boy better. I figure he's gonna tell him that they'll be together soon, or something like that. But that's not what he says. He says, "You go home and make me proud, OK?"

"But I don't wanna go home, Daddy!"

Is it weird that it kinda kills me that Cross is callin' him Daddy? Because this man isn't his daddy. This man doesn't know anything about this boy.

"Oh, this place ain't going nowhere, Cross. It's gonna be here when you turn eighteen."

And I'm thinking, *There it is. That's his plan. Wait until he's eighteen and—* But this thought of mine is cut off when I realize that Sawyer isn't looking at Cross, he's looking at me.

And then, as Sawyer stands back up, he says in a voice so low it's even less than a whisper, "Take good care of him, Amon." And then he winks at me and mouths the words, *Not everything is what it seems.*

The next thing I know Cross is pushed out of the hatch by one of the MP's or whoever they are, and the door is being slammed shut behind him.

"What did he just say?" Ryan asks, still holding his rifle at high-ready just in case.

I look at him, then down at an angry Cross, then back up at Ryan and sigh as I shake my head. "I'll tell ya later. Let's go."

Cross starts his complaining, but I just put my hands on his shoulders and turn him around so we can start the long walk back.

ROSIE

Sheltered they might be, but neither the women nor children of Disciple scare easily. Add in the fact that we spend less than two hours in our secret hiding place under the church before we get word from Collin that Amon is already on his way back and he's got my boy in tow, and what we've got ourselves here is a... *non-situation*.

So it's no surprise, really, that no one hiding down in the secret tunnel below the Edge Security church—which apparently also doubles as a munitions depot—is particularly concerned about the recent turn of events.

Which kinda makes me wonder a little bit. About their lack of concern.

But then, when I take a good look at my own circumstances—boy kidnapped by presumed dead father, taken to a secret underground military city, then rescued by my outlaw security company boyfriend and a standing army of a hundred armed men—I realize that I've got my own problem with lack of concern.

And then I start to wonder where this indifference might stem from.

There's really only one answer: the Revival, of course.

Me and my neighbors have spent our whole lives playing dress-up and pretend. And I myself have taken the game to a whole new level. I mean, I don't just dress up for Disciple, I put in my playtime with Revenant and Bishop as well.

And as nice as that print shop is, and as fun as writing up those 'desperately seeking somebodies' is, and as pretty and feminine my little cottage is... I'm starting to think I've taken it a tick too far.

I might not actually be grounded in reality.

This thought is just beginning its tour through my mind when the door to the hallway opens and Collin Creed comes in saying, "Let's go, people. Fun's over. Ya don't have to go home, but ya can't stay here."

Everyone chuckles as they get to their feet.

Part of me understands that Collin is making light of this because of the kids. But there's another part of me that understands that this is his job. He keeps people safe.

As does Amon.

This is a *job* to them. Danger, and secret hiding places, and coded word puzzles comin' in the mail, and maps of tunnels underneath your compound. It's all in a day's work to these men.

I've never been particularly afraid of anything. I mean, my own sad heart sometimes scares me. But that comes and goes in a casual will-I-end-up-a-spinster kind of way. Not a strange-man-claiming-to-be-my-baby-daddy-just-stole-my-child kinda way.

As I slowly follow-the-leader out of the secret underground hallway that lives beside a secret munitions bunker, which resides below a fortified church, outside of which stands an army of a hundred men ready to go to war with some bureaucrat over my once-missing child, I have an epiphany.

I might not live in the real world.

I'm not sure I know what the real world is.

I'm not sure I want to.

I come out the church doors and the first thing I see is Amon Parrish standing in the long gravel driveway of Edge Security with his hand on my son's shoulder. Like I'm getting off a train or something. Like I just got back from a trip and they're picking me up to take me home.

Cross is angry. I can tell because when I come up to them, he sighs instead of smiles.

I reach out, put my arms around him, pull him close, and hug him tight.

He could pull away, but he doesn't. He doesn't really hug me back, either, but I don't care. We can sort these feelings out later. Right now, I'm just happy he's home.

This is what I really want to talk about, so I turn to Amon. "Can we stay at your place?"

Amon is nodding yes before I even stop talking. "Of course."

"In fact"—I push back from Cross because I'm kinda talking to him now—"I think we should just move in for good." Cross throws me a look of confusion, which quickly turns into suspicion. "I've been thinking, son, that you were right."

"About what?" This comes out real surly.

"About... learning to do important things."

One of his eyebrows cocks up. And when I glance at Amon, he's got one of his up as well.

"Yeah," I say. "It's time for you to learn to be... well, whatever it is you want to be."

"Well, I wanna be like my daddy, that's who I wanna be. I

wanna live underground in a secret city, and do target practice at the range, and take secret trains to restaurants that you don't even have up here."

It amazes me how fast I went from 'us' to 'them' in this boy's mind. But then I remind myself that he's twelve and I can work with twelve. "What would you say if I told you we were gonna quit the Revival?"

"What?" His whole face goes cockeyed. "Why would we do that?"

"Because it's pretend."

"But…" This has clearly caught him off guard. He looks at Amon.

Amon just puts up his hands. "Don't look at me. I've got nothing to do with this."

When Cross looks back at me, I keep going. "Yes, I think it's time to move away. To here." I point down at Amon's house. Which makes Amon happy, because he smiles and nods his head.

"What about Bishop? And those dresses you like? And your paper? And what about—"

"It's all pretend, Cross. This is real. And I know that you've made up your mind that you wanna be just like your daddy, but… take a look around, son. Is there any more secret-spy place than Edge Security? Did you, or did you not, just come out a secret tunnel in an old abandoned mine?"

He's looking in the direction of the woods when he says, "I did."

"And did you know that I was hiding in yet another secret tunnel underneath that church right there?"

His eyes dart over to the church, then he looks at Amon.

Amon nods. "That's right. We've discovered a whole bunch of secret shit around here."

"Can I see it?" All the anger and grumpiness has left my son's tone and he's now excited, and smiling, and his eyes are filled with curiosity.

"If it's OK with—"

But I'm already nodding my head 'yes,' and Cross's kid-sense has detected this permission, so his little feet are running in that direction.

Amon turns to me. "You OK?"

"I'm fine. Why?"

"This is kind of a big move. I mean, you can stay for sure, Rosie. But you don't have to give up your place, ya know? And you certainly don't have to quit the Revival. I mean, we just promised Jim Bob to run security for him so I'm gonna be there every weekend."

"Yep." I nod my agreement. "That's all true. But don't you remember what it was like to live there? To be inside the show, all the time?"

Amon's face goes thoughtful. "Oh, I do. I hated it. I couldn't wait to leave."

"Do you remember why you hated it, Amon?"

"Because it was fake. I mean…" He laughs here, smiling. "The real world is surely lacking its share of authenticity. It's a pretty sick place overall. But when I was a kid, Disciple always felt like a lie."

"And now?"

He shrugs. "Well, now I know better. It's not real, but it's not a lie, exactly. It's just… a show. It's theatre."

"Which is fake."

"Yeah, it's still fake, I guess."

"My whole life is fake, Amon."

"What? Nah. Your life is pretty cool, Rosie. You've got your printing business—"

"Which I wear a costume for."

"Well…" He's kinda stuck for words.

"And the diner? I wear a costume for that too."

"You don't wear a costume at McBooms."

"No?" I laugh. "Maybe you just don't know it's a costume. Maybe I didn't even know it's a costume. I feel like I've been jumping from one role to the next without ever taking a breath. I went from being a kid, to pretending I was an adult, to being a mother, and all that turned into this." I point to myself.

Amon is starting to get confused and Cross is standing on the steps of the church waitin' on him, so I figure I might as well just get to the point.

"I feel fake and I think it's holding me back."

His eyebrow cocks up again. "Pretty dresses are holding you back?"

"It's not the dresses, Amon. It's the pretending. I grew up in a show, and I stayed in the show, and I can't even imagine a life outside the show. And so…" I let out a breath. "I don't know. I'm not making any sense. I like the fake stuff. I do. But I don't want my boy to grow up all fake and get the urge to leave me and this fake place behind. And go join the marines and get himself killed, or worse. I'm suddenly very afraid that I've done it all wrong."

Amon comes over and pulls me into a hug. "If you did your best, Rosie, then you didn't do anything wrong." When we pull apart, he says, "Welcome home. I thought you'd never get here."

AMON

It's been a few weeks now since Cross had his little adventure in the secret underground city beneath Trinity County and I've spent most of that time thinking about Rosie and her doubts.

I guess everyone gets to this point in their life where self-assurance suddenly morphs into uncertainty. Some, like me, get to this place young. And these people do rash things like join the marines the day they turn eighteen, and learn to do things they really shouldn't know how to do, and then a bunch of friends die, and you end up gulping fruit drinks delivered by military courier every Monday while pondering all your bad life choices.

So I get it.

I don't mean this casually, either. I totally get it. I get *her*, actually. I've got a solution for her problem, but before I do that, I gotta take care of a different kind of problem.

It's three twenty-three a.m. when I walk into Cross's room and shake him awake. "Cross. Get up. We got things to do."

He rubs his eyes, looking at me. "What?"

"You've got two minutes to meet me on the porch."

I leave his room and go outside on the porch to wait.

The day after I brought Cross up out of that tunnel, I gave him a job. It has been my experience that a job is a

411

necessary part of life. So I told Cross that his job was to train Collin's dog, Mercy, during the day because Collin and I don't see eye to eye on the whole job thing when it comes to canines. He thinks she should be allowed to sleep on the porch all day like a good-for-nothing layabout. But I'm the dog expert here, and I don't agree.

So every day Cross gets up, goes next door to Collin's house, snaps a lead on Mercy, and takes her to the a.m. training session with all the other men.

Even if Cross wasn't smitten by the dog, he would be smitten by training with the men. He's living his dream.

This morning, though, he's gettin' a new dream.

The screen door bangs open and I catch it as Cross comes out of the house so it doesn't bang closed and wake up Rosie.

Cross is mad. "What the hell?" He has taken to swearin' when his mama's not around and I don't correct him because the last thing he needs from me is a reminder that he's still a boy. "It's the middle of the night, Amon." His eyes are all half-closed with anger. "What are we doing?"

"You've been fired." I jump down the porch steps and shove my hands into my pockets as I stride across the grass towards the kennel.

He jumps down the steps too, then runs to catch up with me. "What? What do you mean? Fired from what? Don't say Mercy."

I stop and look at him, recognizing the look in his eyes. It's fear, but with way more than just a tinge of sadness hooked up with it. "I'm sorry, Cross, but you can't train Mercy no more."

Then I start walking again.

He doesn't follow me. So when I get to the door of the kennel and look over my shoulder I find him standing in the grass under the moonlight. But in my mind's eye I see myself too. The last day I was in the marines as a legitimate soldier.

I had a dog. She was called Angel. She was an all-black German shepherd, just like Mercy, and she was the first dog I ever worked with. That dog didn't belong to me—not legally, at least—but in my heart, she and I were partners.

So, when I left the marines, I left her too and it just about killed me.

"Come on," I tell Cross. "Hurry up."

"Hurry up for what? You said I can't train Mercy no more."

"Ya can't." I pause to shoot him a smile. "Because she's not yours, Cross. And you never wanna give your heart to something that's not yours, because it hurts real bad when that something gets taken away, doesn't it?"

I'm talking about dogs here, of course. But I'm talking about daddies too.

Cross lets out a long breath that I can hear even from fifty feet away. But he nods his head. "Yeah. I guess."

"So that means you gotta have your own dog then, right?"

His eyes go big. "What?"

"Ya need your own dog, right?"

I think he's afraid to really hear what I'm saying because he gets this look on his face like he might cry.

"Come on, then. Let's go choose you a dog." I open the door and hold it open for him.

"What dog? We don't have any extra dogs."

"We *didn't* have any extras… until about an hour ago."

Now he gets it and his smile is so big, he laughs out loud as he runs towards me. "The puppies were born!" He doesn't even pause when he gets to me, just flies past and turns left in the kennel, back to where the whelping room is.

By the time I get back there with him, he's down on his knees, leaning into the box where the puppies are squirming and whining as they fight for position.

Cross looks up at me. "I thought you said they were all taken? I thought you said there weren't enough for me to get one?"

"Well, that was true. The vet said there were twelve puppies coming, but it looks like we got ourselves a lucky thirteen."

Now Cross really does start crying. But it's the happy kind. The kind when you just can't believe that something this good just happened to you.

So I kneel down next to him and I say, "Which one is yours?"

Then I watch, and listen, and be there for him as he points to each puppy and starts trying to figure them out. It takes him hours to choose. It's well past daylight by the time he points to the big sable male—the literal pick of the litter in my eyes—and says, "That one. That one right there is mine."

So I get up, and cut off a piece of red satin ribbon, and hand it to Cross so he can put it on his puppy.

I leave the kennel alone. Cross stays behind. And this was the plan.

Because that boy is mine now too. And there ain't no way in hell I'm gonna take any chances with this kid. When he turns eighteen this little puppy of his will have had six years of professional training and it will be something very, very special.

This puppy will grow up to be his partner. His first love.

He's never gonna join the marines now because if he joins the marines, he's gotta walk away from the dog.

And he's never gonna walk away from this dog.

Having ticked Cross off my list, my attention returns to the love of my life, who I find in the kitchen. She's making coffee, looking a little sleepy—which is more than a little sexy—and sighing as she does this.

But when she turns and sees me, her face lights up.

I make her happy. I know this. She likes it here, I know this too.

But my woman is not quite satisfied with her life at the moment. Every weekend since she made her decision to step away from Disciple she gets up and doesn't know what to do with herself. It's even worse during the week because she has quit her part-time lives as well as her full-time one.

She packed up the entire print shop and she packed up all those dresses in the cottage and she's got both those places up for sale on the private Trinity County market.

I tried to talk her into easing into a new life. She should take it slow. It's a lot of change, after all.

But my Rosie was dead set on going cold turkey.

The problem is, she can't quite figure out what to replace it all with and she's going stir crazy in the house. Especially since I'm doing something in her old stomping grounds every single day because Trinity County has replaced the US government as our number one client.

I do not share her problem because I know exactly what is missing from her life.

"Why are you smiling at me like that, Amon Parrish? You look like a canary-eatin' cat."

"Well, I just gave our son a puppy so I'm feeling pretty damn pleased with myself."

"Oh, they were born! How happy is he?"

"Rosie, that boy isn't going anywhere without that dog. They are gonna be partners in crime for a decade or more."

She slips her hands around my hips and leans into my chest. "Thank you."

I kiss her head and hug her back. "It was my pleasure. And now that Cross is taken care of, it's your turn."

She pushes me back a little so she can look up at my face. "Oh, Amon. I don't want no puppy."

"Silly woman, I'm not talking about a puppy. Dogs are the salve for the wounds of men. But ladies such as yourself require something different." I walk a few paces, but take hold of her hand. "Come with me."

Rosie sends me a sexy look like we're gonna go upstairs and have ourselves a good old time, which I would not mind doin', to be honest. But that's not where I take her. I take her down the hallway to the spare room and stop at the closed door.

She's shootin' me a confused look now. "What are you up to?"

"Open the door and find out."

She lets out a little huff of a laugh, then turns the handle and opens the door. For a moment she doesn't say nothing, just looks around with wide eyes.

I see it through her eyes as well. It's an office, but not just any office. Lowyn decorated it. I told Low, "I'm lookin' for somethin' that says 'eighteenth-century printshop, diner waitress, flower child'. Can you pull that together?" And Lowyn McBride nodded her head and said, "Consider it done."

So this room has been transformed into a mixture of a printshop and a dressing room, with a side of biker and genuine 1970's accents. With a desk and laptop, of course. Because those two things were the entire point of the whole redecoration.

Rosie turns to me. "What is this?"

"This is your office, of course."

She laughs again. "But... why do I *need* an office?"

"So you can write books."

Rosie looks bewildered. "But... how did you know that I wanted to write books?"

She's so silly. "Because we're on the same page, Rosie. We're on the same page."

And from this day forward, that's where we'll stay.

Dogs are the salve
for the wounds of men.

END OF BOOK SHIT

Welcome to the End of Book Shit. This is the part of the book where I get to say anything I want about the story you just read or listened to. It's never edited and sometimes I ramble. One thing is guaranteed, it is unfiltered.

I have been meaning to write this for about a week now. The book has been done for months. I sent Echo on the Water and Comfort in the Brave to my audiobook producers, One Night Stand Studios, on May 1st, I believe. But I had finished Echo back in March, then started right in on Comfort. So anyway, that's how long I've actually been thinking about this EOBS.

And now that I think back I had things to say about this book—very clear ideas about the theme of this End of Book Shit. But I forgot about them. lol And what actually made me remember what I had planned to talk about here was my dissatisfaction with my own life at the moment because I am selling my house and moving a very, very long distance away, several states over, and I'm taking my farm animals.

I had put up a giveaway question on my Rumble and the Glory blog post on my website and all you had to do to enter is leave a comment. I love these giveaways because I can ask a cool question and make your comment, your answer, the way to enter. And then I get to read all your responses. So it's fun for me.

My question for this giveaway was: What are you doing this summer?

That was it. I've asked this for several summers now and it's always nice to get a tiny peek into people's lives. And this summer ya'll are having fun (for the most part). You're hanging out at the creek, or going to the river, or the lake, or camping. Boating, road tripping. So many fun things.

So I was reading through these answers, which, as I write this, was just a few days ago, and I suddenly realized that my summer was not fun. I was not having fun. There is nothing fun about moving, not even buying a new house because it's just all so stressful.

And part of the reason why it hit me this way was because last summer was super fun. I only went on one trip (to Book Bonanza, which was really cool because I was upgraded to the presidential suite) but I was riding the horse like 3-4 times a week, I was writing Vampires, I think. And Sparktopia was next on the list. I was getting ready for the release of Sick Hate—which I love, love, love—especially the audiobook. And life was just pretty good. I was putting it all up on Instagram Stories—and it's all still there in highlights—Summer 23.

Plus we had so much rain. This place I live in (at high altitude and in the Rockies) is like a desert for the most part. We get some rain in the spring and early summer, but it dries up really fast. And last year it rained so much my seasonal pond at the bottom of the valley was like 3 feet deep. Everything was green and lush and it stayed that way all summer. All the way into fall. It never went brown. And I think, maybe, I forgot how hostile this place can be.

Fast forward to this year and it's already getting brown.

We haven't had rain in weeks and there's none on the schedule that I can see. Last year my horses ate pasture all summer. I'm already feeding hay and I have been feeding cubes to supplement (like serious supplement or they will starve) since early June.

It never really got hot last year. We never made it 90 degrees. It was mostly 70's. It was just a good year, I guess. And I think I should've called this place quits back then. I should've sold it last year. I should've gone out on a high note. Because this year is so brown, and hot, and stressful I'm over it.

I told my friend on the phone the other night—I'm not having fun. I'm reading all these comments about people having a fun summer and I'm not having fun. And it's not the weather, the weather is just making it all worse. It's this house—which I LOVE. But I want to sell it. I want to go somewhere GREEN. I'm over this desert shit. Yeah, we get snow so it's not like I'm living in Phoenix. But it's a desert up here in the summer and the winters at 7100 feet can be brutal, and horses in the winter are NEVER fun, and I'm over it.

I was feeling this way because I think back on how much fun last summer was. I really didn't do anything special but I had my first baby goats, and even though my garden got hailed on and my driveway got washed out by a flood, I was pretty satisfied because I had finally gotten up the nerve to get back on the horse. Like literally.

I've been riding horses my entire life. I have had several HUNDRED professional English equitation and show jumping lessons from very qualified and capable instructors. It was my passion as a kid, then in college, and it is again my passion now. And last summer I embraced it —even though I hadn't been on a horse in 15 years, I got back on.

I was terrified—I had a very bad fall in college during a show jumping lesson and really fucked up my right shoulder. I mean, I have fallen off dozens of times. I've gone flying over jumps face first (in front of my horse) and falling is just part of the job. It's like skateboarding. You're going to get hurt. But that fall sent me to the clinic. It was college so I was very poor and didn't have health care. And it hurt for months. It still hurts now, in fact. Every once in a while I'll feel it and it's a terrible ache. The kind you can't ignore.

I had a good reason to be afraid of riding. It's a dangerous sport. And I'm not young anymore. So I was pretty worried about falling off. I was trying to work up the nerve to go out there and do it, but something was always getting in the way. I didn't have the energy.

And then one day I realize that it's just fear. And I hate being afraid of things. I think facing fears is the easiest way to level up. Because you build a thing up in your head and make it so big. And if you just get through it instead, you suddenly realize it's a small thing. Sometimes a tiny thing.

So I sucked it up and got back on. I made my daughter and son-in-law come out and watch the first couple of weeks just in case something went wrong-and trust me, with horses, something is always going to go wrong. Because I didn't know how Mo was gonna react. I hadn't ridden him yet. He is super stubborn, but he's also very sweet. He's not a mean horse at all. I don't even think he's got it in him to be mean the way Annie, my Belgian draft, does.

Anyway, long story short, it was fine. And it was fun. I figured out how to ride a retired work horse, he figured out how to respond to leg pressure, and we did stuff. We went on trail rides (here on the property) we galloped up hills, we did a little road riding (in my very private gated neighborhood, so it was safe) and I had fun.

And this year all I've been thinking about, literally since January, was selling this house and finding a new one, and how none of this was fun. I was not having fun.

Which is fucking STUPID.

Because the thing that made last summer so fun—Moju, my big-hearted, but very stubborn retired draft horse—is still here. He's in my back-fucking-yard. I talk to him twice a day. But every time I think about riding I come up with an excuse. I 'didn't have the energy'.

This is what people say when they don't want to bother. I don't have the energy. What it really means is: I don't care enough about this thing to get invested right now.

If I'm not having fun, and the very thing that makes things fun is literally standing out in my back yard just waiting for me to come get him and tack him up, then it's my fault I'm not having fun.

I realized this yesterday and immediately I made a commitment to find my fun again. I went out in this sticky-hot afternoon sun and rode. We didn't do much, just walked around mostly. But that is my fun and if I couldn't find it, and it was literally standing in my backyard, then honestly, I don't deserve to have fun.

Plus, this year I have a garden. Last year it got ruined by

hail. And it's not doing too bad so that is fun. I really like taking care of a garden. I like watering things, and adding fertilizer, and taking note of how they grow and change every day. Every day, it's amazing.

So even though the house thing is a nightmare, everything outside is still the dream.

And I tell you this because Rosie Harlow says something in Chapter One – She says, "Time is a thing you make for things you like doing."

I felt that line was pretty profound when I wrote it because I wholeheartedly believe in the idea that you find your own fun. You make time for things that create happiness inside you. And this is what spurs on Amon's idea of courting Rosie. Not *dating* her, *wooing* her.

Rosie was something Amon was gonna make time for.

And I just love that. So that's all this EOBS is about.

Make time for the things you love. Not because life is fleeting, either. But just because it's FUN. And we ALL deserve to have fun. We do. Make time for it.

Thank you for reading, thank you for reviewing, and I'll see you in the next book!

Julie
JA Huss
June 26, 2024

ABOUT THE AUTHOR

JA Huss is a scientist, *New York Times* Bestseller, *USA Today* Bestseller, and a cowgirl who rides English. Five of her books were optioned for TV/film, several of her audiobooks have been nominated for the Audie and SOVA Awards, and she was a RITA Finalist in 2019. She has been an indie author in both fiction and non-fiction for seventeen years and lives on a ranch in Colorado with her family, horses, dogs, goats, donkeys, and chickens.